ABOUT THE AUTHOR

Zoje Stage is the *USA Today* and internationally bestselling author of *Baby Teeth, Wonderland,* and *Getaway.* A former filmmaker with a penchant for the dark and suspenseful, she lives in Pittsburgh.

ACKNOWLEDGMENTS

Many stories have a "What if...?" at their origin, and this is such a story. When I was in my late teens, camped with my family at a remote place in the Grand Canyon, a scary person came by—a person who didn't seem to belong there. In real life the scary person walked on, but this book came from imagining "What if he'd stuck around?"

In years past I went backpacking in the Grand Canyon four times. I've been down and/or up the two maintained trails—South Kaibab and Bright Angel—and one wilderness trail, Hermit. And I've camped at numerous places within the Canyon, including Sumner Wash, Clear Creek, Monument, Hermit, Salt, Horn, and Bright Angel—and even spent a night at a deserted Indian Gardens one cold December with my dad. But I have never been out to Boucher or Slate, which play such pivotal roles in this story. I'm indebted to my dad, John Stage, for all the knowledge he shared—the gazillion questions he happily answered—that allowed me to write this with as much accuracy as possible.

I wouldn't get to keep being an author without my unflappable agents, Stephen Barbara and Claire Friedman. And this book wouldn't be in readers' hands without my astute editor, Helen O'Hare. I'm grateful for the entire team at Mulholland Books: Josh Kendall, Sareena Kamath, Pamela Brown, Alyssa Persons, Lindsey Heil, Massey Barner, Laura Mamelok, Nancy Wiese, Pamela Marshall, and Ben Allen. Thank you to Little, Brown for all your support: Bruce Nichols, Judy Clain, Craig Young, and Sabrina Callahan. Thank you to my copyeditor, Barbara Perris, for being the "final eyes" on this manuscript. And thank you to Gregg Kulick for another stunning cover.

I keep being surprised that each novel evolves so differently from first draft to publication, even though my basic writing process is the same. Thank you to Jenny Belardi and Brooke Dorsch for feedback on an early draft. Much of the rewriting of this book happened during quarantine and, as hard a time as it was, I'm grateful for so many Saturdays spent with my "quarantine bubble"—my sister and my mum. As always, sending love to my friends: I miss you!

#PittsburghStrong #NoPlaceForHate

GETAWAY

GETAWAY

ZOJE STAGE

MULHOLLAND
BOOKS

Little, Brown and Company
New York Boston London

Copyright © 2021 by Zoje Stage

Hachette Book Group supports the right to free expression and the value of copyright. The purpose of copyright is to encourage writers and artists to produce the creative works that enrich our culture.

The scanning, uploading, and distribution of this book without permission is a theft of the author's intellectual property. If you would like permission to use material from the book (other than for review purposes), please contact permissions@hbgusa.com. Thank you for your support of the author's rights.

Mulholland Books / Little, Brown and Company
Hachette Book Group
1290 Avenue of the Americas, New York, NY 10104
mulhollandbooks.com

First Edition: August 2021

Mulholland Books is an imprint of Little, Brown and Company, a division of Hachette Book Group, Inc. The Mulholland Books name and logo are trademarks of Hachette Book Group, Inc.

The publisher is not responsible for websites (or their content) that are not owned by the publisher.

The Hachette Speakers Bureau provides a wide range of authors for speaking events. To find out more, go to hachettespeakersbureau.com or call (866) 376-6591.

ISBN 978-0-316-24250-9
Library of Congress Control Number: 2021935941

Printing 1, 2021

LSC-C

Printed in the United States of America

In loving memory of my mum,
Ruth Stage (1942–2020)

GETAWAY

PROLOGUE

It might not have been a beautiful day. In her memory, the golden leaves of a ginkgo tree shimmered in poignant juxtaposition to the harrowing splatters of blood. But in reality, it could have been an ordinary maple tree. And the blood, though it had been shed, pooled indoors, beyond her field of vision.

Within moments of it happening, Imogen lost track of what was real, what was imagined. Had she heard screams? Or were those in her head too? Later, she could only tell the police her name, why she was there, what time she'd arrived, and other unhelpful details. When they asked what she saw, Imogen had shaken her head, distrustful of her awareness.

Unsure of her faith and skeptical of organized religion, she'd been going to the Etz Chayim synagogue for only a month or so. Growing up, her Jewish mother had insisted she was Jewish—it being a religion of maternal lineage—but as a family they hadn't really practiced anything or discussed their beliefs. Imogen was the only one among her old school friends who hadn't gone to Hebrew school or had a bat mitzvah. She'd

1

tried telling people she was half Jewish and half Christian, but even at ten that hadn't made sense. She'd never liked that empty space of not knowing where she belonged.

It wasn't until Kazansky's closed—the deli she'd relied on for matzoh ball soup and Reubens and kosher pickles—that Imogen even started thinking about the culture she didn't know. The matzoh ball soup had satisfied an easy kind of hunger, and without it she wondered what else there was. The first book she read on Judaism made her blink as if she'd just awakened, emerging into sunlight after a long slumber beneath a dusty tarp. She'd never heard of a tree of life that mapped levels of reality, or the possibility that the soul might have five distinct planes. Judaism wasn't opposed to the concept of God as a tree, or the universe; it didn't exclude those who believed one thing in the morning, and another thing in the evening, and nothing the following day. The spirituality of it intrigued her.

Curiosity killed the cat.

Imogen didn't die. But she hadn't been the same since that October morning. She'd gotten in the habit of going early, as that was when a group of the older congregants arrived to socialize: men and women whose parents had gotten them out of Germany before it was too late; Pittsburgh-born seniors who reminded her of her grandparents, dead for over a decade. They were friendly and welcoming, happy that a "young lady" was rediscovering her heritage. Almost thirty-four, Imogen remained petite and youthful, with a smattering of delicate black tattoos (which she kept covered in the synagogue), and had been assumed younger than her actual age for much of her life. She enjoyed their attention and their eagerness to chat with her.

The shooting had started as she'd approached the glass front doors.

That was how she saw herself, in her memory of the morning. Her arm outstretched, her hand never quite making it to the door handle. Frozen.

It was her first time in the vicinity of a human slaughter but she instantly recognized the sound. As loud as a cannon. (An exaggeration.) Flesh ripped through with bullets meant for a battlefield. (Not an exaggeration.) She couldn't decide if her fragile early-bird friends had looked surprised, mouths agape, dentures exposed in shock. Or had they, in their wisdom, always known it was coming.

A part of her had wanted to rush in, find the gunman, launch herself in front of his weapon or onto his back to tear out his hair, puncture his eyes. The part of her that lived in the real world scampered off to the side of the building to hide behind a bush.

She kept trying to call 911 but her hands were shaking too hard and she couldn't even unlock her phone. It didn't matter. The sirens came anyway. And more sirens. And more. And the SWAT team. And television crews. She was still hiding behind the bush when the news alert first broke on the internet and her neighborhood plunged into mourning.

1

They were too busy to watch the sunset, or the moonrise, beyond the two-story windows of Beck's Flagstaff living room: they would be getting up before dawn, and still had a lot to do. The cathedral ceiling was buttressed with thick timber beams that suited the rustic locale and made the space feel huge in spite of the heavy furniture and clutter. Night now hid the pine trees that made a perimeter around the house, but Imogen swore she could still smell them, even through the glass wall.

It looked like a bomb had exploded. Ziploc bags filled with travel-sized toiletries, first aid gear, fire-lighting stuff. Puffy sleeping bags, backpacks, mattress pads—of both the egg crate and inflatable varieties. Hiking boots, padded socks, hoodies, adjustable nylon straps, compact flashlights, bamboo walking sticks, plastic bowls, protein bars, crushed rolls of toilet paper, fuel canisters, water canteens. Of some items there was only one: the small stove; the pot it fit in; the fluorescent orange plastic trowel for burying poop. Of some items there were many:

lumpy freeze-dried food packages that turned into tantalizing dinners with the addition of boiling water.

Imogen's sister, Beck, had lured her out of her hermit's cave with the promise that nature would be healing. The subtext couldn't have been more obvious: *Stop brooding and get out of the damn house.* They'd talked about it on the phone four times in a span of two weeks. When Imogen questioned if she could fly all the way to Arizona by herself, Beck reminded her she'd done it many times before; when Imogen questioned if she was strong enough for such an arduous trip, Beck reassured her that backpacking was in her blood. For every doubt Imogen expressed, her sister was ready with a breezy counter. She'd said "You can do this" so many times that Imogen had started to believe it.

In the months since the shooting, Imogen had cycled through bouts of overwhelming sadness, and fear, and maddening frustration at her own uselessness, all of which had made her reclusive tendencies even worse. She'd started ordering delivery instead of going around the corner to pick up her Vietnamese food. Once a week she headed up Murray to the Giant Eagle for bananas and snacks, and hurried home with her eyes on the sidewalk. The names of her lost friends were still posted in the storefront windows, another tragedy for the Jewish community to *never forget.* Crocheted Stars of David dangled from branches, parking meters, telephone poles, shipped to Squirrel Hill from around the country; a constant reminder that Imogen didn't want to see.

And yet, her hermit's cave was no longer the sanctuary it had always been, where she could shut away the world and make productive use of her imagination. She hadn't believed writer's block was a real thing, but over the past year every story she considered felt empty, unworthy, too trivial to bother with. It was a miracle of good fortune that her second novel, *Esther's Ghost,* had sold just weeks after the shooting; it gave her a slight distraction from the horror and lack of words. While Beck grew ever more cautious about inquiring about the "dry spell" or the "wordless hiccup," Imogen knew it fueled her concern. No doubt that if Beck needed inspiration she'd find it in the Grand Canyon, but would it work for Imogen?

The months of preparation—walking up and down her building's stairs with a daypack full of canned goods—had brought back fond memories of backpacking with her family. (Though she couldn't pretend she'd done nearly enough exercising; every time one of her neighbors exited their apartment she'd scurried back to her cave before anyone could see her.) She'd never had an apartment with so much as a Juliet balcony to stand on to watch a thunderstorm or get a breath of fresh air. But once upon a time, nature had been a balm, an essential thing that satisfied her soul. After Beck had first suggested the trip Imogen realized just how far she'd pushed nature to the back of her thoughts, as something she couldn't have. Her world had been shrinking for many years, even before what happened at the synagogue. She appreciated that her sister wanted to give her a gift and return her to a place where she'd once felt at peace with her surroundings. But it came with its own hiccup, beyond having to leave the safety of her four walls.

Tilda.

Tilda, whose friendship had once filled a critical void and helped Imogen survive high school. No, she'd been more than a friend—the trio had been like sisters, present for each other as their home lives imploded. It was a formative time, their three reckless paths converging as they dog-paddled toward a future they couldn't quite see.

Tilda hadn't called even once to check on her over the past year and it wasn't like she didn't know; the massacre was international news.

Sometimes, when Beck and Tilda were back in Pittsburgh for a holiday, the three of them got together for a museum excursion or high tea at the Frick. Imogen and Tilda could smile at each other and speak in upbeat voices, but they were mere masks of civility. Imogen was better acquainted with Tilda's public persona, which she followed on Instagram. Real-life Tilda scared her a little; Imogen often couldn't read her. They hadn't had a serious conversation in four years.

Their relationship had gotten rocky after their first year of college. Imogen left the University of Pittsburgh during her sophomore year, a consequence of The Thing (though she would've denied that was the reason). They never talked about The Thing, but it left a residue, a rust-colored ring like a half-healed wound; Imogen understood it slightly better now, but only because of how society had changed.

As Tilda and Beck surged forward with their busy, ambitious lives Imogen was alternately proud of their success, and envious of how easily they moved through the chaos of ordinary life. She harbored a more recent, more specific jealousy too; Tilda's six-figure book deal was another thing they hadn't gotten around to discussing. There were periods over the years when they grew closer, but it never lasted. Someone would say something that ruffled the other's feathers, and they'd stop communicating again.

The silences were getting steadily longer. Beck seemed confident she could function well enough as a bridge between them, and that spending real time together as a trio would bring them closer. But Imogen was less sure. Backpacking in the Grand Canyon was difficult enough without the added burden of personal baggage. Yet, here they all were.

With the grace of a dancer, Tilda's pedicured magenta toes found floor space amid the detritus as she held her phone over the scattered piles of gear and snapped photos. Tilda had been documenting her expedition prep on Instagram and YouTube for weeks: the purchasing of her pack, boots, clothing; scenic strolls in the San Gabriel Mountains with her boyfriend, Jalal. When Beck revealed that she'd planned the trip for the three of them, Imogen was certain Tilda would bow out, perhaps at the last minute. Her idea of a vacation was a five-star hotel with its own private crescent of beach. Could Tilda even survive being dirty and sweaty without the refreshing promise of the false-blue water of her Los Angeles swimming pool?

Beck insisted Tilda had been game from the get-go, ready for an adventure and a chance to discover new things about herself: she'd never been so much as car camping or spent an entire night out of doors. (Rather than an "adventure," Imogen thought it more likely that Tilda needed new material for her motivational speeches and videos—and possibly her book.) Imogen was well aware that Beck had cleverly manipulated them both into coming, suggesting to each of them how a week in the wilderness would benefit their personal situations—and tying it up with a bow at the reminder of the twentieth anniversary of their friendship. Dr. Beck liked to fix people, even when they weren't her patients. Imogen didn't want to invest too much thought in a grand reconciliation; she had no idea where Tilda stood on the matter. Even now, Tilda would barely make eye contact with her.

The connection they'd shared as teen misfits was long gone, but for years it had been effortless. The week before the Blum sisters transferred to Beechwood, a private alternative high school run by hippies, Imogen had turned fourteen; Beck was crashing toward sixteen. They were barely past the threshold when Tilda Jimenez sashayed toward them, beckoning them in with her vintage cigarette holder, everything about her as flamboyant as a drag queen. While she was Beck's age, the three had all bonded over shared feelings of parental abandonment: the Blums were workaholics even before the divorce, Mr. Blum a commercial photographer (who preferred his wife's last name), Ms. Blum a local politician. Mr. Jimenez, an engineer, drowned himself in work too, after Mrs. Jimenez's sudden death. At the time, their parents' failings—avoidable or not—had been unforgivable.

Tilda might've been destined for fame. And Imogen might have encouraged it, writing her a starring role in the school musical that earned them all their first press coverage. There was no question that both Blum sisters were impressed—amazed—by how much mileage Tilda had gotten out of finishing eleventh on her season of *American Idol:* she'd turned her fifteen minutes of fame into a twelve-year career. But the more of a public person she became, the less Imogen could relate to her. Tilda expressed things to strangers that sounded more personal than anything she'd say to Imogen. Now Tilda was the opposite of an outsider or a misfit. She lived for other people's approval and couldn't exist without a constant influx of Likes.

Imogen wasn't sure what to expect from her on this

expedition—was Tilda just playing a role? Was this a performance piece for her followers? Would Imogen be expected to applaud? But given that they were going to be together for the next week, Imogen hoped they could avoid any awkwardness by simply being nice—a superficial solution, but potentially effective.

"You look *fit,*" Imogen said, noticing Tilda's muscle definition, even through her leggings.

"Thank you!" Tilda beamed, and stopped taking pictures. "Extra yoga classes. Spinning. Plus my weekly hikes with Jalal. I may not be outdoorsy, but I can handle exercise."

Beck grinned. Imogen had almost forgotten how much game Tilda had when she was embracing a new challenge. She'd always had an enviable, curvy shape, and with the muscles packed on Imogen could admit to being a little jealous. Imogen was like a squished version of her sister: lean and short (bordering on scrawny) instead of lean and long (bordering on majestic). An image came to her of Beck and Tilda dressed as warriors. Beside them, Imogen felt like the hand servant who scurried after them to clean their weapons.

"I like your hair—it changes with the light." Tilda tilted her head, examining Imogen from different angles.

Imogen touched her bobbed hair, which she'd dyed lavender the week before. "I was going for an inspired-by-the-sunset color, but I bet after a week in the sun it's going to look really washed out."

Tilda shrugged. "It's still cool. You were the only one of us to ever make brave hair choices."

That sounded mostly like a compliment, but Imogen wasn't absolutely positive. (Brave, in this instance, could also mean questionable.) Beck had been wearing her sandy-brown hair short for more than twenty years, and for just as long Tilda's nearly black hair could usually be found in a messy knot atop her head.

"Who wants gorp?" Afiya, Beck's wife, floated in from the kitchen, her smile a white gleam against her dark skin. She clutched pint-sized resealable bags in both hands, shaking them like percussive rattles. "I've got the high-protein mix with assorted nuts and seeds, the fruity extravaganza mix with almond pieces, and a big quick-energy batch of M&M's and cashews."

"Ooh, I'll take those." Imogen reached for the baggies with the chocolate candies.

"You can't have all of them," Beck said, irritated.

"I wasn't going to take all of them, but I don't like the others as much."

The three of them descended on Afiya like vultures, stripping her of the proffered food. More calmly, they took a moment to divvy up the varieties of trail mix. Afiya crossed her arms and watched them, an amused smile tugging at her lips.

"Everyone should keep at least one bag in an outer pocket, so when we take breaks it's easy to grab." Beck's intensity softened as she caught Afiya's eye. "Thanks, babe."

"Master Gorp Mixer, at your service." Afiya gave a dramatic bow.

Imogen grinned, relieved by Afiya's presence. But then she started fantasizing about how much better the trip would be with Afiya along rather than Tilda, and her smile faded. Was this a mistake? Afiya wasn't just a better human, Imogen trusted her with her life. The same couldn't be said for Tilda.

2

Tilda and Afiya sat on the sofa performing an elaborate (or so it seemed) tea ceremony with fancy herbal bags that smelled like lemons and fresh-cut hay. Imogen stuck near Beck, sampling the M&M's. She knew she should be doing more, but she wasn't sure what, and she really didn't love her sister's approach to packing.

Imogen had always been well organized when it came to projects, and this was a large project—with no room for error. Had it been up to her she would have made lists (just as she had to get ready to travel from Pittsburgh to Flagstaff), color-coded by pack and person. And if the lists had their own lists, all the merrier. But Beck was the leader of this expedition, the resident Grand Canyon expert, and her system was to inventory everything first, then claim personal items, and then divvy out the rest by weight.

"Need help?" *Cruncha-muncha-crunch.*

"You could stop eating our food." Imogen hated it when her sister chastised her, but Beck shot her a playful smirk—

and handed her a fuel canister. "This can go in your side pocket."

Instead of zipping it into one of the long pockets on either side of her forest-green pack—specially designed for the petite wearer—she tucked it under her arm and watched as Beck put the stove and pot in the main compartment of her own rust-colored Kelty pack.

"Don't you want them together?" Imogen asked. "The stove and the fuel?"

"Too much weight."

"Well, we could distribute the other things in your pack differently, so you can keep them together." Beck flashed her a flinty glare, chafed by her attempt to micromanage. But it made so much more sense to keep the items together that Imogen risked a harsher rebuke and kept pressing. "I'm just thinking, what if—"

"I know what you're thinking." Beck cut her off. The cold look in her eye extended to her voice, but she spoke softly. "But we're not going to get separated, so we don't need to worry—"

"Well of course we wouldn't *intend* to get separated, but you know it's theoretically—"

"Imogen." Beck cut a quick glance behind them to Tilda. In spite of the miles and years that moved between them, Imogen understood what her sister was trying to say: don't scare Tilda. The set of Beck's jaw, her unblinking eyes, made a plaintive case for not reminding their already-new-to-all-of-this friend that, if things went awry, even a hot meal might not be an option.

As teenagers they'd shared Canyon stories with Tilda, including the one where their family had gotten separated for nearly twenty-four hours. Had Tilda forgotten those stories, or had she written them off as adolescent hyperbole? Beck was in charge now, as their dad had been then, and part of her responsibility was encouraging everyone to get mentally and physically ready. If she was this concerned about scaring Tilda over how they *packed,* had she kept other, more serious dangers from her too?

Suddenly Imogen was certain Beck had left things out. If Tilda knew the entirety of the hazards that could befall them—and death wasn't *impossible*—she might not have agreed to the trip. Or might have canceled, as Imogen had anticipated. Something electric short-circuited, sending skittering flames of anxiety through Imogen's gut. It wouldn't matter if Tilda was physically strong if she was mentally weak; there wasn't an emergency exit if Tilda decided she wanted out. Had Beck done her due diligence in helping her prepare?

(Or maybe Beck had realized that Tilda was only equipped for physical training and the mental training would be a lost cause.) *Snarky. Be nice.*

If Imogen and Tilda had been on better terms, Imogen might have had a chance to talk to her about the things her sister wouldn't say. But it was too late now and, unlike Imogen, Beck didn't share a philosophy of preparing for the worst.

"Okay, I was just trying to be careful," Imogen conceded, a bit of whine in her voice. Sometimes (often) she hated how easily she played her old familiar role, as if her life were a theatrical production and certain voices prompted preset responses. She wanted to change that, but for now she put the fuel canister in her pack.

"There are many ways to be careful, grasshopper." Beck's eyes sparked mischief, with the undercurrent of a challenge.

14

Imogen accepted the bait. "If you say so, bull's pizzle."

"'Oh, plague sore! Would thou wouldst burst!'"

Beck's British accent was terrible, but Tilda, overhearing from the couch, erupted with laughter. "Oh my God, you still call each other that?"

"Only on special occasions." Beck gave Imogen a little wink.

"What's that from?" Afiya asked.

"Shakespeare. They started it in high school," Tilda explained.

"Why?" Baffled, and a touch disgusted, Afiya looked from Imogen to Beck.

"Because she was a genius," said Beck, "the next Shakespeare."

"Hardly," Imogen mumbled. (It used to please her that *Imogen* was associated with the play *Cymbeline,* but now such references made her feel like a fraud. She was pretty sure the Bard never suffered from writer's block.)

"She wrote a musical, the whole thing, play and lyrics, when she was only fifteen." Tilda sounded proud, which made Imogen a touch nostalgic. "Our teacher discouraged profanity, so she worked in some Elizabethan insults instead."

"Oh *that,*" said Afiya, finally having context.

"I saw you have the article framed, behind your desk." Imogen was staying in Beck's home office, on a foldout sofa, since Tilda was using the guest room. She hadn't expected to see the article in a place of honor on her sister's wall.

"Really, you still have that?" Tilda asked Beck.

Beck shrugged, but Imogen thought it was interesting too: of the three of them, only Beck had preserved—and displayed— the newspaper piece written just before *Eighty-Seven Seconds* had opened for its two-night run. The musical took place on an airplane filled with strangers who formed last-minute connections with the people around them when they realized they were about to crash. They talked (and sang) about the loved ones they were leaving behind, the mistakes they'd made, and the things they'd always hoped to do. While the first act had teetered between not bad and pretentious, the second act turned into a trippy hallucination of the afterlife.

"Beck's always had so much faith in your work." Afiya said this with such earnestness that Imogen sifted through her words for the subtext, but couldn't quite figure it out.

"Did you get all your clothes in?" Beck asked Tilda, forever engrossed in the task at hand. Tilda bounded off the sofa and she and Beck chattered about socks and windbreakers and if they should bring a few tampons "just in case." Seeing them so bubbly together made Imogen feel left out.

Afiya strolled over and casually rested a lanky elbow on Imogen's shoulder. Towering above her, Afiya had to hunch to whisper in Imogen's ear, bringing with her a scent of soapy apples.

"How're you doing? You ready?"

Those five words registered a kindness utterly different from anything Imogen would ever receive from Tilda, or even Beck. Only Afiya would openly acknowledge her agoraphobic tendencies, which hadn't improved even though the shooting was almost a year behind her. At thirty-four, Afiya and Imogen were the same age, though Imogen always thought of her sister's wife as older, wiser. Maybe it was her drive: Afiya earned a PhD at twenty-three and became the youngest tenure-track professor at Northern Arizona University. It took a few years, but she almost singlehandedly reshaped the cultural studies department, transforming it into the most intersectional

16

program in Arizona. But it was more than that. Afiya carried an understanding of people, a maturity that struck Imogen as motherly.

She saw the concern in Afiya's eyes. "I'm okay."

"It's not too much? All this—out and about?"

Of course Afiya knew that Beck was trying to help her—*fix her*—and for all Imogen knew the whole trip could've been Afiya's idea. But in demeanor, Afiya was by far the most sensitive to Imogen's enduring trauma. She wondered, and not for the first time, if Afiya came by this naturally because of her own difficult start in life. She'd emigrated from Rwanda at three, with her brothers and her mom, and it had taken her mom some time to get the hang of their new country. Afiya's father was never spoken of. The writer in Imogen liked to invent dark secrets for people, but it was also possible that Afiya's goodness came from *not* being burdened with secrets, dark or otherwise.

Imogen didn't feel comfortable answering Afiya's question in front of Beck and Tilda. Too often over the years she'd been at the receiving end of their scorn when they thought she was being ridiculous. They probably wouldn't be so heartless now, given the circumstances, but she remained reluctant to let her guard down. Without being able to fully immerse herself in another world—an ability she'd taken for granted as a lifelong writer—she'd had no extended hours of peace or engagement. The last several weeks had been especially stressful. Even with the airport's security protocol, she'd dreaded wading into the zoo of bustling people. She didn't feel safe in groups; groups were targets.

Afiya seemed in tune with Imogen's thoughts—or perhaps Imogen's face betrayed some semblance of fear. Afiya gave

Imogen a quick squeeze, then spoke to her as Imogen imagined a mom might (though her mom lacked such warmth).

"You're going to be in one of the most beautiful places in the world, with your big sister and your oldest friend—"

"I wish you were coming."

"This is for the three of you. You'll challenge yourselves and see how strong you are. The Canyon's going to give you a big hug and welcome you home." That made Imogen smile. She wanted that. She needed that. "Why do you think we live here?"

"Your dream home?" Imogen knew how proud Beck was to have provided her wife with this magnificent house, on its picturesque parcel of land.

"The Grand Canyon's our backyard. A place where we can forget the unimportant things, and remember the things we most need to know. When we start to lose track, we go there and remember."

Imogen nodded. "I'm ready."

"You *are*."

Unlike Tilda, Imogen knew how hard the journey would be. She'd backpacked in the Grand Canyon four times when she was younger, but hadn't done any real hiking in over ten years. Still, Beck was counting on her. Beck needed her to be reasonably competent *and* helpful, and Imogen didn't want to let her down. That was a worry she carried, almost as heavy as her pack promised to be, that some part of her weakness would jeopardize their trip.

During the past year Imogen had been infected with loneliness, a new condition for her. It was far-fetched, but sometimes she fantasized about being an adventurer, someone at home in every corner of the world. She was a long way from being that person, but thankfully nature in general—and the Canyon in particular—had always made her feel more immune to the anxieties she experienced in her everyday life. Mentally, she could do it. Push through if she got tired or sore, but what if she really was too weak?

A minor stumble in the Canyon could end the trip. A major stumble could send her hurtling toward her grave.

3

It was starting to look like a living room again, not a staging area for a six-night, seven-day trip beyond the reaches of civilization. Imogen dragged her pack over to the couch so she could sit, without anyone seeing the trepidation on her face, and attach her new sleeping bag to the frame beneath the main compartment of her pack. Afiya made a human Roomba of herself and zipped around picking up discarded packaging and stray bits and bobs that Beck confirmed they didn't need. While Tilda played with her phone, Beck secured a Therm-a-Rest sleeping pad to Tilda's burgundy pack. It was all getting too real. They were almost done.

Upon hearing of Beck's desire to go down the Hermit Trail and head out to Boucher, Imogen had balked, and suggested an easier trip out to Clear Creek instead. Her dad still loved to tell the tale of the first time he'd taken Beck, at seventeen, out to Boucher, and how he'd held his breath as she crossed the narrow passage—rock face on one side, an abyss on the other—

hoping he wouldn't have to call home to report that Beck had *oops!* slipped to her death.

Beck had finally convinced Imogen that the trail out to Boucher wasn't as death-defying as their dad liked to make it sound, that the narrow passage was, in fact, a *super-short stretch* and *totally worth it* and she needed to *push past her fears.* Imogen had a habit of letting her sister talk her into things, even when knowing that Beck, who'd backpacked alone at least twenty times, might not have the greatest understanding of other people's fears. She'd promised them more beauty and greater rewards by heading deep into the backcountry, where they could admire the mighty Colorado at ground level, and might—off-season in October—have the desert to themselves.

Imogen had been thinking about that precarious stretch of trail for seven months. She knew the strategy: keep your eyes on your feet. But it still worried her. What if she took one look at it and chickened out? Then she wouldn't even be *mentally* capable. And she could almost hear Beck explaining it away to Tilda, "There's just one tricky section," as if the rest weren't already going to be the hardest walk of her life.

It wasn't a helpful thing to be thinking about, but their dad really had almost died on their mom's first—and last—Grand Canyon trip.

Things had gone awry almost from the start as they'd descended the Hermit Trail. Beck, fifteen and on her third Canyon trip, and Imogen, thirteen and on her second, went at their own pace and were soon far ahead. When their dad blew his emergency whistle they'd feared their parents were in real trouble. They hurried back only to be told that their mom was wobbly on her feet and proceeding slowly; apparently stomping around the city in high heels was *not* effective preparation for clambering over rocks with a heavy pack on. Their dad told Beck and Imogen to hike the rest of the way on their own, and have camp ready when they got there.

By the time they reached the Hermit camping area, Imogen had felt unwell. Hot. Hungry. Tired. But Beck was more worried than exhausted. Even at barely fifteen, she was already inclined to fix everyone's problems: she decided to head back to Cathedral Stairs—a particularly difficult section of trail—and relieve their mom of her backpack. It was getting dark. Imogen didn't want her sister to go. It was too dangerous, and Beck was the one person she couldn't live without. She was alarmed by her sister's sense of duty—her reckless grit—as she set off alone with only her walking stick and a tiny flashlight.

Having backpacked in West Virginia many times, Imogen knew how to set up camp—how to hang all the food from a tree, and lay out the ground tarp and mattress pads so they could sleep when ready. But after that, she sat on her thin bed and cried, imagining her sister swallowed up by a cavernous mouth that only opened when the sun stopped looking, when the surrounding rocks loomed black in their shadows.

She found out the next day that for some number of hours the four members of the Blum family had all been on their own in the dark. Two months later their mom filed for divorce. And six months after that, the Blum sisters started at Beechwood and told their new friend how their dad had almost fallen over a cliff, and they'd laughed and said he deserved it for being so clueless. Adult Imogen knew that wasn't true. Though he might have miscalculated his wife's abilities, when he realized they weren't going to make it to camp he'd hurried ahead to find a level spot where they could bivouac. But night came on too quickly and he found himself racing back so their mom wouldn't be alone. Careless in his panic, he'd stumbled off trail, and soon heard his walking stick go clattering off rocks as it plunged into the darkened emptiness.

"You okay?" Beck asked her now, skeptical.

Imogen realized her face had crumpled and she coughed the tightness from her throat. "Just thinking."

How had it not occurred to any of the Blums to just stick together? Though Beck had forsaken her mission to Cathedral Stairs and returned to camp safe and sound, they hadn't been able to eat a hot breakfast the next morning—not without the fuel in their missing father's backpack.

Imogen wanted to excuse herself to go tongue a few drops of the medical marijuana tincture she used for anxiety. (Later, she'd slip it into her pack with the last of her personal things.) But they were all watching her. Maybe they thought this was what she did at home in the months since the shooting—randomly burst into tears. But these tears were for something else.

Their dad had hoped that backpacking trip would somehow shore up the crumbling infrastructure of his marriage. It hadn't. If anything, it accelerated its collapse. Could Beck do it better?

Imogen and Beck took turns hoisting each pack onto their backs, checking for weight and balance. It would make walking even more difficult if one side was heavier than the other, or if stuff shifted around. But of particular concern to Imogen was that her pack weigh the ten or fifteen pounds less that she'd been promised. Tilda was the most solidly built of the three of them and they were counting on her overall physical ability. Beck, the tallest, was like a slab of wood, thin and hard and strong. Imogen could still buy children's clothes (which she did on occasion to save money).

"How's it feel?" Beck asked as Imogen took a few steps.

"Heavy." But she'd tried the others, and knew hers was lighter. "How's yours?"

"Heavy." Beck turned to Tilda. "Want to try yours?"

Tilda set down her phone and leapt across the room. "Ooh, mine looks like a big burrito."

Hers was the only one of the three with an internal frame. Beck held it up, as if offering an overcoat. Tilda slid her arms through the straps, heaved the belt across her hips. She paced around a bit. "Not bad. Not as bad as I thought it might be."

The Blum sisters exchanged raised eyebrows. Suppressed grins. Yup, the city girl couldn't imagine beyond the room, the level, manufactured floor. But there was no point in telling her. If Tilda still said "not bad" after arriving at Hermit Camp, Imogen would suggest a career change to an Olympian.

"And it matches my toes." Tilda stuck out a foot so they could admire her nail polish. Imogen rolled her eyes. Tilda ignored it, and resumed marching back and forth. "It feels good. Talk about downsizing. If I can fit all this on my back, maybe I should sell my house and live in a van."

Afiya cackled. "Maybe taking this a bit too far."

"Okay, Wonder Woman, don't wear yourself out," said Beck.

Tilda took up the superhero pose, fists at her waist, then used her invisible wrist cuffs to deflect invisible bullets. Beck shot at her with an imaginary ray gun, complete with sound effects, *pkew, pkew.* Imogen sank into the sofa and watched them battle it out; they used to play like that together, the three of them, silly and unselfconscious (or stoned).

24

"Okay children, I don't think you should get this worked up so close to bedtime." Afiya playacted the mom role well. Tilda and Beck groaned—disappointed, bratty imps.

Imogen joined in only when it was time to line their backpacks against the couch, ready for the morning.

"Don't forget to brush your teeth," Afiya said, walking her guests to their rooms.

"You're good at this," Beck whispered, and kissed her cheek.

After an exchange of good nights and sleep tights, Imogen shut the door to Beck's office, glad to finally be alone. This was the last time and space she'd have to herself for a while. She plopped onto the edge of the foldout bed and took off her bra. Their alarms were set for four o'clock and she didn't want to risk not being able to fall asleep; she dripped her marijuana tincture under her tongue.

There it was again, the framed article, with its muddy black-and-white photo. Imogen was in the middle with a smug smile (and a messy mohawk), flanked by openmouthed Tilda (holding a microphone) and Beck, the director, glaring with her arms crossed (the photographer had wanted her to look authoritative). Imogen silently chuckled. At the time, they'd taken themselves so, so seriously—simultaneous to being utterly ridiculous. *We had range.*

She laughed again at the thought. But it was true. They weren't set in their ways then. They didn't know where they were going or what life would throw at them. She realized, looking at her old self, confident without reason to be, that she needed some of that girl back. Was she out there somewhere? Perhaps, in the company of Beck and Tilda, she could find her again.

4

Dawn light slithered across the horizon, a molten stripe.
The Flagstaff public radio station had been playing
classical music since they left, but Imogen, in the backseat,
spent most of the eighty-minute drive half asleep. She came
fully awake as Beck angled her Jeep into the Hermit Trailhead
parking lot, simultaneously turning off the radio.

There was only one other car in the lot, but Beck parked
some distance from it. Imogen unbuckled, eager in her sudden
wakefulness to get going.

"Cell phones?" Beck held out her hand.

"Are you sure we can't—"

"I'm sure." Beck had been ready for Tilda to try one last
argument, even though they'd discussed it a dozen times.
"They're not gonna work anyway, it's just dead weight."

Tilda had known this was coming, it was why she'd
purchased a mini digital camera. Impatient, Imogen passed her
phone to Beck, and stepped out into the quiet, cold dawn. She
half hoped her friend would forget to use her little camera—

not because she didn't want Tilda to have "content" to share on social media, but because wonder was its own blessed distraction. And *this* was a wonder. Imogen remembered her dad telling her, decades earlier, how Nature preferred to reveal her gifts to the truly attentive, and technology would sully that.

In her peripheral vision, Beck leaned over Tilda's knees and slipped all the cell phones into the glove compartment. Imogen intentionally didn't look to see if Tilda sighed or made some sort of pathetic frowny face. A minute later they were all at the tailgate, hauling out their packs. Silently they loaded up, tightened their belts, grabbed their walking sticks.

After locking the doors, Beck zipped the car key into an internal pocket of her fleece, ready to let the Jeep hibernate for a week. "Everybody all set?"

Imogen couldn't wait to leave civilization behind, but the little wings of nervousness took flight in her chest—part excitement for the adventure, part fear of the journey.

"Let's do this," said Tilda.

They were a few hundred yards down the Hermit Trail before the view opened up. It wasn't as expansive as the views from the tourist overlooks. But still. Hermit Trail clung to the eastern side of Hermit canyon, which meant some serious drop-offs, and impressive vistas, all the way down. The difficulty of the walking required eyes-on-feet at all times, so in order to look, really *look*, they needed to stop. They stood there in a row in all their gear, leaning on their bamboo poles, and took in the morning.

Tilda looked as if she'd purchased her entire sporty and expensive (and colorful) trousseau from REI, and probably had. Imogen felt a bit like a pauper by comparison in her baggy cargo shorts and faded black leggings, but they were practical. As a well-paid general practitioner, Beck could've afforded any specialty apparel she desired, but favored a pair of comfy old jeans. They all wore shirts, hoodies, and windbreakers against the chill October morn, but it would probably be less than half an hour before they started peeling off layers. It was a temperate time of year for the Canyon, no snow on the rim, and no blistering temperatures at the bottom. Imogen preferred a bamboo walking staff that rose several inches above her head; she leaned on it with both hands. Beck still had her tried-and-true skinny stick. Tilda had wanted to get a trekking pole like the stores sold, one that looked better suited to a ski slope, but Beck convinced her to go to a garden center and buy bamboo; Tilda's stocky pole came just to her chin.

This was what you did in the Canyon, whether it was the first visit or the thousandth: stand.

Look.

Absorb.

There were no words, so none of them spoke.

Here was a masterpiece, and Imogen was awestruck by the Creator's vision. How had a painter painted this? With so much depth and so many hues? Gray, lavender, sand. Smoky colors that blended and bent and rippled, and, from so many places along the rim, went on for as far as the eye could see. How had a sculptor sculpted this? With its infinite layers and formations, endless temples for countless gods. In some places the universe revealed its soul. A many-chambered heart, the inner canyons carried the tributaries of the Colorado River outward like branches, diminishing yet infinite.

From everywhere along the trail the view would be different. But even if they stood as they were all day the light would change, and with each passing minute a new landscape would emerge. The artist would dip her brush into a vast palette throughout the day—pastels would bleed from blue to pink to buff to the electric shades of sunset—until finally it would be the moon's turn, though she preferred more secretive silks, in tones of ink and silver. It was a view that reminded Imogen of the complexity of time, how water and wind and the forming continents might summon an especially pleasing surprise. And it was a comfort, this spectacularly dissimilar evidence that if the universe made everything—even this great canyon—it had made her, too.

She hoped she possessed even a speck of greatness. As if in response, her skin tingled as something inside her shivered back to life, thrilled that she was really here.

The true beginning of a journey was a daunting task, almost sacred. After an appropriate amount of time, Beck resumed the lead and headed on down the trail. Imogen waited for Tilda to follow after her. For a moment, in Tilda's hesitation, Imogen really recognized her old friend—a girl with a big personality who'd sometimes hovered at the fringes of a room, unsure if she was welcome. But a second later she strode ahead, leaving Imogen to take up the rear.

The first mile and a third of the Hermit Trail descended a toe-crunching thirteen hundred feet in elevation. Ahead of her, Tilda prodded cautiously with her walking stick and watched her feet, acclimating to the conditions. She didn't know yet about the thing that happens to a person's calf muscles after walking downhill for seven steep miles. The agony really couldn't be duplicated through exercise—even by people whose workout routines required them to leave the house. Imogen remembered being barely able to squat for a pee the day after a descent into the Canyon. Yet, it wasn't the sort of pain she feared. *Unlike bullets.*

"Oh my God." Tilda came to a full stop where a section of trail became a slanting rock over an abrupt two-foot drop.

Beck was already a little way ahead, so it was Imogen who stood beside her and examined the ground beneath the drop-off. They made hesitant eye contact. Imogen could almost sense Tilda wishing that Beck were here to guide her. Imogen reminded herself she had been good at this once—good at dancing across the stones in a creek bed, good at gauging the distance her legs could handle when maneuvering along footholds.

"You can use your stick to brace yourself. Then you can step onto…" Imogen pointed with her walking stick to a rock barely the size of an eggplant. "Maybe that one. Do you want me to go first?"

She wanted to prove to herself—and Tilda—that, rusty or not, she wasn't a liability.

Tilda studied the terrain, considering her options. "That's okay. I'll try it."

"Make sure your stick is wedged tight so it doesn't slip." Imogen had made that mistake once—*once*—at nineteen, crossing a pair of boulders farther down this very trail. The pole had shifted midleap, slamming against her ear.

There'd been no one close enough to see what had happened (or hear her cry out), and Imogen had half collapsed, her ear ringing, her head throbbing, certain she was bleeding. Tentatively, she'd touched her ear canal with her pinky finger, unsure what she'd do if her brain was oozing out. It wasn't. After a few minutes she was back on her way, but all these years later if she slept on that side too long her inner ear squawked in distress.

Apparently unimpressed with the eggplant-rock, Tilda sat on the edge of the slab and lowered herself over. Up ahead, Beck had stopped and was watching them.

Once safely down, Tilda raised her walking stick above her head in triumph. It wasn't quite a curtain call begging for a standing ovation, but close enough. Imogen kept any uncharitable comments to herself, though she uttered an "oh dear" at Tilda's back before nimbly traversing the drop.

"Are there a lot of places like that?" Tilda directed the question to Beck as they caught up to her, but Imogen couldn't hold back.

"Yup. Lots. You might not be able to sit on your butt for all of them." She hadn't meant to sound snide, but Beck and Tilda heard it that way and shot her a cold gaze.

"She's not as experienced as you," Beck said, using the tone that made Imogen feel like a bad child.

"I didn't mean it like that," she mumbled as they resumed hiking. Imogen felt herself blushing as something devilish wormed around inside her. No, the thing that had bothered her was the celebration, Tilda's expression of conquest after crossing a relatively small hurdle. What would come next? Would they have to congratulate her after every obstacle?

In spite of the beauty all around them, Imogen was aware of an unfriendly bitterness hovering within her lungs, too easy to express. And this wasn't the place to let something as stupid as envy endanger anyone's safety.

Maybe she hadn't been paid as much money as Tilda for her book, but Imogen was proud of her second novel, *Esther's Ghost*. Sure, Tilda could write a how-to-live-your-best-life book filled with lots of glossy photographs and fat words of inspiration. But she couldn't touch what Imogen had learned to conjure after years of practice and thousands of pages of effort. *Esther's Ghost*'s second miracle (after finding a publisher with relative ease) was that it needed little in the way of revisions—which was fortunate, considering the state of her muse. She'd worked on it long and hard before showing it to her agent, getting feedback from Beck and a couple of online writer friends between drafts. It was a little darker than her debut novel, with a gothic feel, and she'd wanted to get it just right. Her protagonist, Esther, became consumed with finding her assailant after she was assaulted in her bed in the middle of the night. When the clues suggest her attacker was an honest-to-god ghost, Esther's friends start to question her sanity, but she knows the rape wasn't her imagination.

It was now seven months from publication—though, the way things were going, *Esther's Ghost* might be Imogen's last book.

It abruptly dawned on her what her sister had really said: Tilda didn't know how to do any of this—and Imogen did. If she wanted to feel good about herself, a worthy member of the expedition, she could play the role of teaching assistant. And maybe that was what Beck, disinclined toward expending too many words, envisioned for her. If Imogen wasn't sure who she was supposed to be in Tilda's life, at least she could do what Beck expected of her.

"This is probably the *steepest* section," Imogen said now, trying to make up for her earlier cynicism. "But you should anticipate a lot of rough spots ahead, especially once we're past Santa Maria Springs. But we'll be able to rest there for a bit to get refreshed."

In truth, Imogen didn't remember every piece of the trail that well, but part of her own preparation had been talking to her dad. He knew it helped her to visualize things, so her imagination wouldn't run amuck, and he'd happily answered her gazillion questions. Now she had a good portion of their hiking days outlined in her head.

Both Tilda and Beck glanced at her. Tilda seemed to get that she was trying to redeem herself, and flashed a grin. Beck shot her a patented look of disapproval. Imogen was tempted to shout ahead to her, "Use your words!" She was sick of her sister's weighty judgments, made in silence, leaving Imogen to question what she'd done wrong.

She suspected Beck had avoided describing anything as painfully steep or scoot-on-your-butt rough, or mentioned that Hermit Trail was *extremely difficult* on a scale of *already hard*. Beck could be merciless in her belief that people should figure things out for themselves. As a teenager, she'd expounded philosophically about her reticence, claiming that people too easily let someone else's rhetoric color their expectations. At sixteen, that sounded sage and geeky, but in recent years Imogen had wondered if it went deeper, if Beck really was afraid to express herself on some level.

Stop thinking! Too much baggage. Backpacking was supposed to be about packing light, but Imogen had brought a ton of extra shit, none of it useful.

Turning her attention to more constructive things, she watched Tilda on the trail ahead of her. She placed her feet carefully, but Imogen could see her muscles straining against the fabric of her two-tone hiking tights; they'd hardly started, and Tilda was already struggling.

"Keep half an eye on Beck," Imogen said. "See how she

maneuvers down the trail. You'll get more of a feel for the pack soon too, and how to move with the extra weight."

"Okay. Maybe I'm stupid"—Tilda paused to catch her breath, her eyes on the scenery—"but I didn't expect it to be quite so…"

"You're not stupid, you're just used to the word *trail* meaning something smooth and more or less easy to walk on," said Imogen.

"Yes. That. But…it is pretty fucking incredible."

They exchanged grins, unselfconscious for once, and continued on.

"Remember those stories we used to tell you? About tourists we'd come across who were totally unprepared. Thought if it was a tourist destination it must be as safe as Disneyland?"

"Yeah, I get it now. Honestly, if Beck hadn't advised me I probably would've been the same way. Headed off on a day hike in running shoes with a little bottle of water and a protein bar—like I did in LA! I get it. This is some *real* shit. Some not-something-everybody-can-do, don't-take-it-for-granted shit. And I'm glad we're doing this."

From the switchback below them, Beck radiated joy as she called up, "This is the real life."

"The real world," Imogen agreed. The *better* world. Nature didn't fuck things up the way people did.

The three of them smiled in unison.

5

They reached Santa Maria Springs two hours later. The much more heavily traveled Bright Angel Trail—the route the mule trips used—had strategically placed open-walled rock houses every couple of miles where people stopped to rest. But the Hermit Trail just had Santa Maria: a mini three-walled "cabin" with a wood-slab bench.

"Is this it?" Tilda asked, not sounding terribly impressed.

"This is it," Beck confirmed.

Several feet below the rustic shelter, spring water trickled out from between some rocks into a trough.

"It's named for *that*?" Tilda pointed to the dribbling water.

"Yup."

"I was hoping I'd be able to soak my feet." She drooped a little, disappointed.

Beck found a good-sized rock to use as a chair and perched on the edge. She leaned back a little to let the rock take the weight of her pack, and then unfastened her hip belt. "Are your boots bothering you? Are you getting blisters?"

"I don't think so. It just sounded nice, dangling my feet in a pool."

Tilda watched as first Beck, and then Imogen, removed her pack. Beck used her stick, wedged against another rock, to keep hers propped up; Imogen let hers rest on its back, an upside-down turtle. Using the same technique, Tilda soon had her pack off and plopped herself down on the cool, ever-so-slightly damp floor of the hut. While the Blum sisters gathered the canteens and filled them with fresh water from the trough, Tilda took off her boots and socks and pressed her feet into the moist earth.

Tilda might not have fully appreciated their shady sanctuary, but Imogen was well aware that their packs would've been much heavier if Santa Maria weren't such a stable water source. Imogen gave Beck points for that; she'd planned a trip where water wouldn't be a concern. Hermit and Boucher each had its own creek, unlike other places in the desert interior of the Canyon. On previous trips, when they'd gone out to places like Sumner Wash and Salt, they'd had to carry in all the water they'd need to get them through the night. If they got lucky, they might find a puddle nestled in the curves and angles of a boulder and they'd press the mouths of their canteens into the stagnant water, while trying to avoid the twigs and mosquito larvae. They never turned down opportunities to top off their water bottles, even if the puddles necessitated a double dose of iodine tablets. At Santa Maria, the water was so clean they probably didn't even need to purify it, but Imogen dropped a single iodine tablet into each canteen, just in case.

Their chores complete, Beck and Imogen joined Tilda, sighing with relief as they sat on the ground and extended their legs. They passed around a bag of gorp, though Tilda augmented her snack with a fancy organic protein bar.

"If your feet start to hurt don't ignore it—tell us and we'll stop right away," said Beck. "The best remedy is prevention."

By the slouch of her shoulders, the lethargic nod, it was apparent that Tilda was feeling it—the effort of their steep descent. "They're okay. This…not Disneyland," she said with a snort. "Jalal and I did so much hiking—at least I thought we did. Now I see it was more like strolling. I was duped—the San Gabriel Mountains should be demoted. I really thought I was better prepared."

"Don't get discouraged," Imogen said, picking out one M&M for each cashew, a ratio she knew wouldn't last. "Everybody feels like this the first half of the first day."

"Going down is always hardest," said Beck. "And then your muscles start to acclimate, and it gets better."

"So this is only halfway?" Tilda squinted an eye at Imogen.

"More like a third?" She turned to Beck for confirmation. Got it with a bobbing nod that really said *A little less.*

"You said it gets *harder* after Santa Maria Springs?" Tilda asked Imogen, her incredulous voice spiraling upward.

And now Imogen understood better why Beck hadn't given Tilda the full rundown. It pissed her off a little that her sister was right, and too late Imogen realized she might have planted a seed of doubt or worry in Tilda's mind. Indeed "Prepare for the Worst" might not work for everyone.

"There are some level stretches coming up." It was Beck's attempt to save her and Imogen appreciated it, but even to her biased ears her sister sounded cryptic.

"And some *unlevel* stretches?" Tilda asked, her focus back on Imogen.

"Remember the tricky spots I mentioned?" Imogen said, hoping *spots* made it sound less daunting.

"There are some sections with sharp declines coming up, and some rock falls to cross—real boulders, and not just a rock or two. The next three hours might be the toughest section of the trail."

Both Tilda and Imogen blinked at Beck and her matter-of-fact assessment.

Tilda swallowed some water with a loud gulp. Imogen saw her trying to imagine it.

"And after that? Will we be almost to camp?"

"Then we'll hit Cathedral Stairs," Beck said.

"That sounds pretty," said Tilda. "Is it pretty?"

"Sure."

"Are they stairs?"

"Nah. Switchbacks, descending down through the Redwall." Beck closed up her Ziploc baggie of nuts and seeds.

Tilda snapped her head back over to Imogen, a playful smile curling her lips. "And then we'll be at camp?"

"No...not quite." Imogen liked it better when Beck was in charge of the answers, though it felt good that Tilda was consulting her, too. Now that they weren't holding back, she tried to picture the rest of the route. "Then we'll walk a bit more. Hit the Tonto Trail. Head west—a mile and a quarter or so?"

Beck nodded. "Not gonna lie, Til. When you hit the Tonto, and it seems like easy walking, you keep thinking that camp is just around the next bend. And a mile and a quarter doesn't sound that far...And it becomes the longest mile and a quarter you've ever walked."

"Oh." Tilda bunched up her protein bar wrapper and stuffed it in her pack; they'd designate an actual garbage bag later and tie it on the outside of one of their backpacks. "And *then* we'll be at camp?" she blurted, both good-natured and exasperated.

"Yes!" the Blum sisters said with a laugh.

"Now I have the whole plan? No other surprises?" Her gaze ticktocked from sister to sister. Imogen pressed her lips together, raised her eyebrows, and waited to see what Beck would say. Which was nothing. "You're the word person," Tilda said to Imogen. "I count on you to be chattier where Beck's more...reserved."

Imogen hadn't believed for a long time that Tilda was the least bit interested in having a better relationship with her. Now she wondered if her own mixed feelings clouded that perception. Writing *Esther's Ghost* had reminded her of past traumas that she'd never fully examined. Worse, she'd effectively suppressed them until she believed she was a hermit because she *wanted* to be, but she was starting to question that.

"I say exactly what needs to be said," Beck offered in her own pithy defense. "*When* it needs to be said. No more, no less."

Beck took herself so seriously and sometimes it struck Imogen as funny, but she glanced away to keep from laughing; her sister could be sensitive about being laughed at.

"Guess we better get going—sounds like it's a long-ass way." Tilda put her socks and boots back on.

"Agreed," Beck said, instantly on her feet.

"Miles feel a lot longer in the Canyon." Imogen took a minute to stretch out her calf muscles. "Scrambling over rocks takes a *lot* of extra steps."

"A quick pee first." Tilda glanced around, dismayed by her bathroom options. Imogen retrieved a flattened role of toilet paper from the side pocket of her pack and handed it to her. "Where should I go?"

"Anywhere," Beck said. "It's pretty deserted this time of year, no one's going to see you."

"Just don't pee on your boots." They both gave Imogen a smirk. "What? I'm serious, that's good advice—stand so your boots are uphill of your pee."

"Okay." Tilda sighed, tucking the toilet paper under her arm as she wandered a few feet off the trail.

"And don't sit on anything with thorns." This time Beck earned the smirk—and a merry middle finger from Tilda.

The sisters packed up the water bottles and snacks.

"Can you see me?" Tilda called from behind a boulder.

"No," Beck and Imogen said together, chuckling. They both stuffed their windbreakers under the straps that held their sleeping bags.

"Maybe I should take my leggings off before we go," Imogen murmured, feeling a little sweaty. But before she could decide, Tilda let out a shriek and came running from behind the rock. Beck bolted upright, on alert.

"Gross, gross, gross!"

Beck seemed to decide it wasn't an actual crisis, and her whole body loosened. "You'll get used to it. Please don't scream unless it's a real emergen—"

"No, no—" Tilda pointed behind her and Imogen saw real panic on her face.

"What's wrong?" she asked, the hair on her arms tingling.

"Blood, there's a bloody—"

"Are you bleeding?" Beck was all doctor now.

"No, there. I was kicking dirt over my toilet paper and I saw…A bloody…"

Imogen grabbed her walking stick and she and Beck hurried off trail in the direction of Tilda's privy. The writer in Imogen ran through possibilities of what they might find: the bloody carcass of a freshly devoured animal; a severed human limb (unlikely, but a story-worthy idea). What Imogen spotted wasn't exactly dramatic. They squatted down to get a better look.

"Looks like a…T-shirt?" Grimacing, Imogen used the tip of her walking stick to prod it. As Tilda had attested, the lump of cloth, perhaps once white, was covered in brownish-red bloodstains.

"Maybe somebody got their period and didn't have anything," Beck suggested.

"Maybe." As it dangled from Imogen's stick, Beck studied it more carefully.

"No. It was wrapped around something." She pointed at the succession of stains. "It seeped through these layers, see? But not these." She shrugged. "Lots of things to get cut on. I trust they were heading out, not in—that much blood probably needs stitches."

"Should we put it with our garbage?" Imogen dropped it back on the ground and took a step back. She really didn't want to carry around someone else's bloody waste, but it was the right thing to do.

"Why don't we just bury it well. Want me to get the trowel?"

"That's okay, I'll use my stick. And some rocks." She started digging into the dry earth with the end of her pole.

"Got this? I'll make sure Tilda's okay."

As Imogen nodded, Beck retreated. If it had been bright blood, fresh and wet, she might have asked Beck to take over. With its dried, subdued color Imogen could pretend it was something else; it reminded her of a shirt she'd once tie-dyed in mashed blackberries. But that wasn't enough to keep away a momentary flashback of a morning demolished, a memory of screams. They weren't supposed to be here—the triggers of the outside world.

They used the reverse method of how they'd taken off their packs to put them back on. One by one, they tugged each other's hip belts, making them tight to ease the strain on their shoulders.

Beck looked spry, a bounce in her step, as she started down the trail. Tilda's stride and footing were growing more confident, and she was handling her walking stick better too, letting it assist her balance and support her when needed. Imogen's own legs were feeling a bit jiggly after their rest, but her muscles soon warmed up and she felt strong enough, at least for now, to make it to Hermit Camp without slowing them down.

The air around them smelled clean and undisturbed. Tilda's hair, bundled on her head, bobbed as she walked. Imogen's pack made a rhythmic squeaking noise as it swayed with her stride. At the lead, Beck marched on with a sanguine ease and Imogen suspected she was lost in her thoughts. A distance grew between Beck and Tilda, but Imogen wasn't concerned. Tilda paused at another rocky step-down and, unable to look back over her pack, swiveled her whole body toward Imogen.

"I prolly shouldn't start asking every fifteen minutes if we're almost there."

"Prolly not." They shared a grin. And held each other's gaze for a moment longer than they had in…forever.

It had only been a couple of hours, but Imogen already felt different. In the city, in her apartment, her blood was diluted the weak red of being half alive, half out of it. She was always aware of the slowness of her life's journey—how she generally just needed more time than everyone else to figure things out.

Years ago Beck and Tilda had surged ahead and forged busy, enterprising lives full of new people and new experiences. Imogen had watched from afar, watched as seeds germinated and started to grow like a barrier between them. They'd kept growing, tall and thick, sprouting thorns on their entwining arms. If Imogen couldn't finally put a stop to it, the plants would become a hedgerow, as solid as a wall, and she wouldn't be able to fit even her hand through to find anyone.

This is going to work. She wasn't even sure what the thought meant, what it included, but it felt right. Maybe it wasn't too late to catch up. As if to compel her to move everything along a bit faster, find a way through the gap, her sister disappeared on the trail ahead.

6

The feeling of settling in at camp after an interminable day of hiking was like finally finding the home you'd always wanted. The home, devoid of luxuries, that you'd always needed. Watching as Tilda lay sprawled on her one-inch-thick inflatable mattress pad, Imogen knew exactly what she was experiencing: the greatest comfort of her life. No sofa after a difficult but ordinary day could compare. Nor could a prosaic view of four walls or the best in streaming television.

The feelings came back so effortlessly, as if this real world, this better world, had been waiting for her. And it would have waited forever, and welcomed her regardless, but she was glad, so glad, Beck hadn't let her say no to this trip. They'd gone car camping a few times while Beck was in medical school, and when she first moved to Arizona they made one Canyon trip together. But in the intervening decade Imogen had become too intimidated—too poor, too indulgent-of-her-ways—to make adventurous trips. And in the last year she'd even forgone trying to visit her sister and Afiya.

Now, fully immersed in being outdoors—truly outdoors, with no easy way to go back indoors—it was easier to see the meaninglessness of her everyday life. With its to-do lists and routines, its material distractions and petty worries. At home, she was broken and useless; in the Canyon she had the same potential as the raven that flew circles above her head.

While Beck unpacked the things they'd need to make supper, Imogen did a bit of housekeeping. She secured their plastic drop cloth with rocks around its edges, as sometimes gusts blew hard through the inner canyons. They never used a tent in the Canyon, and Imogen had never experienced rain here, though they carried extra tarps for that contingency. In theory, the scorpions came out at night, but they'd never seen one; as a precaution, they always shook out their boots in the morning. But a tent would ruin everything.

It was something of a contradiction that in the city she preferred the familiar and solitary comfort of small rooms, yet sleeping outside had always ranked near the top of her Favorite Things. There was nothing like being snug in a sleeping bag and awakening in a morning fog that made her feel like she was in a cloud. And while she was never fully at ease in the dark, here—with a sky unmarred by the disease of light pollution—the celestial canopy promised wonders of its own. She was hopeful it would feel just as good as she remembered, and in a state of physical exhaustion, she might not even need her tincture to help her sleep.

As Imogen tidied up their mattress pads and sleeping bags, making neat parallel beds, she grinned with the anticipation of the nightly star show. Both she and Tilda had invested in heavier but more comfortable Therm-a-Rest inflatable pads, but Beck still liked her eggshell pad, which accordioned into a featherweight rectangular prism. Imogen made each of them a preliminary pillow using the stuff sacks from their sleeping bags, which she filled with whatever they weren't currently wearing. It would drop into the forties overnight, but the sleeping bags would keep them warm. Until then, they'd wear their sweatshirts and fleeces as the temperature started to fall.

Tilda strolled back from the pit toilets, which they'd passed on their way into camp, the toilet paper in one hand, her camera in the other.

"Gotta enjoy the facilities while I can, right?" Once they departed for Boucher canyon in the morning, they wouldn't have even a pit toilet again until they came back to Hermit for the last night of their trip.

"Squatting isn't so bad," said Beck.

"The *lack of plumbing* isn't so bad," Imogen corrected, "but my thigh muscles aren't good at squatting."

"You've got it so backwards," said Tilda, sitting crisscross applesauce on her makeshift bed. She sniffed her underarms. "I'm still a little unsure of this whole no showering thing."

"No one ever died from being a little smelly." And Imogen should know: with fewer reasons to leave her apartment came less motivation for daily hygiene.

Tilda snapped a few pictures of their camp, then took a second to survey the campsite about two hundred feet beyond theirs, where a small blue tent was set up. "So some people use tents?" she said.

"Silly people." Beck lifted her compact Swedish stove out of the saucepan it traveled in.

"Do you ever, like, go and introduce yourselves and hang out?"

"If you pass someone on the trail you say hello, maybe swap stories," said Imogen, aware that avoiding people was probably a new concept for someone who spent most of her life trying to expand an ever-widening circle of followers.

"But at camp, people pretty much like to do their own thing." Another reason Beck surely liked the wilderness, with its little demand for small talk.

"Don't you ever…worry? About who's around?" Tilda asked.

Imogen eyed the distant tent. She was tempted to say yes, but didn't: at best Beck wouldn't understand why she shared this concern; at worst she might kill Imogen for *scaring Tilda*. At home, she'd added a second lock to her door, even though it was against the rules of her lease, and couldn't sleep with the windows open. She listened now, trying to pick up voices. If she heard women among the neighboring party it would diffuse much of her apprehension. But she didn't hear any voices at all.

"Backpackers are a certain type," Beck said, "especially people who do hard-core trips."

"Like us?" Tilda asked her.

"Exactly."

Per usual, her sister was calm and reasonable, and Imogen perhaps found more comfort in her words than Tilda did, as she knew Beck was right—and once upon a time she'd felt just as carefree. People who loved nature *were* different. Except for hunters. And maybe survivalists.

Imogen loved to binge certain kinds of reality television. Beck would refute its value as "preparation," but over the last few months she'd watched every season of *Alone,* in which contestants tried to survive on their own in an unforgiving wilderness with nothing but a handful of tools. Living vicariously through their adventures, she'd admired some of them for their incredible skills, their knowledge of plants and how to build a shelter. But sometimes the show broke her heart. The squealing squirrel at the end of an arrow. The duck, sick or injured, that sat alone on a cold beach. Imogen wanted to help it, to cuddle it and soothe away its pain. The hungry contestant had other ideas; she stepped on its neck and it pooped toward the camera while it suffocated. While Imogen understood that people needed to eat, she was glad that backpackers weren't trying to win out over starvation.

"Need help with anything?" Tilda asked her.

Imogen appreciated the diversion. "You can get out the bowls and mugs and utensils. I think they're all in your pack."

Beck had set up their kitchen area so the stove was sheltered between two rocks, which would help keep it ablaze if it got windy. The stove was about the size of a thirty-two-ounce can of tomatoes and consisted of only a few elements: the bottom section held the Coleman fuel below the burner; above that, three prongs could be turned outward to stabilize a lightweight pot; and the keylike mechanism that would ignite the flame. Beck struck a wooden match and lit the fire-starter—a gel she'd squirted in the indentation beneath the burner. Tilda brought the utensils and plastic dishes over and set them within reach.

"Anything else?" she asked, genuinely eager.

"You can fill the pot with water if you want," said Beck.

Sometimes Tilda acted like a little kid, with big gestures and silly voices and over-the-top reactions, but this version— the intrepid kid, the *ooh what's next?* kid—was actually kind of endearing. Imogen struggled to reconcile this person with the

Tilda she'd come to know online, who always looked more like an advertisement than a real person. Admittedly, part of Tilda's persona was acknowledging the breadth of her mistakes— "That's how we keep growing!"—but Imogen always found something disingenuous about it, as if such admissions were just another way to earn points.

Tilda splashed most of the contents of a canteen into the pot. Looking quite satisfied with herself, she affixed the lid and balanced the pot atop the delicate prongs of the now-roaring stove.

"After this boils, it'll just be a few minutes before supper's ready," Beck said.

"Great!"

Tilda loped over to see what Imogen was doing just as she finished burrowing through the last of their backpacks. Beside her lay a mound of every speck of food they weren't consuming for supper: snack baggies, freeze-dried dinners, oatmeal packets, the noncrushable container that held their crushable crackers, a half dozen self-contained Cup Noodles, even the coffee and tea bags. The sun was starting to set and she wanted to get the food hung while there was still enough light to see by. She whipped open a blue nylon drawstring bag and started shoving everything in.

"What's all this for?"

"We can't leave the food in the packs overnight," said Imogen, "so I'm going to find a tree to hang this from."

"That's so the bears don't attack you while you're sleeping?"

Catching the gleam of mischief on Tilda's face, Imogen suppressed a giggle, impressed by Tilda's easy acknowledgment of her own naïveté. "If we were in a forest that would be the reason. But here, the problem is squirrels, and other little creatures that might like to chew through our packs and eat up our food while we're none the wiser."

Tilda squatted beside her to help—and promptly let out a squeal of pain, followed by a laugh. "Oh, my poor body—see why I thought a shower was a necessity? A hot bath would be even better."

It made Imogen feel a tiny bit better to know that even someone as fit as Tilda wasn't immune to the Canyon's physical demands. They both staggered back into upright positions. Imogen's legs were as zonked as her friend's, but she knew come morning it would be even worse: after tightening overnight, her muscles would feel as pliable and soft as barbed wire.

"What are we having?" Imogen called over to Beck.

Beck picked up two freeze-dried dinner bags. "Chicken à la king."

"My favorite!" said Imogen.

"And—"

"Even more chicken à la king?"

"Actually, chicken and rice."

"Still good, a close second."

Imogen felt a little bloom of victory when Beck chortled approvingly: Imogen's love of freeze-dried chicken à la king was a long-running joke in the family, but she was getting less good at predicting her sister's reactions. Way back when, on that disastrous trip, after their parents finally made it to Hermit Camp on their second day of hiking (Beck had, in fact, ventured back up Cathedral Stairs in daylight to ferry down their mom's pack), they'd all enjoyed a hot meal at last. Imogen had declared the chicken à la king so delicious she planned on serving it once a week to her future husband (such was her thinking as a thirteen-year-old, optimistic about love, pessimistic about cooking).

"Sounds very…chickeny. Do you need help tying this up?" Tilda asked as Imogen slung the heavy nylon bag over her shoulder.

"Sure." Imogen handed her a length of cord, and they ambled away from their campsite.

"What are we looking for?" Tilda followed along behind her like a puppy. They hadn't passed any other in-use campsites, so proximity to people wasn't the problem.

"A branch strong enough to hold this high enough off the ground, but not so high we can't reach it."

A dubious, confused look settled on Tilda's face as she took in the growing things around them, none especially hale or sturdy. The ground beneath their feet was sandy, spotted with rocks and low, spindly shrubs that Imogen identified as brittlebush and Mormon tea. The trees weren't much better. Runty acacia with narrow trunks and fingerlike branches that seemed likely to bend under the weight of their food bag. The cottonwoods didn't look much stronger, though they flourished elsewhere in the Canyon. Imogen supposed they were too far away from the creek to draw much water through their roots, but their leaves were well on their way to pure autumnal gold.

Above them, the sky was drifting toward purple; she had forgotten how quickly it darkened in the inner canyons. "I think this'll do."

They stopped beside a tree seventy feet from camp where a branch a few inches thick umbrellaed over their heads. Imogen tied a couple of half hitch knots around the gathered top of the bag, then hoisted it onto her shoulder and let Tilda do the rest.

It took Tilda a couple of tosses to get the nylon rope exactly where she wanted it.

"How do you do the knots?"

"Here, you hold this."

They switched places and Tilda held the bag. When Imogen was done tying it off, the bag swayed about two feet away from the tree's trunk, and three feet off the ground.

"Well. Better than nothing." Though a picture came to Imogen of an especially tall squirrel standing on its hind legs, cackling as it nibbled through the bottom of their bag.

"I like all these little rituals," Tilda said as they headed back.

"There's a certain way to do things, living outside. Carrying all your stuff." Imogen liked the rituals too, and liked that Tilda had named them aptly. Beck practically lived for them.

They might not have been traditionally religious as a family, but in many ways the wilderness had served as the synagogue of their youth. There, they were reverential, whispering gratitude and prayers. As a child, Imogen had taken the commandment of *tikkun olam*—repair the world—as a quite literal command to not litter, to protect the earth's water and air. As an adult, she came to learn that *tikkun olam* often invoked social justice, with *mitzvot* as simple as being kind, being generous, being compassionate, and, in more recent years, joining protest movements. That understanding—the *healing* of the human world—drove much of her desire to be better at being Jewish.

"Hearing it described, it sounded...like a pain in the ass," Tilda said as they strolled toward camp. "But actually doing it—with the water tablets, and packing all these little plastic bags within bigger bags. And how everything's rolled and fits together in a certain way, and then unrolled. I don't know, there's something very appealing about it. Like your daily life is a physical puzzle. And everything you have is important."

Imogen grinned a reply. She'd been cognizant of her loneliness, but for the first time since befriending the early-bird congregants of Etz Chayim she felt open to the possibility of deeper relationships. And Tilda, once a best friend, was an ideal start.

Pleased as pudding and fully in her element, Beck held out two vintage Tupperware mugs as Tilda and Imogen made themselves comfortable on the ground near her. "Hot chocolate appetizer?"

"Never say no to chocolate," Tilda and Imogen said in perfect sync. It made them all laugh. Imogen couldn't remember the precise origin of the chorused words, but at some point in high school "never say no to chocolate" became a thing, perhaps because they smoked a little too much weed and often had the munchies. They thanked Beck and took their mugs, stirring up the powdery chocolate with the same slightly bent spoons they would soon eat dinner with.

Maybe it was the old spoons, or the place, or the company, but Imogen sensed a shift in reality, as if they'd gone back in time. It was a good shift—to an age before the hedgerow had sent even an investigatory tendril through the topsoil. An age before The Thing. Once upon a time the three of them had spoken the same language, and maybe some of it still lingered in their subconscious.

"Dinner will be served in three minutes. Give or take," said Beck.

"How can you tell? Without a clock?" Tilda asked, blowing on the steaming mug. The Blums didn't allow technology of any kind on their wilderness expeditions; a watch was even less useful than a cell phone.

"When the chicken's not like pebbles anymore?" Beck shrugged.

"Or the rice," Imogen chipped in.

"I see, so this—backpacking—is a mixture of precision and winging it."

"Exactly!"

"You got it."

A few minutes later they divvied up the reconstituted pouches and hungrily dove into their bowls. The chicken à la king was just as delicious as Imogen remembered.

7

H ow's work?" Tilda asked Beck, interrupting long minutes where the only sounds had been chewing and
satisfied *mm-mm-mm*s.

"Good. The same. Too much paperwork, not enough healing work."

"Our priorities are so screwed up."

"Indeed they are."

"How's your work?" Tilda asked Imogen, somewhat to her
surprise.

"Good. Just finished the copyedits on my second novel,
Esther's Ghost."

"That's awesome, congratulations! Sorry if I missed your
announcement online."

"Thank you." She opted not to say more than that. Tilda
either hadn't seen, or chose not to acknowledge, any number
of announcements: the deal itself, the cover reveal, the book's
acquisition by a UK publisher.

"She couldn't post about it but she got a raise, on her advance," Beck said, chewing as she spoke.

"A little one."

"And they're going to send her on a book tour."

"A little one," Imogen said again. It wasn't that she wanted to downplay her achievement, but it had started to bother her when people assumed that being published automatically earned certain benchmarks of success—like making the *New York Times* bestseller list, or selling the movie rights. Most books lived in a liminal place of near obscurity.

"You really stuck with it," said Tilda. "I'm proud of you."

"Thank you." She appreciated Tilda's better-late-than-never support, but it triggered some guilt at her own hypocrisy. "Congrats on *your* book deal—I meant to tell you before, but…"

And then she didn't know what to say. Tilda's announcement had come via Instagram a few weeks earlier and Imogen hadn't "hearted" the post. From the wording, Tilda was being paid six figures to write a feel-good, you-can-do-it-too book inspired by her post–*American Idol* career. At a minimum, that meant Tilda was being paid five times what Imogen had been paid for her first finally-got-the-damn-thing-published novel.

It had made their impending reunion in the Canyon that much weirder to think about, and Imogen had found herself too often at the losing end of her tug-of-war with the green-eyed monster. It was every variety of petty to be upset by someone else's success, but sometimes her mind morphed into a vindictive screensaver blinking words from the most flawed part of her heart—former waitress, aspiring-but-retired singer (*quitter*), reality-TV star, social media influencer. And then, more urgently, and in bold, capital letters: **NOT A WRITER! NOT A WRITER!**

In the conversational gap, Imogen heard laughter—high-pitched, a woman's—drift up from the neighboring camp. She imagined a trio of women backpackers in their midthirties, lifelong friends, all of them having a great time. In this trio, it was Tilda who finally came up with a response.

"I know it has to seem funny-not-funny, seeing how I've never written anything."

"But you worked really hard," Beck said, perhaps oblivious to the tension.

"I'm really happy for you, Tilda, I am. But you know…I have this belief, about how two diametrically opposed things can exist in the same space?" Judging by her face, Tilda had no idea what Imogen was trying to say. "That means I can be happy for you—sincerely happy—but also be jealous."

Tilda let out a gush of breath, as if she'd been holding it. "Thank you."

Beck looked up from her dinner, unable to track the subtext of the conversation. "You're happy that she's jealous?"

"No. She's happy I admitted it."

Tilda nodded. "If the situation had been reversed, if you announced out of nowhere that you'd gotten a big record deal I'd be like what the fuck?"

"I would too 'cause Imogen can't sing."

They laughed, but without heart.

"I was almost afraid to be with you this week," said Tilda. "I know I'm not a writer, I don't have any of your talent."

"Sometimes books aren't about the writing." Imogen was trying to say something conciliatory, but it didn't sound right. "I mean, I understand it's a completely different kind of book. This is your life, your thoughts, your words of wisdom. I'm sure it'll do really well."

"*If* I can write it. It's probably the most daunting thing I've tried to do."

"Except for this," Beck offered.

"You might be relieved after this to get home and *only* have to write a book."

This time their laughter was more genuine. Imogen was glad it was out in the open, and she recognized Tilda's efforts to understand her perspective. But it still didn't feel quite okay. Tilda's *if* was a reminder of her own predicament. What would Imogen do when *she* got home? Even the poems and short stories she'd dabbled with over the past year were unfinished. She'd always prided herself on her discipline. At times she thought writing about the shooting would help her process it, and at other times she considered trying her hand at something light and uncontroversial—a children's book, perhaps. But all she had to show for a year of effort were dozens of mostly empty Word documents.

"How's the volunteer stuff going?" Beck asked, nimbly—or obliviously—changing the subject.

"Great." Tilda's whole demeanor changed, to something with a high but soft wattage. "I have so much respect for Jalal and everything he's doing. I feel purposeful in a way I never have."

Imogen was clueless. Jalal she knew about, though hadn't met; Tilda had been dating him for over a year, but she didn't share much about him online.

"What kind of volunteer work are you doing?"

Tilda turned to her, still beaming. "I've gotten involved with the immigrant resource center. Originally I thought I'd mostly be helping recent immigrants tap into the resources they needed, but now we're also trying to keep people from being deported. It's gotten so merciless—parents who've lived here for a generation, paying taxes, all their kids born here. The kids go to school and worry that their parents won't be there when they get home. They've even deported people who were adopted from other countries as babies and have never lived anywhere else. Jalal helps on the legal end, but sometimes we're literally just ferrying people around, hiding them from the authorities."

"Oh my God." Imogen thought of all the dystopian novels she'd read. "This is worse than a horror novel."

"I don't understand what's happened to this country. But I wish my Spanish was better." She sighed. Imogen remembered how annoyed Tilda used to get in high school when people assumed she spoke Spanish or came from somewhere else. She hadn't been shy about screaming that her mother was from Texas and her father was from Brooklyn and "We speak English!"

Imogen didn't know Tilda as someone who took on serious issues. "Why don't you ever talk about it online? I'm sure some of your followers would be really interested."

Tilda sucked on her spoon for a moment. "On the one hand I want to, to make more people aware of how bad, how unfair it is. But I don't want to seem like I'm virtue signaling—and a *lot* of people in my space do that." She shrugged. "I'm working behind the scenes, until I figure out a good way to use my platform."

"Wow. That's really cool." She hoped she sounded as impressed as she was.

"When all that's left...," Beck sang, rather wobbly. "Remember that? *When you're so bereft...*"

Imogen groaned. It was a song from *Eighty-Seven Seconds.* A slow, sappy tune that fit the maudlin moment when the people on the doomed plane realized they could perform a mitzvah in their final moments of life by simply comforting those around them.

"Is helping your fellow man—we're all a clan, so take my hand!" Tilda's professional voice hid Beck's wavering notes.

"I can't believe you can still sing that." Imogen meant it as a put-down to her own forgettable writing.

The singing came to an abrupt end. "You always did underestimate me."

The rebuke came swift and sharp. Imogen felt herself shrink; she hadn't meant to insult Tilda. But she didn't correct or excuse herself, because she heard the deeper accusation behind Tilda's words. And the truth of it made her feel like she was naked under a spotlight. In Imogen's mind Tilda was often shallow, self-centered, selfish even—and somehow she hadn't thought Tilda capable of divining her secret opinions. *Surprise.*

The silence that followed made Imogen want to mount some sort of argument or counterattack, and she knew exactly where she wanted to direct her blade. But to do so would mean excavating The Thing. A long time ago Imogen had had to choose between dwelling on The Thing or stuffing it away. She'd gone with the latter. Dwelling, she'd feared, would discolor every choice she made.

Night settled in around them and it was almost pitch black. She struggled not to cry.

"We should get this cleaned up." Beck stacked her dirty dishes and got to her feet. She and Tilda had resumed their easy dialogue, though Imogen had slunk inward and finished her meal without speaking.

Imogen and Tilda both flicked on their flashlights, which had been dangling from their wrists. Together, the three of them rinsed the dishes with the rest of the boiled water, leaving them facedown on a rock to dry. They exchanged light banter in soft voices, as if afraid of awakening someone—or something—best left to slumber. Maybe that was what they all needed, sleep. Tilda's anger hadn't resurfaced, but Imogen sensed it there, like a predator stalking the nocturnal landscape, waiting for its moment. As Beck and Tilda got out their toothbrushes, Imogen dug out her marijuana tincture. Just as she was dripping the slightly skunky liquid under her tongue, Tilda directed the flashlight on her.

"What is that?"

"It helps me relax."

"That isn't your medical marijuana?" Beck asked, her tone well on its way to disapproval.

"It's mostly CBD." Imogen returned it to the pocket of her pack.

"That's not the point. You brought that on the *plane*?" Beck's tone now surpassed disapproval.

"I needed it." She joined them in their toothbrushing huddle.

"It's illegal to travel with—"

Imogen cut her off. "I repurposed a Visine bottle."

Tilda laughed. "Clever."

"Not clever," said Beck. "Stupid."

Imogen shrugged. "Security didn't look twice."

They slithered into their sleeping bags, with Beck in the middle, still in their clothes—though they each pulled off their top layer and added to their pillows. It was cold; Imogen hunkered into her bag and zipped it all the way up. For a time they gazed at the sky, pointing out shooting stars and satellites and bright objects they could almost name. Imogen wished she knew the constellations better, but Beck named a few, and spotted a couple of planets, too.

After a while the commentary stopped and they silently watched the heavens. Imogen, aware of the mellowing effects of her tincture, let her eyes go out of focus. In that blurry place the cosmos enveloped her. She breathed in the night and became the night, with the memory of the Milky Way imprinted on her shuttered lids.

8

Hands on her knees, Imogen stood hunched for a moment, her legs like crab claws. Standing upright would shatter the claws—send pink shards everywhere—that was how tight her muscles felt. But slowly she straightened. Limped a few feet. Greeted Tilda, who was attempting a Sun Salutation on her stripped-down mattress pad. The sun hadn't warmed the air yet, so Imogen layered up with clothing from her pillow.

In the kitchen, Beck already had the stove going, its signature roar like a greeting from another time. They exchanged good mornings, though the morning was a shock for Imogen, who hadn't awakened out of doors in many years. *So much air! So much sky!* The gloriousness of it distracted her, made her forget the stiffness in her calves and down the backs of her thighs. It was so quiet she could hear the murmur of voices from the camp beneath them, and the creek water rippling through its eternal bed. A canyon wren trilled its little song, an almost melancholy series of notes, dropping in pitch. The breeze took a more tactile approach and caressed her cheek—"Hello dear, welcome back."

An outdoor morning was so different from an indoor morning, with a loss of certain creature comforts, but a gain in mindfulness. Back home, there was nothing and no one to acknowledge her upon awakening. In the Canyon, she was part of something elemental, returning to consciousness to resume *being alive.*

"Head to the loo?" she said to Tilda, by way of invitation, as she shook out her boots.

"Yup." Tilda, enviously limber, abandoned her yoga and plucked the partial TP roll from her left boot before slipping her foot into it. "What if we run out of toilet paper?"

"That would suck. Don't overuse the toilet paper."

"Get the food bag on your way back?" Beck asked.

"You got it," said Imogen.

Beck already had the mugs lined up. She was a Coffee Person of the First Order, Tilda of the Second Order. They both had many ways of describing their nonpersonhood when confronted with life before the day's first cup of coffee. At home, Beck's standards for the type and strength of that coffee were quite high. Not willing to sacrifice, she'd brought a small Melitta cone and a wad of filters to make individual "pour-over" cups. Tilda, not needing it quite as strong, had agreed long before they entered the Canyon to take the second cup, so they could reuse the dark grounds and justify this bit of luxury.

None of them were quite awake enough to be sociable, but Imogen was glad for Tilda's company as they headed for the pit toilets. Was this what it would be like to live with someone? A boyfriend, in Tilda's case. A wife, in

Beck's. Someone to brighten your day with companionship? Help you with ordinary tasks? Sometimes Imogen thought she wanted that, and other times she told herself it would be too annoying—cleaning up after another person, having them around when she wanted to be alone, sharing a bed. Arguing.

In college the trio had started out in an apartment together—financed by their busy, guilt-ridden parents—but Imogen had moved back to her dad's when she quit school. A few years later, with her dad's help, she'd gotten her own small apartment. She'd lived alone since then. It was hard sometimes, having to handle every single contingency by herself. Laundry, meal prep, paying the bills. Walking to Rite Aid for ibuprofen in the middle of a migraine. Sitting in the dark alone when the electricity went out. She'd suspected for a while that she might be missing out on something, but hadn't figured out how to remedy it. Joining the synagogue was meant to be a beginning.

After their pit stop they headed toward where they'd hung the food the previous evening. Even a short walk helped to loosen Imogen's cranky legs.

"Did you sleep well?" she asked Tilda.

"Great. Better than I expected."

Imogen beamed; Tilda might be a full-on outdoor enthusiast by the end of the week. She could already hear her exclaiming, "Why didn't you make me do this sooner?" But all her good vibes withered when she spotted their bright blue food bag—not swaying on its branch as it should have been, but resting in the dirt.

"Fuck."

They hurried to the bag. It lay open, on its side.

"I knew I didn't get it high enough off the ground. Beck's gonna kill me."

In a panic, Imogen dropped to her knees and sorted through the contents, taking a quick inventory. If too much was damaged or eaten…She couldn't—simply couldn't—be the reason they had to leave the Canyon early; they'd never had to abandon a backpacking trip before. And she wasn't ready to go. If one day in the Canyon could do so much, who would she be after seven days? She wanted the chance to find out.

Imogen looked for signs of gnawing—tooth marks or ragged holes. She expected to find the spilled contents of instant oatmeal or gorp. But she didn't. And then she realized the drawstring bag had been *opened,* not chewed.

"Imogen?" Tilda's voice—uncertain, borderline alarmed—instantly drew Imogen's attention. "Look." She held the end of the thin rope that still hung from the tree. "I'm not an expert. I'm not anything…But this looks cut to me. Cut with a knife."

"That's…" Imogen wanted to say impossible. But there were no teeth marks on the food or the bag. And the rope…had clearly been *sliced* at an angle. A clean angle.

Had they been robbed?

Her barely awake mind struggled to make sense of it. They'd never had anything stolen while camping. It was a code, unwritten. It just wasn't done. Sometimes backpackers even stashed food or supplies for long trips, and it was understood: if you came across such a stash you left it alone. Someone's life might depend on it.

As Imogen huddled beside the bag, she took a more thorough accounting of its contents. Tilda, wanting to help, tidied the piles of freeze-dried dinners, the different Ziplocs—holding hot beverages and instant soups and cereals. At the very bottom of the bag was the heavy-duty Tupperware container, where they kept crackers, Fig Newtons, and other crushable snacks. Imogen snapped it open: its contents looked untouched—someone hadn't bothered to dig that deep.

"Looks like they took . . . all of your protein bars, and some of the sandwich bags of gorp. That's it."

"You think it's those other campers?" Tilda looked in the direction of their blue-tented neighbors. "Should we go talk to them?"

"No. That wouldn't make any sense." She remembered the previous night's laughter, and the normal morning sounds of hikers getting ready for their day. "If they were in trouble they would ask."

"Well someone didn't ask."

Was there another group staying at Hermit, or a solo back-packer they hadn't seen? Imogen quickly swept all the food back into the bag and slung it over her shoulder. "Can you get the rope down? Still might need it."

As they tramped back to camp Imogen's mind was awhirl. At her side, Tilda radiated worry. In their high school days Tilda had thought the Blum sisters were nuts, sleeping in places without *beds* and *doors*. Though Imogen had carried an unease—*Is it safe? Could I be cornered?*—as she moved through the world, it had never followed her here. *Is there anywhere to go for help?* Tilda had asked that as they'd packed. Help was miles away at best, but they'd assured her they'd never needed help, not even on the trip where they'd been separated from their parents.

And they didn't need help now—it wasn't an emergency, she

reminded herself. But it was unnerving: someone had invaded their space. Her brain refused to zero in on a plausible reason why this could happen. Not *here*.

Imogen wanted a diplomatic way of phrasing the theft to Beck, still feeling on some level like it was her fault: Should she have kept the bag within view of their camp? (As if they could've seen in the dark, while asleep.) But the second they were within sight of Beck, Tilda blurted out, "We were robbed."

"Robbed?" Beck stood as they approached, sounding half concerned and half befuddled. The water started boiling, chugging steam, and she bent over to turn down the stove. "Robbed as in an animal helped themselves to our supplies?"

"Robbed as in someone cut the bag down." Imogen plopped it at her sister's feet. Saying it aloud erased her guilt: this was squarely someone else's fault.

"And then helped themselves to our supplies," said Tilda.

"Are you sure?" In another situation Beck's doubt might have angered Imogen, but she hadn't believed it at first either, even while holding the evidence. "It would be easy for an animal to chew—"

"No tooth marks anywhere. And the rope was cleanly cut."

As if to corroborate Imogen's words, Tilda held out the severed cord.

Beck took one glance at it and dropped to her knees, yanking the bag open to start an inventory of her own. "What did they take?"

"Looks like just snack stuff. Mostly Tilda's energy bars." Watching as Beck counted off their dinner packages, Imogen felt useless—the feeling she hated more than any other. She'd so hoped to leave that, the worst of her failures, at home.

With the right number of freeze-dried dinners heaped beside her, Beck's anxiety evaporated. "Wow. That's never happened. I guess someone…was really hungry. They could've asked."

"That's what I said." Imogen was relieved that Beck seemed so chill about it, but she looked carefully—toward the next camp and beyond. "Someone else must be here though."

"Probably gone by now," said Beck.

"With my organically sourced protein bars." Tilda sat on the ground near Beck. "Not to sound like a jerk, but I wish they'd taken the Fig Newtons instead."

"That wouldn't have made it better," Beck said, a tad self-righteously.

"So says you."

Imogen continued scrutinizing the surrounding rocks—possible camouflage for a boogeyman. It was only *sort of* a ridiculous idea, given that she'd written an entire novel about a woman who believed she'd been raped by a ghost.

"It's okay, Im." Beck spoke gently. "No one's hiding. It was just some asshole, too embarrassed to admit they under-packed."

"I guess." Imogen finally sat down too.

"At least they didn't take the important stuff." Presumably Beck meant the dinners, but she grabbed the coffee and returned to the stove to finish her preparations.

With her own cup steaming, Beck set the Melitta cone over Tilda's mug and slowly poured the hot water over the coffee grounds.

"Thank you."

Imogen, clutching an empty mug, still wasn't sure how she

felt; backpackers weren't supposed to be assholes. Was this a new development in declining civility, or had they just gotten lucky before? It was some relief when Tilda, blowing on her coffee, sounded hesitant too.

"So we're not…? We're still just…? Like nothing happened?" Tilda looked from one sister to the other. Imogen waited for Beck to handle it, but she took a minute to enjoy the first careful slurps of her coffee.

It was only when Beck's eyes sprang open, as if jolted awake by the caffeine, that she noticed them both gazing at her, waiting for her response. "Oh. Well. Nothing's really different."

"Should we leave? Do we have enough food?" Tilda asked.

The morning was still nippy and Imogen, the only one without a hot drink, reached for a packet of hot chocolate. For once she appreciated her sister's nonchalance: Beck wasn't worried, and leaving hadn't even crossed her mind; they would continue on.

"If you're okay with gorp for a snack," Imogen said, pouring hot water into her cup, "we probably have enough."

Beck nodded. "I'm sorry about your energy bars, but we always overpack a little. And we have the crackers, and your favorite Fig Newtons."

Tilda returned Beck's good-natured dig with a good-natured smirk.

Imogen stirred her lumpy chocolate until it fully dissolved. The stuff in the Tupperware tended not to get eaten as quickly, partly because it wasn't as accessible. "We can save the gorp for travel days, and snack on the rest on camp days."

"Exactly. We're in good shape," said Beck.

Tilda sipped her coffee. "I guess for an asshole they were

almost nice about it—didn't take anything that would ruin our trip."

"There ya go."

"Still. It's a shitty thing to do."

"Agreed."

"Speaking of shitty," said Imogen, "if they'd stolen our *toilet paper* that would've been a real problem."

Tilda and Beck laughed, which felt like a victory. Imogen was pleased that they'd worked through this and were forging ahead. Many times on *Alone* a contestant was reduced to tears when an animal invaded their stash and ran off with their last piece of food. By comparison, they had it easy. She tore open two packets of cinnamon-apple oatmeal and poured them into her bowl.

"It'll be better when we're back on the trail," Beck said. "And even better than that when we get to Boucher—probably won't see a single person out there. And undoubtedly someone who came into the Canyon without enough food is already on their way out, or heading thataway." She pointed east, toward the more-traveled inner canyons. "Maybe going to Indian Gardens to get some help, if they're smart enough to know they need it."

Imogen remembered that morning when her parents still hadn't shown up at this very camp. She and Beck had debated their options: head back up the Hermit Trail to look for them; hike over to Indian Gardens to ask for a search party; or stay put and see what happened. They'd opted to stay because they were pooped and weren't sure what to do, and by lunchtime they were all reunited. Later, they told their dad they'd considered heading for Indian Gardens and he was so relieved they hadn't. Their guesstimate had been off by several miles and it would have been an arduous journey for two young kids with incomplete gear.

The little devil in Imogen hoped that was where the snack-stealing asshole was heading. Would serve him right to get in deeper over his head.

9

W e will neither tarry nor hurry," Beck replied when Tilda asked about their schedule.

The three-and-a-half-hour hike out to Boucher was mostly along the Tonto Platform, which was the easiest of Canyon walking—except for the few places where it...wasn't. Imogen was looking forward to getting out to Boucher and setting up their domicile for the next four nights. Even in the out-of-doors it felt good to have a familiar nest to return to; in a few hours, Boucher would be *home*.

They all appeared calm as they prepared for the day ahead, and Imogen was glad no one could see her as she felt inside: purple paisley. Hot and cold swirls, her blood zinging with jitters. She tried not to think about the Scary Spot, where their dad had once feared Beck might lose her life. At home she sometimes took a tiny dose of her tincture while readying to leave the house, but despite its low amount of THC she couldn't risk being even a little foggy here. It was already easy to space out while walking, and she needed to be able to concentrate and not jeopardize her balance.

Two evenings before, Tilda had quite literally tiptoed around the packing operation, but that morning she embraced it—stuffing the sleeping bags one by one into their sacks before rolling up the mattress pads.

"Want me to take your picture? Before you pack up your camera?" Imogen asked her, conscientious now about practicing her peacekeeping skills.

"Sure!" Tilda handed her the camera, and posed, smiling. Imogen took a variety of shots—close-ups, and wider pictures that included the gear and landscape—and then handed it back.

"Thank you. I thought I'd photograph everything, but half the time I forget I even have it with me."

Smiling, Imogen went down to the creek to top off their canteens, leaving Beck to finger-wash their breakfast dishes with splashes of boiled water. As Beck had instructed (or predicted) they neither hurried nor dallied, but soon were packed, their teeth brushed, sunscreen applied, and were ready to embark on the next leg of their journey. Anticipating a warm day on the Tonto, they wore windbreakers over short-sleeved shirts.

On their way out of Hermit Camp they passed the pit toilets and after a cumbersome dismounting of packs, they took turns having a last sit-downish pee.

"*Adiós,* civilization! *Hasta la vista!*" Tilda waved goodbye to the primitive restroom and off they went.

It was a lovely morning, the sky vivid and clear. They traveled in the formation they'd used the day before—Beck, then Tilda, then Imogen—and headed north to climb out of

Hermit canyon. Just a few feet up from the creek and they were on the Tonto Platform, a five-hundred-foot-thick terrace of soft Bright Angel shale. It varied in width from a few miles across to a few feet, and the bottom edge stopped a thousand feet above the Colorado River.

For a good half mile their path was straight, and they all took advantage of the relative ease of the walk to keep their eyes on the landscape rather than their feet. It was effortless, with such surreal terrain, for Imogen to imagine she was on another planet, Mars perhaps—though the Canyon offered more in the way of color variation (and vegetation). Periodically washes came in on their left, plunging into Hermit canyon, which became continuously deeper on their right as they walked on. By the time they turned west, Hermit Creek lay in its gorge several hundred feet beneath them.

The Tonto Trail could become a drudgery, where Imogen felt like the trail went on and on and on and camp seemed hopelessly far away. So, beginning with her first trip when she was twelve, she used a mental trick to help her stay motivated. Shortly before that trip she'd read *The Long Walk*, written by Stephen King's alter ego, Richard Bachman. She'd connected to the young people and their quest to be the sole survivor of a long walk, made nearly impossible by the promise of being shot in the back if they fell below a pace of four miles per hour. It was a grisly mantra to think about in such a heavenly place, but it had worked: *four miles an hour or get shot in the back, four miles an hour or get shot in the back*. Even when she was dead tired Imogen always made good time on the Tonto (though not at the pace of a fifteen-minute mile).

The mantra came back to her now, but instead of helping her pick up her pace it filled her vision with red. Juxtaposed against the golden leaves of a ginkgo tree. Or maybe it was a maple tree. A red maple. *No.* How had imagining a gun at her back ever made her walk faster? *Hide.* She shuttered the mantra and focused on the distant rock formations, the here, the now. With each breath she forced away old images—from a book, from life. Here, now: this was enough. This was everything.

Traveling within the Canyon meant a lot of ups and downs as they traversed inner canyons. Tilda had struggled with this notion of "inner canyons." When the three of them had their first Skype planning session, Tilda had been confused that Boucher was their destination. "But I thought we were going to the *Grand* Canyon?" But any one of the inner canyons— created by creeks that fed into the Colorado River—might be a National Park of its own if it existed anywhere else. Imogen had been shocked when her dad had claimed that Hermit canyon was larger than all of Yosemite. When she explained it Tilda had just blinked and blinked, and Imogen saw her mentally picking up Yosemite, an invisible plastic model, and dropping it into place on the map laid out in front of her. So many things about the Canyon were difficult to describe; maybe that was the simple explanation for why Beck had disclosed to Tilda so relatively little.

Halfway between Hermit and Boucher lay Travertine canyon, which they crossed by descending partway into the dry creek bed and clambering back up the other side. Though the hiking had calmed her nerves to a degree, Imogen still couldn't resolve the mystery of the theft; it blurred the division she'd created between her city life and her return to nature.

After navigating through Travertine, the next landmark on her mental map was the Foreboding Rockslide—which would mean they'd almost reached the section she'd been dreading.

Beck might not have painted a full picture for Tilda, but Imogen's dad had been more than happy to give her every brushstroke (though she came up with her own names).

She'd always been the sort who worried about losing control while walking across a bridge or standing at the high rail of a balcony and suddenly plunging herself into the void. It wasn't a suicidal urge, but a fear of succumbing to a deadly impulse. She remembered a stretch of trail she'd crossed on her last trip with her sister, heading into Clear Creek canyon. There, the footing narrowed to just a few inches, angled at a downward slant across scree. It was like walking on broken M&M's. If you started sliding on the slippery rock particles you'd just tumble on down, with no way to stop until you unspooled at the bottom a hundred and fifty feet below. Twenty-four-year-old Imogen had squelched her dark impulses and crossed with excessive care, firmly planting each step. Later, when she told her dad about the trip, he'd confirmed the peril of it: "Yup, woulda killed you, tumbling at a hundred miles an hour."

The section heading out to Boucher sounded a bit different— not scree, but a passage right on the lip of a cliff. "Exposed," as the mountain climbers would say. With an eight-hundred-foot drop-off. A never-recover-your-body sort of drop-off.

They'd been close to the edge of a bluff for quite a way, the empty space hovering just beyond Imogen's line of sight as she kept her eyes on the ground. Movement made her look over and there was a raven, gliding over the chasm, nearly level with her. It was so close she could hear the air moving through its wings. She could have sworn the bird made eye contact with her before swooping away, and when she faced the trail again she spotted a rockslide ahead of them.

She paused for a second to confirm it was the Foreboding

Rockslide, and the purple paisleys churning in her gut sparked into fireworks. Her father had described what to look for: a place where a large boulder had crashed down centuries before, stopping just inches from the cliff's edge, blocking the trail (or so it looked).

Fuck.

Sure enough, Beck slowed down and waited for Tilda and Imogen to catch up.

10

"ittle tricky spot up ahead," Beck said, a casual understatement for what Imogen had just decided should more aptly be called the Promontory of Catastrophic Possibilities. "It's short, just ten or twelve feet to get around that rock." She pointed with her walking stick toward the ominous boulder, which sat surrounded by the dirt and rubble it had pushed along in its tumble. "Then be prepared to make a left—you can't see it from here, but *don't miss the left*. And keep your eyes on your boots, on your next step. Don't look at anything but where you're walking."

What Beck didn't say was that missing the left turn meant walking off the cliff. Plunging into nothingness. Goodbye.

A line formed between Tilda's brows and her mouth opened but the question didn't leave her lips. She stepped closer to Beck to get a better view of what lay ahead. Like a cartoon character, she stuck her neck out, squinting as she followed the trail with her eyes. It sloped downward, covered in what looked like gravel, the rock wall on the left, empty air on the right.

"Oh dear God," said Tilda.

"It's not as bad as it looks."

Imogen almost laughed. Beck and her refined ability to downplay the worst. Maybe she should've become an oncologist rather than a general practitioner; she was probably fantastic at delivering bad news to her patients.

"I'll go first," Beck told Tilda. "Watch where I walk. Then Imogen can go next if you want to watch another person do it." To both of them she advised, "Steady breaths. Eyes on your feet. Concentrate, and keep walking."

With that, she turned around and headed across the narrow strip that divided their world. She kept her walking stick in her right hand and jabbed it into the gravelly ground ahead of her. Judging by Beck's pack, the trail was little wider than a window ledge, eighty stories high.

A plug ballooned in Imogen's throat, the tears she would shed for her sister if anything happened to her. Sometimes they grumbled at each other, but Beck was *her person*—the person she needed more than her parents, more than her friends.

When Beck was out of sight—as gone as if she'd rounded a building on a street corner—Imogen inhaled deeply. Their dad was right: it was hard to watch. But Beck was fine. The whole discussion and crossing had taken a mere minute; she'd made it look simple.

Now what? Imogen felt abandoned. Who was going to go next? She visualized herself walking in her sister's footsteps, crossing the abyss…and quickly had to smother the little monsters who taunted her with shitty ideas. *Swan dive!*

Tilda and Imogen looked from the trail ahead to each other.

"She didn't tell me about this," Tilda said in a shaky voice.

"She didn't want you to worry."

Though still on solid land, Tilda bore the haunted look of someone who'd already glimpsed the perpetual void. "I'm not sure I can do this. What if I can't do this? I didn't think it was gonna..." The fear abruptly vanished and became anger. "Someone should have told me!"

The glare she gave Imogen implied that Imogen was the one who'd betrayed her. "I haven't been out this way either," she said in her own defense.

"You're the chatty one. Except when we aren't really on speaking terms and then a fat lot of good that does."

"Beck just didn't want you to freak yourself out. I've been a nervous wreck all morning, at least you didn't have time to worry."

"Everything okay?" Beck's voice traveled across the chasm.

Tilda took a step forward, as if that would put her in Beck's face. "Seriously what the fuck! How do you just leave this part out? Don't we need ropes for this? Shouldn't there be something to hang on to?"

There was no point in answering. Where would someone string a rope?

"We wouldn't be here if I didn't think you could do it," said the unseen wizard, the disembodied voice of calm certainty. "I'm serious that doing it is just like walking—it's the knowing what's beside you that makes it difficult."

Tilda made an expression like a grimace, unimpressed, doubtful. But Imogen was bolstered by her sister's confidence. Beck had been right about everything so far—this trip was exactly what Imogen needed—and she wouldn't have given them a test she didn't think they could pass. But Tilda didn't seem to draw on Beck's faith the way Imogen did.

"Do you want me to go next?" Imogen asked. "So you can see another person—"

"No. I understand the concept," Tilda growled. "It's really fucking simple. I just don't want to do it."

Imogen looked at the boulder, smug on its patch of oblivion. She expected Beck to come back around, join them on the safe side and do her smooth-talking thing until they fell in line behind her. But Beck didn't come back. Imogen considered the possibility that this was intentional, leaving her alone with Tilda to figure out—quite literally—how to move ahead.

Tilda leaned on her stick, facing away from the crossing, a childish show of rebellion. This was part of it, Imogen told herself. Guiding Tilda. Having, for once, to be a leader. She put herself in Tilda's line of sight.

"Remember all those years ago? In Schenley Park? You did a handstand on the curb, like a balance beam. If you can do that on your hands, you can walk across a short section of trail."

Tilda considered her. "I was stoned. And young. And an idiot."

"You had good balance. Even on your hands. Beck knows that too. She knows you're strong, she knows you put in the extra effort to be in good shape." Which was more than Imogen had done. "You *can* do it, Tilda. And I know, you're right, I've underestimated you. But not about this. Beck would never want to see you get hurt." *Die.* "I would never want to see that either—and you can do this. You may not *want* to, but you're capable of it."

Tilda sighed. A rivulet of sweat crept out of her hairline. Her anger melted, leaving her defeated. "I don't want to be that person. And I never thought I'd *be* that person—for fuck's sake I make a living encouraging people not to accept defeat. But apparently I've never actually tried to do something that could kill me. Feeling like a total fucking hypocrite and failure now."

"You're not a failure. Most people never face an obstacle like this. And it's scary…but not the *bad* kind of scary." It was almost a relief to see this vulnerable side of Tilda, without her makeup and peppy words. A person with fears was someone Imogen understood.

Tilda met her eyes—no, Tilda peered into her soul, that was what it felt like (cheesy as it was). "I'm sorry I haven't been a better friend this last year."

The apology was so unexpected that now Imogen felt like the cartoon character, blinking and widening her eyes. She nodded, unsure how to respond.

"There were many times…" Tilda faltered. "It's little consolation, but I thought about reaching out. I guess…I didn't want to say the wrong thing."

Imogen nodded again. A memory surfaced, coming on like a lightbulb, and just as quickly she switched it off. A tsunami of emotions—regret, longing, apprehension—flooded her and Tilda was suddenly someone who Imogen really missed. For a moment they were teenagers, in Schenley Park. And then they were adults again, with a gap between them as deep as the gorge.

"I'm sorry I don't know you better." It was almost a whisper.

"Well, there's still time," said Tilda. "As long as we don't die crossing this fucking trail."

They turned around and contemplated the boulder ahead of them. Imogen had a powerful sense of them *being in this together,* which was something she hadn't felt since high school.

"Just see it in your mind as a sidewalk," she said, "with

people on either side of you who you don't want to bump—you do that every day, move around in narrow spaces without thinking about it." Imogen liked that image; she'd try to take her own advice.

"Can you go first?" Tilda meekly asked.

The delay had kept Imogen too distracted to fantasize about spreading her arms open to see if she could fly. No, she would walk. *One foot in front of the other. One foot in front of the other. Twelve steps.*

She counted them as she went. Watched her feet. Used her walking stick to keep from slipping on the loose stones. Ignored the emptiness beside her.

Before she knew it she had made the left turn—and there was Beck, relaxing on a boulder. Imogen exhaled, grateful for solid ground.

"See, toldja you could do it."

Imogen saw pride in her sister's face. She was pretty proud of herself too, and in the happy rush of accomplishment the purple paisleys blinked out of existence. She took off her pack and propped it beside Beck's.

"Is she on her way?" Beck asked.

"I think so."

"You made it seem easy, that should help."

"Thanks." The compliment meant everything. She remembered Afiya expressing how much faith Beck had in her work. Beck believed in the *many* things Imogen could do, even the things she struggled with. It suddenly seemed possible that her writer's block wasn't so different from this Scary Spot. Perhaps she'd allowed herself to become distracted by her awareness of the metaphorical abyss. No one could move forward over perilous terrain by gazing at the empty space instead of the trail.

She felt triumphant, but for now there was nothing to do but wait. How had Beck been so patient? And what was keeping Tilda?

The soft sound of crying drifted across the divide. Beck hopped off her boulder. "Tilda? What if I come back over and carry your pack across. Would that help? You'd have a better sense for your center of gravity. Nothing to throw you off-balance."

The Blum sisters gazed at each other, tense and expectant. Imogen had been so certain that Tilda was ready, that their minutes alone had changed something. What would they do if she really refused?

11

Without being able to see her, Imogen and Beck had no way to gauge how Tilda was processing Beck's idea. Did she think it was a good one? Or was she looking at the trail behind her, wishing they could go back?

"Okay. Let's try that," came the reply a moment later.

The Blum sisters grinned.

"You got this!" Imogen said, cheering her on from afar.

With the walking stick now on her left, Beck reversed directions and headed around the promontory.

Imogen sat on a rock, drank from a canteen. It was Beck's turn and she would help Tilda: infuse her with the special thing Beck possessed—an ability to make people feel okay. *That's why she wanted to be a doctor.* She did it with an invisible wand and sometimes no words. But with a certain look, a quirk of her lips, a person might suddenly feel better.

It seemed like only a minute later that Beck rejoined her, sloughing off Tilda's trendy pack. And seconds after that, Tilda appeared—eyes like laser beams on the path ahead of her.

Tilda walked over to safer ground, gasping with her tongue out, relief graffitied across her face. "Holy crap."

"Wasn't so bad," said Beck.

If Imogen hadn't known better, she might have thought her sister was a hypnotist. "Not as bad as I thought," Tilda said, under her spell.

"You did it!" Imogen rejoiced, throwing her arms in the air.

"I did it!" Tilda embraced her in a celebratory hug.

They wound south. For much of the day they'd had a distant wall of Muav limestone for company—with five hundred sheer, vertical feet of Redwall limestone atop it—and the scrubby bushes that dotted the Tonto Platform. After successfully navigating the Promontory of Catastrophic Possibilities, they'd fallen into a meditative rhythm. Walking. Thinking.

As they started the descent into Boucher, at the elevation of the Tapeats sandstone, things got steep and rocky again. It struck Imogen as funny—yesterday was only *yesterday,* but in the Canyon your legs and endurance acquired their own sort of expertise in a short amount of time. Ahead of her, she could almost see Tilda thinking the same thing. They'd survived going down the Hermit Trail, and inched around a monolith without stumbling. It wasn't that everything became *easy* by comparison, but the body and mind developed new standards by which to evaluate the terrain.

Boucher "camp" appeared to be deserted. It didn't have designated spots, but the whole area was broad and flat in comparison to other places in the Canyon. Beck seemed to know exactly where she wanted to go: she headed toward the creek.

"Is this it?" Tilda asked.

"Yup. Home for the next four nights," said Beck.

"Nice." Tilda looked around for a second, and then resumed following Beck.

Knowing they were only yards away from setting up camp, Imogen let the other two go on ahead.

"You coming?" Tilda asked, turning around.

"Yup, just gonna enjoy…a minute to myself."

Tilda grinned, as if she understood, and walked on.

Back home, Imogen often found it exhausting to be among people for hours on end, even when she was enjoying herself. But that wasn't necessarily true in the Canyon. She wondered why backpacking with friends felt as good as being alone.

Here, the presence of other people felt different; or maybe she was different. Civilization had gone awry, with its buildings and highways, its digitalization and consumption. *Binge-watching TV.* Humans had adapted to a meaningless structure of work and wealth that resulted in a fundamental loss of identity. Here, you could return to the natural order, enjoy the two-part state of doing-the-necessities-to-survive and sitting-around-doing-nothing, unburdened of existential angst.

Maybe she was overthinking it, but it felt different here nonetheless. Imogen inhaled. Searching for archaic memories, she let her breath permeate deep into her lungs, her soul. The colors were so rich she could smell them: flamingo rock, terra-cotta dirt, cornflower sky. The air carried a fragrance full of patterns—lizard skin, raven feather, vaporous cloud. Even the distant night had a scent, the musk of the coming hunt, the deep yearning to survive. Everything spoke softly. Everything remained: the gossip of fossils and the whispered bones of millennia. She heard the agave sigh, the succulence held in its bayonet leaves a private song. Everything sang in the sun.

Imogen might have continued pondering these things, gazing around at the rocks and trees, larger than the cottonwoods had been at Hermit—might have even scribbled a few lines of poetry on her tiny notepad—but something caught her eye. A spark of unnatural color. Shiny lavender.

It was a few paces from her but its iridescence and angular edges drew her attention. Backpackers were pretty good about hauling all their garbage out and leaving the land as pristine as they'd found it. And in such an isolated place she hadn't expected to find litter, especially within moments of arriving. Perhaps it was an oversight, a bit that had blown away?

She squatted down carefully, not wanting the weight of her pack to send her hurtling onto her face, and picked it up. A torn scrap, a corner. Silver on the inside like a candy bar wrapper. But no. It wasn't from a candy bar.

Imogen recognized it. Tilda had brought enough to eat two per day.

The stolen protein bars?

A shiver scuttled up her arms even under the desert sun. She took in her surroundings more carefully. No signs of a tent or gear. It didn't *look* like anyone had been here recently. But the proof in her hand said different. The scrap looked fresh, unblemished by exposure to dirt or sun.

Beck and her dad had talked about Boucher canyon many times. Imogen knew that somewhere nearby was a partially dug mine, gouged right into the billion-and-a-half-year-old Vishnu schist by Louis Boucher himself, back when he'd lived in the Canyon as a guide and prospector. Would someone stay in there? It seemed like a weird idea to her, to choose a cramped rock tunnel instead of enjoying this splendor. But people could be weird. Mr.—or was it *Monsieur?*—Boucher had also built himself a little rock shelter, like an igloo, though she hadn't laid eyes on that yet either. The roof had long since caved in and Imogen didn't consider it likely that anyone would camp there.

Her eyes scanned farther up the creek, past where Beck and Tilda had dropped their packs. There, the opposite bank was a steep wall, fifty or sixty feet high. Erosion had made pockets in the sandstone that resembled cave mouths, and one of them was wide enough and deep enough to camp in. From afar she couldn't discern the shallow cave from other imperfections in the cliff face, but she knew Beck and their dad had found the hidden shelter on a rainy day. If a person was standing just within the archway Imogen thought they'd be visible, but she wasn't sure.

So it was possible they weren't alone. It was possible someone else had come out to Boucher—it wasn't like they could reserve it for themselves. If it was the asshole, at least he wasn't *following* them. But it was troubling if the person who'd helped himself to their food bag was here. And more troubling still if he was hiding.

Or maybe she was being paranoid. Maybe someone else— not necessarily a *he*—with a taste for expensive protein bars had passed through a day or two before, heading east or west— there was no way to know for sure. Or…her paranoia wasn't ready to give in: What if the Canyon meant to test her, in more than physical ways?

In *Esther's Ghost,* after her friends decided she was delusional, Esther had to unravel the mystery of her attack alone. She researched the history of the mansion-turned-apartments where she lived—and the robber baron who'd built it— suspicious that he might have never fully vacated the premises.

But finding someone who had committed a crime became exponentially trickier when he lacked a corporeal form.

The skin of Imogen's exposed forearms looked like a softer version of the prickly pear at her feet. Now she was just spooking herself. It was a good story, but it was unlikely they were dealing with an invisible antagonist.

Imogen tucked the scrap into the pocket of her shorts and continued across the flatland toward the patch of earth Beck and Tilda had claimed as home. If she mentioned it to Beck, it would probably be best to leave out the latest theory, life imitating art and a phantom thief. She could already hear her sister telling her, not for the first time, that she watched "too much TV"—though Imogen spent just as much time with her growing library of scary books. Sometimes it helped to read stories that were scarier than the real world. At least in fiction the protagonist usually survived.

12

They set up camp much as they had the previous after-noon, only this time Tilda helped Imogen with the drop cloth and mattress pads that designated their bedroom. The kitchen remained Beck's domain.

No one was in a chatty mood, which suited Imogen's unease; she didn't like the thoughts that were going through her head. As a writer, sometimes she didn't trust her imagination. In the writer's world, everything had to lead to conflict and tension and *problems,* and she didn't want problems here. She wanted relaxing days, and the chance to keep reconnecting with nature and herself. But she couldn't stop imagining in the silence that they were all spinning fears.

Maybe it would help to get her discovery off her chest.

"Want to fill the canteens?" Imogen asked Tilda, hoping to orchestrate a moment alone with Beck. Her sister could be counted on for a low-key reaction; she was less sure how Tilda would respond.

"I can get it," Beck said, unzipping the side pockets of her pack where she carried her portion of the canteens.

"I thought Tilda might like it," Imogen said casually, retrieving her own canteens. "It looks like it's easy here, and she hasn't done it yet."

Boucher Creek was barely forty feet from their campsite, but Imogen was counting on the constant gurgle of the shallow water to mask their voices.

"I'm game—gimme those bottles!" They handed her a half dozen containers of various shapes and sizes, which Tilda hooked on her fingers. "Should I take the iodine tablets?"

"You can do them when you come back," Beck said.

"Okay!" No worse for the day's three-and-a-half-hour hike, Tilda bounded off on her mission.

Imogen watched her, waiting for her to reach the creek. Beck was on the ground, applying fresh smears of sunscreen on her nose and cheeks, the backs of her hands, when Imogen squatted beside her.

"I found this." She held out the torn wrapper, and pointed back where they'd come from with her chin. "There."

Beck turned the scrap over and over; her face gave away nothing. "Okay?"

Was she being deliberately obtuse?

"Doesn't it look like one of Tilda's?" Why hadn't Beck recognized it right away?

"Maybe. I don't think there's that much difference in… wrappers." Now Beck looked at Imogen, as she might a bug under a magnifying glass. "You think this was Tilda's, and whoever stole it is here?"

"Maybe. I don't know." Imogen looked out, around. A lizard scuttled away in the red dirt. A soft breeze awakened the tree leaves. Far above them contrails from a jet they could barely see left the white signature of its passing. Little else moved. "I mean, maybe they came out here, they could've."

"Low on food? That doesn't make any sense."

"Maybe we should show it to Tilda—she might recognize it." Imogen had anticipated that Beck might not look at the clue and leap to her feet with worry. But she hadn't anticipated her sister's complete denial.

"Aren't you jumping the gun a little? We don't know if this was Tilda's. We don't know if this was left by someone who hiked in or out of Boucher today, yesterday, or two days ago. It looks fairly new. But it could be *anyone's,* from days ago."

Imogen felt like she was being chastised; good thing she hadn't mentioned her more paranoid theory. *So you don't think the Canyon's playing a little round of Find the Ghost?* She nodded. She was just starting to make progress, proving her competency, and she didn't want her sister to start doubting her. Beck could be counted on for a nonemotional response— wasn't that why Imogen had wanted to show her the scrap? To put herself at ease?

"Just being careful," Imogen mumbled.

"It'll be easier to keep the food bag closer here. More trees. We're fine, Imogen, it's not gonna happen again."

Imogen should've felt relieved, but the magnifying glass had been held under the sun too long and she was the bug beneath it, burning. Her sister might trust her with basic backpacking duties, but, like her character Esther, Imogen was afraid she didn't come across as someone truly sound of mind. While they returned to organizing their camp, Imogen privately brooded. They'd had few reasons over the years to fear humans while camping. But it had happened once before, and Beck had been uneasy then too.

Before Beck moved west for her residency they'd done some occasional car camping, sometimes with Beck's girlfriend or their dad, sometimes just the two of them. They preferred to go just off-season—mid-September—when the weather was still good, but people were back to school or work. That was how they'd had all of the Blueberry Patch campground, at Finger Lakes National Forest, to themselves. Well, almost. One spot had been occupied by a man who appeared to be living out of his covered pickup truck.

He didn't do anything—didn't come and say hello (as some men did when they saw two young women on their own), didn't get drunk and sing to the moon or hang dead squirrel carcasses from the trees. Beck had wondered aloud how someone could live in a national forest, and she'd kept an eye on the other camp. That first night Imogen felt real fear, sleeping in the tiny backpacking tent beside her sister like two corpses in a coffin. She might have felt safer without the tent, able to see if anyone approached their camp, but it had been a chilly night and over-cast enough that rain was a concern. Her writer's imagination had gone wild, picturing a giant hunting knife slicing through the thin fabric roof of their tent, stabbing Beck in the chest while Imogen, blind and panicked, scrambled to fight back or get out. *In real life, I would've curled into a ball and played dead.*

Maybe the man had simply been homeless and hadn't de-served to be the cause of their fear. Yet Imogen was glad they'd be sleeping in the open at Boucher. If someone approached them in the dead of night, tripping over rocks and scrub, she was certain it would awaken her. And she'd sleep with her Swiss Army knife in her fist, just in case.

* * *

They ate a hot lunch of Cup Noodles. Afterward they gathered all their food into the bag, and Beck hung it just a few yards away from their kitchen, on the branch of a cooperative tree. They stripped down to T-shirts and shorts and what the Blum sisters affectionately referred to as camp shoes, which were just a lightweight pair of old shoes brought to wear around flat terrain. By comparison to her boots, Imogen's Skechers felt like slippers. They kept a sleeve of Fig Newtons and a canteen with them and went off to explore.

Tilda let her camera dangle from her wrist, snapping a few shots as they meandered. She had Imogen and Beck pose at noteworthy locations: in front of the creek; at the entrance to the unfinished mine; from within the half-collapsed rock igloo. In person, each place looked even less habitable, though Imogen thought she saw something slip away into the shadows at the back of the mine. It was probably a rattlesnake, so she kept the sighting to herself. Sometimes they swapped and Imogen took pictures of Tilda.

They passed the afternoon this way. Ambling. Sitting in the shade, their legs outstretched on the feathery dirt. Sometimes they talked, relaxed tidbits of conversation. But many of their questions drifted away, unimportant and forgotten.

As the sky wrapped itself in an amethyst cloak, they ate supper. Washed up. Put the food bag back in its tree. Earlier they'd found a corner sheltered by two rocks and claimed it as their latrine, digging a shallow trench with their plastic trowel. But Tilda still wanted someone to go with her and Stand Guard. On their last trip before bedtime, Imogen kept her flashlight angled at her feet, waiting to escort Tilda back to camp.

Tilda chatted about something as she squatted, her wad of toilet paper at the ready, but Imogen wasn't listening. High up in the rocky bank on the other side of the creek she saw a flash of light. Though she hadn't smoked since her freshman year of college—when they'd all agreed to cut the worst of their bad habits (at least the consumable ones)—she was certain about what she'd seen.

A match, igniting. The flare of a cigarette on its first inhale. Then darkness.

Someone was up there.

If she could see that, he could see her. Them. Imogen switched off the flashlight.

"Hey! I can't see."

"Your eyes will adjust. It's a beautiful night." Above them hung a bulbous moon.

Tilda grabbed Imogen's elbow as she stumbled on the way back to camp. "Can't we use the flashlight?"

"We don't need it."

"Speak for yourself," Tilda huffed, annoyed.

Imogen really didn't want to agitate Tilda, especially as their truce was so recent and fragile, but she wasn't sure what to do about her suspicion that they were being watched.

"Why is it okay for Beck to use her flashlight"—indeed, Beck had her light on as she zipped up her pack and slid into her sleeping bag—"but we're supposed to walk in the dark? Sometimes your rules seem a little random."

"Yeah, why are you walking in the dark?" Beck asked. She illuminated Tilda's bed as Tilda slipped off her camp shoes and tucked herself in. Imogen managed in the shadows on Beck's other side.

When Beck finally flicked off her light, Imogen rolled over in her sleeping bag and whispered, "Did you see it?"

"See what? What are you talking about?"

"What are you guys whispering about?" Tilda leaned on her elbow, joining the conversation.

"I thought I saw something."

"What kind of something?" Beck asked.

"A cigarette lighting up. Up there." She pointed across the creek. "Isn't there a shelter there?"

"Imogen. I never promised we could have the entire Canyon to ourselves. This was the best I could do."

"I'm not blaming you. But—"

"There could be people here. It's entirely possible. I don't know what else you want me to do."

It sounded like they sighed in unison, vexed in different ways. Tilda noticed too, and laughed.

"We heading to the river tomorrow?" she asked Beck.

"That's the plan."

"Awesome."

On their backs, they watched the sky. Tilda asked Beck a few more questions about the river and tomorrow's walk. Imogen lay there silently, feeling left out, misunderstood. Okay fine, there could be people there. But it meant they were vulnerable at night when their flashlights were on: someone could see their camp from above. And no one wanted to be spied on while their pants were down. The second she thought it, she understood why she shouldn't say it aloud—then Tilda *really* wouldn't be comfortable squatting out of doors.

Tilda fell asleep first. Then Beck. Imogen visualized sight lines and angles, so she could lead them to a better-shielded latrine tomorrow.

It didn't have to mean anything—a person camping in the rain shelter. It could be unrelated to the stolen protein bars. But it bothered her in the same way the man's presence at Finger Lakes National Forest had. A niggling worry. Something—someone—slightly out of place.

Imogen fought the urge to flip onto her stomach, direct her little LED flashlight onto the rocks across the way. Whoever was up there had retreated to a deeper place within the overhang to enjoy his smoke. But she wanted him to know.

We know you're out there. Don't fuck with us.

While she'd intended to keep her Swiss Army knife in her fist, closed, she drew open the largest blade as she curled up on her side, and laid the knife within easy reach of her bundled pillow.

13

Tilda felt okay in the morning, in daylight, visiting the makeshift latrine on her own, though now Imogen was more squeamish about it so they went together. On the way there—and back—Imogen looked for footprints coming in from other directions, or any indications that someone else had been out and about during the night. She didn't see any.

"I sleep fantastically out here!" Tilda declared as they got back to camp and put away the toilet paper and trowel.

"Me too," Beck said with gusto. They were all excited to head to the river; they'd earned a day of glorious sitting around.

"I swear since I hit my thirties, I can't sleep for crap back home. I've bought like four different mattresses, a zillion pillows, a white-noise machine that played rain sounds and made me have to pee all night."

"Same—minus the buying stuff," said Imogen. She was managing to sleep decently here, but they weren't the comatose, worry-free nights she'd been hoping for. Having two strong women with her helped, but she was disappointed that other people, somehow, were still a concern.

Tilda inhaled a deep, cleansing breath, her eyes closed as she faced the sun. "I thought October would be cold, but this is perfect."

In spite of having planned a leisurely day, they gobbled up breakfast as if they were in a hurry to get on with it. Imogen could stare at a rippling creek all day and was looking forward to spending a few hours with the Colorado, watching its microscopic progress as it continued carving its masterpiece, the Grand Canyon.

Their dishes were left on a rock to dry in the sun. As Beck organized the day's snacks, Tilda folded up Beck's mattress pad, which they planned to bring and share as a cushioned seat. Imogen knelt beside her sister.

"I'm thinking we should just take our packs with us."

Startled, Beck peeked over her sunglasses. "Why?"

"Just in case. We can't rule out…I know it's unlikely, but it's not impossible, you know. With the protein bars. And not knowing who's here."

Beck gave the terrain a three-sixty once-over. "I'm not sure anyone's here."

"It couldn't hurt, right?"

"It's kind of a lot to lug down to the river. The trail gets a little tight, walled in."

"Now what are you two scheming about?" Tilda watched them, perched on a rock as she laced up her boots.

"Just figuring out what all to take with us," Beck replied.

"For two sisters who practically never agree, I commend you for how calmly you fight."

"We don't fight. This is just how we…"

"Do things," Beck finished.

Imogen gave her a smirk. "I was going to say communicate."

Beck gave her a what's-the-difference shrug. They both knew that ninety-five percent of the time they resolved their arguments by doing everything Beck's way. Beck was accustomed to winning; maybe that was why neither of them put in as much effort anymore. But Imogen didn't want to give in, not this time.

"I just think it couldn't hurt to be careful," she whispered. She knew how she sounded, with her constant invocation of being *careful*.

Beck considered her. "Will it really make you feel better?"

"Yes."

"What if we just take the food bag?"

Imogen weighed the offer. It was better than nothing. "Okay."

"Okay. You carry it."

Imogen pulled the drawstring closed and slung the bag over her shoulder, ready to go.

"You're taking everything?" Tilda asked, fists at her waist. It didn't look like a Wonder Woman pose now, not while she oozed impatience.

"So critters won't get at our vittles while we're gone," Beck said. But she exchanged raised eyebrows with Tilda, and Imogen recognized that she was being humored.

Beck carried a daypack filled with the actual necessities: fresh water, sunscreen, toilet paper, Imogen's tiny notepad (in case she got inspired), Tilda's camera, and the eggshell mattress pad. They all took their walking sticks.

It was a short hike to the river by Canyon standards, about a mile, right along Boucher Creek. At one point the trail narrowed so much they were practically walking in the water, and they could reach out and touch both of Boucher canyon's steep walls. It was tight, as Beck had said, but plenty wide enough to have accommodated their fully loaded packs.

The Colorado River bubbled with rapids wherever separate creeks came down to join it, the water turbulence augmented by the boulders that had migrated down from the inner canyons. They heard the river roaring its hello. And then they were there, though the river gushed past without acknowledging its human visitors. The Canyon walls rose high and imposing on either side, with white ribbons of Zoroaster granite rippling through the silvery Vishnu schist. The geologic striations made Imogen think of historic costumes, a proud display of finery that told a story—many stories—to those with a knowledgeable eye.

They dropped their stuff and went close to the water's edge. It was like a sacred summoning and they stood there for a moment in silent awe. The water swept by. Before the Glen Canyon Dam had been built, the river had been a muddy brown year-round, not just during the spring floods. Its wild passage tamed, now it shone green. Still, standing on the bank, Imogen felt its power. White rapids knobbed the river's passageway throughout its run through the Canyon. There weren't as many professional rafting trips in the autumn, but if they stayed at the river long enough they'd undoubtedly see some pass.

For Imogen, being in such close proximity to the raging water wasn't dissimilar to how she felt while standing at the top of Niagara Falls, or on a bridge, or at the Promontory of Catastrophic Possibilities—with those whispering little monsters. *Come on, one little step forward.* She took a step backward. And another. And finally made a nest in a sandy spot and kicked off her shoes.

A moment later, Tilda and Beck joined her. Tilda tossed off her sunglasses and performed some kind of side-stretching yoga pose that Imogen couldn't name, though she was happy to dig out the camera and document it. Beck propped her eggshell pad so it leaned against a rock, then secured her canvas sun hat and sat, legs extended, utterly content.

Time passed. They nibbled on a sleeve of crunchy crackers. Took turns napping on the mattress pad. Ventured off alone for short walks. Waved at the yip-yipping rafters every time an excursion bobbed past. Tilda attempted to toss a rock across the wide river. She had a good arm, but the rock splashed into the water and immediately vanished. Imogen wrote a few inadequate sentences in an attempt to describe her surroundings; at least she could blame that on the Grand Canyon, immune to common words, and not her wayward muse. Once or twice she wondered if everything was okay back at camp, but she didn't want to ruin the healing, calming bliss of their first unstructured day, so she didn't dwell on it.

After a couple of hours Beck returned to the river's edge and gazed upstream, as still as a rock formation. For a second Imogen feared something was wrong, that Beck had spotted something alarming. Then it seemed more like an act of meditation, breathing in the environment. As the minutes stretched, Imogen sensed that her sister was troubled, but she didn't know why.

When Beck finally rejoined them, Tilda and Imogen were both watching her. Somehow it wasn't surprising when she took a seat at the point of their triangle, facing them. They sat up a little. Beck didn't often open up in such a formal manner, and Imogen was dying to know what was on her mind. Judging by Tilda's keen attention, she was too.

"There's something I haven't told either of you…"

The admission, even unfinished, made Tilda and Imogen exchange glances.

As Beck went on, her eyes wandered from the dirt beneath her fingers, to the rock wall across the river. "I had an epiphany. After I read Imogen's new book. It didn't come to me right away—it was several months later, actually, after the synagogue…Then I couldn't stop thinking about it."

At the time, Beck had only pointed out a few small plot holes; this was the first Imogen was hearing about a revelation.

"I realized…" Beck stopped, searching for better words. "I planned this trip for all the reasons I told you, but also because…I couldn't figure out how else to get you two face-to-face, where neither of you could run out of the room."

Imogen felt the dread clambering down her spine, a toothy imp who used her bones as a ladder. Where was this going? Tilda looked just as clueless.

Beck turned to Imogen. "There's something that never got resolved…" She turned to Tilda. "And it's affected Imogen ever since. And maybe we can't resolve it completely, but it can't go on like this."

Oh God. Imogen angled toward the river. Could she make a run for it? Jump in so she'd never have to hear the rest of Beck's epiphany? If it involved her and Tilda—and fuck, why had she encouraged Beck to read *Esther's Ghost?*—it could only be one thing. *The* Thing. And Imogen was more than capable of bringing it up on her own, if it was something she wanted to talk about—and she didn't. She didn't think Esther was anything like her, and hadn't expected Beck to connect the book to Imogen's own life. She adamantly shook her head.

"Beck, that was fiction, total fiction."

"I know. I know you think that. And that's part of the problem. It's so deeply in you that you don't think it's a problem anymore, but it is."

Imogen looked at Beck, saw the sheen of tears in her eyes, and quickly looked away.

"What are we talking about?" Tilda asked.

"The Thing," Beck said. "Imogen's book is about a woman who thinks she's been raped by a ghost, because her friends don't believe her."

"*Not* because her friends don't..." Imogen willed herself to dematerialize—as if this whole conversation weren't bad enough, her sister had totally misinterpreted her novel. "Esther *knows* she was raped by a ghost, that has nothing to do with her friends. Her friends don't *believe* it, but that isn't what makes Esther think it was a ghost."

In spite of Beck's obvious concern, she still had the where-withal to give Imogen a pinched-lip look of doubt and disapproval.

"I appreciate your concern for your sister..." Tilda weighed her words with great care. "But I don't think you can force us to talk about this."

"I agree with Tilda. There, we're in agreement."

"You're in *denial,*" Beck said like a bullet. "And it's ruining your life." She met Tilda's frosty gaze. "And it affected *you* a helluva lot longer than you might admit. It didn't go unnoticed how every boyfriend after Rob shared some quality of his—a big laugh, an over-the-top sense of humor—for *years*. And they all flattered you in the same way, and said the words boyfriends were supposed to say, and they were all fake. Or worse than fake, they were exactly what they were: assholes. And you got more and more insecure and turned outward..." She tossed her frustrated hands in the air. "You needed someone's approval, and when you finally realized the boyfriends couldn't give it, you looked for it from everyone else. From strangers."

Rage bloomed on Tilda's neck and cheeks, a deepening purple rash. "That's what you thought? All this time you just went with the flow and never said anything? Great. Great—and here I thought, here I was grateful, that *we* stayed friends."

"We were friends, and we are. And no, I didn't think about it then. I *accepted* it, yes, because…it was normal. It was your 'type,' the kind of guys you liked. I wanted better for you—and you knew that—but I didn't judge you. And I didn't think about *why*. I'm not kidding, Tilda, I'm almost mad at myself—how didn't I see it? You went that way." She made an airplane of her right hand. "Imogen went…" An airplane with her left hand, but it arced downward.

"You think my life's that bad?" Imogen asked, unsure if she should be sad or offended.

Beck slowly shook her head. "I should've seen it before the shooting. That was only the nail in the coffin. You didn't set out to live like a hermit. You had dreams of being in love once."

Imogen intertwined her fingers in her lap, gripping them so tightly she was in danger of breaking something. "I made a decision. A long time ago. Not to…not to dwell on it, because I didn't want it ruining my life. That was a decision."

"I read your book. I've had months to think about it. You're literally being haunted by your own life."

Imogen gazed in stupefied awe at her sister, uncertain if she was right, but impressed by the poetry of her conclusion. For half her life—seventeen years—Imogen had trained herself not to think about The Thing. But that didn't mean she'd forgotten. And the #MeToo movement begged her to reassess what had happened—with Rob, and with Tilda.

The party. The summer after their freshman year at Pitt. Tilda was out of town, vacationing with her father in Mexico. Beck had a girlfriend—her first true love—and they were always off on their own. Imogen had graduated from the Beechwood School at sixteen, an exemplary student, so the trio could matriculate to the College of General Studies together. Everyone called it night school back then, though classes were offered throughout the day. The program was ideal for people who had been out of school for a while, or had questionable grades, or had attended a small alternative high school run by hippies. That was how she found herself at a party without her wingwomen when she was only seventeen.

She'd never liked beer much, but she had a few sips. It was probably the Jell-O shots that got her tipsy. Rob, Tilda's boyfriend, had offered to escort her home. She never figured out why she'd been so stupid. So naïve. So should-have-seen-it-coming. So it-was-probably-your-own-damn-fault. So don't-complain-it-could-have-been-worse. No wonder Tilda doubted her after the fact. Imogen doubted herself, though not in the same way: she'd always been useless. Words—*no, stop, please*—had never been a deterrent against violence.

Imogen withdrew socially after it happened, which, for a while, made her a better student: they'd all struggled at first, unaccustomed to the academic rigor of university classes. Tilda and Beck both transferred to Pitt's School of Arts & Sciences for their sophomore year. Imogen didn't bother; she dropped out midterm. Said she didn't need to waste their dad's money to become a writer. It sounded reasonable enough that no one questioned it. They were already on more solitary paths by then, the trio branching out like the three rivers of their hometown.

Reflecting on it now, with all she'd learned from the women who shared their #MeToo stories, The Thing had been as powerful as a river, carving her as easily as sandstone into a person she wasn't sure she wanted to be.

There was a period—a solid punctuation mark—of uncomfortable silence. The roar of the river became the only audible sound. For so many reasons she didn't want her sister to be right: it would mean Imogen was transparent, and it would mean that she could've been someone else. The very thought nearly brought her to tears.

14

You seriously think Imogen's problems are my fault?" Tilda spat, shattering the moment.

"You didn't believe her," said Beck.

"I wasn't even there! I was barely nineteen, not exactly the most experienced or reasonable age a person—"

"If that's your reasoning, then you understood—or understand now—that your reaction was a problem. And that's exactly why we're doing this."

"I didn't come here for this." Tilda got to her feet.

Beck bolted up, blocking her retreat. Imogen shook out her cramping hands. Her whole body was a knot but she didn't know what to do. It was horrifying and thrilling at once to see Beck fighting for her. Truly, was Beck right? Imogen had thought she'd stuffed everything away so neatly, clamped the suitcase shut and put it on such an impossibly high shelf that she'd never have to look at its contents again.

"I don't think I'm ready for this either." Imogen grabbed the now-vacated mattress pad and dragged it toward her, desperate to lie down and shut her eyes. *Maybe they'll all disappear.* But the drama kept unfolding and she couldn't look away.

"You can't force an intervention," Tilda said to Beck with a sneer.

"Do you really think I'm wrong?"

Imogen realized she'd chosen an unfortunate moment to curl into the fetal position when Beck gestured to her as Exhibit A.

"This isn't my fault. She wasn't even sure if she'd been raped."

Imogen sprang into a sitting position. "No, *you* weren't sure if I'd been raped. I was always pretty clear—"

Tilda emitted a sarcastic snort, brutal enough to stop Imogen in her tracks. "I think you're rewriting history. You only said a thousand times that you weren't sure what happened."

This was Imogen's battle too, and she stood up to claim her ground. Beck moved to form a barrier between them. "You're the one who's rewriting history. Yes, I was very unsure about *why* it happened. I was insecure that I'd done something stupid—I knew Rob, felt comfortable with him, because he was *your boyfriend*. You were the one who didn't want to accept that your boyfriend raped me, because it was more important to you to stick by him than to believe me."

"Look, it wasn't a great time for me either," Tilda said, yelling over Beck's shoulder. "My boyfriend cheated on me with my best friend, you think I was happy about that? But at least he admitted—"

"Oh my fucking God!" Imogen brought her exasperated hands to her cheeks. "You're still taking his side."

"I loved him! What he did hurt me."

"Me too."

In the heavy pause, the Canyon sounds returned. Wind. A

bird trill. The rocks were eavesdropping and Imogen felt the flush of shame, as if they'd seen her naked.

"Tilda." Beck was back to her calm self, determined to mend a festering laceration. "Don't you think that if Rob—who claimed to love you—could be shitty enough to cheat on you, he might also have been shitty enough to force himself on someone? And deny it? And lie about it?"

Tilda spun away, burying her face in the crook of her arm. It was a posture of embarrassment, of guilt. "Things were different then."

"You mean people didn't believe victims then." Now Imogen felt the full weight of her own sadness. It was true; Imogen had spent half of her life in her own grave, buried alive. She trudged away from them a few paces and dropped into a sitting position, half facing the river. Beck gently tugged on Tilda's arm and guided her to the mattress pad, where they both sat down.

"I'm sorry," Beck said to Imogen. "I wish we'd told someone, Mom or Dad, someone."

"I'm glad I never told. It would've made it worse." At the time, it hadn't occurred to Imogen that she wouldn't be believed; she'd feared her politician mother would make a case of it, use the Terrible Act perpetrated against her daughter as a public ploy. She'd never trusted her mother with truly sensitive matters. Something occurred to her, and she snorted. "Remember that photo op Mom did with the drag queens?"

Tilda burst out laughing. "That was priceless."

Beck winced. Their mom really had used her sexual orientation to earn bonus points with voters. "Still. I'm sorry we didn't take you more seriously. Do more."

"You tried." Imogen remembered Beck and her girlfriend,

Jenna, comforting her the next day. Taking her to Planned Parenthood for emergency contraception and an STD screening. It was a lot to handle, and they did what many teenagers do who don't have an adult they trust: they circled the wagons. They made a place in the circle when Tilda got back from Mexico, but she didn't want it. The gaping wound of her absence had been there ever since.

How would they make this okay? Okay enough to not leave them with a ruined trip—days of awkward interactions—and a friendship in irredeemable tatters. Imogen watched the Colorado rushing past. It could wash her away. Carry her into oblivion. Her bones could become silt and in another million years maybe a creature would come to rest at this very spot, unaware of a girl called Imogen who was now a sliver of the rock tapestry.

"I've thought...," Tilda began. Imogen glanced at her tentatively, but Tilda had softened. "I've thought about it over the years. You might not believe me, but I have. There were so many things I struggled with, that didn't make sense, that didn't seem fair. I thought Rob was a good one. I'd had boyfriends since I was thirteen, since like the second my mom died. Rob seemed by far the best. Someone I liked, who liked me just as much. He was funny, generous, always there for me. You know how important it was to me to feel like someone considered me their number one priority—it's not my dad's fault, I know he was trying, but it was really hard after my mom died. For both of us—it took me a long time to really understand, so many things in our lives were never the same. But for years I missed feeling...important to someone. Doted on."

Tilda cast them a slightly guilt-ridden look. "I mean, I had you guys, obviously. But I wanted..." The light had shifted away, but she slipped her sunglasses back on. "When you told me…well, I felt ambushed, honestly. It seemed like an attack, on me—you, Jenna, Beck—like you'd all just been waiting for me to come home, like it was my fault because Rob was *my* boyfriend.

"I've thought about that night I found out. And how quickly I put my walls up. And with the walls up it was easier to believe that it wasn't like you said it was. I wanted to think Rob was lonely and drunk and I was on vacation, and that in some stupid way it was about me, him missing me. I know it's fucking asinine—yes, the years have given me clarity on that."

Imogen recalled a line from a Leonard Cohen song and something within her cracked a little, willing to let the light in. But Tilda wasn't finished; something inside her had opened too.

"After that I didn't trust my judgment at all. If Rob was the *good* boyfriend, the boyfriend I *loved,* what did that say about me and my shitty taste? I had hoped that if maybe you were wrong—a *little* wrong about what actually happened—then maybe I was only a little wrong too. I mean, how was I supposed to tell? What's a *good* man, a *nice* man? Rob was good to me, nice to me. But if he wasn't, in the end, good or nice…So I've wondered ever since then with practically every man I've dated: What *might* he do? Or what has he done in the past? You can't have that constantly in the back of your mind and have a healthy relationship with someone."

"I know," Imogen said, trying to give Tilda a pointed look.

Tilda nodded, but with the dark lenses on Imogen couldn't tell if she was looking at her. Imogen hadn't expected this to flip around and become about Tilda's insecurities, but Beck was apparently right about The Thing affecting her life too. Imogen had never contemplated Tilda's attraction to assholes or why she needed so much attention, so much approval. In recent years Tilda had matured, and from everything Imogen knew about him Jalal was a genuinely decent human. Yet Imogen heard, in the multiple times that Tilda had insisted it *wasn't* her fault, that on some level she'd always felt like it was.

It wasn't an apology, but it was better than nothing. Now that they were so close to it, she realized an apology might be something she needed. And she understood another important thing, something that Tilda might need.

"It wasn't your fault. What Rob did was never your fault."

"We never even considered that," said Beck.

Tilda let out a slow, measured breath, as if she were doing yoga.

Suddenly it felt like they'd been sitting there all day. Imogen's butt was sore and she needed to walk. As she stood, the others did too. They gathered up their things and started back along the creek, the mood heavy but not oppressive. Imogen wondered if, once they were moving, Tilda's missing *I'm sorry* might joggle loose. But apparently the talking was finished.

"Cook up some dinners when we get back? I could use a real meal." As the one who'd blown up their lazy day, Beck tried now to reestablish a lighter mood.

If someone had told Imogen that this confrontation was the trip's true agenda, the day's true plan, she wouldn't have come. Of course Beck had known that. Dr. Beck—Little Miss Smarty-Pants—was right about more things than Imogen was ready to admit.

"Sure," she said, trying to sound chipper. The last thing she wanted was to give them any more reasons to think she might fall apart.

"Do we have anything other than chicken?" Tilda asked. "Not that I don't love all your chicken dishes, but we're a little skimpy on the veggies."

Imogen sensed they were all trying to play it light, reassure each other that it didn't have to be weird. That was probably a good sign, though who knew what would happen once Imogen and Tilda had real time to ponder Beck's secret hand grenade.

"Toldja you shoulda brought the seaweed—veggie with protein," said Beck, mock-reprimanding.

"I know," Tilda whined. "I just *can't,* unless it's wrapped around some sushi."

Food talk put everyone in a better mood. The blue bag, now slung across Tilda's back, held all their choices, chicken and otherwise, but they discussed their options as if there were a restaurant waiting for them back at camp.

Their chatter sputtered to silence as they arrived.

The camp had been ransacked.

Their backpacks.

Their personal belongings.

The vital necessities they'd so carefully packed. Strewn everywhere.

It was impossible to tell at first glance what all was missing, though Beck's sleeping bag wasn't with the other two, weighted down with rocks.

"Oh fuck. Holy fuck." Terror made rapids of Imogen's blood and she clutched her chest where the roiling converged. She'd been right, about everything—the robber was *here*. How could she, after all she was supposed to have learned, not have trusted her intuition? "I told you—I fucking told you!"

She wanted to explode. Why hadn't she put more effort into the debate? Little Miss Smarty-Pants wasn't *always* right, after all. Being angry felt safer than being scared, but Imogen couldn't keep it up for long. The minute she looked at her sister she was overcome by something even worse than fear.

15

Beck trembled, her face awash with a sickness that was part horror, part heartbreak. Ever since they were tiny children there was one thing above all others that brought Imogen to instant tears: Beck, in any sort of emotional distress. Even as a child Beck was stoic, and when her pain surfaced Imogen felt it as if it were her own.

Tears stood in her sister's eyes. Imogen knew everything she was feeling: this wasn't supposed to happen. Not here. Not on Beck's watch. Not when people were counting on her. *And not when I'd warned her.* There was a faceless *who* out there, indifferent to the sanctity he'd shattered. Imogen felt exposed again, like she had the night before, knowing someone had been watching them. There was nowhere to hide. He would take what he wanted.

"I'm sorry, Beck, I didn't mean…" To blame her? Imogen was equally mad at herself.

But Beck wasn't listening. Her shock abruptly became urgency and she darted to the biggest pile—ditty bags upended, socks and underwear and toiletries—and dropped to her knees, searching, making a frantic exhumation.

"What's happening?" Tilda asked, confusion and panic in her voice. "Were we robbed again?"

"I told you I saw a flicker of light." There was no point in adding *and no one believed me.*

"The same person who took my protein bars?"

"We don't know!" Beck kept digging, sorting her urgent piles.

Imogen looked up toward the rocky embankment. Tilda took off her sunglasses and gazed with her. "What did they look like?"

"I couldn't see—"

"Look, we still don't know if it was the person from Hermit," said Beck. "Other people are allowed to camp here."

"Two different thieves?" Tilda snarled. "Seriously?"

Imogen hated everything she was feeling: anxiety, dread, guilt. And her old enemy, futility. She was afraid if she tried to help Beck she'd only be in the way, but she didn't like the sarcastic hostility Tilda had turned on her sister. At this point she and Beck would look even stupider if she admitted to having found a remnant from a wrapper suspiciously like Tilda's.

"This is so fucking…" Tilda anxiously glanced around, as if a taxi might come by and carry her away from this unruly place.

"We've never had anything like this happen before," Beck snapped. "It didn't seem possible that it could happen again."

"That's illogical, Mr. Spock—if it happened once of course it could happen again." Tilda glared at Beck.

"Wrong," Beck countered. "If something unlikely happens, the odds don't change—it's still just as unlikely to happen."

"Guys, this isn't helping." Imogen really didn't want to put herself in the middle of their fight, but bickering over semantics, or statistics, or whatever the fuck they were arguing about wasn't going to fix the situation. "We should've done things differently. But we did the best we could with the facts we had. At least we have all the food."

Yes, Imogen was sticking up for her sister. Beck, ultimately, was the leader, but Imogen couldn't fault her for being skeptical. Even now, they had little in the way of hard facts: stolen protein bars (when the thief could've taken much more); a torn wrapper (which could've been from anything); a camper in the rock shelter with a cigarette. *Colonel Mustard in the library with the candlestick.* Only someone like Imogen would connect those dots, and the odds were always in Beck's favor that they were unrelated.

"Even I didn't think I was right," she said. Which wasn't exactly true, but she worried about such things so often that she didn't always know what was real. She felt a twinge of guilt knowing it was her own neurotic behavior that made it easy for them to dismiss her. But alongside it came a stab of anger; hadn't she earned the right to be taken seriously? And couldn't they see how the Grand Canyon had already restored a missing piece of her confidence?

"Okay." Beck, with the mess hastily sorted, bolted upright, on a mission. "Here's what we're going to do." She looked at Tilda. "Can you get this stuff back into its proper bags—the fire ditty, the toiletries, get the clothes and stuff separated?"

Tilda hesitated. "Yeah…I guess?"

"Is that a yes?" Beck, no-nonsense, wanted confirmation. Seeing her take such decisive charge, Imogen felt a glimmer of hope. Maybe everything was going to be okay.

"Yes," Tilda said.

"Good." Beck turned to Imogen. "You and I are going to go have a talk with our neighbor."

Beck snatched up her walking stick, already on the march, heading for the creek. Tilda and Imogen exchanged open-mouthed expressions of flabbergasted dismay. Imogen had zero interest in confronting an unknown thief who was hiding in a rock shelter, spying on them. And why had Beck chosen *her*? Nothing about Imogen's stature or presence said *Ooh, I'm so tough and scary!*

"Uh…Beck?" Beck must have grasped that Imogen hadn't fallen in line. She stopped. Imogen couldn't shake the impression that Beck had become a soldier, the walking stick her rifle. "Think this is a good idea?"

"This is *not* a good idea," Tilda insisted. "We don't know who this guy is."

"He could be…dangerous." This, Imogen told herself, *wasn't* paranoia; this was a logical conclusion drawn from the mayhem at their feet.

"Maybe he already booked on out of here with our stuff, but we have to try."

"Maybe he *didn't* book on out of here with our stuff," Tilda said. "Maybe he's thinking 'No way those stupid chicks would come after me, not if they know what's good for them.'"

Beck considered her words. And quickly formulated a new plan. "Okay. Let's all go. You have your knife on you?" Imogen nodded. "Bring your walking sticks. Let's try to look like we mean business. I know you're upset. I know this is fucked up. But we can't let this guy win. We have to demand our stuff back, and look like we won't take no for an answer. Okay?"

Imogen and Tilda exchanged another round of stunned looks. Where was levelheaded Dr. Beck, and who the fuck was this reckless person who'd taken her place?

"Why don't we sit and talk about this." Tilda took her

best shot at calming Beck down. "We're mad, upset, this is a violation of our space, of our beings, but the worst has already happened. We don't need to rush in and put out a fire."

"Yes, we do." Beck, wired, was ready to go. "Look, I'm sorry if there's something else I should've done. I'm glad you had us bring the food bag—"

"We should've taken our packs." Imogen hadn't meant to blurt it out, but the truth of it was so obvious. They wouldn't be in this position now if they'd just lugged their damn packs the one mile to the river.

"Maybe." Beck sighed. Her zeal for the mission wavered for a moment, and the pain returned to her face. Pain, and sadness, and worry. "We have a problem."

"No shit," said Tilda.

Ignoring Tilda, Beck kept her gaze on Imogen. "He took the iodine tablets."

In spite of the sweat in her armpits—part nerves, part the flurry of activity—icy dread plucked at Imogen's skin. Now she understood her sister's call to action. Something electric passed between them.

Tilda looked from one sister to the other, desperate to know. "What's going on? You guys can't keep leaving out the important parts!"

Beck hadn't bothered to mention the loss of her sleeping bag; on the priority scale, it wasn't critical. But without the iodine they couldn't purify their water. They'd have nothing to drink, unless they risked having untreated water—and whatever ailments that might cause. Without the iodine tablets they couldn't stay even if they wanted to, and fleeing the Canyon would become a painful exercise in dehydration. Or worse.

16

None of them spoke. They walked quickly, an army of three, unhappily determined to do what they needed to do. Beck led the way, and Imogen and Tilda stayed a step behind. Now that they were on the march, Imogen was buoyed by the conviction blooming inside her. Beck was right—they couldn't let this asshole win. And they'd been planning this trip for a long time, and had their own unfinished business.

The creek was only six feet wide where it flowed through the camping area. With the aid of their walking sticks it was easy to step on rocks and scamper across. As they started scrambling up the steep, rocky slope on the other side, Imogen recognized the overhang she'd seen from camp. It arched twenty feet at the top and extended a good thirty or forty feet across, but everything within lay in shadow. Up close, it reminded her of the Anasazi homes she'd seen on previous trips to Montezuma Castle and Canyon de Chelly, where people once used ladders to reach their rock-ensconced dwellings.

This rock shelter could've used a ladder, but all they had was a gravelly hill without even a path.

Near the top, Imogen glanced behind her. She could see the colorful specks that marked their camp—backpacks, clothes, the food bag they'd hastily hung. Their neighbor had an easy view of them every time he peeked out from his ledge. He'd needed no stealth to know when it was safe to come down and raid their stuff.

When Beck came to a stop, fully upright beneath the towering eave of the shelter, Imogen and Tilda immediately flanked her. Imogen had never been so happy to be in Tilda's company. Now that she had her game face on, Tilda looked formidable, the very picture of don't-fuck-with-us. Imogen had to stifle an inappropriate giggle. With their walking sticks gripped tightly, they could have been cosplaying the warrior women of Wakanda. Her nerve lasted about four seconds, and then a man emerged from the darkness.

"Y'all about as quiet as a pack a rhino."

He blinked away an interrupted sleep. He was tall and scraggly, in dirty, ill-fitting clothes. His buzzed haircut showed blotchy bits of scalp, scars where his strawberry-blond hair wouldn't grow. In contrast, the hair on his chin and face, though short, grew thick and coppery. He looked weary and unhappy, and something about him reeked of trouble. Yet Imogen was almost relieved: standing before her was a real person; he wasn't a phantom, a figment of her overactive imagination. And the others could see him too.

"We don't want any trouble," said Beck.

"Y'all are trespassing," he said.

"It's a National Park." Imogen couldn't believe she'd blurted such a retort; first impressions pegged him as utterly the wrong kind of man to sass. But it pissed her off that he should claim a wonderland for his own—in *addition* to their belongings.

"We just want our things back," Beck said. She didn't sound nervous or angry, just matter-of-fact. "And we'll leave you alone."

The man came a few steps toward them, into the light. That was when Imogen noticed the blood. His shirtsleeves were rolled up to the elbows and the left cuff was tinged with a brownish stain. Much of his left forearm was streaked with fresher blood, and he'd used Band-Aids to patch a wound deep enough to still bleed through the bandages.

They kept the iodine tablets in the first aid ditty and Imogen suspected he'd stolen the whole thing for the medical supplies, not the water-purifying tablets. She remembered the bloody T-shirt they'd found; it could've been his. It brought her an immediate rush of reassurance. If that was all he needed, maybe they could get everything else back and continue on their journey. She felt a touch of sympathy for him too, with the evidence that his need had been great.

Beck took in his injury. "I can fix that. It looks deep. Probably needs stitches."

"You a doctor?" His bright blue eyes scrutinized Beck; then he considered Tilda and Imogen, with a directness she found unnerving.

"Yes," Beck said, standing up straighter. Perhaps she, too, felt less vulnerable seeing his condition. "We don't carry large quantities of medical supplies with us, but I've got a little of all the basics. Well, you have them now—they're with the stuff you stole. Give you some antibiotics too, take care of any infection."

His eyes traveled over them again, suspicious and evaluating, before settling on Beck. "You'd do that? Fer me?"

"I'd do that for anyone I could medically help. Even the jerk who took my stuff."

"We could make it an exchange," Imogen suggested, suddenly seeing an opportunity. "She patches you up, you give us our gear back."

"Sounds fair," said Tilda.

Beck nodded. "Deal?"

He looked shifty, like an animal that wasn't sure if the creatures before him were a threat. "How'd you know where I was?"

"Saw you light a cigarette last night," said Imogen.

"And I've been out here many times," Beck said. "Everyone who comes out here knows about this shelter."

"And here I thought I was just lucky."

"Maybe you're luckier than you thought." Beck nodded, eyes on his wound. "Looks like a serious injury. What happened?"

He glanced at his left forearm and lifted it a little, revealing that it was patched up on both sides. "Doesn't hurt that much, all things considered, but it bleeds like a motherfucker. Just when it's all scabbed, I move round and it rips back open."

"So what do you say?" Beck said. "We don't need to get in each other's business, but we *do* need that stuff you took—and it looks like you could use a bit of assistance."

"Well, thing of it is…" He sniffed with his crooked nose. "You seem like nice enough girls 'n' all, but I need some a this stuff."

Imogen reconsidered him. What sort of person didn't accept help and a fair exchange? It was easy to envision, by the coarse look of his hands, his trip-wired posture, and that unfortunate nose, that he probably hadn't had an easy life. Maybe he was used to living on the streets, or roughing it in the outback. She wondered if, somewhere in the shallow cave, he had a back-pack and at least basic gear. What was he doing here? Why didn't he just leave and go to a hospital?

Her mind raced back to all those episodes of *Alone*. Every contestant had a satellite phone and could call for help when they couldn't take it anymore, when they got too hungry or too lonely or too cold. But the call meant giving up on the game. The more determined contestants tried to push past their un-lucky mishaps—a broken tooth, a fishing hook embedded in a thumb. But eventually they got too concerned about infection and permanent harm. Every injury ultimately signaled the end of every player's shot at the prize. What was this guy's story? Why was he risking his health to stay a little longer? Beck, even without Imogen's reality-show acumen, was thinking along the same lines.

"You probably need your arm too, and that hand even more. It would really suck if you got gangrene."

Imogen had to admire the way her sister was playing it. She'd seemed to know right from the start that something about him was off, and had found a way to make herself useful and not a threat. Imogen wanted to help her out, if she could. She hadn't done any theater, on or off the stage, since she was a teenager, but she gave it her best shot.

She uttered a gasp and wrinkled her nose in disgust. "You aren't going to cut his arm off, are you?"

"Ewww!" Tilda grimaced and turned away, as if the sawing were about to begin.

Beck took the bait, but not in the way Imogen expected. Beck rolled her eyes at the silly girls, trying to share a traitorous moment with the thief, *Can you believe how ridiculous they are?* He chortled, and she leaned in to get a closer assessment of his wounded arm. "It's not to that point yet, it's not turning black or green. But it could. You want to keep an eye out for any red streaks radiating from the wound—that could be a sign of blood poisoning, and that would be life-threatening. If an infection in the blood reaches the heart…" She looked around at the canyon behind her. "I'm not trying to be dramatic, but they wouldn't be able to get you out of here in time."

"I'm not looking to get outta here, just trying to lay low fer—"

"I suspect you aren't looking to die either."

There was a silent standoff. Imogen saw Tilda holding her ground, but her eyes gave away her unease as they shifted between the man and Beck.

He abruptly turned and headed into the darkness behind him. They heard him rustling around. Imogen froze in place, unsure what was about to happen.

"What are you doing?" Tilda whispered to Beck. She managed to keep the volume of her voice almost nonexistent, even as it registered alarm. "He looks like a rabid fucking dog, let's just leave."

"Keep calm, it's fine," Beck said. "Remember there are three of us. And he's injured—we've got bargaining power."

Imogen wasn't feeling as confident as her sister. Had the man retreated to get their first aid ditty—or something else?

17

To Imogen's surprise, he returned with Beck's sleeping bag, hastily stuffed into its sack, tucked under his right arm and a faded army messenger bag—likely full of stolen goods—over his shoulder. One of their canteens dangled from his finger. And he'd put on his belt, to which was attached a camo sheath with a hunting knife.

"Let's go."

"Where are we going?" In spite of Beck's command to stay calm, Imogen was starting to tremble. She hadn't expected him to return with a knife—one a lot bigger than hers.

"Camp. You got a good setup. You can fix me up there, and we can eat some a that stuff you cook in that little pot. Could use a warm meal."

He headed out, scrabbling—amateurishly, Imogen thought—half on his bottom as he made his way down the slope. Watching him slip and bumble, she guessed he was a city person, with shitty mountaineering skills. But then again, he didn't have either arm free to help his balance (and one of them was bleeding), and somehow he'd managed to hike all the way to Boucher in cowboy boots. What he lacked in grace he made up for in determination. Like a survivalist. He was as ill equipped as the *Alone* contenders.

Oh shit. *Shit shit shit.* He wasn't just some injured man, down on his luck, lying low. Imogen flicked her eyes from Beck to Tilda, begging them to understand, to see: he was *crazy.* Crazy the way survivalists were, proud of themselves for the suffering they could endure. Willing to do anything. Beck didn't understand who she was negotiating with.

Tilda might've been close in her assessment of him as a rabid dog; it would be better not to let him sniff out their panic. Imogen needed to control her wildly beating heart, it was making her unsteady. She probably looked as scared as she felt, so she tried to emulate Beck and Tilda, who appeared cool, almost bored. As they crossed the creek and walked back to camp he kept an eye on them, wary for his own reasons. Imogen couldn't figure it out: he hadn't actually agreed to the terms they'd offered, and his actions—joining them—were the opposite of the leaving-him-alone that had sounded so promising when Beck had proposed it.

What the survivalists on *Alone* longed for more than anything was company, an end to their solitude. Could that be what he wanted?

Was he planning on spending the night with them?

Maybe she could dump the rest of her marijuana tincture into his food so he'd fall asleep (or at least get sluggish). Then they could get the iodine tablets back and leave him to whatever the fuck it was he was doing out here.

She started plotting it out in her mind. She'd need to let Beck know, so she could distract him. Maybe she could let

Tilda in on it while Beck was stitching him up. Imogen would offer to dish out the food (and hope his portion didn't taste too obviously of skunk). It was a very civilized plan. A very this-will-be-easy plan. Which probably meant it wouldn't work.

Stop thinking like a wimp! She needed to start thinking like someone who was in the presence of a crazy person. Something was wrong with this man, and judging by his clothes and lack of preparedness, "lying low" could mean he was on the run—from a bounty hunter, or the redneck mafia, or his girlfriend's husband. They needed to anticipate something more than a pleasant dinner. Could Beck be thinking the same thing? Was that why she'd reminded them they were three against one? Were they going to have to launch some sort of attack?

If it got to that point, Imogen had her Swiss Army knife—though the largest blade was barely two inches. Hitting him with a rock was an obvious option. Tilda had well-muscled arms but was she prepared, mentally, to hurt someone? Would Beck do it, or would the oath she'd sworn—"first, do no harm"—prevent her? Imogen wished she were stronger, that she could handle a physical confrontation by herself. As surreptitiously as she could, she glanced around for a sharp rock—small enough to grip tightly, but large enough to have some heft, some power.

They were almost back to camp. She was running out of time and the uncertainty of what they were getting into was making her more anxious by the second. While she understood Beck's logic in attempting to get the water-purifying tablets back, she was less and less sure it was the right move. A cacophony of warning bells blared inside her. He wasn't the asshole they were expecting; he was potentially something much more dangerous.

* * *

He sat down and made himself comfortable, taking a long drink from the canteen he'd stolen, as soon as they were among the detritus of their camp.

"You want to get supper on?" Beck asked Imogen, kneeling in front of the man. "I'll take care of this wound."

"Okay." She was glad for something to do, something to put the brakes on her runaway thoughts. Fuck giving him the tincture, she needed it herself. Beck poured water over one hand, and then the other, scrubbing them as well as she could.

"What kinda supper choices we got?" the man asked.

"Chicken."

He either didn't notice or didn't care about Tilda's curt answer. "I like chicken. Sounds real good."

"I'm going to need the first aid bag."

Instead of handing Beck the bag, he kept it on his lap and opened it, reaching in with his uninjured hand. "Whatcha want first? We'll do it like those hospital shows, I'll hand off everything ya want."

Was he not going to give up the bag—or anything else? Or was this his weird version of fun? Imogen lit the stove and set a pot of water on to boil, one eye always on Beck and her patient.

"When did this happen?" Beck asked him, removing the Band-Aids and cleaning off his arm with first water, and then alcohol swabs.

"Few days ago."

"Looks like the bullet went straight through." Gently, she examined both sides of his forearm.

Tilda and Imogen snapped their heads toward Beck. Did she say *bullet*? Beck ever-so-briefly met their eyes, but proceeded with her work, unflustered.

"What happened?" Beck asked.

"Got into a little situation. Dumb fucking unfortunate dumb shit that never shoulda happened."

"The other guy okay?" Beck was fishing, smooth as could be.

"Really just a misunderstanding," the man said, maybe not even aware of Beck's question. "But Doug's gonna kill me fer what happened to his car. But what was I gonna do?"

Tilda's muscles unclenched and she breathed a mini sigh of relief. She set to work sorting out the mess from their dumped-out backpacks. It seemed stupid to Imogen—probably to Tilda, too—to kill someone over a car, but whatever this man's misdeeds were, they were between him and Doug. People probably got shot over less. Still, the less time they spent with him—and his volatile cohorts—the better.

"Hand me the syringe?" Beck held up her palm.

He got leery. "What's that for?"

"It's lidocaine, it'll numb the area so the sutures don't hurt."

She only ever brought a single syringe dose of lidocaine for just such a contingency, though they carried an anesthetic gel for burns or stings. Instead of retrieving it from the bag, he looked skeptical.

"Sure you ain't trying to knock me out? I don't need it."

Dr. Beck gave him a you're-trying-my-patience glower. "Yes. You need it. This exit wound is a mess, and I'm not going to have you wriggling around. Don't be a martyr."

After a momentary standoff, he relented and gave her the syringe. He didn't even wince as she injected small amounts of the numbing medication around the freshly cleaned gashes in his flesh. But he was more compliant after that, and let Beck do her work without questioning her.

"I can't guarantee there aren't bone fragments in here, I'd recommend you get this X-rayed as soon as you can."

He snorted. "I can move it okay."

"Still. It's good it went straight through, but that doesn't mean it didn't damage anything. Do what you want, but it's my professional opinion you should have this looked at as soon as you get out."

"I am out. Fair and square."

Beck and Imogen both looked at him, struck by their differing interpretations of *out*. That was how they'd always referred to leaving the Canyon—heading out, getting out. What did it mean to him? *Prison.* The word appeared in Imogen's mind with bold certainty. He was an ex-con, she'd bet on it. His hard days weren't spent on the streets or in the wild, they were spent in a prison cell. It begged the question: What had he done?

"I'm just saying you still might need surgery," Beck patiently explained.

He shrugged, indifferent.

There wasn't any way to talk openly, to plan—to tell Tilda or Beck what she'd deduced. The man's eyes wandered continually, somehow watching all three of them at once.

"Where you girls from?"

Imogen's impulse, again, was to assault his semantics: they were women, not girls. She let it slide, but before she could answer Tilda jumped in. "Ohio."

"Never been there."

"It's not that thrilling." Tilda sounded annoyed.

While Imogen understood her impulse to lie, she wasn't sure

if this was the right person to deceive. She could imagine him taking great offense at any effort to insult his intelligence, or play him, should he figure it out. They needed to be cautious, a warning she tried to convey to Tilda under her breath.

"Careful."

"All you from there? You two look alike in the face, though nowhere else. Sisters?" Beck nodded. To Tilda he added, "Not you though. You a Mexican?"

"We're all from Ohio," she said, turning her back to gather up the bowls. She gave Imogen a pleading, what-the-fuck-are-we-doing look.

"I grew up in Mississippi, but my ex—my first wife—was from Texas and I ended up there longer than planned. I wanted to see more a the West, was heading to Nevada when this…situation came up. Know this is some kinda world wonder, but this fucking hole seems like a weird place to come fer fun. Y'all have fun out here?"

"We *were* having fun," Beck said, terse, concentrating on her stitch work.

"You can call me Gale, if ya want. It's not my name, not really. Well, part of it, but people been calling me that forever. It beats Red Fred. Not commie red, but…" He pistol-pointed at his strawberry hair and rolled his eyes.

"Gale, I don't mean to be a jerk," said Beck, "but I have a needle in my hand, and your skin between my fingers. We need to settle our arrangement. I'm going to finish this. Give you the antibiotics, as promised—I'll even throw in some ibuprofen. We're gonna share a nice dinner. And then my friends and I are going to pack up and go. If you're looking, as you said, to lay low, I'd recommend you head west—that way." She pointed. "Few people come out here, but even fewer head out to Slate and beyond. We'll give you some basics, but we need stuff too, so we can get out and go along our way."

Beck sounded firm, reasonable. Imogen watched him, hoping Gale would finally accept the deal.

He gazed westward, where Beck had recommended he go, but instead of agreeing he asked, "Y'all have names? Might as well be acquainted, if we're gonna break bread together 'n' all."

He sure was congenial for a guy whose friends would kill him over a car. Shouldn't a guy this guileless be able to patch things up over a couple of beers? Imogen couldn't think straight in his presence. Everything about him was begging for a good story, but whenever she started to get a picture of him, it went blurry again.

Before Tilda could invent new names for them, she said, "I'm Imogen. That's Beck, and this is Tilda."

Tilda shot her a look, but Imogen didn't care. She didn't trust that Tilda had a workable plan; she understood Tilda wanted to get away from him, but other than shoving a few things into her own pack, she'd been only marginally useful since they got back. Imogen's strategy was to pay close attention to the man's words, to Beck's cues, and it wouldn't hurt to find…There. She spotted a triangular rock a few feet away, twice the size of her fist. Perfect for crushing a man's skull.

If Beck's negotiations worked, they wouldn't need to rely on her violent fantasies. But just in case…Imogen waited until Gale looked distracted, watching as Beck wrapped his forearm in a gauze bandage, and then casually kicked at the rock, as if she were clearing a spot on the ground to sit. The rock came to rest inches away from where Tilda was kneeling by the stove, setting out the bowls and forks.

The water came to a boil. Imogen opened her knife's scissors tool with its tiny one-inch blades, but to her surprise, Tilda reached for it.

"I'll do it."

As Tilda cut open the bags, Imogen squatted down and lowered the stove's flame. For a moment, instead of pouring the boiling water into the pouches, Tilda just gripped the pot's handle. She flicked her eyes to Gale. And clenched the handle tighter. Imogen's mouth hinged open in dawning realization: Tilda was ready to spring. She looked to Imogen for approval.

We're not ready! They didn't have any kind of plan, they couldn't even grab their stuff and run, not with everything still scattered around. At the very least they needed to have canteens, and their walking sticks, and the blasted iodine tablets that had gotten them into this predicament in the first place.

Imogen wasn't sure what her expression said, her features felt stuck on and mismatched, but Tilda deflated, frowning, and poured the water into their chicken dinners.

"We don't have enough bowls," she murmured, defeated.

"What's that?" Gale asked, standing up, wiggling the fingers on his injured left hand. "Good as new. More or less."

"We only have three bowls with us," said Imogen.

"You sisters can share, right? Or maybe one a you is lezzies with the Mexican. You more likely," he said to Beck. "I know I'm being judgmental, on account of yer short hair. But you and yer sister both dress like boys. The Mexican's got a nice figure."

Imogen didn't need to look at Tilda to know she was seething. In one of Tilda's viral videos she'd ranted about how her body was the first and sometimes *only* thing men noticed, and it increasingly pissed her off.

"I'm not a framed painting on display," she'd barked to the camera, describing an encounter she'd had in the subway in New York City. She'd been too tentative to say anything back, to do anything but smile with gritted teeth and look away; you could never predict how men might take a perceived rejection. Imogen had watched the video more than a dozen times—*that* Tilda, the public Tilda, would never have doubted that she'd been raped.

Whatever Tilda was thinking now, she kept it to herself. This situation was worse than a man in the subway with loose eyeballs and casual assumptions. Much worse. Even if this asshole-survivalist-ex-con-crazy-person intended his comment as a compliment, it was harder to know what exactly *Mexican* meant to him. He could have used a more racist term, if those were his leanings. But his very need to classify them—and he wasn't wrong about Beck's orientation, or their resemblance as sisters, or Tilda's ethnicity—was unnerving. He was smart and observant.

"Supper ready?" Beck asked, seemingly oblivious to any danger.

18

Gale ate heartily from one of their bowls. "Pretty good."
As he'd suggested, Beck and Imogen shared, and
Imogen used a spoon, which she preferred anyway, since they
only had three forks. She'd been hungry since they left their
peaceful spot at the river, but her intestines were more like coil-
ing vipers now and she could barely make herself swallow.

"Eat as much as you can," Beck said softly.

Imogen heard: *I know you're scared.* She heard: *You need to
stay strong.*

The canyon walls around them were changing colors as the
sun sank on the horizon. As much as she didn't want to spend
a night anywhere near Gale, Imogen wasn't looking forward to
hiking in the dark, per Beck's plan. The minutes stretched and
the shadows deepened and her antsiness grew.

"You girls are probly real talky when I ain't around, right?"

"No offense, but we don't know you," said Imogen, trying to
be as nonchalant as her sister. "And this is kind of…a strange
way to meet."

He gazed at each of them in turn, masticating his food in a noisy, predatory way. "This is decent fer grub from a bag, not as good as home-cooked but better than…" He slurped up another mouthful and didn't finish his sentence.

Prison.

"You all always this skittish?" He kept his eyes on Tilda now, who sat between Beck and Imogen and hadn't uttered more than a few words since the rock shelter. "You think you know something about me?"

"We know exactly: you're the guy who robbed us. Twice. In a place where people are usually chill and considerate." Beck somehow managed to sound both no-bullshit and, to use her own word, chill.

"That's why yer all so weird around me?"

"You don't think that's reason enough?" Tilda asked. The vibe he gave off would have made them wary even if they'd met him elsewhere. Like in the subway, demanding a smile.

"Gale, seriously—I understand you're in a bind, and we're not without sympathy," Beck said, "but this isn't just some friendly get-together. You completely fucked up our trip. Between the food you're eating and the snacks you stole we don't have enough to stay. And giving you some of our canteens and iodine tablets means we have to be very careful rationing water just to get back out. I think you should be a little more thankful, and understand that none of us are super happy that you messed up our vacation. We'd been planning this for a long time."

Tilda stopped chewing. Imogen felt it too, the risk of blaming this man for anything. But she understood Beck's approach: treat him as honestly as they could.

Gale chewed, eyes on his bowl. "I'm sorry. I guess I owe you girls an apology. Obviously I'm here kinda spur a the moment. Figuring out what's next. But you've been helpful. And volunteered more than I expected. Thank you—fer my arm."

"You're welcome."

He sounded sincere—something probably none of them were expecting. Imogen's intestinal snakes calmed a bit, and she scooped up more of her dinner.

"You don't owe me anything. You don't owe me shit, but…if we could do something, like whatcha said before. I'd be grateful. I just want to lay low here. Seems like a good place to figure things out, think about yer life. That why you come out here?"

Imogen saw Beck nodding, and found herself nodding too.

"This is a good place for that," Imogen said. In a matter of seconds her view of him shifted back to what he'd first been—a troubled person. She knew that no child set a life goal of becoming a troublemaker, and whatever had happened— whatever he'd done—the criminal justice system had a way of swallowing the poor. "Everything seems quieter here, even the stuff in your head."

"You got shit in yer head too?" Gale asked, his voice tipping toward surprised.

"Pretty sure everyone has shit in their head. Life is hard. Makes you doubt what you're doing, what you *should* be doing, how you got here…how you might have ended up somewhere else if things had been a little different."

"Yeah," Gale said quietly. "I think about that too."

Imogen met his gaze. In the waning light he looked sad. The empathy she felt for him came quickly and naturally. He didn't seem like a mean person, a little (a lot) rough around the edges, but even as a thief he'd attempted to stay out of their way. It was possible they'd even scared him, showing up at his hiding place. She cursed the part of herself that assumed everyone was sinister in some way—especially when she forgot that she, too, didn't always make a good first impression. Everyone who met her probably thought she was standoffish, maybe stuck-up, because while her mind assessed people at a million miles a minute, she wasn't quick to be friendly, open, warm. *Like Afiya.*

She remembered something that informed her writing, a thought given to her by a teacher during her first semester at Pitt, in the only acting class she ever took: *No one thinks of themselves as evil.* (It worked just as well to replace evil with *bad,* or treacherously *wrong.*) The other students had looked puzzled; they protested, and then started tossing out the names of history's villains and dictators. The teacher clarified that she wasn't saying that no one *was* evil, but that no individual would *label* themselves that way. And Imogen, who'd been reading *Richard III* at the time, immediately understood: through the experience and lens of one's own life, all actions were reactions building toward the goal of ending the endless *want,* to fill the empty place where the true self had been robbed by circumstance.

A boy didn't set a life goal of being evil, bad, wrong. A criminal. He set a goal of being loved. And then things went awry.

When they were done eating, Imogen had Tilda do the washing up. Usually something of a clean freak, now Tilda only swirled a little water in each bowl, and halfheartedly wiped away the debris with a dishcloth. While Beck and Gale worked on their negotiations—what he wanted versus what Beck would give up—Imogen packed what was left of their things as they went along; they still had miles of night hiking to do and she wanted to be ready to go.

Gale wanted a backpack—Beck's, but she refused; it was like asking for a part of her body. Tilda offered hers. "It's not like I'm ever going to use it again."

For some reason the pronouncement made Imogen sad, but this wasn't the time to try to change Tilda's mind—Imogen wasn't sure herself if any corner of the world remained a safe haven.

Gale wanted the stove and pot, but Beck talked him out of it. "You'll run out of fuel in a few days and then what? Useless dead weight. We'll give you most of our crackers, nuts, and snacks. Matches are more useful. And the fishing ditty—that's where we keep a few hooks and some fishing line. You can figure out the rest."

He agreed. They didn't have a fishing ditty, but Beck stuffed bags and snacks into "Gale's" pack. The lie indicated to Imogen that Beck worried about what Gale would consider *enough*. She let him keep her sleeping bag—this was now going to be their last night in the Canyon and she'd bundle up on her eggshell pad and rough it for one night. They gave him a second canteen to replace the crappy Mountain Dew bottle he'd been using, and the majority of their iodine tablets. Beck rationed out enough to purify their water for the following day. If they were careful, after refilling at Santa Maria Springs, they'd be fine.

Gale wasn't knowledgeable about the specifics of what they had or what he needed, so Beck figured it out for him. She gave him a tarp, a bowl, a fork and spoon, a tiny roll of toilet paper, the first aid stuff she'd promised, and a Ziploc bag full of miscellaneous items that included the "fishing stuff." In addition to her pack, Tilda donated a sweatshirt to his cause. Maybe it was because of Imogen's small size, but she lost none of her personal items. Gale asked for a walking stick and Beck told him to find his own. She gave him a pair of her padded socks instead.

It was almost dark when their supplies were redistributed and packed.

"One a y'all have a cigarette? Outta smokes, could really use one." They shook their heads. "Didn't think so. Where you girls heading? Don't have to rush off. Ain't it too hard to hike at night?"

Beck and Imogen quickly hoisted on their backpacks. Tightened their belts. They were a little heavier than they'd been before: they hadn't given Gale a full third of their gear, and what was left had been hastily divided between their two packs.

"Back to Hermit. It's mostly Tonto, we'll be fine." Beck had been playing her diplomatic game for so long—hours—but her patience was dwindling; it was time to go.

"Y'all just looking to get away from me?" His instincts were scary-good. It was too dark to see his face, but Imogen feared he was about to go back on his word.

"Thought you wanted to do your own thing," Beck said.

"We have to be out by tomorrow or we'll run out of stuff," Imogen added, as benign a reminder as she could muster of all they'd given him.

"Yeah. Makes sense," he said, not very convinced.

Stick in hand, Beck turned, ready to lead them away. Tilda switched on her flashlight.

"Hey, you got an extra one a those?" Gale asked, taking off his cowboy boots as he sat on Beck's sleeping bag.

"Sorry," Beck said, and kept walking. Tilda fell in right behind her, smartly angling her light on the path ahead of them. Imogen took up the rear, grateful that he hadn't ransacked their stuff with more care.

"Really?" Gale called.

"We don't usually hike at night," Imogen said.

"It's easier to see the stars in the dark. Good luck to you," Beck said from the front.

"Thanks." He sounded farther away with each step they took. "Bye now."

"Take care." Imogen couldn't help herself. She wished him well enough, even as the instinct to get away from him grew with each step.

She tried to pray—for their close call, for their safety—but the slithery words wouldn't coalesce and all she heard were their boots on the scrabbly dirt and their heavy breathing. The terrain heading out of camp wasn't difficult, but for hours they'd been holding back everything they might really have wanted to say—about Gale, about Beck bringing them together under false pretenses. Inhaling and exhaling became its own language, universal and less dangerous than speaking aloud. Imogen concentrated on the sounds behind her, anxious—half convinced—that she'd hear footsteps chasing after them.

They started the steep ascent out of Boucher. Imogen desperately wanted to get out her own flashlight—Beck probably did too—but she knew better than to let Gale see another bright beam in the darkness. They'd have to wait until they were farther away.

"Where are we going?" Tilda's voice sounded small and frightened.

"Travertine," Beck answered. "That's about three miles. It'll put us halfway back to Hermit, and there's a flat spot just as you head in. It's the best place to camp that isn't too far, and it won't add that much to our hike out tomorrow. I'm really sorry, guys."

"I'm sorry too," said Imogen. "I should've...I really didn't want any of it to mean anything, the wrapper, the cigarette—"

"What wrapper?" Tilda asked.

"I found a torn scrap, maybe from one of your protein bars."

"It could've been from anything," Beck maintained.

Away from Gale, Tilda regained some of her tenacity. "Doesn't either one of you have any common fucking sense? He was *following* us—"

"That's not true." Imogen cut her off. Maybe it was her allegiance to her sister, or a need to defend herself, but Tilda's distorted interpretation pissed her off. "Technically we were following him. He was at Santa Maria Springs *before* us, at Hermit, at Boucher—"

"What's the difference?" Tilda spat.

"Big. He wasn't stalking us. It doesn't make it right, but it's a bit..." To Imogen, that reality seemed better—that reality made Gale less of a predator and more a criminal of convenience—but she didn't have the energy to argue the point. "It was bad luck, happenstance."

"Whatever," Tilda mumbled.

"It just..." A twinge of emotion tore a space in Beck's words. "It seemed impossible. Not here. Of all places."

This man had done more than scare Beck or wound her pride. He'd stolen some of the holiness from her chosen synagogue. And Imogen fully understood, fully agreed.

Finally they were far enough away and Beck flicked on her

flashlight. As Imogen switched hers on, she thought she heard something behind her. A scampering. She swung the light around: there was nothing there but the luminescing beam and a shroud of inscrutable darkness. Maybe it had only been a mule deer, startled by their crossing. What else might be out there... Elk? Javelina? Mountain lion? Coyote? Something hungry.

The last thing they needed was another animal in need of food.

19

They paused for a short rest and a sip of water when they reached the Scary Spot.

"Are we really doing this?" Tilda asked. "It was barely passable in daylight."

At least it was a question and not a refusal. Imogen thought it might be better to have only the trail visible in the beam of her flashlight; she could pretend the drop-off wasn't there. As it was, hiking at night felt like walking in a dream. Nothing seemed quite real.

"It's actually easier from this direction," said Beck, "heading uphill rather than down."

"Can I go first?" Imogen asked. She wouldn't have been able to explain her eagerness; all she knew was she didn't want to be the last to go, to watch Beck and Tilda disappear around the boulder and blink out of existence like the snuffed flame of a candle.

"Sure." Beck let her pass.

The extra weight Imogen was carrying compressed her hips;

her bones seemed to grind in their sockets in protest. So far it had been manageable, on a trail without lengthy inclines or uneven crossings, but she wasn't sure she could carry her pack all the way back up the Hermit Trail. The packs should've been lighter at the end of their trip, depleted of food and fuel, not heavier.

Before she crossed, she turned to Beck. "Hey. Maybe we could take turns with the packs tomorrow."

"Sure, that would be good—that should help a lot. Up for that, Tilda?"

"Yeah." She sounded worn out. "Are we almost where we're going?"

"Almost. We'll be to Travertine soon."

Where they could finally—finally—relax. Talk about what had happened (or not). Sleep.

Imogen headed up the path at the edge of the gorge. It might be less perilous from this orientation, but now that she was here, with her flashlight on the finite ground in front of her, she felt even more the dark absence at her side. Beyond the beam, the world simply ended. The nothingness beckoned to her. *It won't hurt at all.* She kept her eyes on the trail and walked with resolve.

Behind her, Beck asked Tilda, "Want to go next?"

Tilda must have agreed—or maybe Beck had performed her hypnosis trick. A minute after Imogen reached the other side, Tilda appeared, strolling casually, head tilted toward the circle of light at her feet. Beck followed just a few steps behind.

"See," Beck said. "It really is—"

"Let's just get to camp." Grouchy Tilda had taken over. Nobody could blame her.

* * *

The rest of the walk was undemanding and they moved more swiftly—or so it felt—than Imogen would have predicted, given their exhaustion and the darkness. Beck, with the aid of her flashlight, had no trouble keeping track of the trail, whereas Imogen was fairly certain she would have wandered off to God knows where without her sister's guidance. *That's how Dad almost tumbled off the cliff.*

There was one tight spot—literally, a place where they had to squeeze and clamber between two boulders—but then Travertine was right there, a few feet beyond. Imogen recognized it from the morning before: Had it really been just yesterday? The dry creek bed was flat and mostly level, making it a safe area to maneuver in the dark.

Beck exhaled an emphatic puff of air, releasing hours of tension.

"Set up camp?" Tilda asked.

"Yup." Beck unbuckled her hip belt.

"You guys really think…" Imogen held her flashlight high enough that it cast a glow on Beck's and Tilda's faces. "Is this far enough? I mean, we could keep going a little?"

She was tired, but willing to push on if it put more distance between them and Gale with his questionable past. Tilda rubbed one weary eye.

"Are you serious? Why?"

Imogen couldn't really shrug with her pack still on. And she knew if she bungled the explanation they wouldn't listen to her. "He's…He's a survivalist—have you ever seen the show *Alone*?"

"You watch way too much TV." Beck set her pack down.

"No, I'm serious, there's something about him—"

"We know, Imogen, believe me. He's bad news, and that's why we gave him half our stuff and left. But he's not looking to go where we're going."

"And there's no way he's crossing that fucking deathtrap in the dark." Tilda retrieved her stuff from Beck's pack.

"I know it's not perfect," said Beck, "but we're okay. I did everything I—"

"I know," Imogen said. "I know, you did."

And Beck had. She'd used her doctoring skills, her calm-under-pressure skills. Sometimes it struck Imogen how truly unalike they were. Beck the left brain, and Imogen the right. Imogen would keep inventing scenarios, keep reimagining Gale as a character, fluid to the needs of her story, no matter how far away they got from Boucher. Perhaps someday he'd show up as a character in one of her books.

All of their remaining food was already in its nylon bag and Beck quickly found a place to hang it. "And now it's time to get some sleep. We'll have a hot meal in the morning. And we'll take a real break on our way out and cook a good lunch."

It sounded comforting, but Imogen knew that had nothing to do with why Beck had refused to hand over the stove—or her pack or walking stick. Where Imogen had an emotional attachment to a large percentage of her belongings (stuffed animals, books, knickknacks), Beck was more discriminating when it came to bonding with inanimate objects. Beck reserved her fondness for things that were useful or provided a sense of companionship (or both). Her little Swedish stove had been an essential and reliable companion on many a journey; Imogen understood why she hadn't wanted to let it go. Especially not to the man who'd defiled their sanctuary.

Tilda wasted no time blowing up her mattress pad. "I should've just given that dickhead all my overpriced hoodies and socks," she said, balling everything into a pillow. "I'm never wearing this shit again."

"Your clothes might have been a little too girly for him." Imogen was hoping to lighten the mood, but even in shadow she saw Tilda's unamused smirk.

They were both annoyed with her, at least that was how it felt. The longer Imogen stood there with her pack on, the more she wanted to lie down and go to sleep. Finally, she took her backpack off. With all the shuffling and reorganizing, she'd lost track of her little Visine bottle. But she made a quick search, to no avail.

Their flashlights rested on the ground, directed toward their activities as they finished laying out their mattress pads and stashed their boots for the night. Imogen couldn't see her sister's face, and almost didn't want to. How much of this was she blaming on herself? Imogen was a pro with the if-onlys; if she were in Beck's position she'd probably start with *If only I hadn't staged an intervention in the middle of nowhere.* Imogen wasn't ready to digest everything that had been said. It was out in the open now, which was potentially a positive start, but nothing with Tilda felt resolved. And Imogen had her own inner work to do. *I let him change me.*

"You know, this is the kind of thing we'll be talking about thirty years from now," said Imogen, needing a distraction. In a weird way, it could end up being a bonding experience beyond what any of them had hoped for.

"Let's just get through tonight," Beck said, tucking her laces into her boots.

Tilda wriggled into her mummy bag. Imogen pushed her

mattress pad flush with Beck's, and proceeded to unzip her sleeping bag all the way around to make a blanket. It was out of character for her, but while the other two had retreated inward, Imogen was in the mood for talking. She wasn't sure if she could fall asleep; she was weary, but her thoughts were as unsettled as a plundered beehive.

"Maybe when we get back to the car we can head south," she said. "Find a nice hotel, sunshine, a swimming pool?" A hotel always had been more Tilda's speed. "We need a couple days to relax, process. Want to?"

Tilda sighed, turning away from them. "Maybe. Okay."

As Beck curled up on her eggshell pad, Imogen floated the faux-down "blanket" over the two of them.

"You don't have to," Beck said.

"Don't be silly."

"It's barely big enough."

"So we'll cuddle." Hadn't they done that long ago, as kids? Though maybe they'd been face-to-face then. Whenever they stayed overnight in a new place they would take turns reciting their favorite story, "Rumpelstiltskin." They'd done it at their Bubbie and Zayde's house, or on those rare occasions when they found themselves in a hotel with one of their parents in the adjoining room. Except for that fateful Canyon trip and a few family visits to Kentucky, the Blum sisters had usually traveled with one parent or the other, rarely both.

She spooned behind Beck now. Even with all their layers on it promised to be a chilly night, and the narrow sleeping bag left Imogen's butt hanging out in the cold. Beck tucked her half under her chin. Imogen felt her sister's silent, shuddering sobs, and wished she remembered the whole tale of the hobgoblin who promised to spin straw into gold.

"It's gonna be okay," she whispered in Beck's ear, unable to give her a bedtime story.

They were awake for a long time, shifting restlessly in the dark, probably whirling close calls and do-overs in their head. Finally Tilda's breathing settled, and then Beck's. Imogen still had too much going on inside. Too late she realized she hadn't gotten her Swiss Army knife back from Tilda. It would've been some comfort to hold it in her hand as she tried to sleep, but Tilda would probably kill her if Imogen awakened her to ask for it.

She longed for her own bed, her comforter, the safety of her small apartment. *Advantages to being a hermit? Shit like this doesn't happen!* She thought of how two diametrically opposed things often exist side by side: that was how she could like the confining walls of her apartment as much as she loved the wide-open out-of-doors, with little regard for anywhere in between. But, for the first time in Imogen's life, the wilderness had become uncomfortable.

Instead of sleep came the memory of another night when she'd lain cramped beside her sister, filled with swallowed tears.

Every summer Imogen and Beck (then Becky) went to Kentucky to visit the Blankenbillers. (Their dad, once known as Bobby Blankenbiller, became Robert Blum after his marriage, much to his family's chagrin.) When Imogen was nine and Becky eleven they stayed at their cousins' for the first time without their dad. That was when Imogen came to fully understand the difference between *her home* and the word as it applied to where other people lived, which was more antihome. Aunt Barb reacted as if her discomfort were wonderfully amusing and inquired about Imogen's homesickness multiple times a day, seemingly with the hope that it was getting worse.

Her aunt and uncle insisted Imogen looked just like her mother (whom they clearly didn't like), and teased her for every little thing. Her buckteeth. (Two years later they practically rolled on the floor laughing at her over-the-head night brace.) Her distrust of glow-in-the-dark-green pistachio pudding. Her jeans, which she liked to wear rolled up to keep from getting muddy. Becky was exempt from their judgments, and held in high esteem because she didn't mind helping with the sheep and chickens.

Imogen was familiar with house cats and fish tanks, not farm animals. The chickens looked sort of friendly and she almost gathered the courage to help collect the eggs. But then Aunt Barb came out with an ax and chopped off one of their heads. The chicken ran flapping and headless and Imogen didn't understand what it meant: Did things not die *instantly*? Was the chicken watching its own body run around? The sheep were different. Stinky, for one. They were giant woolly mammals that behaved like schools of fish. Young Imogen couldn't wrap her brain around it. What were all these creatures *thinking*? The headless chicken and the herd of cotton balls?

One night the cousins decided it would be great fun to have a slumber party in the back of the pickup truck. Aunt Barb layered the hard bed of the truck with blankets; the five girls were to sleep width-wise like sausages. Imogen wasn't keen on sharing a bed with anyone, ever, and she got stuck in the middle, with Becky on one side and their youngest cousin on the other. She lay on her back, afraid to move, gobbling the night air. It smelled sweet, of fresh-cut hay, but she couldn't shake the sensation of being in a grave. Imogen's lungs started to collapse. Her heart raced.

The bodies around her squirmed and giggled while Imogen gasped for air.

"Becky! Help me!"

The cousins were a chorus of *What's wrong?* and Imogen didn't want to cry in front of them. But she wanted out. *Out! Out!* Becky helped her climb over the side of the truck. She walked her to the house and opened the door. For once, Aunt Barb's concern wasn't tinged with glee. Becky returned to the truck while Aunt Barb led Imogen to Tammy's room, where she got to sleep in her eldest cousin's big bed all by herself.

"You're just a little homesick," Aunt Barb said for the sixty-third time.

But Imogen knew she'd been misdiagnosed. Yes, there were things about her home she missed. But the real problem she had while summering in Kentucky was an endless lack of having her own space. Privacy. Alone time. A door to close. She'd had no way to explain to Aunt Barb or anyone else the ways in which she didn't feel okay. Her dad thought it was fun for them, spending time in the country with girls their own age. But the cousins were only fun during the day. Come night, Imogen yearned for her own room.

Afterward, she'd longed to be a snail, carrying around its beautiful spiral of a home. Or a turtle, which could draw in its extremities and say *bye-bye*. Yet, for all the hours Imogen spent as an adult cocooned in her apartment, she still wasn't sure if she'd ever felt truly at home *anywhere*. Sometimes in the company of a tree—or a creek, or a moss-covered rock, or a desert night haloed by the Milky Way—she felt the tension inside her finally relent. There—*out there*—was a place where she belonged. But it had always been fleeting; she could never stay *out there*. Not then. Not now.

This wasn't the trip she'd hoped it would be. Though a dormant part of her had started to revive, ultimately her fears were proven to be valid: destructive men lurked everywhere, willing to wreak havoc to get what they wanted.

The one positive thing she'd done following the incident at the synagogue was to refuse to give the shooter space in her head. She never saw his face; she shut her eyes when they showed him on the news. Rather, she held the images of everyone who had been injured or killed; they were the ones who deserved to be remembered, not the insecure bigot with the gun. When she got home and started to process this misadventure, she'd forget Gale and focus instead on Beck and Tilda. Maybe, where Tilda was concerned, there was still something to salvage. And with Beck's epiphany held close, Imogen wouldn't let herself regress further. If nothing else, she understood now that she didn't want to end up late in life with regrets over things she could've changed.

As she gave herself over to the moment, breathing in the pure air and reflecting on the dark whimsy of her childhood summers, an idea came to her. A dark fairy tale about a girl who had to go on an extraordinary journey to understand who she really was. Pieces of the story materialized instantly—the girl, her best friend, wise women, a glorious forest. Imogen saw the allegorical world unfold in her head and smiled. This, finally, was an idea that excited her.

She hovered near sleep, wondering if home wasn't a physical location after all, but a state of mind—the place she entered when she filled a page with words. At least she'd found the first upside of their situation: she couldn't wait to get home. And write.

20

Someone kicked her in the back. It was a shitty, confusing way to wake up, but it was only as Imogen regained consciousness that she realized how deeply asleep she'd been. The sky was radiant with color; the sun, too, was just peeking over its nightspread, blinking at the new day. Her first thought was that Tilda or Beck (or both) must be anxious to get going and she was impeding their departure. But then she felt Beck's warm, sleeping presence at her side.

And another kick in the back.

"Tilda, what the fuck—" Imogen rolled over.

Initially she was too shocked to even gasp at what she saw. The instinct to get away made her push backward, trying to crabwalk an escape. But her hands encountered sharp pebbles and her elbow collided with a small but bruising boulder.

"Ow, fuck."

"Rise and shine, sleepyheads," Gale said.

Beck was the only one yet unaware. Imogen wished with all her might for it to be a nightmare. But as she locked eyes with

Tilda and the heat of peril throbbed in her spine, she was all too awake. Gale knelt beside Tilda, the hunting knife at her throat. Her friend appeared almost dazed with terror. As Beck startled into wakefulness and took in the situation, her instinct was to lurch forward, toward Tilda. Gale stopped her by tightening the grip of his other arm, squeezing his prisoner against his body.

For a moment they all froze, unsure how to proceed.

"Sorry to wake y'all up like this, but I was tossing and turning all night, bothered by something I couldn't quite point a finger at. And luck of luck, y'all didn't get as far as I thought."

Beck reached for her boots. Force of habit meant she still turned each one over and gave it a shake before putting them on. Imogen would have preferred to keep retreating, away from the tableau, but without that option she had no choice but to crawl the length of her mattress pad to get her boots.

"What are you doing here?" Mornings, even on the best of days, were an existential struggle, and being wrenched from sleep by a madman made it infinitely worse. Was this really happening? Imogen's heart was in her ears, a muted storm. How had reality caught up with her imagination?

"Just get yer things together. Come on."

"We're heading *out,*" Beck protested, quickly folding up her mattress pad.

"That was a mistake." Gale glanced around, surveying the trail both before and behind them, nervous. "Let's just get back. Better there, no one around."

Beck and Imogen exchanged frantic looks. Going back to Boucher with him was like getting in the car with the kidnapper: doom. No one who wanted to survive an abduction went along without a fight. Imogen was certain her sister was thinking the same thing.

"Can't we just talk about this? We'll make some coffee and talk here?" Imogen said. Beck's brain would be sharper with an infusion of caffeine, and they desperately needed to be alert. His desperation had been obvious—how had they underestimated him so badly? But hindsight was the devil's mirror, and of course it was clear now that they'd made a terrible miscalculation.

Gale, the knife still at Tilda's throat, jerked his head around, looking this way and that. He was jumpy. Too jumpy. His knuckles were white and the silver blade almost grazed Tilda's windpipe. He was in no condition to hold a rational conversation. But Imogen would almost rather plunge into an abyss than follow him anywhere. Nothing good would come of it. She'd created a dozen different story lines for him in her head, and in none of them was he a kidnapper. And if he was capable of even worse things than what she'd imagined...

Before complete terror took hold, she made eye contact with Beck. Gave one shake of her head. "We can't," she mouthed.

"There were people over there." Gale gestured with his chin in the direction of Hermit. "Worked good fer a couple days, got some necessities. But you know I don't wanna see nobody else. Didn't even wanna see *you,* but glad I caught back up 'cause here's what was bugging me." He scrutinized Beck. "Maybe you already seen me on the news, or heard something. I know they're out there putting two and two together—even if Doug didn't say who borrowed his car—thanks to DNA and other things I couldn't make disappear. And you girls are gonna tell someone 'bout me the first chance ya get. Being a doctor, ya gotta report a gunshot wound—"

"I wasn't going to report anything," Beck insisted. "And we have no idea who—"

160

"It's the law, ain't it? You know whatcha learn by breaking the law? You learn how many damn laws there are. Now hurry up, get a move on."

"You're wanted by the police?" Imogen, disoriented, toyed with the possibility that she was lost inside one of her own stories. She wanted to ask what he'd done, but why bother when she was a conjuror of nightmares and could simply guess and be close enough to right.

Beck remained calm, her face unreadable. She efficiently packed their loose things while Tilda looked on helplessly. "I can't guarantee no one else is going to come out to Boucher," Beck said in her smooth hypnotist's voice. "People *do* go out there."

"Didn'tcha say I could keep going, head west? Maybe we'll do that. But let's—"

"Why are you doing this?" Imogen begged as dread started to boil inside her. Maybe Beck was thinking that, for Tilda's sake, they needed to comply, but Imogen wasn't ready. It felt too much like giving up. "We *helped* you. We gave you our stuff and fed you and Beck fixed your arm."

The hand at Tilda's throat relaxed a little. "Yer not gonna do anything stupid?" he asked her.

"No." Her voice was a croak.

Gale released her. Tilda scampered out of arm's reach, releasing a sob, and quickly put on her boots. Imogen held her breath. Had she gotten through to him?

"Last night. I was so tired and I shoulda been asleep. But I kept thinking; I made so many mistakes. Gave you my name. That's what I do 'cause I'm a friendly person, but I shouldn'ta done that. And you know what I look like. And I let slip a few things I probly shoulda kept to myself. Fuck it if I ain't the biggest softy at heart, when I see a person as a person and I relate to them. But it gets me in trouble, sometimes keeps me from doing what needs to be done."

Was he saying what Imogen thought he was saying? That if he wasn't such a people person he wouldn't have let something like three innocent, mortal women get in his way?

"We won't get you in trouble, Gale. We really don't know who you are," said Imogen. His other name came to her, Red Fred. He was right in a way: if he'd been less chatty they wouldn't have known anything about him other than the nature of his injury. And Imogen had no idea if that alone would've made Beck report him to the authorities. But now that he'd come after them, they knew he was wanted by the police. And if he expected to be on the news, he was either a narcissist or had done something really, really bad.

"We promise we won't tell!" Tilda said.

"There's nothing to tell," Beck maintained. "You're a random…guy. I don't care why you're here. I was perfectly fine and serious about going our separate ways and calling it a day."

"You"—he pointed the knife at her for emphasis—"are a big fat liar. Big fat doctor brain. Think yer smarter than everyone. I'm not stupid—wanna know what I know? Lit a few matches as the night wore on—hate being in the dark, fucking hate it. I'da had a *flashlight* if I hadn't been worried 'bout how you girls were gonna hike in the dark! See? Then this morning, soon as the sun started up, started going through the stuff, seeing what's what and if there were more matches. And you know what I found? No fishing tackle. No line, no hooks." His face twisted; his nostrils flared. He looked like an injured bull sick of playing games with the matador. "You don't appreciate.

How *nice* I was trying to be. Fucking bitches trying to get over on me. Now come on." He flicked the knife toward the trail.

Beck's expression gave away nothing, but Imogen wanted to kick herself: she shouldn't have let Beck try to pass off the lie. Gale had already proven himself to be observant, and if Beck and Tilda hadn't noticed—or understood what that meant about his character—Imogen should've been more assertive. And while she was at it, she could've made a better argument for pushing on toward Hermit. For someone who made her living with words, she sure didn't use them well when it really counted.

Before she could come up with another line of negotiation, another stall tactic—which was itself dangerous, considering his bad mood and jitters—a helicopter swooped past. The discord was an invasion, complete with the gunfire of rotary blades. But it was a common sound within the Canyon: some people preferred to gain a dragonfly's perspective, a quick hover before darting away. They were simply tourists out for a morning excursion, but Gale jumped back against a rock, plastering himself into a shadow.

"See?" he said, when the chopper receded.

"It's just a sightseeing flight." Given Gale's new distrust of Beck, Imogen considered it her duty to take over the talking.

"They're looking fer me."

"Not *them,*" Imogen insisted. "Gale, honestly, we don't mean you any harm. I'm sorry—we're sorry—about lying about the fishing gear. For what it's worth, we always talk about bringing some, but never do. We just wanted to finish our trip in peace, and let you get on with your own business."

She was trying to be clever, emphasizing their willingness to be candid *and* discreet. But her hope that he'd reconsider lasted less than two seconds.

"We can talk about that back where we were. Come on, stop dillydallying."

Imogen turned to Beck, pleading with her eyes, unsure what to do but certain she didn't want to follow him back to Boucher. Gale's knife had been sharp enough to cleanly slice the cord on their hanging food bag. And if he'd had an altercation with someone with a gun—and won with a knife—they never wanted to see that knife in full action. Beck gave the tiniest of shrugs, and then a barely perceptible nod. She shouldered her backpack and after a second's hesitation, Imogen did too. Beck had some sort of plan, Imogen was sure of it. She handed Tilda her walking stick.

Tilda flared back to life. "You're going with him?"

"It'll be fine," Beck said. If Dr. Beck ever had to tell someone they had cancer, that was surely the manner she'd use. Gentle; unflappable.

"No, wait." The sisters had taken a step forward but stopped at Tilda's urging. "I can't help you with anything," she said to Gale. "I don't know anything about outdoor survival, I'd never even been in a sleeping bag before a few nights ago."

Imogen looked at Beck, jolted that Tilda seemed on the verge of bargaining for her own release. Was this a clever ploy to try to get help, or something more selfish? The situations were radically different, but the last time they'd encountered trouble in the Canyon they'd foolishly not stuck together. Judging by the fury that flashed in Beck's eyes, she was thinking the same thing.

"I had nothing to do with planning this trip," Tilda went on, pleading to Gale. "You can have the rest of my gear, there's nothing else I can do to help you. And I'm not a doctor, I don't have to tell anyone about anything."

He looked like he was considering her offer, but then he chuckled and turned to Imogen and Beck. "True colors. Always find out who yer friends really are when the shit comes down." His amusement vanished as suddenly as it had arrived and he took a step toward Tilda. She tried to retreat, but he grabbed her arm. "Pretty sure that makes you the phoniest a the bunch. The one I need to keep my closest eye on. No more debating," he bellowed to all of them.

Beck strode forward, ready to scramble through Travertine's demarcating boulders and lead them back to Boucher. Everything about this felt so, so wrong.

"After you." Gale, mimicking a gentleman, indicated with a sweeping, bladed hand that Tilda should fall in line next.

There they were, proceeding as they would have on any other hike—Beck, then Tilda, then Imogen. Only this time Gale took up the rear position, where none of them could escape his observant gaze. For an instant the air rippled as reality divided itself. Imogen had experienced this before, when time demarcated a Before and an After. They were in an After now.

From behind them, Gale started to warble a hoarse but jolly tune.

"You are my sunshine, my only sunshine, you make me happy when skies are gray…"

21

Imogen really wanted a drink of water. And a pee. A sliver of her was grateful it was a fairly short walk back to Boucher, ninety minutes or so. But the rest of her rampaged with regret that they hadn't pushed on the previous night. Gale was right: there were probably people there. He might not have risked going all the way back to Hermit to kidnap them, and even if he had, they might have had a chance to call out for help. But the extra miles hadn't seemed crucial then: they'd parted with Gale on decent terms, and he hadn't threatened them in any way.

In the light of day there was a whole new litany of should-haves, sharpened by the mirror of Imogen's remorse. They hadn't known why he was lying low or who was after him—and wouldn't know now if he hadn't come unglued by his own paranoia. Imogen hated to think that they had that in common.

Gale wasn't singing anymore, but she wished he weren't at her back. His eyes felt like hot darts burning all the way through her backpack. What was he thinking? Was it better or worse that he was winging it, making decisions on the fly? He was good at improvising, but his brash actions were dangerous—for all of them. But maybe he didn't see it that way, or worse, maybe he didn't care.

To distract herself from the bottomless what-ifs, she concentrated on the rhythm of their three walking sticks. *Tap-tap-tap.* Lift, lift, lift. Swing forward, forward, forward. Plant again, one by one. *Tap-tap-tap.* Maybe they could use their sticks for something, defensive or offensive. When they were little, Becky and Imogen liked to sword-fight and joust with them while backpacking in West Virginia. A bamboo walking stick had many applications: it could support your weight as you crossed a creek, or become a tent pole if you jammed it into the ground. At the very least, the sticks could help keep the man and his weapon at a distance.

Or maybe... The Scary Spot was coming up. Tilda would probably hesitate again; they might be able to use her lack of confidence in some way, a stall tactic if nothing else. And if they could keep just the right gap between them...could they—one of them—use a walking stick to push him into the gorge?

It would come with a risk. If Gale grabbed for the stick as it prodded him, its holder would have to let go—fast—lest his momentum drag them both off the edge. But it would be a quick way to end this, and a tidy way to dispose of him. If they could pull it off. And if they were ready to resort to such means to restore their freedom.

Could Beck be thinking something like that too? If only they could exchange even a few words. If he went first could one of them rush forward and stab him with the bamboo pole hard enough so he'd lose his balance? What if he went last? That might work better; he wouldn't be able to see any of them on the other side of the Promontory. They could surprise him with a quick thrust from the blind side of the rock. She could already imagine him falling, hear his scream diminish as he hurtled toward his death.

I'm not a murderer. But that's the perfect murder. At least it would be if she were writing a book.

They approached the spot soon enough.

"Stop," Gale commanded, and Beck, Tilda, and Imogen all came to a halt. He strode past them and surveyed the crossing. The downhill footing from this side would always make it harder, even if they weren't being shepherded across against their will.

Beck swung her head around and as soon as they made eye contact Imogen took up her stick like a lance and made a quick stabbing motion, hoping her sister understood. Beck nodded. They had only seconds before Gale turned back around, but it was enough to convey a general idea.

"I hate this fucking bitch of a trail," Gale grumbled. "What kinda people call this fun? Was expecting a desert, lots a rabbits to eat and some big cactus—you can get water from some kinds a cactus, ya know, purer than rain. Not this…fucking cliffs." He scowled. "Bet you all'd love to see me topple right off that ledge, probly think it'd serve me right."

No one said anything. He looked at each of them. Imogen hoped her face didn't display any eagerness, or guilt—about this, at least, Gale was right to be paranoid.

"You go first," he said to Tilda. "Then I'll figure out what to do with these two. I'm betting they're better at it, more experience and not so *posh*. Probly got yerself a Chihuahua back home, carry it around in a little handbag—a Mexican dog fer a Mexican girl, right?"

Tilda stepped backward. "No. You're right—what kind of people call this fun? I'm not doing this again."

Her whole body was rigid, spring-locked, like it had been the evening before as she gripped the pot of boiling water, trying to decide. Imogen didn't stop her this time. Tilda didn't have a pack on—with adrenaline and good health on her side, she might be able to outrun Gale to Hermit. Gale started to turn his head away from her, perhaps to order Imogen or Beck across the divide. Tilda bolted.

One second she was there, the next she was gone, replaced by a wake of dust. She was *fast*.

Beck and Imogen instantly thrust their walking sticks at Gale's torso, trying to block his pursuit. He tried to defend himself, grabbing for their sticks, but after a couple of jabs in the gut he held up his hands, amused, and side-stepped away. He reached behind his back and untucked his shirt—

It happened in slow motion. It happened in the blink of an eye. But she knew what he was reaching for.

"Oh fuck!" Imogen screeched.

—and pulled a handgun from the waistband of his pants.

Beck spun toward Tilda's diminishing back. "Tilda! Get down!"

Gale pointed the gun. Aimed. Fired. Fired again.

The sound exploded. Imogen felt it inside her, shredding the soft membranes of her sanity. She gripped her ears and howled in torment.

Tilda sprawled on the trail, a graceless collapse of limbs.

Beck shouted something. Maybe Tilda's name. Imogen still heard a barrage of bullets, the faint memory of distant screams.

Tilda turned over, looked back at them.

Beck grabbed Imogen, hugged her hard around the neck. "She's okay! It's okay!"

Tilda knelt in the dirt, her eyes locked on Gale. He grinned, the black pistol now in his relaxed hand, pointed toward the ground.

"Aimed way over yer head," he called. "This time. Now get yer dumb ass back here." He turned to Imogen, whom Beck was still trying to console. "I didn't shoot yer friend, you can calm down."

"It's okay, you're okay."

"She's the scaredy one, huh?"

Tilda watched Gale the whole way back. She made a wide berth around him and huddled with Beck and Imogen.

"You okay?" Beck asked her.

"Now y'all know what's what, okay?" Gale said. He fiddled with the handgun. "Safety back on. Safety first, second, and always. Got this little souvenir from the cop who pulled me over. He didn't need it no more." He tucked it back in his pants. "I never like having to hurt people, goes against my grain. But I wasn't gonna go back to prison just fer driving across a state line. Now, shall we try this again?"

Beck held a canteen to Imogen's lips so she could take a sip; her own shaking hands wouldn't cooperate. Then she handed the water to Tilda. Tilda and Beck shared a complicated look, a silent attempt at communication with pinched eyebrows and angry eyes. Were they mad at Gale, or each other? Imogen's heart was finding its way back into the center of her chest, done with its stomping around. Should she have shaken her head to stop Tilda? At least they knew now. He had a gun.

Gale had shot a cop. Gale was on parole. Gale had borrowed Doug's car to drive to…where had he said? Nevada. But why risk his freedom? *I am out. Fair and square.*

"Guess it don't matter who goes first now, right?" Gale said. "Better this way. Just do what yer told and it's all easy."

"Okay? Everybody ready?" Beck asked them. "Want me to go first?"

"I'll go," said Tilda, retrieving her walking stick.

"Don't do anything stupid," Gale said. "Anything *else.*"

Tilda glowered at him. "That was really subtle. For someone who wants to lay low. Firing off a gun." She seethed, skirting around him again.

They watched her cross. Her runner's legs were more tentative now, taking small steps aided by her bamboo stick. Imogen wondered if it could possibly be true: Could the sound carry far enough? Could anything other than the rocks and the ravens have registered the gunshots? There'd be no SWAT team, but anyone—a lone ranger—would be better than nothing.

"That girl's got pluck, give her that. But damn, disloyal. Probly thinks she's too good fer everybody else. Seems more like a big-city girl than Ohio."

The smirk he gave Beck and Imogen said it all: he knew they weren't from Ohio. Fucking Gale missed nothing. Perhaps he assumed everything they'd ever uttered was a lie.

Imogen went next, so she wouldn't have to be alone with Gale. She dreaded what lay ahead: the fear and uncertainty; the terrible possibilities of a forsaken life. She shut off her mind. Ignored the heaviness of the pack, the thirst, the rumbling from her insides that was either hunger or the collapse of the world she'd known.

Beck was only a couple of strides behind her, followed by Gale. They'd really done it. Gotten in the car with the kidnapper, and shut the door.

22

Her mind raced during the rest of the hike back to Boucher. Where once her mantra *four miles an hour or get shot in the back* had been a macabre form of motivation, now it was sickeningly real.

Gale corralled them back to their camping site, which he'd evidently left in a hurry: the ditty bags were upended; Beck's sleeping bag, three-quarters unzipped, had been carelessly tossed aside, its two halves like crumpled butterfly wings.

Imogen couldn't read Tilda's or Beck's expression, aside from their obvious apprehension. It was beyond frightening how well Gale handled his multiple hostages. As if he'd done it before. He didn't even need to keep the gun in view, having successfully taught them that he would use it, though he kept his knife drawn. They were the flock and he the attuned sheepdog. Imogen hated the image of herself as a sheep—hated it so much she decided to make use of it, let it fuel her fortitude. Farm animals were butchered; she wouldn't allow that to be her fate.

He gathered the three walking sticks and stashed them near his own disorderly collection of stuff. Then he allowed Imogen and Beck to take off their packs. With the knife, he directed them where to stand: in a line, two feet apart from each other.

"What are you going to do with us?" Tilda asked.

"As little as possible." After positioning himself where he could watch all of them, Gale ordered Imogen to retrieve their nylon rope. "Know you got it, to tie yer stuff up in a tree."

It took Imogen a minute to search through the packs. Gale didn't hurry her. All things considered he seemed rather cheery and calm, a marked improvement from how jumpy he'd been at Travertine. Tilda's escape attempt had bolstered his confidence; he'd established the pecking order. He sipped from a canteen and watched Imogen scurry about.

"Yer gonna be my little helper," he said to her, "'cause this one lied to me, and that one's a piece a work. Yer the only one who ain't pissed me off yet. And you are little." He grinned at his own wit. As Imogen handed over their bundles of cord—some short pieces, and some quite long—he beamed as if she'd delivered a bag of gold. "Perfect. Thin and strong, just how I like it. All righty then."

He clicked his tongue as he pointed at Tilda. "Where ya wanna sit? Over here? Against this rock?"

"I'm not going to run again—across that fucking deathtrap."

"While I kinda believe you, it don't matter. This is how it's gotta be now, and you got no one to blame but yerself."

As Tilda walked over to the rock he'd indicated she scowled at Imogen and Beck as if they were the ones about to tie her up. She plopped down in the dry dirt and kept her head turned away, refusing to look at any of them as Gale bound her wrists together. With a quick slice of the knife, he cut a second piece of rope and knotted it onto the cord above Tilda's hands. She clenched her teeth and rolled her eyes as he wrapped it under her legs and tied her ankles together.

"Really?" she asked. "I'm that much of a threat to you?"

Imogen's heart skipped a beat and she glanced at Beck. Tilda was known to crack a joke when a situation overwhelmed her, but Imogen feared her sarcasm and hostility would only antagonize Gale. They really didn't need the twitchy side of him to resurface; the twitchy side might not aim *over* their heads. Beck stared at Tilda, maybe trying to mesmerize her into acting more rationally, but Tilda wouldn't look at her. Fortunately, Gale laughed it off.

"There, keep you outta my hair fer a bit." He shoved the rest of the cord in his pockets and strolled back to Imogen and Beck. He carried the knife casually, indifferent to its pointy tip as he used it to gesticulate. "I don't like having hostages, ya gotta understand. It's baggage I don't need. But maybe it ain't so bad." He winced a little, holding his injured arm against his belly. Was the morning's activity getting to him? At least he had a weak spot. "Got my own doc and tour guide—and a personal assistant. Why don'tcha make us all some breakfast. Oatmeal and coffee sure sound good."

Imogen decided to risk that his mood was as congenial as it seemed. "Can I pee first?" she asked.

Without missing a beat, Tilda said, "I have to pee too."

"Oh fer fuck's sake. The sisters can pee, but the Mexican's gonna have to wait until after breakfast—I just did up those knots, why didn'tcha ask before?"

If it had been a scene in a movie Imogen would have laughed. Everything was backward, the wrong people getting mad about the wrong things.

"Sorry, I've never been kidnapped before!"

Imogen didn't understand how Tilda could think her anger was a good move, but once again Gale didn't seem to care.

"Fine," he said to Imogen. "I'm coming with ya, a course."

She got out their toilet paper and Beck led them to their preferred rock.

"'Kay, do whatcha gotta do." He turned around without being asked, which Imogen supposed was decent of him. But she hesitated. Was it safe to drop her pants anywhere near a man like this?

"Come on," Beck whispered.

Gale half glanced behind him. "Hurry it up. Ain't gonna wait all day."

Imogen squatted beside her sister, one eye on Gale as she emptied her bladder. "What do we do?" she mouthed.

"Wait. Watch."

As Imogen and Beck started the stove and got out what they'd need for breakfast, Gale patiently unpacked their things, investigating with a thoroughness he hadn't bothered with before. When possible, he did everything one-handed, and Imogen hoped Beck was plotting a new way to "help" him that might involve a misuse of her medical expertise. In the meanwhile, the three women could do nothing beyond cast each other glances, checking in to make sure they were all okay.

He found Tilda's camera and examined it with interest. He held it up to his eye, and looked at each of them through the viewfinder. "Smile!" But instead of clicking the shutter, he got to his feet and dropped the camera to the ground. Smashed it with his boot. "In case y'all got any photos a me."

When it was in pieces he sorted through the debris and retrieved the memory card. That he pounded with a rock.

"Can I have some water?" Tilda asked somberly, watching the destruction of her work.

Imogen took a canteen to her and helped her drink.

"Front pocket," Tilda whispered.

"What?"

"Cut me loose."

"What're you two yakking about?" Gale asked.

"We should refill the canteens," Imogen told him, disappointed to have to turn away from Tilda before she could figure out what she was trying to convey.

Gale scanned the creek and nodded. "Stay where I can see you."

The creek was barely forty feet away. Imogen took three canteens. Refilling them wasn't an urgent necessity, but it was the first thing that had popped into her head. Now she cursed herself for a missed opportunity. Her brain wasn't in full working order, a deficit caused by stress and hunger. Tilda had been trying to tell her the Swiss Army knife was in the kangaroo pouch of her sweatshirt. She wouldn't have used it to free Tilda, that would've been too obvious and taken too much time. But Gale didn't perceive Imogen as a threat, and she needed to take advantage of that. She'd try again—Tilda would need more to drink, or help eating, and Imogen would pick her pocket then.

As she filled the canteens she kept one eye on the camp behind her, in case she needed to dash back. Gale just sat there making piles of their belongings. He handed her the iodine tablets when she returned with the fresh water.

"Thanks." It felt weird to thank him, but the habit was ingrained.

Beck busied herself with the coffee preparations, nervously watching Gale. Imogen started toward Tilda, but Gale stopped her with a word.

"Hey. Now what're you doing?"

Imogen held up the dripping canteen. "Thought she might like some cold water."

"She already has to pee, give the girl a break. And just 'cause yer little and ain't pissed me off yet doesn't mean you can wander around doing whatever you want. Breakfast almost up?" Beck nodded. Gale turned back to Imogen. "Sit. Chillax—do the kids still say that?"

Imogen sat cross-legged near Beck; she rubbed her wet hands over her face. She felt Tilda staring at her, her gaze scorching with disappointment. Beck flicked a questioning look between the two of them. She knew the iodine needed thirty minutes or so to do its thing and not nearly enough time had passed.

Almost finished with his examination of their gear, Gale lined up the *three* flashlights at his feet. Imogen felt his earlier friendliness—if it could be called that—start to evaporate.

"Can you untie *one* of my hands? So I can eat?" Tilda asked, oblivious to the change of mood.

"I'll tie up the sisters after breakfast and you can go to the john and eat then."

"I'm sorry about the flashlights," Imogen said, trying to stay a step ahead of his fury. "We really did need them. We really were just going to leave and not cause you any trouble, and I didn't know you were afraid—didn't like the dark." She prayed he wasn't a man who'd want revenge for a perceived slight on his masculinity.

Beck gazed at the flashlights, proof of another lie, and shut her eyes for a second. Maybe she was concerned about retaliation too, or maybe she anticipated what was coming next. Gale dug out Beck's Swiss Army knife from deep inside her pack.

A wicked grin traveled from his lips to his eyes, but to Imogen's bewilderment he didn't explode. It was good he didn't have a short fuse, but unhelpful in predicting his behavior that it burned at an unsteady rate.

"Everybody keeps some secrets to better their own chances," he said, his voice ominously soft. "What else you hiding?"

He sprang up, tucking Beck's folded knife into his pants. "More of a girly knife but might be useful. You each got one then? Turn out yer pockets." Imogen balked, not because she had anything to hide, but because she knew they were about to lose the last of their weapons. "Turn 'em out or I'll pat you down."

Beck and Imogen got up and emptied their pockets. Dirty facial tissues. Lip balm. Imogen's little notepad. A small piece of schist, meant as a souvenir. They made sure Gale could see they didn't have anything else, and Imogen hoped he'd leave it at that. But no, he went to Tilda.

"Any pockets in these?" he said as she squirmed. He ran rough hands around her hips and backside.

"No!"

He reached into her sweatshirt pocket. "Bingo! Can't believe I didn't check that before tying you up, I'm getting sloppy. So that's two. You got one?" he asked Imogen.

"That's hers," Tilda said before Imogen could reply. She was telling the truth, of course, but Tilda's continued eagerness to separate herself was becoming more than a little annoying.

179

"That true?" Gale asked. "You know she had it?"

"Yes," Imogen said. "She used it to open our freeze-dried dinners."

Gale swirled his tongue around the inside of his mouth, his eyes hard and evaluating. What conclusions would he draw?

"You didn't ask us to hand anything over before," Beck said. "We bring these as tools."

It felt like he stared at them for an hour before finally passing his sentence. "We got everything out in the open now?" They nodded. "Don't need to do a strip search?" They adamantly shook their heads.

After a shrug and a huff, Gale reeled back and threw Imogen's knife as far as he could—far enough that they didn't hear it land. They'd never find it.

"Don't ask, don't tell." He chuckled, amused with himself, and approached Beck's neat row of brewing coffees. "Can't fault you fer following the basic rules a common sense—so that one's on me. My bad. Been off my game fer days, a wonder I'm not dead. I'll even forgive you fer the flashlights, 'cause if I'd wanted y'all to die last night I woulda found a more direct way a doing it than leaving you to stumble around this shithole in the dark. Now, why don't we sit a spell like civilized people."

Civilized people who casually threaten other people's lives? Imogen lowered herself into her former cross-legged position and gathered up the detritus from her pockets. Gale claimed Beck's mug of steaming dark-roast coffee. He sat near their kitchen, but with enough separation to keep an eye on everybody.

"See, we can keep it all friendly. Makes everything easier."

He took a slurp of the coffee. "Coffee's good. Been a minute. Thanks, Doc."

Beck took the second-darkest cup. Tilda's mug sat there on a rock, cooling off. Away from the rest of them, her wrists and ankles bound, Imogen watched a tear slide down her cheek.

23

Beck made only one packet of oatmeal for each of them. Imogen knew they usually made two per person but Gale didn't, and she understood her sister was rationing. Gale expected Beck and Imogen to share a bowl again, but Imogen took the double serving over to Tilda and for every spoonful she ate, she fed one to Tilda. It was one thing to leave her without coffee, but Imogen couldn't just let her watch them eat. Fortunately, Gale didn't object.

After a minute he proposed that Tilda scoot over on her hiney so they could all eat together. And with a little help from Imogen, she did. In spite of Tilda's bindings (and questionable behavior), Imogen felt safer sandwiched between the warm blockades of the two strongest women she knew.

"This is good. Thank you, girls." He looked at them, an expression Imogen would have shockingly described as *appreciative* on his worn-out face.

"You're welcome." There was no rational reason for it, but in that moment Imogen felt more relaxed than she had all day.

There were times when she caught glimpses of the normal person in Gale. In fleeting instances he could even seem good-natured. The more she thought about it, this realization might actually be the best thing she could contribute to their survival. Beck saw him as a challenge to be conquered by out-maneuvering, and Tilda perceived him as a menace to escape from posthaste. They were valid perspectives, but ineffective if applied without a better understanding of what made him tick. If Imogen could look past her fear and hold in her mind an awareness of his vulnerabilities, his fundamental needs and wants as a human being, she might be able to connect with him in some important, lifesaving way.

Like the young heroine she'd been conjuring the night before, who had to endure an arduous quest to find her true self, Imogen realized she might now be on such a journey too.

"Yer the soft one," Gale said to her, alarmingly in tune. "See you thinking, but what *you* worry about is if yer fickle friend is thirsty or hungry, and is yer big sis gonna make it all okay. She's older than you, right?"

"Yeah, a little. Less than two years. You're good at reading people." The compliment was genuine.

Gale shrugged. "Everybody gotta be good at something. Coulda used a slightly more practical skill, like being handy with tools or good with a computer. But you take whatcha can get."

Ha. Gale probably hadn't meant that as a double entendre, but it worked. In another situation Imogen might have coun-seled him that reading people could make him a good writer or actor, or a good therapist or salesman. It was unfortunate that he'd found other ways to use his talent; she might have guessed his criminal aptitude would make him a con artist, if it weren't for the evidence of his violent side.

"What's your plan?" Beck asked Gale, bursting into the conversation, impatient. "Even rationing food there's only enough for a few days, and possibly less fuel if you're spreading it over more meals."

"Always using that fat brain, aren'tcha? Well, from where I'm sitting things ain't so bad. Just enough people come through here to get what I need, but not so many to rat me out."

In a matter of seconds, the atmosphere felt more foreboding and less like something Imogen could work with. She nudged her sister with an elbow: the chitchat had been going just fine. Beck nudged her back. It was the closest they could come to arguing without speaking.

"We can't stay here with you. And believe me, I have way more interest in getting home to my family than I do in reporting some random gunshot injury that I don't give a shit about. In a few days when we're not home we'll be reported missing. And if, as you say, there are people looking for you, then it's not in your best interest for us to be hanging out together when the search parties come out here for *us*."

Imogen didn't like how cantankerous Beck sounded. Sure, her points were accurate, but what if Gale decided they were all just a pain in his ass and not worth the trouble?

"You girls get what's happening here?" he asked in his quiet voice. "I'm keeping you with me 'cause the alternative...I ain't some serial killer kills fer fun, kills fer a hard-on with no conscience. As long yer with me yer alive, you get that?"

Imogen's heart suddenly felt like the needle on a record player, skidding off its groove. The spoonful she was feeding Tilda dribbled, and she wiped it from Tilda's shirt with shaking fingers. She heard Gale threatening their lives, but Beck wasn't having it.

"Great. So?" She sounded combative, as if intentionally picking a fight. Imogen wasn't sure why. They didn't have a thing at hand—rock, knife, or other—to overpower him, and one-third of their trio couldn't use her hands or feet. The two of them couldn't consider taking him on unless they first relieved him of the gun or the hunting knife—or both. Even then, Imogen suspected he was a scrappy and ruthless fighter. She would've preferred to be having an entirely different sort of conversation with Gale. But Beck had other ideas. "We don't have to stay *here,* where there's nothing—that's what I'm saying. We can hike out together, I'll *drive* you somewhere."

The suggestion came out of nowhere. Imogen felt as surprised as Tilda looked. It hadn't occurred to her, but it wasn't a bad idea.

Gale considered Beck's offer. "Can't say I fully trust you."

"Same."

"Where would we go?"

"Mexico?" Imogen suggested.

"It's the opposite direction a where I was heading. But probly safer."

Beck nodded. "It would take about…seven hours to Nogales."

"Ya got any money?" he asked.

"We'll get some," said Tilda, finally joining in on a current of hope.

"When you're across the border," Beck said, "you really won't need us. You can disappear. No one will come after you."

They could almost hear his brain grinding, recalibrating. But then he seemed to push the thought aside. "I'll think on it."

The women exchanged glances. It could work. A possible way out, though Imogen wasn't so sure about going from the kidnapper's metaphorical car to a literal one. It would get them back to civilization, to people, but what then? Would they become accomplices in his getaway? Or would Gale exact some other sort of guarantee for the next stage of his freedom? Beck wasn't stupid. Maybe she'd already thought about what would come next.

The more they talked, the more at ease Gale became, as if they were simply shooting the breeze at an ordinary picnic.

"Y'all really didn't see anything on the news about me?"

They shook their heads. "I don't watch the news that much," said Imogen.

"Nothing about a cop? Texas highway patrolman got killed in a routine traffic stop?"

The trio froze, momentarily in sync. It was startling to hear it so casually uttered.

"Maybe they didn't start reporting it until after we were in the Canyon," Beck suggested.

"Yeah. Could be right." Gale acted as if this were just a thing that had happened, like a flat tire or running out of gas. "Wasn't supposed to turn out this way. Just wanted to see my daughter in Nevada. What's the point a being out if you don't got the freedom to live yer life, see yer people? Only been on parole three weeks, knew it was a risk, but...Whatever yer thinking, 'bout all a this, I ain't no cold-blooded killer, that's the truth. I panicked, that's all. Didn't have a valid license, and the car was a buddy's, not in my name. I was almost to New Mexico, pretty obvious I was leaving the state. Knew the second that cop started looking into it he'd see what's what. I had to strike fast. He still got a shot off, but just the one. Only wanted to see my girl. Totally fucked now. You get it now, why I got no option but to lay low?"

Imogen directed her empty gaze to the pocked sandstone embankment across the creek. He'd admitted, with no real remorse, to what he'd done. She couldn't help but wonder if he was willing to be so open because there was nothing left to debate, no further compromises to be made.

"How'd you get here then?" Beck asked, seemingly unaffected by his story.

"I got across the New Mexico border. Then left the car. Hitched a ride from a Navajo kid. Real nice kid, friendly. He was heading this way and seemed like a good option. No one'd look fer me here, right?"

"I'm sorry everything got…so fucked up." Imogen wasn't sure why she was apologizing. Most of the regret was for herself, and for Beck and Tilda, yet a fragment of it was for him; he had a way of getting under her skin. For all the street smarts he likely possessed, he lacked a simple understanding of how to live in the real world. In a similar way Imogen was book smart and life dumb. She couldn't help but commiserate with someone who couldn't mold their plasticine life into the shape they'd set out to make.

"Well, I'm glad we're putting it all on the table now. Easier if we can be honest. Now fer real, where y'all really from?"

"I live in Los Angeles. Beck lives in Flagstaff. And Imogen lives in Pittsburgh, which is where we're all from. Okay? No more bullshit."

He considered Tilda, and nodded. "Good. Good."

Imogen still couldn't tell if Tilda was sucking up to him for her own benefit, or to benefit all of them. But she felt the moment open up; perhaps there was still a chance to reason with him. "We truly just want this to work out for everybody. I get that you don't trust us. But you have to realize we don't trust you either." She saw a slideshow in her mind—the severed food bag, their ransacked camp, a bullet whizzing past Tilda—and hoped Gale was seeing the same imagery. "But if we could help you figure it out, four heads are better than one, right? If you want to get to your daughter, maybe we can help."

"Maybe we're not part of your problem but part of your solution," said Tilda. It was the kind of thing she'd say to her followers, but would it motivate Gale?

He seemed to weigh the possibility. "You girls have some decent qualities, I do appreciate that."

"I was serious about what I said before. This doesn't have to be complicated," Beck said, as all-business as ever. "We hike out and we'll *drive* you somewhere. No one will be looking for you if you're with us—as long as we get this done by the date we're expected home."

"When's that?" he asked.

"Three days from now, late afternoon. Gives us plenty of time to get to Nevada and back, or Mexico and back."

"You got a car here?"

"At the Hermit trailhead." For proof, she unzipped the inner pocket of her fleece and waggled the key.

"Better idea: why don't we just *give* him the key," Tilda said, glowering ever-so-slightly at Beck. "He can leave ahead of us. Get in the car. Go wherever he wants, we'll be none the wiser."

"We legit couldn't tell anyone where you were then," Imogen added. And she had to agree: unless there was a genius second part to Beck's plan, Tilda's idea was better.

Beck and Gale both started nodding, picturing their separate escape scenarios. *Holy shit, is this working?*

"So then...Even if you say ya won't tell anyone you've seen me, you'd report the car stolen?"

"We'd be stuck for a while," Beck said. "Have to wait for someone to show up to ask for a ride back to the visitor center or something. And we could give you a full twenty-four-hour head start. You'd already be where you were going by then, north or south, whatever you choose."

Gale turned to Tilda. "Wanna come with me to Mexico? Show me around? Be my translator?" She cocked her head and gave him a silent *fuck you* smirk. "Kidding. Learn to take a joke." But he grew somber, disappearing into his own deliberations. "So...you want me to believe you wouldn't just call fer help? Minute yer phones get a signal? Not sure where that is, maybe up top. Wait—I didn't find...You girls don't have phones?"

"They're in the car." Tilda rolled her eyes. "Beck's dumb tradition."

Gale blinked. Some kind of mechanism was spinning in his head and Imogen could almost see it, like a slot machine, as three matching symbols lined up and *ding-ding-ding* he was on his feet, enraged.

"See? This is just the kinda shit I'm talking about!" He paced, with his hand on the hilt of his knife. "You send me off in yer car, don't tell me about the fucking phones. And later the feds track me down with yer GPS—"

"The phones aren't even charged, they've been sitting for *days*!" said Imogen.

Gale ignored her, his anger focused solely on Beck. "Yer always trying to get one over on me!"

"We leave the phones in the car because they *don't work* here," Beck yelled, to Tilda as much as Gale. "And *I* wasn't the one who suggested letting you drive off in my brand-new Jeep. *I* suggested we drive you, so you could keep an eye on us and know we weren't calling anyone or turning you in."

As Beck glared at her, fear skittered across Tilda's face. "I'm sorry," she said, looking from Beck to Gale. "I was just trying…I thought I had a good idea."

Gale scooped up his mug and downed the rest of his coffee. He half turned away from them, scanning the otherworldly terrain. It was cloudier than it had been, and quiet except for some light gusts rattling the vegetation.

Beck, Tilda, and Imogen watched him, simmering in dread: Now what?

24

This time it was to their benefit that Gale didn't stay in one mood for long. He abruptly sat down and grabbed up his bowl with its last few bites of oatmeal.

"Yer still the sneaky one," he said to Beck, now sounding more sullen than hostile. "The Mexican's not a good enough thinker."

"Please. Call me Tilda," she said, bristling.

"Yer plan has some appeal, I'll give ya that. But there's probly something I'm not seeing. I'll think on it. Roll it around till I see it from all sides. Think I shouldn't trust you."

"I fixed your arm," Beck said, back to her calm, nonchalant self.

"Not as good as it felt yesterday. You probly poisoned it." He clenched and unclenched the fingers of his left hand.

Christ on a cracker, he sounded petulant. Imogen's snort and chuckle slipped out before she could contain it. Gale quirked a grin at her, much to her astonishment.

"Does it look worse?" Beck asked, undaunted by his capricious temperament.

He peeked under the bandage. "No."

"You need to rest it. Take a couple of ibuprofen for the inflammation."

Imogen wondered if, behind Beck's calmness, she was hiding something—some aspect of the plan that Gale would never agree to. She wished there were a way to warn her sister: *Don't trick him.* If he agreed to something and later discovered a trapdoor they wouldn't get another chance.

He nodded a little, like a chastised schoolboy who realized the teacher was right.

"We'll come up with something, okay?" said Imogen. The breadth of his emotions actually gave her hope: he wasn't a ruthless, one-dimensional cartoon character. "We're not trying to be sneaky." She shot Beck a look, *Right?* "We really do all want the same thing."

"Doubt that," he said, still pouting. He scraped out the dregs of his oatmeal, polishing his spoon with big, shameless licks. Then he wiped his mouth with the back of his hand. "Any a you girls married? Got kids?"

"I'm married," said Beck.

Gale swiveled to look at her. "You? Didn't have you pegged fer…Oh. You married to a dyke?"

"A woman."

"You the butch one?"

Beck peered at him over the rim of her plastic coffee mug, but declined to answer.

"I didn't mean no offense, I got nothing against gays. Or Mexicans. Or"—to Imogen—"whatever you are, with that weird-color hair." She almost laughed again. There was something genuine about him, genuine enough to make her believe that his failings didn't include being superficially hateful, in spite of crass generalizations. To Beck he asked, "Ya got kids?"

"Not yet." Beck flashed a look at Imogen and there was something in her eyes, a message, but Imogen wasn't sure what it meant. Beck and Afiya wanted kids, but Afiya had already had two miscarriages.

"What about you two?" he asked.

Imogen shook her head.

"I have a boyfriend back home," Tilda said. "No kids."

Gale nodded, and didn't make eye contact as he spoke. "Well, I got me some kids. It goes without saying I been a shitty dad, locked up most a their lives. But that doesn't mean I don't love 'em. My daughter—I got just the one, and two boys with a different mother. The boys...Maybe it's my fault, bad role model and all that. But my daughter, Crystal, she's a good girl. She was born when I was twenty-one and now she's twenty-one and having her first baby. I feel like that's...We got a special connection. I shoulda named her Diamond, 'cause she's priceless. She's having a little girl and I suggested she name her Diamond.

"Anyway. I wanted to be there, that's all. Crystal's gonna have that baby any minute and I just wanted...to hold her hand. Kiss the baby's head. Thought I could drive there and back and not miss my parole officer. I didn't think that was too much to want, just to see my newborn grand-daughter. Didn't think the effort was gonna...Hoped to be fer Diamond what I couldn't be fer Crystal. That ain't a bad dream, is it?"

Nothing about Gale's appearance spoke to a tender heart. But even Tilda, practically hog-tied, wore an expression of wounded understanding. Every daughter—and Tilda more than some—needed a father who'd show up for her. Beck's eyes were filmy with tears. Was she really that moved by his story?

"Parole is ridiculous," Imogen muttered, thinking aloud. It always sounded like a cruel game of Simon Says, played in whispers.

"Agree with ya there."

"It just sets people up for failure." The criminal justice system was only punitive, designed to minimize the odds for reformation. This entire chain of events led back to the rules of his probation. Now a cop was dead, three women's lives were in the balance—and who knew what had happened to the Navajo kid—just because Gale wasn't legally allowed to attend his first grandchild's birth. "It was a good dream. A dream you should've been able to have."

Something in her words or her tone made Beck turn a questioning glare on her.

"Yup. Shoulda. Instead…I never learn, even when I know better."

"Let us help," Imogen said. He might yet be convinced to hike out, take the Jeep, ditch the phones, and accept that there were no other booby traps, aside from the ones of his own making.

Gale tossed his plastic bowl and cup over to her. "You can help by washing the dishes. I'll tie up yer sis and take the Mex—Tilda—to the john, as promised."

Beck laid her dishes and spoon at Imogen's feet. She turned herself over to Gale, hands clasped together. He took a bundle of cord from his pocket and quickly wrapped it tight, and Beck was soon immobilized where she sat. As Imogen used the last of the now-warmish water to clean up, she watched Gale work. The sympathy she'd felt for him only moments earlier was already waning.

"Gale, just take the car," she said. "It's the fastest way you'll get to Crystal."

"That's fer me to decide."

Tilda winced; he tugged the knots away from her wrists before successfully freeing her. "Can't one of them come with me?" she asked.

Imogen might not have been able to relieve herself if her sister hadn't been beside her. They already felt vulnerable in this man's presence, and Tilda had never acclimated to squatting. "I don't mind coming."

But as she said it, Beck's face hardened and she gave a little shake of her head.

"It's this or nothing. I'm not gonna have you three always trying to get yer way. Yer not calling the shots here. But I'm a gentleman, keep my back turned, just like before."

Tilda radiated panic, rubbing her wrists, but she tucked the toilet paper under her arm. Gale took her by the elbow. "Be back in a minute. Don't do nothing stupid."

"We won't," Imogen promised, though Beck's clamped jaw looked less inclined to make such a vow.

They watched him lead Tilda up-camp, away from the creek. At least Imogen would finally be able to exchange a few words with her sister—but she wasn't prepared for what Beck had to say.

"Run to the river! Now!" she whispered.

"But—"

"Flag down some rafters, tell them we're here and ask them to call—"

"We'll make it worse, he's almost ready to take the car—"

"This was my backup plan," Beck hissed, "if we couldn't push him into the gorge. Tilda wrecked that before we could even try, but we can't give up."

"He'll kill us!" The next time he took the gun out, it wouldn't be for a warning shot.

"He's gonna kill us anyway! We're running out of options. Take a canteen. Hide somewhere, in case he comes looking. Go!"

There wasn't time to keep debating Beck's plan. Suddenly deluged with adrenaline, Imogen grabbed a canteen and bolted for the creek.

25

She stayed hunched over, hoping some of the rocks and shrubs in the flat area around camp would hide her if Gale looked over. His back was still to her as he led Tilda to their latrine area; she could hear him whistling that grating sunshine song. Imogen needed to get farther up the creek as fast as she could, to gain the protection of Boucher's rugged walls. Her mind was racing faster than her legs, faster than her heart. If Gale couldn't hear her scrambling over rocks, he could probably detect her heartbeat, as subtle as a fighter plane breaking the sky, rolling out fat scars of thunder.

A whimper escaped her throat. She wanted to cry. She wanted to huddle into a ball and roll away. Too many emotions were surging through her and she didn't know where to put them. But there wasn't time to cry.

She ran. How much time did she have?

Even if it took less than fifteen minutes to dash down to the river, Gale would know she'd run off within five— maybe slightly more if Tilda couldn't easily relieve herself. He wouldn't know, at first, which direction she'd gone. Maybe he'd assume she'd booked it back to Hermit—Tilda's plan, and the only area he was personally familiar with. Or maybe Beck would feed him misinformation, tell him she'd fled up the Boucher Trail to the rim. (No one *fled* up the Boucher Trail; it was even worse than Hermit.)

A part of her was tempted to turn back. It might've been a decent backup option if Tilda hadn't already tried running off, but now they knew too much about Gale. *Fuck.* If only there'd been time to weigh the pros and cons of their various strategies. Getting Gale in a pissed-off frenzy was not a good idea. And they'd nearly reached a point of mutual trust, or so it seemed to her. This could be a disaster—unless Beck was right, and Gale was only biding his time until he was ready to dispose of them. Still, she didn't want to put Beck and Tilda in even more peril. If she failed now, he'd never trust them again.

As her breath grew more ragged a squeal slipped through, but she wouldn't wail, wouldn't scream: if it echoed off the walls Gale might find her.

Her only hope was that a commercial rafting excursion would come by in good time—and good time meant within minutes of her reaching the river. She wasn't sure if the smaller, private groups carried satellite phones, but she expected—as obviously Beck did—that the commercial outfits would. Without satellite phones they'd have no way to call for help if something happened to one of their tourists, and they couldn't risk a week or more on the water with no way to summon assistance. She tried to remember how often they'd come by yesterday. At least twice, but she hadn't bothered to notice if it was on any kind of schedule.

Panic and desperation drove her. She kept expecting to hear

footfalls coming up behind her, slipping on gravelly rocks as he chased her down, but so far she was alone. Ahead of her, the rapids grew louder. The roar built, a dramatic crescendo, as she reached her destination. Panting, she gripped her knees and tried to catch her breath.

Throughout most of the Grand Canyon sheer cliffs came straight down into the river and the Canyon continued its process of majestic erosion, gaining incremental depth. River-banks existed only where a creek flowed out of an inner canyon and joined the Colorado. Imogen took a moment to get her bearings. It looked different under the current circumstances, no longer the place the trio had come for respite. Now she surveyed places to hide, to stay out of sight if—when—Gale came crashing down the creek.

There was a cluster of trees growing some distance from the river's edge, but Imogen feared they were too far away: the rafters would slip past before she could run down and wave them over. She had a couple hundred feet of walkable land on either side of the creek-river intersection. On the far side, the strand was narrow and she didn't see any hiding places, with the ancient wall of schist so close to the water. Maybe there was an outcropping there big enough to hide her, but she couldn't be sure without crossing the creek.

Desperate, the clock ticking, she looked for something closer. There were stands of tamarisk. The invasive shrubs had wispy trunks and leafy, frondlike branches. They grew in clusters in the river's wet soil and Imogen didn't care that they threatened the native ecology, they were the best option she had. She scurried over, found a promising, dense clump, and hunkered down. Here she was, hiding in a bush for the second time in her life, hoping a gunman wouldn't spot her.

Her pulse pounded in her temples and the river thumped in her ears. There was still no human movement behind her, just the swaying of the river-fed plants and the gushing creek.

"Come on, come on," she prayed, her eyes glued to the curve where a fleet of rafters might appear. Her throat felt raw. She took a sip of water. And waited.

Beck was being optimistic, sending her with water in case she succeeded in evading Gale and was on her own for a while. Even while they were separated, Beck was looking out for her, though Imogen couldn't shake the horrible, clawing feeling that Beck was being naïve, that she'd misjudged—and that she and Tilda might pay a steep price for it. Imogen would never recover if something happened to Beck as a result of her own inability to win a damn argument.

It didn't take long before her thigh muscles started to tremble, so she abandoned her squat—better for leaping into action—and sat on the slightly damp ground. The roiling water was mesmerizing, a repetitive wash of fluid movement and white noise. It was easy to fall under its tranquilizing spell. But she couldn't.

What else? There had to be something she, or they, hadn't thought of yet. Some other way to signal to people, some other way to handle Gale, some other type of weapon they could make.

Suddenly inspired, she patted at the left hip pocket of her cargo shorts. It was there—her tiny memo pad and the half pencil. Frantically, she scribbled a note. That long-ago morning when their parents still hadn't made it to Hermit, she and Beck had deliberated hiking back to the small ranger station. They'd known it was just a locked shed, but they'd considered writing a message and leaving it on the door. Now, Imogen would leave a note behind, and if Gale found her too soon, another backpacker or rafter might discover it.

We've been kidnapped. Gale shot Texas trooper. At Boucher maybe heading west. Rebekah and Imogen Blum, Tilda Jimenez. Help!

Checking that the coast was clear, she darted out of her hiding place to get closer to the river's edge. She quickly assembled a cairn of four palm-sized rocks and slid her note between two of them. Cairns were typically made by rangers or seasoned hikers to help mark a trail; she hoped someone would notice the little rock tower and investigate. Her task accomplished, she dashed back to the tamarisk and resumed waiting. Waiting. Waiting.

How often did the rafts go by? It no longer seemed like such a brilliant idea to come out to a remote place in the off-season. The one time they *needed* people and they'd set an itinerary that almost guaranteed they wouldn't see any.

"Come on, come on, please, please." She stood long enough to scan Boucher Creek: still no signs of pursuit. What had Beck done to keep Gale from coming after her? The river chugged along, hurrying in an indifferent way.

She gasped. A raft was coming. And another. *Oh my god, this might really work!* She jumped out of the tamarisk and raced to the edge of the river. Waved her arms.

"Here! Over here!"

It wasn't quite what she'd been hoping for—two rafts towing kayaks, a small noncommercial excursion—but it was something. The sight of people practically made her burst: with tears, with hope. She could already see herself in a near future, reuniting with Beck and Tilda, victorious.

"Hey! We need help!" She waved and jumped.

The rafters concentrated on rowing hard through the rapids to keep their inflatable boats driving down the channel they'd chosen.

One took a second to wave a greeting.

She didn't want a greeting. She thrust her arms in the air, fingers spread wide, and screamed, "Help! Please! Help!"

Another waved. The roaring water carried them—grinning and oblivious—swiftly past.

"Help…!"

And then they were tiny specks, rushing on downstream.

"Come back!" No. No no no. She pivoted upstream—maybe more were coming. "Please, please…"

This was another reason why she needed a commercial operation: raft after raft—enough of a parade that someone would figure out she wasn't jumping up and down and waving both arms because of an exuberant desire to say "Hi!" *Amateur idiots.* Even without a satellite phone, eight outdoorsy men and women could have provided some solid backup for handling Gale.

She couldn't hold it in any longer. With hiccupping sobs, she wept.

How had she failed? She might have toyed with the possibility that—*Beck was right*—she was a ghost, visible only to those who fervently believed in her existence. But two of the rafters had waved, they'd seen her—but they'd been incapable of imagining a grotesque scenario in the midst of this beauty. She and Beck had thought like that once too. Now they knew. Monsters roamed everywhere.

Tears streaming down her face, she retreated to her leafy hideaway, trying to recall what she'd once learned about the rules of the river. Rafters left from Lees Ferry at least one hour apart. But then what? After days on the Colorado, did everyone still follow the rules? Camp where they were supposed to? Keep their distance from other parties?

Would she have to wait at least an hour before more rafters might go by?

26

Time was the scraping gears of a malfunctioning clock. The cogs ticked and ticked and nothing changed. Imogen longed to know what was happening back at camp. As much as she didn't want to be with *him,* being without Beck and Tilda made her anxious. What if no one else came by today? How long was she going to be alone? The optimistic partial canteen of water now seemed insufficient. Could it get her through the next day? It was still overcast and she had absolutely nothing in the way of gear. What if it dropped below freezing overnight? Or what if those clouds let loose a cold rain?

She was the safe one, but her mind made it an utterly miserable experience. When she ran out of ways to worry about herself, she returned to worrying about Beck and Tilda. What if Gale forced them to continue on with him? Where would he go? Slate? Or was he crazy enough to try to get unwilling hostages all the way up Hermit Trail to Beck's Jeep? He could go faster without them—would he leave them behind? Tied up? Or...?

What if she never saw Beck again?

A noise interrupted her anguished thoughts. It took her a moment to home in on the sound and its direction—reverberating off the rock walls, it seemed to be coming from everywhere. With a mixture of dismay and fear, she finally recognized what it was.

Splashing. Scraping. Scrambling. Someone—or more than one—was coming down Boucher Creek, quick and sloppy.

Then she heard recognizable voices. *Goddammit.* A minute ago she'd been afraid of never seeing Beck or Tilda again, but if she couldn't stay hidden now, this attempt at rescue would be lost.

"Stop!" Tilda screeched, her voice ringing with a distress Imogen had never heard.

"Come on!" Gale responded.

Imogen could imagine Gale yanking on Tilda, her wrists tightly bound, not caring if he was making her stumble. Of all the dangers they'd discussed—and encountered—a simple thing like a sprained ankle was potentially disastrous. Gale wasn't going to summon a mule or helicopter rescue if one of them couldn't hike out.

His steady banter to hurry them along was punctuated by Tilda's outcries.

Wait. She didn't hear Beck. Where was Beck?

Oh God, what if he'd killed Beck…

Her heart did that crazy thing again, slamming against her ribs as her pulse ricocheted in her skull hard enough to make her reel. She needed to know if Beck was with them. She fought the urge to pop her head out, see what was going on, and hunkered deeper into the leafy fronds instead. *She's the scaredy one.* Their footsteps quieted as they reached the soggy riverbank. She didn't need to see them to understand what was happening: Gale was looking for her, scrutinizing the terrain.

Scrunching down even lower, she was able to glimpse an incomplete picture through the striped gaps between the narrow trunks. Legs. Hands—tied behind their backs. They were all there—Beck, too!—standing close together. Gale had a length of cord wrapped around his fist as a leash; Tilda and Beck were tethered together, Tilda in front.

"Know yer here! Come out, come out wherever you are!"

Fear razored up Imogen's spine. She'd made things worse. Never mind that she'd followed her sister's instructions, it hadn't worked and Gale's tone was menacing. And impatient. She debated if she should give herself up. Beck wouldn't want her to, and she was afraid she'd already ruined everything, regardless of whether she surrendered or stayed hidden.

"Come on now, I ain't fucking around. You girls've pissed me off one time too many."

And part of her knew: it was a matter of minutes, maybe less. Her hiding place was inadequate. She felt like a zebra against pink froufrou wallpaper, pretending that holding still was sufficient camouflage. Every second would piss him off more, but she couldn't come out. Didn't want to come out. Didn't want to face him again, or her own defeat.

He spotted something, and resumed dragging Tilda and Beck along. *Fuck.* Imogen shut her eyes, condemning herself for a lifetime of mistakes. Even her good ideas were bad ideas. Gale kicked over her little tower of rocks. The note started to flutter away, but he snatched it up. Read it. Barked a laugh.

"You girls think a some crazy stuff."

"Maybe someone picked her up," Tilda said. "Maybe she's already way downriver."

If only. The hope in Tilda's voice was heartbreaking.

"Yeah. And maybe she tied a note to one a those big black birds and it's delivering it to Harry Potter." He laughed again. Crumpled her cry for help and tossed it toward the river. "My boys loved those movies."

His mood was improving. Imogen knew he could sense her, a predator with a whiff of his prey. The thought of her getting away had pissed him off, scared him, but now he was confident that she was nearby. The more they failed to escape, the more cocksure he got.

"Okay, you had yer fun. Know yer hiding here somewhere, all scared behind yer rock."

Almost worse than her desire to stay hidden was Gale's understanding of who she was, as if the word *chicken* were branded on her skin for all to see. Or it could be a sign that this was the moment to surprise him—to sprint out and clamber onto his back to tear out his hair, puncture his eyes.

He turned to face the stands of tamarisk.

"Ya know, yer not the one that's gonna get hurt. I already had to hit yer sister. She ain't as tough as she looks." He didn't call out this time and his quiet voice was grisly. His soft tone made her think he was speaking directly to her, having already detected her purple hoodie among the greenery. Her view was still limited to the lower halves of their bodies. What was wrong with Beck? Was Beck's silence a precaution, or had he done something to her?

"Know this was her idea, you just taking orders. I'll letcha pick." It sounded like he was at her side and she almost felt his breath hot on her ear. "You got two choices fer a neck kill. A quick jab in the carotid artery, and bleed out like a stuck pig. It's the better way to go. Probly hurts less too. Or you cut the windpipe and then you die all panicked and unable to breathe. Some people, if they got little control, just cut ear to ear and go fer everything."

Imogen wanted to scream. She couldn't fathom what was happening. How could this man say such things in such a placid tone? Was he really asking her to choose how he should kill Beck? Tilda quietly wept.

"Or, since I know you really like yer big sis, I could put a fast bullet to the brain. That's more merciful. Yer call."

Imogen stumbled out of her hiding place. Without even looking at Beck she collapsed to her knees, her hands in front of her on the dirt as she prostrated herself, sobbing the only prayer that mattered. "Please don't kill my sister. Please don't kill my sister."

She finally dared to glance up. Through her tears Gale multiplied, so she wiped her arm across her eyes. While Gale had the gun pointed at Beck, he was clearly more interested in the strange slug at his feet. The crying slug with the lavender hair. It seemed as if he'd meant to step on the slug, but now the creature rather captivated him.

"Okay. What about this one?" He swung the gun over to Tilda. She clenched her eyes tight and whimpered, instinctively hunching.

There was a moment. A moment in which Imogen took in Beck's lip, fat and bleeding, her left eye swollen and starting to bruise.

A moment in which Imogen was glad the gun was no longer aimed at her sister. No one spoke for that moment, though Gale started to grin.

"No—please!" Imogen begged, a second too late.

Gale bent his arm, redirecting the muzzle toward the sky. But he knew which one she'd choose. And apparently thought it was funny. Imogen was grateful Tilda's eyes were closed; maybe she hadn't noticed the hesitation. The guilt shimmied inside Imogen, made her want to slough off her skin.

"You gonna follow along peacefully, or you wanna join the chain gang?" Gale wagged the makeshift leash, and Tilda finally opened her eyes.

"I'm coming." Imogen kept her hands raised as she got to her feet.

"You lead the way," Gale told her, tucking the gun away.

As she passed Tilda she said, "I'm sorry."

Tilda clenched her jaw and looked ahead.

Gale and his captives stayed close behind Imogen as she headed back up the creek. She was glad no one could see her face. She felt sodden, defeated; it was an effort to lift her legs and make them work. But she was also furious. Beck might've been the leader of their expedition, but if Imogen continued obeying her every command Beck was going to get them all killed.

Every second now might be a wasted opportunity, but for what? Only Imogen had her hands free. Only she could *do* something, right there, right now. Should she turn on him, weaponless? Shove him against a rock? Push his face under the shallow water and hope Beck and Tilda could help keep him down, even with their hands behind them?

Uncertain, she looked back at him. His eyes met hers instantly. He was a master of self-preservation, always aware of the darkest options. While one fist held the rope-leash that kept

Tilda and Beck's hands tied—together, and to each other—his other casually rested atop his sheathed knife.

It would slice through the soft flesh of Imogen's belly, damaging precious organs as it went in, in, deep into her abdomen. *It would hurt so much.* (*Worse than a bullet.*)

The thought—the fear—made her turn back and keep marching.

Weak. This was who she was and what she spread wherever she went. She was a coward, more scared now than she'd been on that long-ago night—or that Saturday morning—when at least it had ended quickly.

She remembered how she reacted during the rape. It was one of the things she never wanted to give much space to: the reality that she hadn't fought back. Should she have fought harder? Or had her *passivity* saved her then from further harm?

Wasn't that also why she (*hid in a bush*) hadn't run into the synagogue to try to save her fragile friends? Because sometimes passivity was the smarter move?

It was the one thing they hadn't tried with Gale: fully cooperating; going along with everything he asked. It was a submissive approach and Beck and Tilda wouldn't understand its merits. But Imogen was the only one of them who'd survived any potentially life-threatening situations, and she'd survived *twice* by not making any brazen moves. Maybe she, and everyone else, underestimated the role of meekness; maybe it didn't make her weak or a coward. Was it possible that her past attacks were rehearsals, preparing her for *this*?

Beck and Tilda wouldn't agree to capitulate. But their efforts to negotiate or flee hadn't worked, so what else was left? If only the three of them could really *talk*. The trio wasn't on the same page, that was for sure, and didn't know each other's minds well enough to consult from the same book.

Yup, they needed to have had their great bonding vacation *before* they got themselves kidnapped. Imogen resisted the bitter urge to chortle. Their inability to communicate was as dangerous an enemy as Gale.

27

As soon as they were at camp Gale ordered them to sit. Beck and Tilda, though attached, kept their backs turned to each other. Before Gale could tie her up or stop her, Imogen dug out a washcloth, and doused it with the water from her canteen. She dabbed at the blood on Beck's lip and chin.

"You okay?" She'd never seen her sister injured before, nor had she ever seen the fresh wounds made by another person's fists. Beck's face looked swollen and sore, but she gave a tiny nod, her good eye always on Gale. He paced, looking west, looking east; Imogen saw him weighing his options, trying to figure out his next move.

"Sorry," Imogen whispered to Beck. "A pair of rafts came by but I guess they couldn't hear me over the rapids."

"That was the dumbest fucking thing you could've done." Tilda practically spat the words at them.

"You're one to talk. At least I had a plan." The words slurred; Beck sounded like her mouth had been shot up with Novocain.

"I didn't know he had a gun then," Tilda hissed.

Stuck between them, Imogen wasn't sure what to do. She folded the washcloth in quarters and soaked it, then laid it gently on her sister's puffy eye. Gale strode an antsy patrol back and forth a few feet away, and she feared his paranoia was skittering back in.

"We have to overpower him," Beck said, inching around to include Tilda.

"No." At Imogen's refusal Tilda and Beck both looked at her. "That won't work."

"You have an idea that will?" Tilda's rancor betrayed her belief that none of Imogen's ideas would ever work.

"So what are you thinking?" Beck asked, curious.

"We have to seem like we're going along with—"

Not only did Imogen stop speaking, she stopping hearing. Something exploded against the left side of her head. A bomb of pain that instantly made her dizzy and nauseous. She was already sitting, but her muscles gave out and she wilted. Tilda's body was there to catch her, to keep her from tipping over onto the ground. She saw Beck's mouth moving, saw her livid face looking up at someone, yelling.

I can't hear.

The thought lasted only seconds before the buzzing of a familiar agony set in. Gale's face came into focus. She swayed, trying to sit straight; she knew what had happened. Gale had punched her in the head. In the same ear that hadn't been quite right since the incident with her walking stick. This time she didn't need to wonder if her brains were oozing out—she could feel something warm and wet. The nausea lingered though the sharpest pain started to fade. When she touched her ear her finger came back with a pinkish spot of blood.

"You punctured her eardrum!" Beck's red face was now equal parts injury and rage.

Gale knelt. Tilda tried to squirm away, but couldn't. He was close enough that Imogen could smell the regrettable dereliction of his body, his teeth.

"Sorry I had to do that," he told her. "Know yer the soft one, but you gotta learn to stand on yer own two feet. Can't listen to everything yer damn sister says—"

"I told her it was a bad idea." Imogen's voice was shaky. She wasn't trying to sell her sister out, but she wanted him to know that she agreed with him.

"She says 'Jump!'" Gale said, "you gotta learn to say 'Fuck you!'" Tilda bobbed agreement, glaring at her. "I expected more from you."

Imogen felt dazed. Part of it was the ringing in her ear, the rest was an unexpected barb of remorse. Gale seemed to have faith in her ability to do better. No one ever told Imogen her instincts were good; she felt a little sorry for letting him down.

Perhaps it showed on her face. He patted her shoulder. Then stood and said to all of them, "And fer the love of fucking Jesus y'all need to stop with this plotting and scheming. You said ya wanted to help? This ain't helping."

A few heavy drops of rain splattered on their pants and shoulders, on the surrounding dusty dirt. Imogen cupped her throbbing ear and, with the others, turned her face skyward. Her brain was still helter-skelter and the odd thought came to her that in this moment they were all in sync: an unhappy deity had demanded their attention with flicks of water, and they'd all looked upward in obeisance. What was It going to tell them? Something that would set them all free?

Apparently the others only saw darkening skies, laden clouds.

"Great," Tilda said under her breath.

"We should move to higher ground," said Beck. "In case the creek floods."

"That happen often?" Gale asked, looking from the sky to the overhang in the cliff face where they'd first accosted him. What a mistake it had been, approaching the dragon in his lair.

Beck shrugged. "Depends on how hard it rains."

"Been near a flash flood once. Got no desire to do that again." He burst up and started shoving stuff into their packs. All of Beck's and Imogen's gear was in their sloppy postexamination piles, and Gale's acquisitions were still scattered around. "You," he said to Imogen, "help me get this packed up. Don't matter what goes where."

She got to her feet, but didn't get far before she tottered and had to stop. The world spun and she kept her hands on her knees. Everything in her stomach was lurching around, in contra-rhythm to the sway of the earth. A groan escaped her mouth, which was preferable to vomit.

"Dizzy?" Beck asked.

"Yeah." *Dizzy* sounded like a cute word compared to how she felt.

"She's got vertigo," Beck said to Gale. "She could even have a mild concussion. Why don't you have one of us help you?"

"Too late fer that." He snatched at whatever was at hand and jammed it into the nearest pack. "Come on, let's go."

The dribbles of cold rain helped Imogen focus. She let it wash away the feverish green feeling, until finally she could stand upright. She'd push through, because they needed her: it would help nothing if their supplies and gear were swept away in a storm.

Imogen gathered up armfuls of their belongings and filled

215

Beck's pack. Just a few nights ago they'd been in Beck and Afiya's living room and Imogen had been annoyed at Beck's disorganization; how silly that seemed now. She wished she could shut her eyes and transport to the safety of that cozy room with its cathedral ceiling. She wouldn't say no to a mug of Afiya's earthy tea. If Imogen was thinking about this, Beck was too. And Tilda probably longed to be in her own home, away from the Blum sisters and their abominable ideas.

It was only early afternoon, but the clouds brought a mood that made Imogen want to find a nest and curl under a fluffy blanket. "Could use a nap," she mumbled, strapping her sleeping bag to the bottom of the rust-colored pack.

"Just my plan," said Gale. "Need some shut-eye myself. Not ashamed to admit I ain't thinking my best and I don't wanna make no more mistakes." He looked at the sky again. The rain hadn't gotten worse, but there was no hint that sunshine might return. "Ready to put that on?"

Imogen struggled into the bulky pack. The cliff shelter was the ideal place to go if it was going to storm, but she couldn't imagine how she would sleep, or do anything else, while confined in a rock prison with the dragon.

He picked up a walking stick—Tilda's, as it happened—and handed it to Imogen. "You head on up. I'll watch these two. Hurry, in case the rain comes down harder."

Once upon a time she'd contemplated how to use a walking stick as a weapon. Now she needed it to keep from stumbling. She glanced back as she started off. Though he'd ordered her to do it, it didn't feel right leaving Beck and Tilda behind, again.

Her emotions had been caroming inside her since Gale had kicked her into wakefulness. She'd intermittently been a lump of ice or a puddle: solidifying when called to action, and melting in defeat as things worsened. Now she felt herself shrinking, losing substance; she couldn't sustain this level of stress. On top of it, she was still queasy. She wanted to close her eyes, make everything as motionless as possible, retreat to a place of stillness and quiet so she could recharge. The stress was exhausting, and they couldn't afford any more slipups.

As she clambered up to the overhang she dreaded the thought that Gale intended to use her as a mule, ferrying the packs to the shelter one by one. It would be faster if he carried Tilda's next time, then they could complete their move. In her current state Imogen was the worst person to be hauling heavy backpacks, though maybe that was intentional, part of her punishment for running off.

Imogen walked into the rock shelter and unbuckled the hip belt, slipped her arms out of the straps. The backpack dropped to the ground. While only eight feet deep, the interior felt roomy with its high ceiling and wide wings. Twenty people could sleep beneath the overhang, but it was still too small if one of those people was Gale.

He'd said he wanted to take a nap. Undoubtedly he planned to arrange things so they would be helpless to escape or attack him as he slept. But maybe they could finally talk. Imogen needed to make them understand how they might win him over by expressing more sympathy, treating him with respect. Common wisdom recommended trying to make your abductor see you as a real person. She wanted to take that a step further and convey that they could be *friends*. That would require, at the very least, getting Beck on her side: Beck could be a master manipulator when she wanted to be. Somehow, they needed to convince Gale that letting them go was what *he wanted*.

Her skull ached and she still felt wobbly, but with the walking stick's support she hurried toward the yawning mouth of the overhang, eager to get back. But then she paused beneath the towering umbrella of rock, stunned by what she saw across the creek.

She blinked hard, in case it was a mirage, in case her head injury was making her hallucinate. But no, it looked real. Her heart screamed *go-go-go* and she hurtled on, half slipping down the steep incline.

There was a man. A backpacker in full gear. Heading toward their camp—toward Gale. The backpacker would have easily spotted them on his steep descent into Boucher; much of the camping area was visible from the trail. With Beck and Tilda facing away, and Gale busy packing, they hadn't noticed him yet.

Imogen recognized his approach for what it was: their best chance to end this.

28

Imogen charged across the creek, splashing in the inches-deep water. "No no no no…" The man couldn't take this on alone—he might have sensed something was wrong, but he didn't know what he was walking into. He didn't know about Gale's weapons.

Gale saw the backpacker emerge from the scrub when he was thirty feet away.

"Everything okay over here?" the man asked. Was he close enough to see Beck's and Tilda's hands, bound behind their backs?

Gale took a step forward and held up his hand, a halt command that the backpacker didn't heed. "This ain't none a yer—"

"Help us!" Tilda screamed—and kept screaming.

"What are you doing, what's going on?" Alarmed, the man veered away from Gale to get closer to the two women.

Imogen raced across the level ground, her bamboo stick pumping freely at her side as if she were a locomotive, gaining speed.

"Stop! Stop!" she bellowed—it didn't matter who it was for, she just needed to stop the impending collision. The backpacker looked at her, his face a frightened question.

"He has a—" Beck's warning came too late.

Gale thrust his knife into the man's chest, upward, under his ribs.

It couldn't have been more than a minute from when Imogen spotted the backpacker to when Gale decided to end his life.

She flew the remaining yards, breathing hard, tears streaming down her face. Tilda shrieked, lurching backward against Beck. Maybe it wasn't too late, maybe the man wasn't dead, maybe—

"Nooooo!" Imogen cried.

Gale knelt beside the backpacker and thrust his knife in one more time. Ripped it out. Satisfied, he stood back and watched the growing pool of blood.

The man gurgled, twitched a little, and went still.

Imogen collapsed to her knees, skidding to a stop on small rocks that dug into her flesh. The man was on his side and the bulk of his pack shielded Beck and Tilda from the worst of it. But Imogen saw every detail.

—the harrowing splatters of blood—

The salt-and-pepper of his unshaven face. His gray eyes, surprised but sightless. The canvas hat that had tumbled off his head.

—flesh ripped through—

His dusky-green T-shirt bloomed with wet, dark stains; red rivulets streamed from the slashes in his chest. The man's mouth had frozen in the shape of the surprised scream he hadn't been able to utter.

—dentures exposed in shock—

The land spun and Imogen wasn't sure what sickened her most. She crawled away and vomited.

"Why did you do that?" Beck howled at him. Tilda clung to her and they buried their faces in each other's shoulders, sobbing.

Gale stood there gazing down at what he'd done, traces of disappointment on his face. "Yer smarter than that, Doc. Nothing else to do."

Imogen wept uncontrollably. She wept until she started choking, and then coughed and wiped her drooling mouth.

"Why does she get like that?" Gale asked Beck. He sounded confused, but also maybe concerned. Imogen made wheezing noises as she tried to breathe.

Beck extended her foot toward Imogen, the only part of her body that could get closer. "Some things have happened. In her life."

Gale nodded, watching Imogen. "Sorry you had to see that." He grabbed her under her arms, practically picking her up off her feet, and moved her so she was closer to Beck and Tilda—where there was less gore. He wiped his knife clean on the backpacker's rugged shorts before resheathing it.

Imogen felt safer in the proximity of Beck and Tilda. Her throat still burned from her lost breakfast, but she quieted as something occurred to her: What if he wasn't alone? What if the man had mates, walking at their own pace? Maybe another person—or a few—would yet stroll into Boucher. Gale might not think about that, but she knew seasoned hikers didn't feel the need to stay in sight of each other. She fought the urge to look behind her, toward where the trail came into camp. It was better if he didn't know this might not be over.

"On the bright side, y'all have been concerned about running low on provisions. This should help." Gale compared the size of his foot to the dead man's. He squatted down and loosened the laces before tugging off the man's boots.

Aghast, Beck and Tilda gawked at him as if he were a demon, casting off the garb that had allowed him to appear human. But Imogen thought he had a point: he'd get less rattled, feel less pressure, without the constant worry of running out of food; this could buy them some time. She didn't mean to be heartless—the man's murder was unforgivable—but Gale's response to her had been almost kind.

Gale yanked the heavy pack off the dead man's body and an unwanted image flashed in her mind of an animal being stripped of its pelt. She wanted to vomit again, but all she could do was stare, hoping the film would burn in the projector so this horror show would end.

"Now. Where we gonna put this guy?"

None of them uttered a word. He looked at the dark clouds.

"Rain's holding off. This is good. This is real good. A pack fer each of us." It was almost pitiful the way he was trying to convince himself. "Can you take this on up?" he asked Imogen, tying the boots together and draping them over the pack.

With a glance at her sister, Imogen got to her feet. She didn't want to approach—Gale or the body—but he was keeping the pack upright, ready to lift it so she could slip her arms through the straps. She shuffled forward, eyes on the backpack. Alive, the man probably had almost a foot on her and a good one hundred pounds. She started shaking her head, already seeing herself falling to her knees from the crushing weight.

"It looks like it weighs as much as I do."

Gale considered her for a second, then chuckled. "Yeah, my bad. Okay—you take yer little pack up and I'll figure this out."

Still shaky, Imogen managed to get her pack on and fastened, but then she realized she couldn't bend over and retrieve the walking stick, not without teetering. Her queasiness now extended beyond the lingering damage to her ear.

"Can you hand me the stick?" she asked Gale.

He complied, and continued to study her. "Look a little green around the gills. You ain't still dizzy?" She nodded. "You need to toughen up. You know life ain't no picnic."

She nodded again, and made eye contact with her sister before heading off to the shelter. Beck's face was ashen, stunned, an injured mask that barely resembled the woman she'd been only a few hours earlier. Imogen couldn't assess how Tilda was faring: her knees were up, her face pressed into them.

As she crossed the creek again, Imogen feared time was looping on itself and she'd get up to the overhang only to see another hiker approaching. Another hiker getting stabbed for trespassing into the dragon's territory. There was a thrumming in her head. She struggled to get her feet in focus, her boots blurred into four, then two, then six. Perhaps the punch to the head had only exacerbated what she already felt: this couldn't be real.

29

When she reached the back of the shelter something startled her. She dropped her pack and spun around; Gale's silhouette drifted across the opening. He looked like an ogre with the bulge of the dead man's gear thickening the shape of his torso. Had he been behind her the whole time? Had the timpani of her own pulse been so loud she hadn't heard him? Or was he that quiet, that stealthy. *A hunter.*

"We got what we need. Everything's gonna go smoothly now."

We. Were they a *we*? Who did that include? Beck and Tilda, too, or just Imogen? She gave her head a shake, as she would a Magic 8 Ball when she needed a different answer. With alarming frequency she was having thoughts she didn't understand.

Gale set the pack near the entrance and summoned her with an impatient wave. "Come on, the girls are waiting. Had to hog-tie 'em a bit, just real quick so they won't take off."

Imogen's feet moved, following the ogre back to…she

couldn't think of it as camp anymore. Reality had turned fuzzy, dangerously fuzzy, like she'd taken a weird marijuana tincture and her thoughts flitted about like hummingbirds that wouldn't land. She couldn't afford for her wits to abandon her, not when the situation had so escalated.

The high-pitched whine coming from her left ear drew her attention; she used the sound to settle her concentration, to ground herself in this space and time.

"Yer sister very helpfully suggested that old tunnel as a place to put the body."

"Okay." She was on autopilot.

Tilda and Beck were on their sides, both with their ankles hastily wrapped and knotted at the back, but Beck had squirmed to orient herself so she was looking toward the trail that came in from Hermit. *In case the man had friends.* So Beck was thinking it too. She wormed back to face Imogen and Gale as they returned. Imogen didn't see any movement or unnatural colors that might indicate someone else was on the way, but experienced hikers could be twenty or thirty minutes apart, or more. There was still a chance.

"Okay, so here's what we're gonna do…" Gale unsheathed his knife. Beck, Tilda, and Imogen froze, eyes glued to him, uncertain of his intentions but well aware of his proficiency with his favored weapon. Looking at Imogen, he issued his next orders. "You untie 'em both, and then we're all gonna work together and carry this guy to his final resting place. And we all agree? Keep everything nice and chill and nothing stupid?"

They nodded. Gale handed out more instructions as Imogen worked on untying the knots. When Beck was free, she was to position herself at the left leg—hands on—ready to lift and carry. Imogen would take the other leg. Tilda's wrist knots were harder to undo and Imogen wondered if she had been straining against them, inadvertently making them tighter.

"Tilda can take one arm, up front with me," said Gale.

She shook her head. "You can drag him, you don't need me—"

"Don't be squeamish now, he ain't gonna bite. And if we drag him it's you and me, baby, you look strong." His eyes wandered over her body, over her hiking tights. "I like that. Girls who don't waste what they got."

Imogen gave Tilda's forearm a reassuring squeeze. "Just do what he says," she said softly.

"You just obey every fucking person who gives you a fucking order," Tilda spat.

Imogen didn't have time to process the insult before Gale stepped in.

"Hey, I been real tolerant so far, but I don't actually like when girls swear. I think we can agree now everyone's a little touchy and we need best behavior. Right?"

"Sure. Best behavior." Tilda glowered at him, rubbing her wrists as Imogen finally managed to free them. The cord wrapped above her boots was much easier to undo; even knotted at the back Tilda might have eventually gotten her legs free. Imogen made a mental note: his bindings could be undone, if given enough time or the opportunity to work together. Did Gale still want that nap? And fuck Tilda for insinuating that she wasn't invested in trying to get them safely freed; that was *all* she wanted.

"I'll take that." Gale reached out to take the pieces of nylon rope. Being helpful was part of her strategy, so Imogen coiled the cords as neatly as she could and handed them over.

Beck was already squatting, ready to use her lower-body

strength to help lift the dead man. Imogen took her assigned place beside her, faltering for a moment before gripping the man's leg. She hadn't touched a man in a long time and had zero interest in ending her dry spell. His legs were pale in comparison to his forearms (*where did he live?*), and his calves were well muscled. Grimacing, she gripped him below his knee. It should have been the blood congealing within his flesh that revived her nausea, but instead it was the short, coarse hairs brushing against her own skin.

"I think I'm gonna puke again..." She turned her head to the side.

"You okay?" Beck asked. Imogen nodded. "I'll take a look at your ear later, but there's probably not much I can do. Ruptures usually heal okay on their own."

Imogen appreciated her sister's concern, but if her ear was going to heal, they needed to get out of this alive. She did her best to shake it off. Gale was right—she needed to toughen up. She told herself to imagine it was something else: an old log softened by rot.

"I'm good, I'm okay." Imogen fortified her resolve, and dug her fingers into the dead man's flesh.

Tilda stood where Gale had directed her, but kept her arms crossed. "I'm not carrying him. I can't."

"Let's just get this over with," Beck said.

That Tilda still had some fight in her was good, but the evidence of Gale's capabilities was literally at their feet. Imogen couldn't understand the when-what-whys of Tilda's behavior, and it was pissing her off.

"Tilda, please just be helpful," she said through clenched teeth.

"So much blood, there's so much blood..."

Tilda was near tears. The anguish on her face made Imogen rethink her friend's reluctance. Imogen understood that distress.

"Come on, girls, I got other things to do today."

"He deserves a proper burial, it's the least we can do." Imogen hoped to appeal to Tilda's sense of right and wrong. "I know it's hard; pretend it's something else."

"I can't! You don't understand. I want to help, I do—but I *can't*!"

"What's going on?" Gale threw up his arms. "This'll be over in five minutes, this ain't dangerous, I ain't making you cross a cliff."

"I'll just walk with you, to the tunnel, you don't need me to...touch him."

Gale rolled his eyes. "Fer fuck sake. I ain't asking again. We need to get this done. Now."

All Imogen could think about was how quickly he'd drawn the knife on the backpacker. And there was still the gun in the back of his waistband. Imogen wasn't insensitive to Tilda's suffering, but this was a bad time for a meltdown.

Beck got up from her crouch and took a step toward Tilda. Gale immediately pivoted, the knife in his hand like a sword.

"Get back where yer supposed to be."

Beck returned to her spot beside the body, her voice an urgent warning: "Tilda."

"It's my *mom*!" she said, frenzied.

Confusion washed over Gale's face. "This ain't yer mom?" He looked to Imogen.

She thought back to what she knew of Tilda's mother's death. It had happened a year and a half before they met her, the summer after Tilda finished eighth grade. It was the thing that threw her adolescent life off course. Tilda never talked about it much, but had once used it as part of a theater exercise. The other kids congratulated her, impressed by her intense emotions, not realizing the story was true.

An animal in the road. A utility pole. Tilda in the passenger seat, not yet fourteen, startled but unhurt by the airbag. Her mother at the wheel, mortally injured; the antiques she'd just purchased, undamaged in the trunk.

"Her mom died in a car accident," Beck said.

"What does that have to do with—"

Tilda contracted inward, her feet seemingly glued to the ground, as she covered her face and wept. "There's so much blood, I can't I can't I can't..."

"Please," Beck said to Gale. "She's traumatized, she's not trying to be difficult."

Imogen stood, ready to comfort Tilda. To her surprise, Gale nodded. "Fix her. Fix this, so we can get it done. Don't have all day."

Beck and Imogen rushed to Tilda, took her in their arms.

"He's right," Beck said. "It's not your mom."

"But all the blood!"

"Shhh, it's okay. We're gonna get through this," said Imogen. A person could live through trauma, even when it was retriggered. She knew that better than anyone.

"I never think about it," Tilda said, her face in her hands. "Never. But I touched her. I got out of the car. And we were all alone and no one came *forever*—I waited forever. And I wanted to help her. She was still breathing, really ragged. And I called, 'Mama! Mama!' and I got her door open and touched her shoulder and there was blood all over her face. She coughed and all her teeth fell out, there was so much blood, and then she slumped forward…" The memory overwhelmed her, stealing her words, and she could do nothing but cry.

Her mom's airbag had failed. Tilda believed that if everyone had had cell phones back then, her mother wouldn't have died. As a teenager she'd blamed her mom's death on having to wait on that rural road for someone to come by and help. When she told the story at school, she'd blamed herself, too, for not knowing what to do.

There wasn't time to ponder it, but it struck Imogen how quick young Tilda had been to blame herself for misfortune—and how that might have shaped Tilda's denial about The Thing. How much of her life was a wall, an illusion, meant to separate Tilda from her sense of guilt?

Imogen and Beck held her—held each other.

"You're okay, we're okay," Beck said, to both of them.

"You can do this, Til."

"I couldn't help her," Tilda wailed. "I was all alone."

"You did the best you could," said Beck.

"It wasn't your fault. Look at me." Tilda met Imogen's eyes. "It emphatically wasn't your fault. And you're not alone now."

Tilda gave the tiniest of nods.

"We're here." Beck squeezed them all tighter, so they were almost cheek to cheek. "We're gonna do this together, okay? Everything, from now on, together."

As quietly as she could say it and still be heard, Imogen said, "When he falls asleep don't strain against the ropes, they're easier to undo. We'll untie each other."

Beck quickly added, in an audible voice, "I'll take the front, okay?"

Tilda started to nod, snuffling back her tears. She got a dirty tissue out of her pocket and blew her nose. They took another minute as she collected herself, made some sort of peace with what they had to do. When they returned to the body, Beck took the front position beside Gale, ready to do the heavy lifting. He studied all of them as if he were watching a television drama unfold, the story line and characters captivating in some new and unfamiliar way. When Tilda reached down to hoist up a leg, sniffling one last time, Gale turned to her.

"Sorry about yer mom."

Huffing and straining, they carried the stranger across the defiled grounds of the Boucher camping area.

30

Hunched over, they hauled the body into the darkness. The abandoned mining tunnel was only about forty feet long, dug out of the billion-and-a-half-year-old, silvery-gray Vishnu schist. It wasn't such a bad mausoleum, all things considered, though this was probably a temporary arrangement for the backpacker. Boucher canyon might not be the world's most frequented place, but more people would come here, and some of them would investigate the tunnel, and one might even swallow their fear of snakes and cobwebs and venture all the way in to see where it ended.

The stranger would be found someday, Imogen was sure, and his remains would tell his story. He would not be forgotten. She was less sure how her own story would play out.

Imogen and Tilda held the man's knees cradled in their elbows and Imogen, especially, struggled; her muscles trembled. Her sorrow and fear were quickly receding and resentment slithered in to take their place. He was a heavy fuck and she didn't want to lug him around anymore. Just as she was about to suggest they'd gone far enough, Beck stumbled and fell forward. She and Gale had almost dropped the man's torso a couple of times on the way, their hands slippery with blood, but this time it was the loose rocks that tripped her up.

"Aaah!" She landed hard on her hands and knees. The body lurched, and by silent agreement the rest of them let the backpacker slide to the ground. Beck sat in the dirt, clutching her knee, her face twisted in pain.

Tilda got there first and knelt beside her. "Are you okay?"

Beck didn't speak for a minute. With her eyes clenched tight, she breathed with intention, in-out, in-out, trying to recover. A selfish thought came to Imogen: they'd be worse off if Beck was seriously injured. Her busted lip and black eye were one thing, but their ability to get through this might depend on Beck's prowess as a navigator. Imogen didn't have the skills to replace her—to lead them in the dark—or the strength.

"Landed on a rock," Beck said, wincing. "Small, but sharp."

"Can you walk?" Imogen squeezed in at her other side, taking her arm, ready to help her up.

"Probably."

"Come on, it's creepy in here," said Gale, crouching as he turned and headed toward the daylight.

Tilda and Imogen, each with an arm around Beck's waist, helped her hobble out of the tunnel.

"Don't think anything's broken," Beck said, but she limped heavily, reluctant to put any real pressure on her right leg.

"That's good." Imogen and Tilda exchanged worried glances. What would Gale do if one of them became dead weight? *I could put a fast bullet to the brain.*

"Can we stop at the creek?" Beck asked. "Some cool water could really help."

"Yeah, okay." Gale looked at the cloudy sky. Except for some random sprinkles, the weather had held, but it was as overcast as Imogen had ever seen it in the Canyon, and it smelled richly of ozone. Without a doubt, more rain was coming.

At the creek's edge, Beck let go of Tilda and Imogen and lowered herself to the ground on her good leg, keeping the right one as straight as possible. She tugged off her boots and socks, rolled up her pants.

"Doesn't look too bad," Imogen said, hardly an expert. There was a small gash in the center of her sister's swelling, purpling kneecap.

Beck laid her leg in the creek and swept water over her knee. It seemed to soothe her; tension drained from her shoulders. She scooped up more water, gently splashing it against her face.

As if they'd verbalized an agreement, they all—even Gale— took off their boots and socks and found a place to sit at the creek's edge. Silently, they scrubbed the day's bloody work from their hands and arms.

"Better?" Imogen asked Beck after several minutes.

"Think so." She tested her knee, bending it a few times. If it was an impairment, she didn't let it show beyond a tightness in her features. Knowing her sister, nothing would stop Beck from walking on that leg, but Imogen wondered how much pain she was in. What a fucked-up day.

"We should get on up to the shelter." Gale already had his socks and boots back on.

Imogen, Beck, and Tilda scooted away from the creek, but before they could reach their boots, Gale zoomed in and grabbed them. While they waited for some sort of explanation, he scanned the sky, the land, concentrating, the bootlaces bunched in his fist.

"Tell you girls what, I'll give ya a choice. I could letcha walk up to the shelter barefoot—don't think you'd try to run or do anything crazy in yer bare feet. Or you keep the boots and I tie you together again."

Before they could weigh the options, Tilda chimed in. "Bare feet."

Imogen and Beck weren't won over. Sure, the illusion of freedom might make for a nice psychological break, and there were places—especially in a forest with moss or pillows of decomposing pine needles—where nothing felt better than being at one with nature. But not here, not now. They'd need to step carefully to avoid cutting their feet on rocks or thorny bits of brush, and Imogen would feel better knowing she could *run*.

"It'll take longer without boots." Beck looked at the lowering ceiling of clouds.

"We still have one more pack," Imogen said. If Gale expected her to carry it, it would be impractical to do barefoot.

"Boots," Beck said. And the way she said it left so little room for argument that Gale simply tossed them over.

"Make you a deal," he said to Tilda, "since the sisters overruled ya. You haul the last pack up and I won't tie you. Deal? See how nice I can be?"

"Deal."

Gale had his system down; he wasn't taking chances. He supervised as Beck tied Imogen's hands in front of her, and then Tilda tied Beck's. The knife was sheathed, but he kept one hand at his back, ready for a quick draw if needed. Even when he looked comfortable, at ease, he was in their heads, looking through their eyes, trying to anticipate his own blind spot. He'd made it clear: overpowering him would never be an option.

* * *

When they reached what remained of their camp, Tilda shouldered her own backpack. Gale swept his foot like a broom over the bloodstained earth to make it less conspicuous, while Imogen bent over and grabbed with her tied hands the miscellaneous items that hadn't gotten repacked: a sock, a bottle of sunscreen, her sister's sunglasses. Gale gripped all the walking sticks in one hand and told Tilda to lead the way. Imogen considered asking him to let Beck use her stick, but held off in case Beck didn't want to seem too vulnerable, too damaged. Beck gingerly put weight on her right leg, but she limped along without complaint.

Before heading up to the shelter, Gale stopped. "Probly should do yer business here. Can't guarantee another chance tonight—got no clue what time it is, but I vote we eat some grub and call it a day."

It wasn't until he scrounged around in Tilda's pack for a roll of toilet paper that Imogen grasped the situation. He let them do their "business" one at a time, practically where they stood, while the others kept their backs turned. Fortunately, with their hands bound in front, squatting wasn't much more difficult than usual, but Imogen felt her frustration and angst zinging around inside her like a bouncing ball. It was getting harder to separate hunger from distress, exhaustion from fear. Tilda let her exasperation slip out as they trudged into the gloom of the rocky overhang.

"This is getting ridiculous," she said. "I know we fuck—messed up, but the logistics of getting water, going to the bathroom, sleeping. You can't keep us tied up forever."

Beck and Imogen fired off glares: *Steady now.*

"So I should trust you all of a sudden? You screaming fer help at the first possible chance?"

Tilda looked at the ground. Was she thinking that what had happened to the backpacker was her fault, because she'd called out? Gale was going to kill him regardless, Imogen was sure of it. Once the hiker saw the tableau and walked toward it he hadn't stood a chance—unless Imogen had been able to get there faster, warn him not to get too close. Even then, Gale very likely would've drawn the gun instead of the knife.

"I'm doing my best to keep you girls comfortable, fed and watered 'n' such. But we're doing this my way and I can't risk you fucking it all up. And before ya say I shouldn't swear, I know. But it's better on me, I'm not some fancy, educated lady or whatever."

Tilda was smart enough to withhold a response beyond a stone-cold glare. Gale helped her take her pack off, but before it could be mistaken for a gentlemanly act, he uncoiled a length of cord from his pocket and proceeded to bundle her wrists together.

"Now you three go sit over there where I can keep an eye on ya." They moved into the deepest part of the shallow cave. "A foot apart."

They kicked aside some loose stones to make a smoother surface, then sat in a row as ordered. Gale made a busy bee of himself and Imogen was glad to rest for a while.

"Sorry," Tilda whispered. "I wasn't trying to make—"

"And no talking," Gale commanded. "No plotting, no fussing, just chillax fer a bit, all right?"

It grew steadily darker in the recesses of the overhang, and finally the clouds fulfilled their promise and let loose a torrent of rain.

"Good timing! Got a little lucky there." Gale hurried to the front where he'd left the stranger's pack and moved it deeper into the shelter where it wouldn't get wet. He jogged back to the entrance, unzipping his fly, and let loose an arc of urine. Imogen looked to Tilda and rolled her eyes; Tilda released a grin; they still shared the pet peeve that men would piss anywhere and everywhere. It felt good to find common ground with her.

As Gale had done with their stuff, he inventoried the dead man's belongings. He had the right gear for a solo backpacker—everything Gale needed. Clean clothes, proper socks, underwear, good hiking boots, plus a trendy stove, fuel, and extra rope. When Gale got to the food, Imogen and Beck leaned forward to better see his collection of freeze-dried dinners. Judging by the quantity of pouches, the man must have had a hearty appetite—or else he'd planned on a long trip. Imogen's stomach gurgled just thinking about a hot meal. She craved food and sleep—ordinary comforts—as if they were the cure for this nightmare that wouldn't end.

Gale laid their three mattress pads at their feet (though he left the Therm-a-Rests uninflated), with their sleeping bags on top. It was the most orderly thing Imogen had seen him do. Apparently when he wasn't in a panic, he had a tidy side. He positioned the newly acquired sleeping gear near the shelter's entrance, blocking the path they'd been using to get in and out. If it had been windy, it might not have been a particularly dry place to sleep, but so far the rain was coming straight down. Unlike their own things, the dead backpacker's gear was long enough for a man of Gale's height. Next, he lined up all the packs in a neat row near where he would sleep. Finally he got out Beck's stove and fuel.

How strange it was to sit passively and observe him work. Imogen had the sense she was participating in a reality-TV show (that she hadn't signed up for). *Kidnapped: Wilderness Survival Edition.* Hopefully this story line allowed for more than one winner.

"All righty." Gale plunked himself down. "Since I don't trust y'all near a fire, you can tell me how to do this."

It was understood he was referring to Beck. With almost unnecessary precision, she talked him through the process of putting fuel in the stove, and fire-starter around the ignition ring. The mood was bizarre: in good cheer, their captor prepared a meal for his hostages, as the oblivious stove emitted its happy roar.

As they waited for the water to boil, Gale chucked off his cowboy boots and changed into cargo pants, a T-shirt, and a fleece pullover. He was careful with his injured arm, pulling the fabric gently over his bandage. However much he'd bragged about the stitches not hurting, the arm was still bothering him. He sat down to lace the hiking boots, then got up and paced a few feet each way as he gazed at his feet, as if he were in a shoe store.

In clean clothes he almost—almost—looked like a completely different person. If only he hadn't strapped on the knife belt, and tucked the gun into a deep hip pocket.

31

W hen the food was ready, he brought them each a spoon and a bowl filled with portions from all three reconstituted bags: beef stew, macaroni and cheese, and chicken and dumplings.

"Y'all can sit on yer beds if ya want, a bit more comfortable."

They came forward, away from the dark shadows. Tilda and Imogen took a minute to blow up their mattress pads. As they sat back down they let out audible sighs of relief; it felt like days since they'd rested on anything soft. All three of them sat crisscross applesauce at the foot of their beds, with their bowls on the ground in front of them to accommodate eating with bound hands. The food was utterly delicious. Gale even placed a canteen within easy reach, and by all appearances he'd divided the meal equally among the four of them.

"Thank you," Beck said. "This is really good."

"Really good," Imogen agreed. "Thank you."

"Yer welcome."

For several minutes they enjoyed the feast. The rain had

started strong but didn't last; it brought cooler temperatures, but beyond the overhang the cloud banks were starting to drift home, disappointed by the brevity of the party. Finally, Gale let out a contented sigh.

"See? This is better. You girls have the wrong idea about me."

Was this really his idea of better? Imogen regretted ever thinking anything charitable about him if three tied-up hostages was his concept of more agreeable company.

"What I'm thinking is…I'll take tonight to sleep on it, make sure it still seems like a good idea in the morning. But I'm thinking we head west. More private there, ya said?"

"Hardly anyone goes out to Slate," Beck confirmed.

"It far?"

"Five miles, about a two- or three-hour hike."

"Good. Good, that's what we need. I wanna take yer advice and let the arm heal up a bit better. Lay low another day or so, where nobody's gonna be. Then maybe…" He chewed as he pondered. "Mexico might be better. Much as I wanna see Crystal, she's probly already being harassed by cops. Get to Mexico, lay low there…Maybe later I can try heading north, when things've calmed down."

Gale did his polishing act, cleaning his fork with his tongue. Imogen stopped chewing, absorbed in analyzing his every word. The trip to Slate sounded like a *we;* after Mexico it was *I.* Was he planning to let them go at Slate? Or leave them behind (*kill them*) in Mexico? She wanted to ask, but didn't. His answer wouldn't matter anyway; they knew they needed to get out of the Canyon and away from him.

"I want you to know…It's important to me that you understand the difference about killing someone." Tilda nearly choked on the water she was drinking. Their dinner suddenly wasn't as tasty and they set their utensils down, their eyes fixed on Gale. Perhaps it was the intensity of their attention, but he wouldn't look at them.

"Here's what people don't understand: you don't *want* to kill someone. Like I said, only a serial killer feels good about that—they got nothing in their souls but a devil. But most of the time it's just a quick-flash decision to stop one bad thing from getting worse. Sometimes it ain't even that but self-defense."

Imogen wasn't completely sure that was true; Gale fed on his indignation the way a firecracker consumed a flame, thrilled to reach the point of detonation.

"The long 'n' short of it is, most people don't sit up *planning* to hurt someone. It's just a moment. And maybe you get angry—too angry. Or yer afraid what's gonna happen if you don't carry through. But it's still just a mistake and you'd be wrong to think nobody feels it. The authorities—cops and judges and lawyers—think they got it all figured out, armed robbery and rape and first-degree murder and second-degree, depending on how it all goes down. But they're assholes, they don't get it. They don't think about bad *timing* or the whole *chain of events* that led to that fucked-up moment. They just judge you by one shitty minute of yer life.

"Now I'm not saying it's right. I'm saying you *do* know right from wrong, yer not some savage animal. But it starts this chain—one small fuckup, and another, and they're gonna lock you up, bad egg, not fit fer society. And then ya get madder, and badder, and ain't fit fer normal life when ya get out, even if that's whatcha really want. And even if ya do try, you try and fix the situation…Sometimes you only know ways to fix things that are just new ways a fucking up. And no one ever factors in the *trying,* the wanting to do it better."

Imogen nodded, because once again she understood him. Gale was the hero of his own journey, and every setback, every obstacle—even in human form—was a threat to his goal. Ultimately, if he succumbed to a *quick-flash* impulse to kill them, would he feel okay about it because he really did *like* them and didn't really *want* to do it? If Imogen played by those same ruthless rules, what would she have to do to be the hero of her own journey?

"I know my future now," he said. "Got no illusions. What I done to the cop…that's the needle in my arm. Texas'll kill ya fer a lot less. There's no other outcome, if they catch me. You girls get that? This is my *last* bit a life."

A heaviness settled around them, as dense as ash. Imogen was afraid to breathe, afraid to get it in her lungs. She felt the closing of a door, saw the spinning of the lock as if on a vault. Gale couldn't have said it more plainly. She heard *Nothing left to lose.* She heard *You won't get in my way.* Her blood turned to sludge; her meal curdled in her throat.

"I can't letcha rob me a that. This is all I got left."

This was his last bit of life—and maybe theirs, too. He wasn't going to let them go. Even a twenty-four-hour head start wouldn't be enough, not for a man who wanted every minute, every second, of his remaining time. If set free, Imogen, Beck, and Tilda would click the stopwatch, turn over the hourglass— initiate the beginning of his end.

"But what about Crystal?" Beck asked, her voice foggy, her future tottering toward a void as she reached the same conclusion Imogen had drawn. He couldn't be won over now; Imogen's more compliant approach didn't stand a chance if he'd given up on seeing his daughter, his grand-daughter.

He shrugged. "Maybe she don't want me showing up. Disrupting everything—again. Disappointing her—again. Maybe she'd think I was just putting little Diamond in danger. I'll think on it, sleep on it. But it might be better fer everyone if I disappear."

Did he mean for them to disappear with him? Beside her, Tilda and Beck turned to stone.

32

They lay like corpses as Gale prepared for sleeping. Imogen didn't mind being squashed in the middle; it wasn't like it had been with her Kentucky cousins, that lonely summer long ago. Now the warmth of bodies, three spoons tucked tight, meant they were still alive.

He repositioned their hands so they were behind them, and after binding their ankles he used additional rope to attach their feet to Imogen's walking stick. The idea she'd had to wiggle around in the night and untie each other was foiled. They wouldn't even be able to roll over and, unless they made a well-choreographed effort to rise simultaneously, they couldn't easily stand. If they managed it, they'd have to hop together to get anywhere; Gale wasn't going to sleep through that—and all his precautions spoke to his expectations of an unbothered slumber.

His movements were unhurried, but efficient. He unzipped their sleeping bags and blanketed them. At least they wouldn't be cold (*if he slits our throats in the night*). No one spoke. There was too much to think about. Too many horrific images to replay or avoid.

Soon after he'd hunkered down in his own sleeping bag at the mouth of the shelter, the sky a fading mauve in the cloudy dusk, his breathing became rhythmic. On every inhale, something made a soft grinding noise in his throat.

In the silence, Imogen's ear buzzed even louder. The desire to clap her hand over it to stop the noise was making her antsy. As much as she needed a good rest, she wasn't sure it would be possible without her tincture. At her back, Tilda sobbed.

"Everybody doing okay?" Beck whispered. "Imogen? Your head?"

"Yeah, I'm feeling better." And thank God she'd be lying on her right ear all night, not her left.

"What are we going to do?" Tilda begged.

Imogen didn't want to say what she'd been thinking, that they were beyond reasoning with him, and they'd never overpower him. Her once-reliable imagination was failing her, and her reservoir of ideas had run dry. Sometimes she was so resigned to her fate that she felt wisps of her soul drifting away. She couldn't tell them how empty she felt, so she lay there in the dark and said nothing.

Beck must've been battling her own demons, and for a stretch she, too, didn't speak. After a while she said, "I'm sorry."

The apology was so earnest, so final, that Imogen wished she'd never heard it. It sounded as hopeless as Imogen felt.

"It's not your fault," Imogen whispered, because it hurt her heart too much to think of her sister dying with the belief that vanquishing Gale had been her responsibility.

"I brought you guys here."

Imogen considered all the reasons why Beck had organized

this trip, full of so many good intentions. She'd wanted to help them—Imogen *and* Tilda. She'd tried to give them something, in the only way she knew how.

"You didn't bring that ginger Sasquatch here," Tilda snarled.

A moment ago Imogen had thought herself incapable of it, but she laughed. After a second, Beck gave a halfhearted chuckle.

"Okay, true."

"I'm not sorry we came," said Imogen. "Sorry all this shit happened. But not sorry we... You were trying to do something good, for all of us."

"Yeah." Beck sounded distracted. "Ever wonder why I have that article on my wall?"

"The play?" Imogen asked, caught off guard.

"Yeah."

"I have a copy of it somewhere," said Tilda. "But not on the wall. I looked like I was about to give the microphone a blow job."

"Tilda!" Imogen hissed the word, but she wasn't angry. She appreciated Tilda's ability to be snarky at inappropriate times now that Gale was asleep.

"Sorry—yes Beck, I had wondered about that," Tilda said.

"I was trying to remember—to remind myself—that people listen to me. Sometimes take me too seriously. And I have to be more careful about what I say."

"What is she talking about?" Tilda whispered to Imogen.

"When I was directing the play I learned that if I was unclear about something—stage direction, or a lighting cue— then people would get confused. But if I was very specific, I got the results I wanted. It was kind of a power rush. And it's like that with patients sometimes too. There's a part of me that likes it, being in control, but I don't want to be a dictator. I want to help, I want people to have results that work. But…"

"You can't control everything," said Tilda.

"I know. You *shouldn't* listen to me all the time."

Imogen wished she could see her sister's face. "No, that's not the problem. I *should* listen to you, but you should listen to me too—we have to listen to each other, all of us. So yes, I will do what you tell me. But if I have an idea you should listen in return. We keep missing each other's cues. We're running out— We have to keep trying."

"Agreed, yes," Beck said, sounding a bit revived.

"If only we could get the gun from him," said Tilda.

"Maybe, somehow, we can get him to stay—here or at Slate—long enough to trigger our rescue," Imogen said, thinking aloud. She wasn't quite sure how they'd cope with so many more days in his volatile company, but at least they'd be alive. "Afiya would be the first to know we weren't back, how long would she wait to call someone?"

"Knowing her, about fifteen minutes past the ETA I gave her. Especially if I didn't call or text."

"That could work," Tilda said.

"You guys…" Beck's voice faltered, full of emotion. "I hate to put her through all that worry. She's pregnant and you know how hard it was…" She choked on her words.

"She's pregnant?" Imogen leaned up a little, and felt Tilda do the same.

"She wasn't showing," Tilda said. "She didn't say anything."

"She'll—we'll—be crushed if we lose another pregnancy."

"Oh, Beck—"

"And I *have* to be there for her, for them."

"You *will*." Imogen wanted to embrace her so badly. All she could do was inch her shoulder a little closer, blow a kiss toward the back of her neck.

"She'll be at thirteen weeks when we get back. We were going to tell you then."

"I'm sorry, Beck," Tilda said.

Imogen was sure Tilda knew about one of the miscarriages, but maybe not both. Imogen was in awe of the strength and faith it took for Beck and Afiya to keep trying. It wasn't fair that their love wasn't enough to give them the child they both so wanted.

"And I'm sorry I'm saying sorry when I should be saying congratulations."

"Maybe you should tell him," Imogen said, suddenly inspired. "He might think you're lying now, but maybe he'd understand, sympathize. He started all this to try to see his daughter and granddaughter—why didn't you say something?"

"We told people too soon before. And there's no way he was going to be the first person I told."

For all Beck's ability to boss people around, it struck Imogen that she could be a little clueless about human nature.

"Imogen's right. He's a fucking monster but he has a soft spot for babies. This is something you could really connect to him with."

"I don't want to connect with—"

"It's a strategy, Beck," Imogen snapped. "Remember how I just said we should listen to each other? Tell him every fucking thing—tell him how you're going to decorate the baby's room, tell him what names you're considering. For fuck's sake, tell him about Afiya's miscarriages. Make him see you as someone he relates to, that's what the experts would say!"

In the silence that followed, Gale's snores were oddly reassuring.

"You really do watch too much TV," Beck said, ending the standoff.

Sometimes when Beck told her that, Imogen interpreted it as a judgment. But now it helped to squelch her anger. "Yeah. I'll save your dumb ass with everything I've learned from TV."

Behind her, Tilda snorted, and Imogen had the sense for the first time in eons that Tilda was really listening to her.

Beck conceded. "Okay. When I get a chance, when it feels natural and not like a ploy, I'll tell him."

"Good." Tilda sighed—tired or satisfied or vexed, Imogen couldn't tell.

"But…we should prepare ourselves. Mentally. To be ruthless. Because that could be what it takes. We can't shy away. You've seen what he can do."

Maybe, given the evolution of their captivity, their options were only going to become bleaker, more desperate. But hearing Beck verbalize the need to kill him brought home a reality that Imogen wasn't sure she could face. She was notoriously bad at fighting back—though this time she had advance warning. She needed to wrap her head around it. Change her inner monologue and start thinking of herself as a survivalist, willing to do *anything*.

"Can you do that? Kill him? What about 'First, do no harm'?" Tilda asked.

Imogen had been wondering about that too. "Is Gale technically your patient?"

"That isn't actually part of the Hippocratic oath," Beck said.

"Seriously?" said Tilda.

"Nope. Nothing even close. And Gale understands self-defense as a means for doing whatever's necessary. We have to be able to do that too. Train yourself now, mentally. Think about what you don't want to lose. We may only get one chance."

"I want to have kids someday too," Tilda said softly. "Jalal would be a good dad."

"You finally got a good one," Beck said.

"I did."

They were the last words any of them spoke for the night.

Imogen didn't want to know what Beck was mulling over, what brutality she was replaying in her mind to ready herself to act (*like Gale*) without hesitation. Or maybe she was only dreaming about a future where she held her infant son or daughter, with her brilliant, gorgeous wife at her side. Tilda was probably creating a family for herself, too, the future she didn't want to lose.

Who was Imogen supposed to live for?

No one knew, but in recent years she'd started fantasizing about being a mother. Sometimes children appeared in her mind out of nowhere to live out a moment—sharing a meal, talking through a difficult life lesson. Occasionally she would wonder what her day would be like if the girl or boy she passed in the library or grocery store were hers. But her maternal love was for the possibility of a moment, not a duration of forever.

Oh, how emotional she could get, her heart well trained from years of writing to fully bloom for even the less-than-real and most ephemeral of souls. *Because I'm a writer.* A false narrative had lurked in her subconscious for a year, telling her her contributions to the world—to *tikkun olam*—were inconsequential. But it wasn't true. Even a creepy mystery book could look meaningfully at the human condition. And just then, the young heroine from her unwritten fairy tale appeared in her mind—to remind her she didn't yet exist. To beg Imogen to bring her to life. *I have more stories to tell.*

That was reason enough, wasn't it? Something to fight for? She had as much right to be who she was as anyone else. And she was remembering more of the dreams she'd long since buried.

Though she didn't want to be a mother, she pondered the possibility of being an aunt.

She didn't have much experience with babies, but she made herself imagine swaddling a niece or nephew, its little face bursting with delight as Imogen cooed and described, in a baby voice, the adult doings of the world. It hadn't seemed urgent, after the earlier announcements, to put a plan in motion; she thought she had seven months or more to figure it out. Not this time. Now she knew there was only *right now*.

Should she move to Flagstaff? Was that even realistic?

So many things, even under preposterous conditions, reminded her of the race she was losing—the race she hadn't bothered to sign up for. The race in which she watched everyone speed past her while she made no effort to keep up. She didn't mind that Beck was winning the race, but she didn't want to be left so far in the dust that she couldn't join the celebration at the finish line. She wanted her sister's child to know her. One way or another, she was certain she wanted to have a meaningful role in this child's life.

First things first: they all had to get home. Imogen drifted to sleep with images of herself enraged and ferocious. She might be able to kill for her sister's chance to be a mom, and her own chance to love someone unconditionally.

33

Imogen was outside, sitting cross-legged in the middle of
Beck's backyard. A tiny brown child ran around her in circles, squealing, and the ponderosa pines, silent but friendly
neighbors, waved and grinned from the sidelines. A warm
wind swept through Imogen's hair, across her skin, so comforting, until...it turned from warm to hot, hot to blistering, and
the sky morphed from blue to orange. The child started
screaming, its curly Afro alight with flames.

The screaming woke her. Beck's dream home was gone and
in the darkness Imogen wasn't sure where she was. Beside her
something writhed, the frantic undulations of...Tilda. Tied
up. Bucking against her restraints. A banshee yell ricocheted
off the rocky enclosure.

A flashlight blinked on and a haggard man—their captor—
stumbled over.

"What's going—"

"Help me!" Tilda wailed. "Help me!"

"What's the—"

"My hand!"

Beck and Imogen tried to roll over, to see what was wrong, but of course they couldn't do more than strain their heads. Gale directed the flashlight toward something behind them, presumably Tilda's bound hands.

"Oh shit!" Suddenly more awake, he fumbled around, grabbed a fist-sized rock.

"What is it?" Imogen screeched. But given the hour and where they were, she knew it was likely one of two things, and both were bad. Both were poisonous.

Gale slammed the rock down a few inches beyond Tilda. For good measure, he picked it up and hammered again.

"Scorpion." He sounded relieved, now that it was dead. Tilda, no longer screaming, sobbed, twisting in pain.

"What color was it?" Beck asked Gale.

"What the fuck, I don't know." He looked dazed, wrenched from his deep sleep.

"Then we have to assume it was a bark scorpion, they're the most common. And venomous—she needs to be treated." Her words were a little slurry, a combination of her swollen face and being groggy.

"Please!" Tilda begged.

"Fine, what do I do?" From what Imogen could see of his face, he looked honest-to-God scared. It struck her as a thoroughly human reaction, the instinct that came with middle-of-the-night emergencies. She could almost see him rushing to Crystal's bedside as she cried from a bad dream.

"Untie me!"

"Not gonna do—"

"It's okay, Til, the binding will work like a tourniquet, slow down the venom while Gale cools it down. Pour cold water on the sting," Beck instructed Gale. He ran to the makeshift kitchen and came back with two canteens. "Pour it slowly and just keep pouring water on it. Try to relax," she told Tilda.

"Is this gonna kill me?"

"No, you'll be achy. Maybe pins and needles for a couple of days, hopefully nothing worse. But after Gale cools off the wound he'll give you some antihistamines and ibuprofen—they're in the first aid kit."

Tilda pressed her face into Imogen's hair and wept. "Please just let us go."

Imogen reached with her tied hands, grasping for Tilda. All she got was a piece of her sweatshirt, but she held on. Wan daylight filtered in; the colors of their clothing and sleeping bags emerged from the gloom. Now that she was more alert, Imogen registered how stiff she felt—the pressure on her right shoulder and hip, and the tingling in her hands and feet from being in one position for so long.

"Is it feeling any better?" There was a crackle of nervousness in Gale's voice as he stepped back, holding the empty canteens. He looked to Beck for further guidance.

"I guess," Tilda said. "Can you please? Please, Gale—whatever happened before. We just want to go home."

"I'll get you those pills." He went rooting around in the disorganized packs. Tilda whimpered.

"You're okay." Imogen squeezed the fistful of sweatshirt, hoping Tilda was even a tiny bit soothed.

"The pain will subside in a few minutes. You'll be okay," Beck said.

"I'm not—we're not. None of us are okay!"

Gale squatted beside her and helped her sit up a little. "Two a both?" he asked Beck.

"Let's start with one of each."

"See? I'm helping," Gale told Tilda. "The sisters are right, you'll be okay. I got bit by a cottonmouth when I was a kid. 'Bout scared me to death—my momma too—but lived to tell the tale."

Unable to sit fully upright, Imogen and Beck squirmed, trying to keep an eye on what was going on. Tilda hesitated to take the pills from Gale's cupped hand, but finally she accepted them and the fresh canteen he held to her lips. She swallowed them down.

"So fine," Tilda said, flopping back to the ground. As had become a pattern with her, anger crept into her misery. "I won't die of a scorpion bite."

"Sting," Beck corrected.

"Does it matter?" she spat. "It still hurts like a—" Imogen gave her sweatshirt a yank, trying to remind her of Gale's admonition. "Like the male child of a female dog."

"The ibuprofen will kick in," Beck said. "It's not that different than a bee sting, as long as you don't have any sort of allergic reaction."

"Good thing we got a doc with us." Gale paced to the overhang and gazed out over the morning. Imogen wished she could see it: the gelatinous light finding purchase on distant rocks. From where she was it looked as if the sky had fully cleared. Maybe it would put him in a more optimistic mood than the one he was in when he went to bed; maybe he'd suggest heading to Nevada after all. With his back turned he asked, "You girls get some sleep?"

"Yes," they mumbled.

"Good, me too. Needed that." He unzipped his fly and pissed on the dawn. After stretching his arms over his head and arching his back, he came back over, refreshed. "Might as well get up, first light as they say. I wanna get away from…whatever ya call this place. Before anyone else comes by."

He started breaking down their camp—letting the air out of his poached Therm-a-Rest, stuffing his sleeping bag into its sack.

"Can you leave us here? Please?" Beck asked. "Just as we are, tied up? Even if someone comes into Boucher, no one's going to spot us up here and you'll get a good head start. Eventually we'll work ourselves free and head out, but we understand now, about not telling—"

"No." His tone was a warning, a command. His good night's sleep hadn't changed anything; the day was off to a terrible start. He took several minutes to reorganize the contents of the packs.

"Can you untie our feet at least? So we can sit up?" Imogen wouldn't have taken the risk of asking, given how quickly his concern for Tilda had dissipated, but she was desperate to change positions, move her aching muscles and release the pressure from her hip and shoulder.

"Soon," Gale answered.

When Gale was finished repacking, instead of untying his captives he started on a new project. Among the dead man's things he'd found a small roll of duct tape. With that and a length of thin cord he proceeded to fashion himself a spear, attaching his knife to the end of Tilda's walking stick.

Imogen, Beck, and Tilda—awkwardly supporting themselves on their elbows in their half-twisted positions—observed him. What conclusion should they draw that his first task of the morning was to make a weapon? And the spear was a good one, useful at close range, as well as a few feet away. And if the distance grew farther there was always the gun; its weight made his pocket droop.

He looked quite pleased with himself. When the blade was firmly attached, he leaned the spear against the rock wall. Imogen had almost forgotten he still had Beck's Swiss Army knife until he withdrew it and opened the main blade. As he approached them, their instinct was to retreat, but their only option was to lie back down, pressing themselves into the rocky ground. But the backup knife was just for show; he wouldn't cut their bindings if he intended to reuse them.

It probably wasn't because she'd asked, but he untied Imogen's feet first. He took her elbow and helped her stand. She stumbled, her feet half numb, and shook them out, encouraging the blood to circulate. He led her, hobbling and wincing, a few feet away, then redid her wrists so they were in front of her. "Better fer getting stuff done," he explained.

Apparently she remained the one he liked to boss around. A part of her was almost flattered by his trust even as the other part was insulted, but it was undeniable that she felt safer as his servant, unbound—even if the ability to make a run for it was an illusion. She eyed the spear; it beckoned like a fickle lover with its casual stance, indifferent to her burning need. Gale had her dismantle Beck's and Tilda's beds, never mind that it left them lying on the hard, cool ground. She pulled the sleeping bags and mattress pads out from under them as they lifted their feet, their hips, to assist her. She rolled and stuffed and moved back and forth to attach their gear to their packs. While she worked, Gale claimed a rock near the entrance to sit on. He whistled in a lazy way with the spear across his knees.

As daylight slowly brightened the shelter, details emerged

from the shadows. Beck's puffy lip had a scab on it, but otherwise didn't look worse than it had the day before. The swelling around her eye, however, had inflated overnight, a rainbow of affronted colors that virtually sealed the eye shut. Imogen couldn't see Beck's knee, but didn't expect it was much improved, not after a night with no blood circulation. Her legs had surely stiffened, but hopefully she could still walk.

Tilda complained about feeling "weird," but Beck promised her that was normal, a combination of the medications and the sting, and that she would be okay. None of them were really okay, Tilda was right about that. Imogen felt like her brain had been replaced with a wet wad of cotton; she couldn't think straight and her head sloshed when she moved. Her balance was rickety as she packed up the last of their stuff. She hoped the hike over to Slate was as easy as Beck had implied—though walking might be the least of their concerns if Gale followed through on his plans to *disappear*. Most people who wanted to disappear didn't take three unwilling people with them.

"We need to refill the canteens before we go," Beck said.

Gale nodded. "Gather 'em up," he told Imogen.

She could've used a drink of water. Some breakfast. Even after a big meal the night before, she always woke up hungry. Beck was probably dying for some coffee, but she and Tilda remained bound on their sides, tethered to Imogen's walking stick. Everything else was ready to go. Imogen grabbed four canteens and headed out of the shelter, relieved to see the sun, normal and rising.

The crisp air roused her a bit, its movement across her face a fleeting reminder of the dream she'd been having when Tilda's screams awakened her.

34

She thought Gale meant for her to go to the creek alone and her mind moved its scrabbled tiles around, trying to form a coherent idea: What could she do? When he came scurrying along behind her, spear in hand, she swiftly rearranged them: What could *they* do? Could Beck and Tilda get themselves untied? Waylay him upon their return? Gale must have been feeling confident but Imogen knew her sister would do *something;* Beck wouldn't let this opportunity go to waste.

He made her scamper along faster than she would have liked, so she tried to think of ways to distract him, ways to slow them down, if only a little. Give Tilda and Beck that much more time.

"Is your arm feeling any better?" They were almost to the creek.

"A bit. Yer sis is right, helps to rest it." Gale held the spear like the walking stick it was, blade pointed to the sky. He looked out toward where the man had come across the day before, as if he expected company any minute. Imogen had long given up hope that the backpacker had companions, but that didn't mean other people weren't on the way.

She knelt by the edge of the water. It could only sluice into the canteens at its own rate, but she prayed for it to run a little slower. *Please? For me?* Maybe there was still a chance for her to strengthen her connection to him; she still worried she was the only one capable of it, despite Beck's personal ammunition with Afiya's pregnancy. Beck and Tilda didn't believe they had anything in common with Gale, but Imogen understood that certain desires and fears were universal.

"Maybe this sounds weird," she said, "after everything that's happened, but…we appreciate how you're trying to look after us. And know you don't want to hurt us." She hoped she could get him in a chattier mood. At least Gabby Gale could seem like a sympathetic person, and Paranoid Gale was always bad news. "And we understand now, about time, how precious it is. Maybe this is all you have left." She looked up at him, hoping to draw his attention, wanting him to read her sincerity. When he met her eyes, she went on. "I know you might not believe me, but…I think we all have empathy for you. For how this got so…out of control."

He scoffed. "I know what yer feeling fer me and it ain't 'poor Gale.'"

"Actually it is. Sort of." She closed up the first canteen and started on the second. "I understood it, Gale, what you said before, about how things can go wrong. In life—not just one day. My life hasn't gone as I thought it would. There are things that've happened that…messed me up, messed up everything else. There were things I used to want, and I pushed them away for so long, until eventually I believed I didn't want them anymore. But the truth was, I didn't know how to do anything differently, with my life. Beck was the one who really saw it. Sometimes it's hard to look at your own crap. But I want to try to fix it. I see that in you—see you wanting to try to fix the things that got all screwed up. I know it's not easy."

And she really did see that, his desire for things to be different, his desire to change and be better than what he was. Beyond his regrettable actions, she believed he possessed the capacity to love. And he'd shown glimpses of kindness. The only real difference between them was that she'd directed all her frustrations and anger inward, attacking herself, while Gale directed his outward.

"Sometimes people get turned around," she said. "If things had been different…I know you didn't want to end up here."

"So ya get it then." He nodded—at nothing, at the distance. "I fucked it all up, I admit that. And it's too late fer me now."

"Are you sure?" She meant that earnestly. There were times when the *thought* of him, the fear of what he might do, was worse than his actual presence. Talking with him one-on-one, her optimism returned. "It might not be too late—and even if you feel like it is for you, it doesn't have to be for all of us. I think you feel bad, about a lot of things. You don't have to add me and Beck and Tilda to your conscience."

She finished another canteen, set it aside, and immediately started on the next.

He shifted his jaw, chewed on the inside of his cheek. Imogen thought he might be fighting back tears. "I like you girls, I do," he said softly. "Yer different, from other people I met. Kinda weird, but ya got pluck. I like that. I kinda wish…wish we could sit around a campfire and share stuff, real stuff, about our lives. I think…I think you'd actually listen. *You,* anyway."

"I would." It touched her, more deeply than she expected, that he saw something of value in her—patience, or compassion. An ability to listen to and understand someone else's story. "We should do that. Maybe later, when we get resettled at Slate."

The thought of it brought her a warm rush of hope. *It's working!* But Gale was lost in another universe.

"I wish..." He sounded dreamy, wistful. "I wish we had some poison, and we could have our meal, eat up everything we got left, and then...drift off to sleep. Peaceful."

What? How could he be fantasizing about them all dying together while she was trying to give him reasons to let them live?

He snapped back to the here and now, his tone turning harsh. "You finished?"

Imogen pressed the last of the canteens deeper into the water, now urging it to hurry. He sure knew how to suck the oxygen out of a room.

"That's enough, come on. There a creek out at the other place?"

"I don't know—"

"Don't matter, this is enough." He shooed her away from her task and she twisted the lid on the last canteen. She carried all four, and they hung heavily by the fingers of her manacled hands. Gale strode slightly ahead of her with his spear–walking stick, fast enough that she had to jog to keep up. But he stepped aside, grinning, to let her take the lead on the final scramble up to the overhang. "Just in case they got an ambush planned, they'll club you first."

Imogen needed a second for her eyes to adjust to the shadows at the back of the shelter, but whatever she'd been hoping Beck and Tilda might conjure in Gale's absence...They weren't free, hiding in the wings, ready to attack. Everything was just as she'd left it. Tilda and Beck were lying on their sides, a gap between them where she had once been. As Imogen secured the canteens to the packs, she studied their sleeping area more carefully. Was the dirt more scuffed up than it had been? Had Beck and Tilda shifted around? And wiggled back into place so it looked like they hadn't been up to anything? Or maybe Imogen was seeing what she wanted to see.

"How far out to the other place?"

Beck lifted her head to answer him.

"Maybe there's somewhere better," Imogen suggested quickly, locking eyes with her sister. After hearing his morbid thoughts at the creek, Slate was the last place they should go— they needed to head *toward* people, not away. Counting on his ignorance, she threw out an idea. "Maybe Phantom?"

There were always people at Phantom Ranch. It even had small, year-round cabins; their dad still sometimes mentioned celebrating New Year's there, if they could get it together to make reservations far enough in advance. Tilda looked from sister to sister, cautious and uncertain. Imogen couldn't read Beck's tense face. The walk to Phantom Ranch was ridiculously long, two solid days of hiking, but reaching it wasn't her goal. Heading that way would take them back through the main corridor of trails, where they'd start passing other backpackers with increasing frequency.

"That closer?" Gale asked.

"Farther," said Beck.

"More private?"

Beck gave Imogen a tiny, sad shake of her head. "We'd have to go back through Hermit. And cross the Tricky Spot."

This information was for Imogen, not Gale, and she got it: her sister was afraid to cross the gorge, hands bound, one eye out of commission, and with her knee still a question mark. Beck considered her odds for survival better at Slate. Oblivious, Gale strapped on his backpack.

"Ferget that, let's stick with the other place. Better get 'em untied." Gale gestured with his head and Imogen went to Tilda first, and started to undo her knots. "How long's it gonna take?"

"No more than two or three hours," said Beck, "and it's a level walk."

"Great. We'll have breakfast there. Get away from..." He made an impatient, sweeping gesture—toward the walls, toward the world beyond the overhang.

It struck Imogen that he had no names for the things he was running away from. This canyon. The next one. The man he'd murdered. The thousand ghosts fast on the wind, threatening to catch up to him.

35

They were a mule train, packs on their backs, hands bound in front. As Gale demanded, they stayed within three feet of the person ahead of them: Beck limped in the lead, her pace slower than previous days; Tilda was in the middle, sniffling, maybe crying. In the full light of day she had what looked like an enflamed blister just above her right pinky, the venom a halo of red that engulfed half her hand. Once again, Imogen hiked behind them and in front of Gale. He'd tied the other two walking sticks to the back of her pack, "In case we need them." She still felt conflicted about the fact that Gale didn't view her as the least bit formidable. His spear made it easier than ever for him to swat her away like a pesky gnat.

Beck led them along Boucher Creek, in the opposite direction from the route that had taken them to the river. After a few hundred feet she paused, and they all stopped to consider the large cairn, a three-foot tower of rocks that someone had made to mark the trail. Usually cairns were smaller, three or four or five rocks; three was the minimum number to use as a trail marker, since two stacked rocks could be a coincidence. Beck pointed with her bound hands.

"We'll take these switchbacks up to the Tonto, then it's level the whole way from there."

Beside them was a wall of Tapeats sandstone a hundred feet high. Short switchbacks zigzagged along the ledges, leading them out of Boucher canyon. As they clambered up, a realization slashed a wound in Imogen's mind: they were off schedule now, no longer adhering to the locations indicated on their backcountry permit. It was too soon for anyone to think they were missing, but it would be harder to find them now, if someone did come looking. Imogen wanted to drop some crumbs—pieces of thread or fabric from her clothing, anything that a searcher might follow as a clue—but Gale was too close at her back.

Once they reached the Tonto Platform, Imogen scanned ahead for the trail out to Slate. She spotted pieces, but it was faint, a delicate demarcation of trampled red dirt. Beck said it was an easy walk, which physically seemed to be true, but without her in the lead they probably would have gotten lost. Imogen had never been on a path so little traveled, in the Canyon or elsewhere. It wound around washes and sometimes smudged into nothing, disappearing between the scraggy foliage that mottled the rolling desert.

Beck came to a full stop, scrutinizing the terrain ahead with her one functioning eye. Imogen immediately realized the problem and bypassed Tilda to stand beside her sister.

"Somebody coming?" Gale pointed his spear at Beck. Uh-oh, Paranoid Gale was emerging.

"No. There's a split in the trail." With her bound hands

Beck indicated the left path, and the right. "I have to figure out which is the real one."

"Won't they end up at the same place?" he asked.

"No, probably not. All of the trails…they were originally animal tracks, and the animals aren't necessarily trying to get from the same Point A to Point B that we are." She shielded her good eye with her elbow, the best defense against the light that she could manage. The sun had reestablished its dominion, the drunk clouds long gone.

Gale scanned the terrain too, but whatever he was looking for it wasn't the trail. "Get going, we don't have all day." He mock-thrust the spear in her direction.

"If I get it wrong we'll have to backtrack."

"Pick. I don't like being so out in the open here." He looked skyward. Eastward. Round about.

Did he think a satellite could detect him? Or that drones were hunting him down? Did he think he was so important that such resources would be allotted for his capture? Then again, they couldn't be sure what else he'd done since killing the highway patrolman; maybe he was being pursued by law enforcement in multiple states. Strange to think that the worse his crimes, the more diligence would be put into apprehending him. Imogen wasn't sure where that left her, or what she should be praying for. Tilda looked more forlorn than Imogen had ever seen her, gazing out with glassy eyes on a relentless wasteland.

Imogen blocked the glare with her forearm, eager to help Beck. Gale's antsiness was infectious; she was feeling exposed too.

"Look near the head of the washes," Beck advised her.

"Okay."

"It can't be that hard." Even Tilda was getting impatient.

Beck and Imogen studied the land, trying to figure out where the missing pieces of the maze would lead.

"Aw, come on…" Fidgety, Gale struck out with his spear. Tilda shrieked, though she wasn't the one he'd clipped. He might have intended it as a move-it-along nick, but the knife was sharp. A trickle of blood oozed through Beck's shirt where he'd stabbed her upper arm. She gasped, her attention diverted to the gash she couldn't reach.

Imogen grasped her sister's arm in both hands and squeezed, trying to stanch the blood. "Come on, we're really trying!" she yelled at Gale, a frantic whine in her voice.

"Sorry." In his browbeaten apology Imogen saw a boy who trudged in shame on weekly visits to the principal's office.

"Cut the bottom of my T-shirt and tear it off, we can use it as a bandage." Imogen had never thought of herself as the bossy type, but Gale did as he was told. He lifted her sweatshirt out of the way and sliced off the bottom two inches of the shirt beneath it. "You okay?" she asked Beck.

"Think so."

How many times in the past few days had they asked each other if they were okay? Tilda held her cuffed hands below her chin, her arms tight against her body as if she were freezing. She looked more hurt than Beck, a dazed despair on her face.

"I'm okay, Til," Beck told her, and Tilda nodded *yes yes of course,* wild-eyed.

Gale yanked open the hole in Beck's fleece to get access to her wound. He wrapped the strip of T-shirt around and around her upper arm and tied it in a knot. "It ain't deep," he said with the confidence of a man who knew about stab wounds.

Imogen's palms were red. She didn't want to see her sister's blood smeared on her khaki shorts, so she bent a little to rub it off on her blackish leggings. For an instant she flashed on the synagogue, stained by violence, splattered with hate, desecrated by murder.

"Please girls, everybody just do what yer supposed to do."

I thought we were. But aloud Imogen said, "I think it's that one." And gestured with her chin toward the path on the left.

"I think you're right," Beck said.

"See, no need fer so much fuss."

Beck limped on as if nothing had happened, and the mule train fell into line.

The walking became monotonous. The creak of shifting packs. A distant whir of a helicopter. The faint song of a canyon wren. The muffled sound of their boots, swallowed by dust. Their heartbeats begged the prayers they couldn't speak.

It might not have been a terribly long walk but it seemed interminable. A palpable shroud drifted above them, a white windingsheet waiting to ready them for burial. Imogen struggled for words. She couldn't concentrate on the present for her fear of the future. When she tried to examine her thoughts, her emotions, she found them in a state of evaporation, as if written in invisible ink, leaving her with an endless, wordless nothingness. There was only one question that mattered: Where was he taking them? And the answer: *The end of the road.*

There rose in her an impulse to scream. Her lungs filled, ready to release it, but Gale stole the air again.

"Y'all never chitchat while yer walking?" he asked. "You just...plod on, lost in yer own thoughts?"

His questions angled toward irritation. Did he really think they'd stroll along and gossip as if death weren't on their heels?

270

"Walking's good for thinking," Beck replied.

"Well, it's bugging me. All this...quiet. I thought girls were chatty but I know a dozen grown men who talk circles round all a you."

Instead of reminding him of the circumstances, Imogen simply said, "If you want to talk, we'll listen."

He sighed. "I'd rather do the listening. Need some distraction. All this quiet and thinking, it's like being stuck in a storm cellar."

It was, rather. But Imogen was no longer in the mood to swap personal regrets or insecurities. She waited: perhaps Beck would take this moment to wax poetic on the greens and yellows and soft wood hues of a genderless baby room. Or maybe Tilda would tell them more about the life she was planning with Jalal. Imogen hadn't realized, before the previous night, just how serious their relationship was getting. Tilda used to post boyfriend pics online, romantic dates, interesting excursions, or lessons learned from a recent argument. But, as with her volunteer work, she kept Jalal more private, and maybe that said everything about Tilda's true priorities.

Judging by their reticence, Imogen sensed they were so deep in their own thoughts that they'd already forgotten he'd spoken. Gale seemed concerned about that possibility too.

"Well?" he said loudly.

More and more, Imogen felt the need to take charge. Not only was Beck in rough shape, but Imogen had been right since the beginning. So many times she'd thought of herself as useless, but her paranoia had been valid. Paranoia could be an early-warning system, like a siren that blares for an approaching storm, or a reminder of a lesson from the past. She took a step sideways, trying to draw Tilda's attention and lure her out of whatever miserable reverie she was lost in. "Seen any good movies lately?"

"Nah," Gale said, either oblivious to the direction of the question or more eager to talk than he'd admitted. "Was binging some TV shows. Could never keep up with everything on account a spending so much time locked up."

Imogen was about to ask him what shows he liked, certain he was a fan of *Alone,* but Tilda came back to life and joined the conversation.

"You haven't missed much in the way of movies," she said, sounding authoritative. "Mostly comic book adaptations. It's like all of Hollywood has given in to some superhero fetish. Jalal and I have been trying to see more independent and foreign films, so the market won't totally die, but we don't go out that much."

"Jalal? That yer boyfriend?"

"Yes."

"What kinda name is that? He an Arab?"

Tilda stopped and swiveled, giving Gale a short, hard look. "He's from Portland. His family's from Iraq."

"He one a those Muslims?"

"Don't bother," Imogen said quietly. She gave Tilda a little push to set her going forward again.

"I'm just asking. I don't have nothing against Arabs or Mexicans or anyone, I just like to know who's who because contrary to popular belief, we ain't all the same. And that doesn't mean some are less and some are more—think I like being considered white trash?"

"Jalal is an atheist. A lawyer, for a group that provides pro bono services to nonprofits and families, mostly immigrants." She kept her eyes straight ahead, but spoke with a raised, defiant voice. "He enjoys cooking—especially Indian food. He has the worst taste in comedies, but he laughs so hard I end up laughing with him. He's three years younger than I am and we've been seriously talking about getting married. A small wedding. With purple bridesmaid dresses. Or Beck can wear a tux with a purple tie, if she likes that better. And we're thinking about having a baby. Or adopting. Because we're concerned about the climate crisis and what kind of world our child will inherit and who are we to just keep populating the earth when we haven't figured out how to coexist with the other living things on the planet. Or maybe we'll buy a house together first, and see how that goes." She stopped again, turned. If Tilda had possessed superpowers, her glare would have obliterated Gale.

He probably missed everything she was actually saying, but Imogen heard it loud and clear: *I have a life, with wonderful people, and dreams and hopes, and fuck you for jeopardizing everything.* And then Imogen wondered if she'd be invited to the wedding. Tilda had been talking about purple bridesmaids' dresses since high school, back when Imogen had no doubt she'd be there to accompany her best friend to the altar.

"Can we have some water?" Beck asked, taking advantage of the mule train's pause.

"All right." Gale sounded a tad grumpy, but he took a canteen out of the side pocket of Imogen's pack and handed it to her. "Pass it round."

"Thanks," she said. Imogen took a drink and handed it to Tilda, who did the same and handed it to Beck.

It was unlikely Beck was dying of thirst (unless it was from lack of coffee), but she was smart to put a halt to their conversation. There was nothing they could chat about that wouldn't make someone mad or sad. Knowing her sister, Beck might never share the news of Afiya's pregnancy with Gale, not if she couldn't hold herself together while talking about it. It was a tricky balance to keep your reasons to live present in your mind while not letting them become a distraction, or a source of destruction; Beck understood she couldn't fall apart.

After a quick sip for himself, Gale put the canteen away and they resumed heading west.

36

Imogen wasn't sure if she should hope they were almost there or hope they weren't. Walking in the sun had helped dry her wet-cotton brain and her thoughts weren't leaking away as much. But she wanted breakfast. A part of her was growing more resolute, and she needed to feed it. She needed sustenance. There was a tension snapping, vibrating amid them, as if the trio were tethered by rubber bands, and she suspected Beck and Tilda were readying themselves, too: there was going to be a showdown. They weren't going to casually walk to the middle of nowhere only to lie down and die.

In spite of the physical and psychic discomfort, the rhythm of their mule train was meditative. Sometimes when Imogen listened to music with an intense emotional buildup she felt it inside her, lifting her, magnifying her strength. That was how it was now—with the glorious scenery, hiking in a row, breathing in unison.

But Gale couldn't leave well enough alone.

"Wanna play a little game?"

"Like a word game?" Imogen asked. She and Beck used to play them as kids while dying of boredom in the car, or as adults before falling asleep while camping. They'd usually start with a few rounds of Twenty Questions, but their minds synced into telepathy so quickly that they'd soon find themselves guessing the secret person without having to ask a single question. Maybe they could use that now, if she could think of a movie hero or a book heroine with a good solution for a kidnapping. "We could try Twenty Questions—that's easy and fun."

"Nah. I'm trying to figure something out, and maybe y'all could help me."

"Okay?" Imogen was intrigued. They'd offered to brainstorm with him before, but he'd wanted to do everything his way. This could be progress.

"So," Gale said, a bit singsong, "if I were to let one a you go, or even two a you, who should it be?"

All three halted and spun to face him. He'd called it a game, but he looked perfectly serious.

"You'd do that?" Beck asked.

"Dunno. Maybe."

"Why not all of us?"

"Might need one, fer collateral."

Tilda and Imogen looked at each other, hope bursting to life on their faces.

Beck nodded, considering his question. Then she started firing off her own: "How would we explain it? If we're not supposed to say anything, but two—or one—of us don't make it back with the others?"

"I know, that's a problem. But I was trying…wanted to at least entertain a scenario, as they say, where I don't have all a you on my conscience." He flicked a glance at Imogen on *conscience*. "We almost there?"

"Probably another mile or so," said Beck. "Let's think about this."

Heads bowed, they continued walking, now with the accompaniment of a new sound: the clicking of cogs, spinning faster as they pondered his words. At least that was what Imogen heard. A *tick-tick*ing, but not from the counting down of a clock. A solution needed to tumble into place, the combination that would open the door.

Could one (or two) of them guarantee their safety if they conjured a good enough excuse for the missing member(s) of their party? Would one (or two) of them be willing to leave someone behind? Imogen wasn't sure she could do that. She could never walk away from her sister. But if necessity demanded, she might be able to walk away from Tilda.

Oh my God. She regretted the thought the instant it occurred to her. Was this a game, after all? Was Gale just trying to divide them? Then again, he already knew that her loyalty was to Beck—would he let the two of them leave, or want the two of them to stay? Or, if he was feeling especially cruel, he could divide them up. Imogen imagined volunteering to stay behind. So Beck and Tilda could get home and start their families. At least that thought somewhat redeemed her for the earlier one, though Beck and Tilda were probably evaluating their priorities too. Fucking Gale.

"I was thinking 'bout it on my own," he said a few minutes later, "who I'd keep, if I just kept one. I could keep the Mexi— Tilda—but my reasons... they're shitty reasons. Nice legs. But yer personality ain't so hot. Doc's got the most practical skills, but yer my least favorite, no offense. Or the little one, yer kind of a mix. Some skills and, I don't know, you might be okay company."

What a fucked-up contest they were vying to *not* win.

"So I thought maybe you girls could figure it out, by yer own terms."

"We're not going to do that," Beck asserted, marching a little faster.

"Why not?" said Tilda. "We don't all have to—" Instead of saying *die* she speared Gale with another hateful look.

"Because it's not going to happen," Beck said. "He's not going to do it, so don't get your hopes up."

"And we couldn't choose anyway," Imogen added. "We couldn't choose someone to leave behind." The ethical turmoil of it aside, she would never stop thinking that *together* they stood a chance; the numbers were still in their favor. Even with injuries, *three* could potentially overpower him—if he fumbled the gun, or lost his footing. The likelihood diminished if there were only two, and all but vanished if it became one-on-one.

"Speak for yourself," said Tilda.

"Excuse me?" Imogen's rancor flared.

"If you couldn't make the decision, I *could*."

Gale chuckled. "Knew that one wouldn't be shy about saving her own ass."

"*Some* of us have a lot to live for," Tilda growled.

"Wait a second…" Was Tilda really implying what Imogen thought she was? Could Tilda, even in such a terrible moment, weigh the value of their lives—and find them *unequal*? "Are you saying I don't have as much to—"

"Guys, stop it," Beck said. "This is the game. We're not playing."

"No, we *should* talk about it," Tilda insisted. "If we'd been able to talk more we would've entertained this exact possibility: what we would do if *one* person had the chance to get away. He's giving us the chance to talk about it openly, so we should."

"No, he's giving you the chance to sow bad feelings."

"Beck's right," said Imogen.

Tilda whirled around so fast that Imogen almost barreled into her. "You always think that! Even when you argue you still agree—you're always on each other's side! I'm alone out here. No one has my back!"

"That's not true," Imogen protested, even as a part of her acknowledged the sliver of truth.

"You can't just write me off, make me the sacrificial—"

"We're not!" Beck said, joining the fray (much to Gale's amusement).

"I have a lot of promising things happening in my life, and maybe it's not as goo-goo gaa-gaa special as Beck having a baby but I have a fuckuva lot to live for!"

Tilda's fury reverberated in the air. For a moment it was incomprehensible to Imogen that this quartet of people should be standing elbow to elbow in the middle of a desert. As they sweated under the Arizona sun, Imogen realized none of them had washed for days and they smelled skunkish and feral. While the trio cast silent, judging glances at each other, Gale looked only at Beck.

"Yer pregnant?" Behind his shock was a whisper of something else. Guilt? Regret?

"Her wife," said Tilda, and Imogen had the urge to snatch Gale's spear and stab her oldest friend. Because she discerned the spite that had driven Tilda to clarify: if Gale believed Beck was pregnant, he really might let her go.

"You can be a real cunt," Imogen said with quiet savagery.

"Whoa! Language, Jesus!" Gale gaped at Imogen. "Mighta underestimated *you* a little bit, didn't know you had that kinda fight in you."

It was the nicest thing anyone had ever said to her.

"Tilda, Imogen...I was serious," Beck said. "Don't fall for this. This is the opposite of helpful."

She resumed walking, clearly hoping they would fall into line. Silently fuming, Tilda and Imogen resumed trudging along behind her.

"Congrats on the baby," Gale said from his post at the rear. "Not exactly up on how that works, with two ladies, but...babies are full a promise."

Here was her chance, but Beck opted out of elaborating, or even replying. Imogen thought of Crystal, his daughter, and wondered if she'd given birth yet. What kind of person was Crystal—her father's daughter, or someone very different?

"I just meant...before." Though apprehensive, Tilda also sounded determined to make her point. "That if there's a chance—any chance—that some of us, or one of us, can make it home...don't you want that?"

"Of course," said Imogen. Remorse crept in. How often did she misconstrue Tilda's words and their significance? And what did it say about Imogen that it was so easy for her to think the worst?

"I thought that's what Gale...I thought one of us might get to go." With her vitality deflated, Tilda seemed sad and lost once again.

"It's pretty clear now that you girls can't be in charge a deciding that. But you get it now don'tcha? How when it comes to yer own life the rules change? How yer own life is more important than anything—or anyone—else? And y'all proved why girls can't be in charge a things 'cause they get too emotional and can't make—"

While Imogen wanted to stuff a sock in his mouth, it was Tilda who shut him up: out of nowhere, she started belting out a song.

"We're going down—don't call it a crash!
We're changing around, we're evolving fast!"

Imogen actually laughed—and Beck looked back, a misshapen grin on her battered face. It was from *Eighty-Seven Seconds*. Sometimes the songs popped into Imogen's head, but it still surprised her that both Beck and Tilda had such good recall. Surely Tilda's throat was as dry as her own, but she sang with real power.

"We've got minutes left—what are you gonna do?
We're evolving fast, I'm almost someone new!"

"You've got some chops," Gale said. But he didn't know the chorus was coming up; Beck and Imogen joined in, full throttle and out of tune—but the trio sang it together.

"Boom boom we are going down!
Boom boom here comes the ground!
Boom boom we are going high!
Boom boom now watch me fly!"

Only Tilda could hold the last note. For a song about an imminent plane crash, the melody was ridiculously upbeat and catchy—like an old-fashioned Broadway number where tap dancers emerged from the wings, swinging empty suitcases around.

"I love that stupid song," Imogen said, in a brighter mood than she'd been in in days. The singing made her head wobbly again, but for that moment she didn't care.

"Me too," said Beck.

"I actually sing it all the time," Tilda said, "every time I'm having a bad day. I'd considered recording it for the intro to my videos—there's no thinking more positive than turning a plane crash into a chance for personal growth! But I was afraid no one else would get it—it's a little cheesy."

Imogen laughed so hard she thought she might cry.

"I don't get you girls. At all. At each other's throats one minute, singing the next."

Maybe it was his grouchiness, maybe it was the infectious nature of laughter, but Beck and Tilda started laughing too. Imogen's face cramped and, sure enough, tears spilled down her cheeks.

"Emotionally unpredictable."

Everything Gale said made it worse. They were in hysterics. Just glancing at each other brought on a new volley.

Short of breath and light-headed, Imogen reached out to stabilize herself on Tilda's backpack. "I'm gonna pee my pants," she squeaked.

"Please don't," Gale said, getting sulky, left out of the joke. "Crazy fuckin' girls," he muttered.

You have no idea.

The trio had learned important things about collaboration during their high school theater days. No other deadline could compare with the vulnerability brought on by the curtain rising on a live show. Except for this. Now they were at their most vulnerable. Counting down their days with Gale. And despite the rocky dress rehearsal, the impending show's success was critical. Their very lives depended on it.

37

It was the easiest camping area Imogen had ever entered. No scrambling ascents or descents, they just walked right in and were greeted by a rushing creek. And an amazing view. They stood there for a moment and took it in; the world's beauty hadn't faded simply because they'd been dragged away from their ordinary lives. Out in the open as they were, the Canyon's distant monuments were on display—peaks and formations, layers of Kaibab and Toroweap limestone, Coconino sandstone, Hermit shale, the Redwall. All the vibrant colors of a divine palette.

"That's the North Rim," Beck said, pointing both her index fingers toward the other side of the Canyon. Imogen had always wanted to go to the less-visited, more remote North Rim; it was only open five months of the year. But *more remote* didn't hold the attraction it once had, and the words *maybe someday* didn't exist anymore. She found herself incapable of projecting herself into any sort of future.

"Time to eat, yeah?" Gale said, gazing around. "What's a

good spot? Look like all good spots here." He took a few more steps, found a relatively smooth area beside a cluster of small boulders, and unbuckled his backpack. He took it off and leaned it against a rock.

"Time to pee," said Tilda.

"Coffee." Beck made the word a prayer.

Gale untied Imogen and watched her take off her pack; she left it there, on the hip-high rock she'd chosen to ease the weight. He let her do the work of untying Tilda, slipping off her pack, retying her hands—"Front again I guess, 'cause we're gonna eat"—while he stood a few feet away, leaning on his spear. Imogen wondered—maybe stupidly, and always aware of the heavy weight in his hip pocket—if a handgun was anything like a bottle of champagne: Did it suffer any consequences from bouncing around all day? Would it explode if rattled too hard?

She went through the untying, retying process again with Beck, and then Gale summoned Imogen over so he could redo her hands. Keeping hostages tied up required a methodology and patience that she wouldn't have had, though she supposed that if she were the kidnapper she'd just have to bark orders and look malignant. Being a hostage was tedious in a way she'd never considered.

"Grab some TP," he said. "You girls definitely have a disadvantage in the peeing department."

Imogen went first, slipping behind a boulder—a little close to camp for a latrine, in her opinion—as Gale kept his spear pointed at the two who weren't doing their business. It was easier to relieve herself with the rock standing guard instead of Gale. But she had to give him some credit: he wasn't lewd.

When she returned, Beck was doing a little dance, kicking

one boot and then the other, like she could barely hold it, and Gale let her go next. Once they were in a row again, he had them turn their backs to him. A zipper unzipped. Followed by the hiss of piss, the splashing of it on the ground.

Tedious.

He directed them onward to the creek, where they scrubbed their hands, washed their faces. Imogen was tempted to cup the water, so cool and refreshing, directly into her mouth, but didn't in case it wasn't as pristine as it looked. Slate's creek, similar to Boucher's, was several feet across and only inches deep, but in places the arrangement of rocks created little pools. As they squatted there, Beck kept glancing at Imogen, a steely, determined look in her eye. Imogen wasn't positive what she was trying to say. Get ready? On her other side, Tilda had withdrawn again, her focus a dreamy stare at the gurgling water.

Imogen, Beck, and Tilda sat cross-legged on the ground, a foot apart, as Gale bustled around. He could've made Imogen do this part too, but beyond the distrust issue, she suspected he liked fiddling with the gear. He set up both stoves; the dead man's was different from Beck's and he took a few minutes to figure out its workings. When he had both ablaze, he lowered two pots of water on to boil. Mesmerized by the little blue flames, he leaned against a rock and stretched out his legs.

"Reminds me a cookouts. Used to do that in the summer, Fourth a July 'n' such, when I was home. Always liked that. Everyone sitting around, shooting the breeze. Kicking back with a cold beer, burgers or ribs. Back in Mississippi when I was a kid we put whatever we'd caught in the river on the grill. It was real special when the kids were little. Didn't see

Crystal as much, but my boys…loved to run around outside. A hot day and a hose and they were happy. Or on the Fourth, some sparklers, cherry bombs. Kids love that."

Earlier Tilda had implied that Imogen didn't have as much to live for, but perhaps she'd been trying to say that she didn't have as many *people*. Beck had Afiya (and fingers crossed a baby). Tilda had Jalal. Imogen had struggled throughout her adulthood to even make new friends. *Unless Gale counts.* Strike that—another of those out-of-nowhere intrusions. But Imogen was less insulted thinking about it now, because she knew the value of her life didn't depend on how many people attended her funeral. And they needed to take advantage of these opportunities to discuss loved ones. Gale had a strong sentimental streak.

"It sounds like…you had some really good times," she said. "With your family."

"Yup. In between fucking it up. I was in and outta prison before I did this seven-year stretch, and even when I was out I came and went. Regret that now. Shoulda stuck around more, *tried* harder. When I was younger, kept thinking I was gonna find that right *thing,* ya know? The right job or the right opportunity. And most a my…" He sighed. Went silent for a moment as he cut open bags of freeze-dried dinners and set out cups and bowls. It was still morning, but apparently he wanted something heartier than skimpy oatmeal packets.

"I went looking in the wrong places, let's put it that way. Kinda dumb like that, I shoulda learned. You wanna trust yer buddies, yer kin, when someone says they heard about some great way to make some easy cash. Know now, ain't no easy cash—not without consequences. And whatever yer thinking, my priority—in between being a drunk asshole—was wanting my kids to have better. Dreamed of them growing up and getting good jobs, respectable. Crystal did all right. Ain't met her husband but he sounds okay, works hard. Everyone want coffee?"

"Not me, thanks," said Imogen while Beck and Tilda nodded. "How old are your boys?"

Gale spooned the dead man's instant coffee into three mugs. Imogen guessed he probably had no clue what to do with Beck's Melitta cone; normal people brought instant. "In body, seventeen and fourteen. In the head, young dumb brats. A little slow, maybe got it from me."

"You're anything but dumb, Gale." And Imogen meant it.

"Book dumb."

"Books aren't everything, and I say that as a writer of books. You're smart."

"Well, Crystal's mom was smart to get away from me when she did. Saw I wasn't gonna change and got the hell out. Made sure she gave Crystal the life she deserved—but never shut me outta my daughter's life. Always love her a little fer that. My boys…" He shook his head and scowled. "They're a disappointment. I can't blame 'em 'cause it's my fault, taught them the wrong things even when I didn't mean to. And their momma ain't any better. Those boys are angry. Oldest one's locked up. In and out of juvie since he was thirteen. He's mean and hard and thinks with his fists. Probly gonna get himself killed. I worry on that. Worry on it a lot. Still have a tiny bit a hope for Henry. He's got a soft side. Maybe he'll straighten out in time."

The water came to a boil. Gale filled the three mugs. As Imogen watched the steam swirl toward his face, an image came to her of Tilda and Beck, splashing their coffee into his eyes. He turned his back to rummage around for a spoon and she snapped her head toward Beck, then Tilda, and made a little gesture with her bound hands, pantomiming flicking a mug. Beck's eyes widened, and Tilda nodded—though she looked less keen to scald him than she had…when was it? Two days ago? It felt like they'd been with him for a month.

As if it were the most compelling thing they'd ever seen, they watched him stir the three coffees. Imogen was ready to do her part: spring up and grab the spear as he screamed, clutching his scorched face. But when Gale was done stirring, he held out a single cup—for Imogen to take. "You serve."

She faltered, caught off guard. He wasn't going to hand Tilda and Beck their steaming mugs. And once Imogen handed off the cups, Tilda and Beck weren't close enough to do any real damage. They would jump up to help her, but if anyone was going to douse him with boiling coffee it would have to be Imogen—one mug, that would be her only chance to blind him and seize the spear. Seconds were passing like hours, she was taking too long; she should've already done it—

Accepted the mug without hesitation, tossed it in his face—

"Hot coffee's a weapon in some places," he said, reading her like a book. "Yer sister's gonna be real sad if ya don't deliver her coffee."

The half-amused smirk on his face said everything: he knew what she'd been debating, and knew she'd failed to act. Ashamed, Imogen got up and handed out the mugs. Tilda, again, wouldn't look at her. Imogen could almost see her teenage self through Tilda's eyes, lying there inert beneath her boyfriend. Deciding later that she needed a good story so Tilda wouldn't kill her. *That's not what happened.* But it was believable. Imogen mouthed "sorry" to Beck, who mumbled her thanks and started blowing on the steaming liquid.

As Imogen was about to sit back down she tottered

off-balance, spilling over onto her elbow when her tied hands couldn't break her fall. The world was spinning again. She hitched her shoulder up to her ear so she could rub it, as if that would help.

"Good thing you ain't a coffee drinker," Gale said with a laugh. He kept his distance, manning the stoves, coffee in one hand, spear in the other. "Boiling water hurts like a bitch, know so a bit too well. Also know none a you ever stop thinking a ways to take me out." His gaze traveled from one of them to the next. "Weird how my whole life brought me here. Brought you, too."

At least he wasn't angry. If anything, he seemed contemplative, calmer than he'd been since their reckless first meeting; perhaps Slate was finally remote enough to ease his paranoia.

Imogen couldn't rewrite history, but in hindsight most of their attempted efforts at self-preservation were asinine, starting with that march to the rock shelter to reclaim the iodine tablets. Would it have been so bad if they'd just hightailed it back home? No one ever died from disappointment. And what was the worst that could've happened from drinking untreated water? Diarrhea? A regimen of antibiotics? A brain-eating parasite might've been better than this.

Beck would never have organized this trip if she'd had another way to force Imogen and Tilda to autopsy their relationship. *They're here because of me.* It wasn't the most linear thought, but Imogen felt the burden of how her floundering reactions—decades' worth—had led them to converge here, now, just as Gale had said. They'd fumbled their opportunities to leave, and she wondered if that meant something too—if there was something she was supposed to do here, unfinished business that only she could rectify.

38

Imogen could have gone for some hot chocolate, or just a cup of water, but she didn't want to ask and draw the wrong kind of attention to herself. Instead, there was something she wanted to focus on while Gale was in a reflective mood. Maybe this could become the "campfire" chat they'd discussed that morning.

"Can I just say, while you all sip your coffee…" Beck, Tilda, and Gale gave her their attention, but she spoke to Gale. "We're more similar than we are dissimilar."

Tilda squinted, dubious. Beck slurped, looking at Gale over the rim of her mug, studying his reaction. Gale gave Imogen a pointed but jocular glare. It was hard to maintain eye contact with him, but she forced herself to stay connected.

"That so?" He oozed doubt.

"Yes."

"You see yerself in me? 'Cause I don't see myself in you."

That threw her off for a second, but she didn't let it undermine her mission. He was right that their superficial similarities were minimal. "It's something deeper, inside—not about where we were born, or the specifics of how we grew up and what we became. It's more like...we've reached a place where we know we want something different than what we have. But at some point you have to make peace with what you *can* do versus what you *wish* you could do. That's how you stop feeling cheated by what you thought your life *would* be, versus the life you actually end up living. And it's *hard,* life is hard, even for the people who make it look easy." She tried not to look at her sister, but her eyes drifted to her anyway.

"Everybody feels...maybe they're disappointed, for a time. But the thing that's harder to accept, to get over...is feeling like no one really gets you. Like there's some fundamental part of you that isn't understood." This time she looked at Tilda. "And that's what makes people feel lonely, makes them doubt everything else, even if your life looks great from the outside."

She hoped he grasped even a tiny bit of what she was trying to say; it was a difficult thing to express, and she didn't think she'd said it well.

Gale was still in a joking mood. "And everybody laughs in the same language blah blah blah and enjoys a good shit and a good fuck. That yer point?"

It kind of was, but she felt him deflecting. Maybe she'd approached it all wrong, too vaguely, or maybe no one had ever tried to have an intimate conversation with him. "It's not bullshit."

"So you know me—*that* yer point?"

"Not very well. But maybe we have more in common than you think, in spite of how different our lives are. And from what I've seen...you're an interesting person."

Gale snorted. He spooned out hearty portions into their three bowls and the dead man's plate, which he seemed to prefer. He'd made too much again, even more than last time, and it was obvious he didn't care about rationing. Did that portend they'd *all* leave the Canyon at some point, or that none of them would? Imogen remembered the two of them refilling the canteens at Boucher Creek. He'd talked about poison. A nice big meal. *A last meal.* A peaceful drop into a never-ending sleep.

Had the dead man possessed something that Gale could have slipped into their food?

"She's a book writer?" he asked Beck, who nodded in confirmation. He turned back to Imogen. "That's nice a you wanting to think well a me, but doll, you ain't living in the real world."

The jab hurt. She'd always considered her imagination an asset as an author, while fearing that her lack of life experience would eventually show. She didn't think it was wrong to analyze things deeply, or find commonalities between diverse or disparate individuals. And it wasn't as if she'd never visited the real world; it intruded on her fantasy life more than she preferred.

"I know everything about the real world." She spoke with such solemnity that they all looked at her, as if not quite sure who she was.

"Serve 'em up!" Gale held out the bowls and Imogen distributed them.

She sat back down carefully, afraid of another dizzy spell; hungry, she didn't want to spill her food. Before she started to eat, she studied Gale, still concerned that he might have added something to the dinner pouches. Should she warn Beck and Tilda? But even if the dead man had been carrying medications—prescription or otherwise—they hadn't seen Gale grind up any pills. The only other toxic things Imogen could think of were the fuel and fire-starter, and surely they would add a noxious flavor to everything. Gale ate with casual gusto, and Tilda and Beck, though watchful for other reasons, ate without wavering. And without grimacing at a bad taste.

"It's real beautiful out here." Gale chewed and looked around. "It's funny, all that hard work to get down that damn trail, but here it's easier and nobody comes."

"Too inaccessible for most people," said Beck. "And for a lot of people…the Canyon trails are really exposed, a lot of cliff edges. Like you said, it's too hard for casual hikers or tourists."

He nodded, his focus lingering on the astonishing horizon. The painted stripes of endless rock. Perhaps the formations had been sharp and jagged in their infancy, but age had blurred them, creating stone phantoms that rippled with the light. "Glad I got to see this."

"Beauty. Should add that to your list," Imogen said. He scrunched half his face into a question. "With shitting and fucking—your words. Everybody appreciates beauty. Sometimes we find it in different places. Sometimes not."

He aimed his fork at her. "Know what yer doing. Getting all psychological. But I already see what I see and know what I know."

"I know you aren't heartless, Gale." She didn't want to give up—couldn't give up.

"Selfish, though." He shrugged, looked away again. "Selfish as fuck. You'd understand everything better if you remembered that."

It sounded part warning, part apology.

Beck stopped chewing. Damn, her sister cogitated loudly,

even when words weren't spoken; she'd heard only the warning, and reached an instantaneous conclusion. Imogen scrutinized Gale, which was easier to do with his attention focused on the landscape. Tilda, absorbed in her meal, wasn't really paying attention, or parsing words like the Blum sisters. It took Imogen a moment to dig down to the bottom layer of what he really meant.

Selfish as fuck. You'd understand everything better if you remembered that.

Her sister cut to his truth like a surgeon. Imogen had to stop looking for the soft parts, the distracting things that made her see him as a fellow human. She tried harder to put herself in his shoes. What would she do if she was selfish as fuck? She certainly wouldn't waste an ounce of compassion—or anything else—on someone like Gale. He would be as meaningless, his life as worthless, as... She looked at her spoon. Her bowl. And wondered for the first time if he even differentiated living things from the inanimate. Did any of it matter, to someone who was selfish as fuck? A living backpacker or a dead one, they were just stuff. Stuff he needed, stuff he wanted. His personal doctor and little assistant. The curvy girl he liked to ogle.

And then she knew. She saw the sparklers and heard the cherry bombs. She felt the juices dripping down her fingers as she gnawed the rib bones, hot off the grill. She saw, through his eyes, his family, his people, his children. And she knew: no one else mattered.

Beck didn't matter. Tilda didn't matter. She didn't matter.

Had never mattered.

Were never going to matter.

Selfish.

Everything he did was to serve his own needs.

Selfish.

They would never sway him from his course. He didn't care about promises. He didn't care if Beck's child was short one mother—he might say it was a shame, but it wouldn't impact his decisions.

Selfish.

Now she heard it everywhere. In the whistling sound the wind made. In the beating of a raven's wing. In the rustling grasses that lined the creek. The creek itself all but screamed it, a cascade of warnings to listen, *listen, listen.* How had she not heard it before?

She'd been a fool, a dreamer, to believe reason and compassion would turn him around. She'd been duped by his apparent complexity. Or had it only been her desire to see him that way? Her wishful delusions had so preoccupied her that she hadn't seen Gale for what he was: a man so enamored of his own privilege that no one else, ultimately, mattered.

Every moment of his life was more important than anyone else's.

Everything he desired superseded even her—or Beck's, or Tilda's—right to live.

Beck had advised them the previous night to be ready, to *think about what you don't want to lose.* But even then Imogen hadn't heard the subtext: *Be selfish.* Finally Imogen realized that she couldn't save anyone else until she was selfishly, irrevocably committed to saving herself. It was fine to believe she had a purpose for being here—here, now, with Gale. And equally fine to have empathy for his heroic worldview. But it would come to nothing—she would accomplish nothing—until she viewed her journey the way he viewed his, as the *only* thing that mattered.

I wasn't all in before. Gale had seen that—that was the real reason he'd made her his dutiful servant.

She'd wanted to believe in a goodness in him that wasn't there. Anne Frank had done that, but believing that *people are really good at heart* hadn't kept her from dying at Bergen-Belsen. Imogen often thought of young Anne, and the tragic irony that her physical life had expired but the fragile pages she'd written in pencil lived on. How had Imogen been willing, for so long, to accept the microscopic degrees of Gale's humanity? *Stupid fucking cow.* Things had gone so far because she was weak.

Gale wasn't wrong when he said she didn't live in the real world. Even her most recent book was about a woman raped by a ghost, not an actual man. But she was right too: she knew more than she cared to about the real world. He would never shed his demon layer, but Imogen could still slough off the useless parts of herself.

Feral with energy, she gobbled up the rest of her meal.

39

Gale remained composed and relaxed through breakfast. Old Imogen would have seen it as a sign that he was changing, becoming more introspective as he neared his moment of enlightenment. New Imogen didn't give a shit.

She studied him: scrawny, in spite of the big meals he'd been eating; skin patchy with the discoloration of sunburn, scars, jailhouse tattoos. The dirty bandage was still on his arm where Beck had sewn him up. He was strong, but fallible, and not immune to pain. Eyes, throat. Those were always good places to jab a man. Balls, of course. You could kill someone with the heel of your hand, rammed upward to force the nose bone into the brain. But it looked like someone had already tried that on Gale, and failed.

Once there'd been a seventeen-year-old Imogen who kept still, waiting for it to end, afraid to lash out, to make it worse. And once there'd been an Imogen who hid behind a bush at the synagogue, because she was no match for a weapon of war. Now, here, the thing she'd repressed for so long was ready to emerge. One way or another there would be an endgame, a fight to the death. And this time she would not be still, she would not hide.

Gale yawned. Stretched. "Wanna bring me the dishes? In prison we'd kill for those spoons, make fine shivs."

Imogen stacked their bowls and carried them over. Could she shove a spoon, even unsharpened, up his nostril? The spear lay across his lap and she'd have to bend over it to reach his face. *Hmm, not yet.* The picture of obedience, she set the dishes down beside him and returned to her spot.

It would have been easy enough for Gale to pour the leftover boiled water onto the dirty dishes. The stoves were off, the meal done, but he didn't bother washing anything.

Was this their last meal?

Her heart rumbled, a roll of thunder that smashed away the tranquil sounds of creek and wind. Fuck him. They couldn't all die here. Gale didn't get to play God, wipe away their lives because he'd fucked up one time too many. If he was resigned to his fate, so be it. She couldn't fault him for not wanting to be executed. She *could* fault him for thinking a few hours of his life were worth more than the collective decades Beck, Tilda, and Imogen had coming to them.

Selfish.

For a minute his placid gaze wandered over each of them in turn. They sat as still as the rocks, hyperaware: it was coming.

"D'you think I'm going to hell?" He scratched at his unshaven face.

No one responded right away, but Imogen was pretty sure it wasn't a rhetorical question. She was also pretty sure that Beck and Tilda didn't believe in the literal realms of heaven and hell—though they might be rethinking that since meeting Gale, a creature from the underworld.

"In Judaism—" Imogen stopped short. Though he'd been quick to label them, Gale didn't seem to hold repugnant beliefs about their differences. But now she feared the limits of his tolerance; the world was becoming more anti-Semitic by the day. He appeared to be waiting for her to continue, so she did. "In Judaism, it's about what you do with *this* life, the one you're living. This is the only life that counts."

His fingers turned a pebble over and over and he gazed at it and nodded. "You Jewish then?"

"Yes."

"Figures. You too?" he asked Beck.

"Only in the most superficial way."

"Still. What happens when you cross paths with a Mexican, a lesbian, and a Jew—sounds like the start of a joke."

"It's the reality of living in a world full of people," Tilda said, with a hearty dose of snark. "Can't all be white men pretending to be Christian."

"S'pose. Can't help but think it's some karmic justice."

"You believe in that?" Beck said.

"Maybe. More 'n' more." He flipped his pebble around and around and they waited. "So here's the thing…" And they waited some more. "I accept—I know what I done was wrong. Know I can't undo it. Can probly only keep making it worse. So I've been thinking. And I've about made up my mind." He looked at them. The three captives exchanged glances, on edge, both ready and not ready to hear the pronouncement of their fate. "I'll let you *all* go—letcha go tell the world. It'll take ya what? Two days to hike out?"

"Yes," Beck immediately replied.

Imogen's eyes widened, shocked by the direction the conversation had taken.

Gale went on, "So you do that, take yer two days. Tell whatever ya want to whoever—I won't grudge you that. I'll keep going, probly off trail—this place, if I wanted to hunker down and disappear…they ain't gonna poke around in every nook and cranny. Even if you tell them where ya last saw me, I'll be long gone, you understand? I can live out my time here. Maybe it's a week, maybe it's a month, a year…I'm thinking now this was meant to be the plan all along—I started down this path, no way I was gonna stay outta prison fer good. God's telling me 'You fucked this to hell, here's yer minute a heaven. Enjoy it.'"

Just when Imogen had abandoned all hope for his enlightenment.

"Okay." There was a question in Beck's voice, a *What's the catch?* It was too soon to celebrate, the captives all knew there was a catch. Imogen fought the urge to jump up and kick him in the teeth—before Gale could wreck their hope. Again.

"Yeah, so…What I want in return…Some men want a last meal, but I don't care if I starve. It's a better way to go than the needle. I want…I feel awkward 'bout asking, but yer all there is."

He hesitated. The silence stretched. And Imogen knew—the thing he wanted and couldn't voice. The thing all men wanted when language failed them. She almost laughed. After all his shameless behavior, he got sheepish about asking for *this*? What untrustworthy devil had designed men with insatiable urges and no easy way to satisfy them? But then again, at least he was asking, not taking. It showed a remarkable amount of restraint and civility—or so the old Imogen would've thought.

300

The new Imogen started the process of armoring herself, a steel plate for each precious organ, a muzzle for the soft voice of her conscience. This was why fate had brought them together. Her moment was almost here.

"You know before," Gale said, finding his words. "I said my first choice was Tilda. Most attracted to you." He looked at Beck next. "I guess yer pretty much outta the question, swinging the wrong way 'n' such. But, you know, I want you all to have a say—contrary to things I've been accused of I ain't a rapist. And I'm guessing none a you really *want* to, but then there's are you *willing* to fer the sake of our agreement and then I'll letcha all go after—"

"Wait. You want one of us to have *sex* with you?" Tilda's expression mingled astonishment with revulsion. Imogen's only shock now was that it had taken her friend so long to grasp the situation.

"As an arrangement, I think that's pretty fair," he said.

Imogen stood up. "I'll do it."

She wasn't sure which was the chicken and which the egg when it came to redemption and revenge. But whatever he really intended, only she had the real-world experience to summon the necessary rage.

Beck's and Tilda's jaws dropped. But Gale only sighed in relief. "Good. Was hoping one a you would see the value of what I was offering, even if I ain't yer type. But that's the one thing I want before I say goodbye to everything and walk away. I'm a lover at heart. My whole life has been stops and starts and that's the most selfish thing I regret when I fuck up again, 'cause I was never a bitch fer anyone. I waited, and when I got out I got my ladies fair and square and never raped *no* one. And you girls, well, you might not believe in this sorta thing, but I really think, karma and God and all, that this was meant to happen."

"God brought us all here so you could have one of us? As your last wish on earth?" Tilda was full-on disgust now.

But Imogen agreed with him: this was meant to happen. God had brought them together, and she wasn't going to waste this gift. This time, she was going into it with her eyes wide open—not caught by surprise.

"Figures it's you," Gale said to her, ignoring Tilda. He got up, slapping the dirt from his hands, ready.

"Imogen don't, you don't have to." Beck held herself in a tight ball.

"Imogen." Tilda staggered to her feet. She went to Imogen, faced her, gazed in her eyes. Quietly but firmly she said, "I'll do it."

"No."

"I'm sorry. It emphatically wasn't your fault." Tilda spoke the identical words Imogen had expressed to her. "I believe you, believed you, it was never about *you*. I owe you. Let me do—"

"No." Imogen gripped Tilda's fingers, hoping her friend would feel how strong she was, how prepared. The apology meant a lot, and the offer meant everything, but this was Imogen's journey.

"Girls fighting over me, this is better than I coulda hoped!" Gale cackled.

Tilda and Imogen reeled, nuking him with hard blasts of hatred, and he had the common sense to swallow his mirth. Imogen turned back to Tilda, starting to panic with the crush of time: she couldn't explain—didn't want to explain—

Gale's spear appeared between them, forcing them to take a step back. "Don't need to talk so close."

"Tilda. Thank you. Thank you. I love you."

"I love you, too."

"I'm going to do this." They were more than a foot apart, but Imogen only now released Tilda's fingers. "And then we're all going home."

A tear trailed down Tilda's cheek. She nodded. Imogen didn't want to see her sister's face and whatever anguish it held. She stepped closer to Gale as Tilda lowered her head and sank to the ground.

40

I have two conditions."

Gale looked down his nose at her, a touch amused. He didn't see that she wasn't *the soft one* anymore. "And what's that?"

"I'm not into S&M and bondage and whatever. So I'm not going to be tied up like a..." She held up her fettered wrists. "And I'm not going to do it with the threat of a gun at my head. So unless you toss that gun and untie me, this will be rape. Either I do this freely—as a free person—or you make yourself a rapist. That's on you."

It felt good to make demands of him—though it was a gamble and he could refuse. For the first time Imogen was electric with confidence: her empathy might've been misplaced, but she understood him, his pride, his inane self-serving logic. She'd crawled into his head and sat there now on a pillow of brains, gazing out the windows of his eyes. He took a moment to ponder.

"You got an interesting way a thinking. You girls, man... Gladder than you know that we could work this out, 'cause yer all okay. I can't just...get rid a this." He took out the pistol, admired how it fit in his hand. "Might need to hunt something. But what if I stash it somewhere?"

"That's fair."

"Turn yer backs."

Imogen turned around. Beck glanced up at her, looking a little relieved, a tiny bit reassured. She didn't know all the things Imogen had been thinking, and Imogen wasn't entirely sure what her plan was, but they both recognized that the whole thing would go better with the full use of her hands, and without the gun's facile threat. Gale moved around twenty or thirty feet behind them. She heard the clatter of shifting rocks. And then he moved again, and more rocks clanged together. She wanted to bark at him to hurry up—prod him with his own spear.

Finally he came back. "Okay. Now these two. If we're gonna...go off on our own, don't want these two getting up to anything." He pulled the extra lengths of rope from his pocket and bundled them around his fist, eager. "So we'll tie the two a you up while we...That agreeable?"

It was so juvenile that he couldn't say it—yet another thing he didn't have a name for. He wasn't capable of calling it what it actually was: only a rapist would consider this arrangement consent.

He surveyed his options. "Any trees around here?"

Slate was flat and open, with greenery along the shallow creek, but nothing larger than a shrub. Imogen knew her sister might be thinking that she'd lost her mind. They locked eyes; she wanted Beck to see her toughness, her mettle. Whatever was about to happen, Imogen was going to be okay—*they* were going to be okay. Beck had her hard face on, the steely look she wore when she was determined. With its bruises and lumps, it was almost a scary face and Imogen imagined her going berserk as soon as Gale slipped from sight, turning into the Incredible Hulk and bursting out of her restraints.

"You can change your mind," Beck said to her in a wounded voice. Imogen shook her head. Beck sighed, and gestured with her chin. "A few hundred feet."

"So we all agree?" Gale asked.

No one said anything. Agreeing and accepting weren't the same thing. Leaving the packs and gear behind—except for the spear and Beck's mattress pad—they headed upstream, consumed by their own thoughts. Imogen couldn't risk making further eye contact with Tilda or Beck, lest they telegraph something—pity or fear—that might sabotage her courage. She was actually glad when the little grove of trees, sun-beaten and wizened, came into view: her valor might not last. It was best to proceed before it slipped beneath the water, like a sentence, an idea, that never made it to the page. Every second was making her decision more real.

"You sit against that tree, you against that one." He pointed his commands and Beck and Tilda did as they were told. "Wait. I think yer hands should be behind you—or maybe wrapped around the trunk?"

Beck rotated her upper arm so he could see the bloodstain on her makeshift bandage. "Rather not tear that open. If you latch on to our wrists and then around the tree, we'll be sufficiently held in place, don't you think?"

In Beck's attempt to lay on the guilt, Imogen wondered if she had a motive beyond discomfort. It was easier to do many things with their hands bound in front. Gale had to know that, and had to be thinking, as she was, that Tilda and Beck would try to wriggle free as soon as they left.

"Want me to tie them up?" Imogen asked Gale.

"If ya do it good and tight."

After Gale freed her she gave each of her wrists a hard rub and shook out her hands to get the blood flowing. He hovered over her, directing her on how the cord should be knotted around Beck's existing bindings, and then wrapped multiple times around her waist and the narrow trunk before finally tying it off at the back. Tilda wouldn't look at her as Imogen tied her up, but this time Imogen thought it was because of shame, not annoyance. Once again, Gale periodically yanked on the knots to make sure they were tight enough.

There was a weird moment after she was done. Beck and Tilda, their hands imprisoned on their laps, their legs stretched out, were so firmly attached to their scraggly trees that Imogen thought only one of Gale's knives could get them undone. Both wore expectant, nervous expressions. Was Imogen really going to go through with it?

Was she?

She didn't intend to go *completely* through with it—she'd fight as hard as she could—but what if she couldn't find a way to overpower him?

"So..." That was the only goodbye she could come up with.

"Go far enough away so we can't hear you, okay?" Beck said to Gale.

"What, yer sister a screamer?" he replied with an uncomfortable laugh.

"Just, please...That would make for a really...Not the memory I want."

"Well you two look comfy enough. And we probly won't be long." Something about the way he tucked Beck's accordioned eggshell mattress pad under his arm made Imogen fight a wave of nausea. She covered her mouth, close to gagging. His jaunty gesture, as if they were going off for a romantic tryst, made her head throb. Would she have to lie down on that? She blinked, trying to clear her vision—she absolutely could not afford to be wobbly, physically or mentally.

He held the spear like a walking stick and looked at her. "Ready?"

Should she have asked him to leave all his weapons behind? He wouldn't have agreed; he might have denied *all* her demands. The knife had already killed at least twice. It felt like a third person was coming with them and Imogen hadn't agreed to the ménage à trois.

Beck gave her the steeliest gaze, as if trying to infuse her with a reserve of her own strength. "See you soon." Imogen heard *You can do this.*

Imogen's mouth was too dry to reply. There were no words left. She turned and followed Gale into the void.

41

Gale let her take the lead, though he gave her verbal commands—"Straight," "A little left," "Let's go up past this rock." Imogen scanned everything, clueless as to where they were going or what she was looking for. Unable to even grab a rock for protection, she loped along, hoping she appeared casual, compliant.

"So...you actually like me? A little?"

The question so startled her that she wheeled to look at him. She recalled his struggles in life, his love for his daughter. "Um...I don't think you're *all* bad."

He chortled. "I thought this might be like—what do they call it? Stockholm syndrome? That really happens, I guess. I think some people like to be told what to do, have their choice taken away."

"Do *you* like that?" she asked him, confused by his interpretation.

"No!" He chuckled again. "Though there're times when it makes things simpler. Prison rules is easier to follow than life rules. But some people really want—wish they could just have someone in charge, know who's boss. Follow the top dog, all that."

"I don't know anyone like that." She wished he'd shut up. Although, now that he'd brought it up, she realized that she, Beck, and Tilda were all basically their own boss.

"Well, whatever. I hope ya weren't offended, that I didn't pick you first." With her back safely to him, Imogen rolled her eyes. "With yer friend, it's just, ya know, the physical. But yer nicer, and petite. And kinda cute, even with that unnatural-color hair. Reminds me of a toy."

Oh the urges she fought—to scream, to puke, to lunge at him. She hadn't ruled out the possibility of trying to strangle him with her bare hands, but it wasn't her best option. She took deep, even breaths, afraid she would do something rash. To the degree that she could, she needed to let it play out. And hope he stripped off his clothes. He'd be at his most vulnerable then. And if she survived this, she swore to never have pastel-colored hair again.

Thankfully, they continued on in silence. She wondered what Beck and Tilda were doing. At the very least they'd be talking—and they might be able to concoct some sort of strategy, right? And if they got themselves untied (*how?*) they could go back and find the gun. *Yeah right.*

They were the wrong things to be thinking about. Imogen couldn't entertain even the flicker of hope that they would somehow come to her rescue. She'd already been disappointed once that day, upon returning from the creek with Gale. No, she had to be *all in*. They weren't here and she was. They weren't here and Gale was.

Gale came up beside her and stopped. Surveyed the terrain.

She'd spaced out for a few minutes, walking on autopilot. How far had they gone—a third of a mile? more? They'd come to a flattish area, partially enclosed by boulders. It gave the impression of a half wall, like an office cubicle that only pretended to provide privacy. The rest of the Canyon seemed to gaze down at them. A lizard scurried under a dead-looking bush. Maybe it thought it was hiding, but Imogen could still see it.

Gale laid out the mattress pad. "Think this will do. Good spot, yeah? Little bit a heaven?"

Imogen had no clue what to do next. Frozen in place, she felt her pulse pounding in her ears. Gale sat on the eggshell pad and laid the spear beside him.

He pulled his shirt off.

—groped under her dress, squashing her into the corner of the couch—

She remained standing, but the world started to spiral. *No no no.* Everything inside her disobeyed her preparations. The armor loosened and threatened to slip off. Her damaged ear trilled a siren and the ground began to buckle.

—he tugged at her panties and she tried to kick—

What if she couldn't do it? What if, instead of fighting, she just lay down and let the bile rise in her throat. He'd promised to release them. Faster and faster, everything spun. Maybe she'd pass out. Then she'd have no memory and he could do what he wanted to her and then let them all go.

"You gonna sit?"

—she couldn't push him off—

Before she could overthink it, she dropped down beside Gale. He stank. It was more than unwashed pits and unbrushed teeth; something inside him was rotting. His chest sprouted sparse, wiry red hairs and his ribs were countable slats of bone.

He started to untie his boots. The spear was on his right side—
the *other* side. *Fuck.* She shouldn't have sat down; she couldn't
reach across him.

"The sun feels real good. Should take yer shirt off."

She bolted up. Took a few steps away and turned her back to
him. He was watching, she could feel it. She'd gotten skittish
and maybe he was getting wary.

Eyes wide open. Not caught by surprise. The armor slammed
back into place. She throat-punched the little voice of doubt.
This was her moment, years in the making. She whipped off
her shirt, threw it on the ground beside her. Her sports bra,
in patterned turquoise and reassuringly tight, gave her the
illusion of protection: she wasn't naked.

"Don't the sun feel good?"

*—promised herself to never drink again, never go to a party
again—*

"Yeah." It did. On her shoulders. On her upper back. A
warm caress. Fresh out of rational thoughts, she felt the sun's
fingers. The sun was a goddess, there to protect her, help her.
She looked skyward, shut her eyes, soaked in the rays. Let
herself get drunk on the goddess's fiery power.

"Don't be shy. Promise I won't bite."

She glanced back. One boot off, he yanked at the other.
The pants would come next. It was almost time. She came
closer, until she stood right in front of him, and bent over to
unlace her own boot. He wasn't in a hurry. It was so easy for
him, to live with his decisions. His wants. His effortless (*selfish*)
justifications.

"S'pose I should thank you. By doing this…maybe yer not
just saving yer friends, but saving some part a my soul. See, I
been thinking about whatcha said, 'bout my conscience."

So maybe he meant it. About letting them go.

Didn't matter. She had her own shit to resolve.

She didn't know what to say, but her dry mouth wasn't co-operating anyway. Out of habit, and to slow things down, she coiled the laces of her boot and stuffed them inside. She debated whether to leave her sock on or off. The warm earth would feel nice against the sole of her foot, but the sock provided at least a little padding, in case she needed to run.

As she was about to tug on her other shoelace, Gale stood. Unfastened his pants. Lowered them. When they reached his knees...

The sun made her as light as air. Gave her wings.

The lizard darted off onto a tumble of rocks. That was the only movement she consciously registered—not her own, pouncing. Seizing the spear. Gale bolting upright.

Her reptilian brain took over, did what it had to do. Gale stepped forward, reaching for...

She thrust the knife end into his flesh.

They both froze.

In her peripheral vision the lizard got away.

—*"Catch ya later." He let himself out, like it was nothing*—

Gale gazed at the blade in his belly, the blood dripping down to the waistband of his stolen boxer shorts.

They looked at each other, mirroring surprise. Imogen, aware of her hands on the spear, the spear in his gut, wrenched backward. Gale gasped, weaving his fingers over the gash. More blood rushed out. Still, they both reacted as if in a trance.

"Didn't think you had it in ya. Glad I could teach ya a little something."

Slowly, from pain or caution, Gale bent over and hoisted up his pants. Fastened them.

"If that's how it's gonna be...least I can die with my pants on."

A bolt coursed through Imogen's body, making her fingers sizzle. Everything came into sharp focus. They were here. This was happening.

He stood as stoically as he could, his hands cupped against his wound. Imogen felt the tension in her arms, her knuckles white as they gripped the spear, ready to thrust again. But she didn't thrust again. Wasn't he going to fight back? She'd made the first move, but now in the aftermath she remembered who she was.

Had she done enough? Would he bleed to death if she walked away?

Gale shook his head. "Girl. Sweetheart. You gotta learn to take yer moment. You earned this, one way or another. You got a beast in you? You need it, to survive."

She didn't disagree, but unlike him she wasn't a cold-blooded murderer. She couldn't just shut off her mind, her conscience. A human stood before her; she couldn't stop seeing him that way, even after everything he'd done.

For a moment there was just the standoff. The impatient warmth of the sun. A *drip-drip*ping louder than a ticking clock, the blood loss a warning. Deafening. Silent.

Imogen stared at him so hard his image started to blur, then dissolve. She cursed herself for hesitating, for not knowing what to do.

He smiled. His face became the chiseled red of a devil. Deep lines, all menace. From somewhere came a laugh. Was it him? Her? It bounced off the Canyon walls. It bounced around her insides, ricocheting off her steel-plated organs.

Gale lunged. His hand connected with the bamboo stick right below where the knife was attached. Imogen swung upward and he lost his grasp. In the same sweeping motion she carved the blade through the air, around and across—slicing open the skin along his fluttering ribs.

He hurled himself at her. She fell onto her back with a *whoomph* and though Gale landed on top of her, she had just enough mobility left to shift the bamboo pole hard across his face, rupturing his nose.

"That's how you fight." His words bubbled with blood, but he sounded approving.

This time he was the one who hesitated, spitting aside a gob of blood, and Imogen took advantage: with the stick still between their prone bodies, she heaved it up against him and squirmed out from under his weight.

He was an experienced fighter, accustomed to pain. They scrambled to their feet at the same time. Imogen jabbed and jabbed, hitting every part of his body that he held forward in defense—his hand, his forearm. Always he kept grabbing for the spear, but Imogen was quicker.

"Proud a you," he said, as if they were sparring, the master demonstrating his final lesson. "Girl, remember me fer this—okay? For teaching you how to—"

The words imprinted, but the meaning of them came later, with the memory of her guttural cries as she thrust the spear. And the softer, more nightmarish whispers of a blade slicing through flesh.

The air smelled of rust. Of desperation. Of the urine seeping through his dusty pants. It was as if he'd bathed in blood. She cut and stabbed.

He fell to his knees, holding out a surrendering hand.

She panted. The blade wanted to keep going but she held it still, took in what she'd done.

While her mind had been shut off something feral had taken its place. He wasn't dead. Yet. But it was inevitable. Blood nearly black streamed from his mouth; she must have punctured a lung. His entire torso dripped red, vibrant shades of death. And his arms, his hands.

"I got soft, didn't I?" He spoke quietly, his energy nearly spent. "Untying you?"

"I finally got selfish."

He gave her a wet grin. "Glad it was you. Love you."

The fragile creature that lived inside her, often hiding its head beneath a wing, came to the surface and saw the consequences of her wrath. It wanted to weep. It wanted to erase time and bring him back to life. It thrived on love and wanted to love him harder, better, so none of this needed to happen.

Go to sleep, soft one.

Feral Imogen wasn't finished. This wasn't love. This was sick. And gross. She plunged the blade into his neck. Ripped it out in a gush of death. He toppled over.

She thrust and thrust, pocking his bare back with red slashes that looked like sneering mouths. They barely bled, his heart no longer pumping.

"Imogen!"

"Imogen!"

Who could be calling her name? Who could be standing at her side?

"You're okay—"

"Thank God—"

Their voices overlapped. Then she realized. Beck. Tilda. On either side of her.

She wanted them to know she hadn't been afraid to fight.

Not this time. She resumed stabbing at Gale's unmoving body. "I did it. Fair and square, I fought him…"

Her sister's hands gripped the bamboo stick. Tilda's strong arms wrapped around her waist, her shoulder.

"You did it, Imogen." Beck pried her fingers off the pole, released the weapon from her dripping hands.

Tilda tugged her away from the macerated body at their feet.

"I fought fair and square, I won…"

"You did, you won." Tilda sobbed.

Something was crushing her; for a moment Imogen didn't understand why she couldn't breathe. Then the world as she knew it came back. Her sister and her best friend hugged her so tightly. Their three bodies heaved in unison as they all wept.

42

The vultures were already circling overhead.

Beck held out Imogen's discarded boot and she stepped into it. They dressed her: Beck tied her laces, Tilda put the shirt over her head, guided Imogen's hands through the armholes. Reality was slightly out of alignment, nothing seemed quite right. Beck and Tilda whispered to each other like she was in a coma and they were afraid to awaken her.

"What should we do with the knife?" *Whisper whisper.*

"Are you going to want your stick back? For walking out?"

"No."

"Then leave it."

They held Imogen's arms, as if she couldn't walk on her own. No one spoke as they made their way back. They went directly to the creek. Everything was so ceremonial that Imogen wondered for a time if she had died. They helped her sit. Took off her shoes, her socks. Eased her to the edge of the water. Took off her shirt.

She had died and they were bathing her body. It felt so good.

The cool water. The sun's warm fingers—the goddess hadn't forsaken her. Together, they'd slain the monster. Imogen finally looked at her crimson hands. Arms. Belly. She was as blood-spattered as a murder scene. She was murder.

No, she was course-correcting. Course-correcting for the violence that had interrupted her life. She'd experienced what one man could do. One man who didn't care about the web of misery he left in his wake. One man, and another man, and another man.

This was what one woman could do. Bloody as a newborn.

Beck sent Tilda to dig through their things in search of their washcloth, their biodegradable soap, Imogen's clothes.

It seemed like hours before they got the blood off. They washed her hair. They scraped the red from under her finger-nails. She closed her eyes and they scrubbed her face. At some point, a moment that went unnoticed, they all became naked in the water, to keep the stains from spreading. *We are goddesses.* Beck, so flat and slender, pale as a moon. Tilda, with her fertile breasts and hips, glistening like a holy chalice.

Beck dried her with their little hand towel. Tilda dressed her in clean garments. They brought her back from death. Rebirthed, they made her presentable for the coming life. In everything they did Imogen saw the mothers they would become: tender, strong, capable, protective.

When had they all stopped speaking? Or maybe they were speaking. Perhaps Imogen couldn't yet register their mortal voices, their imprecise words. She understood the creek and the creek said everything that needed to be said.

Clean

Clean

Clean

* * *

Things happened around her while Imogen sat in her half trance on an inflated mattress pad and watched. Tilda took everything out of the packs. *Here's Beck's living room, the night before our trip.* She reorganized, redistributed, refolded. With an orderliness that made Imogen proud, Tilda arranged their things as they once had been, in the right packs, the right pockets. Everything that didn't belong to them was set aside for the stranger's backpack.

Beck tended to her own wounds, her knee, her arm. She had Tilda help her with some butterfly stitches, and then she checked Tilda's sting and Imogen's head. As she sat crisscross applesauce beside her steady old stove, flames licked the edges of the pot, but the water wasn't in a hurry to boil. She scrubbed at the bloodstains on Imogen's left boot.

At her fingertips, Imogen found a canteen and drank, long and deep. It was delicious and cold. Tilda and Beck glanced at her every other minute or so as they went about their tasks. The tableau was ordinary, familiar. The hearty roar of the tiny stove. The creek, happy and pure. The infinite landscape of rock formations, donning their deep imperial colors as the sun sank lower.

Everything was so calm, so easy. Imogen felt herself in a parallel dimension where the trip had gone smoothly, where Beck held her intervention and apologies were exchanged with declarations of love. Where they bonded during the days and rested contented in their sleeping bags each night, so appreciative of the all-encompassing and simple joys. But wait. That had really happened—not all of it, but enough. Enough to revive her, to make this dimension real.

"Did you find the gun?" Her voice startled them.

"No. Not yet," said Tilda.

Imogen nodded. There'd been a question, scratching on a door at the back of her mind. "How did you get free?"

"You didn't know?" Beck asked, surprised.

"Know what?"

"That we had a plan, for cutting the rope." Tilda looked at Beck, then Imogen, her confusion becoming something more like shock.

"How could I know that?"

"You went with him? Really not knowing?" Tilda sounded astonished.

"Of course. That was the agreement."

Beck's face reddened, but she didn't let herself cry. "We had shards, of the rock Gale used to smash the scorpion."

"Ohhh." They *had* slithered around while alone in the shelter.

"Stashed in the back of our underwear," Tilda said with an abrupt laugh.

"They were too big, too risky to hide in a closed hand."

"We had a chance to move them when we squatted for a pee—Beck's idea. Slipped them into our boots." Imogen remembered Beck's little boot-kicking dance, and understood now she'd been signaling to Tilda. "Then it was just a matter of waiting until we were sitting again—"

"As long as he kept our hands in front."

"The second you two headed off we grabbed our shards and started slicing."

"It was a long shot, weren't sure they'd be sharp enough. But the rope was thin. You really didn't have any idea?" Beck asked again. "You went out there…"

"I just…I was prepared. Knew I'd have my moment."

Slowly, Beck and Tilda nodded, their gazes dawning with awe. And respect. And if Imogen saw in them a little uncertainty, too, a little fear, well, even she hadn't known the extent of her own power.

"What now?" Imogen asked.

"Spend the night here," said Beck. "Tomorrow we'll walk to Hermit for our last night, and leave right on schedule."

"Wow." *Right on schedule.* A surreal conclusion to a surreal week.

"We can't get out tomorrow? Hike it in one day?" Tilda asked.

"It's too far," said Beck. "It's not practical to push ourselves, and with our injuries we should be cautious. I'm just glad Afiya won't have any reason to worry."

While they'd been plunged in a nightmare, time had kept its steady rhythm. No one knew what they'd been enduring. Imogen found something reassuring in that; everyone they knew had gone about their lives, with Imogen, Tilda, and Beck probably far from their thoughts. Out of sight, and out of mind.

"Everyone else is fine," Imogen said contemplatively. "Like nothing ever happened."

Beck exhaled through her nose and Imogen saw her thinking of her unborn child, of the family they were still going to be.

43

They ate Cup Noodles and crackers for supper, and Beck mixed up a batch of instant pudding for dessert. It was runny and lumpy, but chocolatey in the best way. Imogen knew they were low on freeze-dried dinners, but instead of using the dead man's food, Beck had made them a meal heavy on carbs and comfort. It was just what they needed.

They'd entered a place where the shared experience made conversation unnecessary; this was how soldiers bonded for life. There was a lot to think about. They needed to nudge parts of themselves aside to make room for a new kind of existence. It would take time. But in the meanwhile, some things needed to be discussed. Imogen was hesitant to tell them what she'd been contemplating, afraid they would be dismissive or critical, but she had to try.

"I'd like…" Her words broke a spell. They looked up from their spoons. "I'd like to not tell anyone. What happened here."

A seriousness descended like a curtain on Beck's face and

Imogen knew she was weighing the ramifications of their silence.

"Why?" Tilda asked. "We didn't do anything wrong."

"It's not that."

"What about the other man?" Beck asked. Because of course she'd found the most ethically problematic complication: not alerting the authorities—or the man's family—to his whereabouts.

"I was thinking…Maybe we could leave something, plant something of his, just outside the tunnel. To help them find him. Once it's known he's missing, hopefully soon, they'll be searching and when they spot it they'll look in the tunnel."

Beck considered that. "Maybe his permit." She got up and crossed to his backpack, untwisted the wire that attached his permit to a zipper. She scanned the info as she sat back down. "He was heading straight out to Slate. Planned to spend a couple nights. That's better."

"Than what?" Tilda asked.

"Than if he'd planned to stay at Boucher—how could we not have seen him then? But if we'd been at the river, or day hiking, we legit might not have seen him pass through Boucher."

"But he didn't pass through," said Tilda. "He didn't even get across the camping area."

"But how would we know that, if we weren't there all day?" Beck was building an easy case for plausible deniability.

"They may ask us, at some point," Imogen had to concede.

"They'll contact me first," Beck said. "I registered our permit. But yes, we should be prepared. Are you comfortable saying you didn't see anything?"

"We can say we were hardly at camp—which is true. Telling the truth is easier than lying," Tilda said.

"Agreed. But...Imogen, have you thought this through? Remember last—" Beck didn't say *time*, but Imogen knew that was the word she wanted. "It might have gone better then, if we'd told."

Imogen shook her head. "Please. Please trust me. It's not that I don't want him to be found—I do. And I want him to have justice. It's just, I don't...I don't want Gale to be found. And we can't really report one without reporting both."

"You *saved* us. They're not going to blame you," said Tilda. "You're not going to be in trouble."

"That's not it." It sounded like they might be willing to honor her request. But that could change when they heard the full reason. She took a deep breath before proceeding. "I want to give Gale his final wish. To disappear. He can disappear, if we don't say anything."

He wouldn't want it, to be dragged out of the Canyon. Autopsied. Dissected. Put on display to be judged by the World Wide Web. And Imogen didn't want that either, for herself.

"You don't owe him anything," Beck said, her brows pinched with concern.

"I know. But...if he escapes the end of his story, then we can escape it too." She didn't want to beg, but she prayed they would really *hear* her. "This will be *attached* to me—to us. Attached forever. It won't matter that we were defending our-selves because what people will say is that we were *terrorized*, we were *victims*. They'll choose all the words and decide who we are. And whatever else we do, for the rest of our lives—they'll write it in our obituaries, that we were kidnapped by cop-killer whatever-his-full-name-was. And if we tell them everything then everyone will know. I won't be *me*—no one will see the rest of me ever again. I'll be That Author Who Killed Her Kidnapper."

"It would be good press," Tilda said with an impish grin. Then, more seriously, "No, I see what you're saying."

"I don't want to be seen as a victim—or a killer. I don't want these words attached to me. I want to leave this here. We didn't do anything wrong…" She faltered, not entirely at ease with what she'd done. "I don't want people to know my name, for this. He can disappear. We can be…who we are, on our own terms."

Beck nodded. Tilda chewed her lip. "What about Gale's body?"

"The vultures and ravens will be done with him in a matter of days," said Beck. "Maybe no one will ever find him. Or someday, maybe they'll find his bones." Imogen glanced over at the dead man's pack. They followed her gaze. "We'll leave it near Gale. If he's found, they'll put two and two together and know he killed the backpacker, for his provisions."

"So you're okay with it?" Imogen asked.

"I am." And Beck sounded certain. "I don't want this attached to me—it would be worse than a ghost. We'll leave it here."

Imogen turned to Tilda. "What about you?"

"More than okay. It's hard enough to have a public persona, trying to keep it grounded in reality—this would blow up my life. This is ours. What we endured. Whatever we feel…it might change over time, but we'll have each other. We survived this. We should get to say who knows and who doesn't."

"What about telling our significant others?"

"Do you want to?" Tilda asked Beck.

"I don't know. I'd have to think about it. Maybe I'd tell Afiya in some distant future. It would scare her now, even to see that

I'm all right. I don't want that kind of...fear, changing our relationship, setting boundaries. We'll need to process this—us, the three of us—alone, and maybe together."

Tilda and Imogen nodded.

"So we leave it here?" Imogen looked to both of them. "I know...we don't know how it'll manifest in our lives...but for now, for as long as we can? Between the three of us?"

"It's ours. It belongs to the three of us."

"Agreed," said Beck.

44

What followed were unexpectedly peaceful hours. The trio marveled at the Milky Way as they lay in their sleeping bags. They awoke and were thankful that the night had been kind to them; they'd slept well. The redness and tingling in Tilda's stung hand weren't as bad. Beck's knee was stiff when she first got up, but after walking around she declared it a bit improved. Her face was still a rainbow of sickly colors, but the swelling was receding. She planned to tell Afiya that she'd taken a careless tumble while rock-hopping across the creek. The slash in her arm, she'd say, was courtesy of the agave plant she'd landed on. Imogen's injuries were mostly invisible, but she was hopeful they would heal better than her previous ones.

Before they left Slate, Beck went alone to where they'd abandoned Gale's body. She disposed of his spear in a fissure between two boulders, and left the stranger's pack nearby, stashed under some brush. Their intent was that his gear wouldn't be spotted before Gale became skeletal remains, so no one could easily determine his cause of death. Let them think he died of stupidity, not a savage fight. Maybe they'd wonder if he'd had a fatal reaction to a snakebite, or died of an untreated infection; it wasn't as if Gale would've sought help. Or maybe the Canyon would erase him, an irrelevant speck in a vast domain. The vultures, as Beck reported, were well on their way.

Imogen and Tilda never found Gale's gun. Given the illusion of distance, and how hard it would be to tell one cluster of rocks from another, Imogen doubted if he ever would have recovered it.

They took only a short rest when they reached Boucher. Imogen secured the stranger's backcountry permit to a twiggy bush near the entrance of the old mining tunnel. She wanted to affix it well enough that it wouldn't blow away, while making it look as if it had simply gotten snagged there. Tilda crumpled it and tore it in half first, trying to create the impression that it had been ripped off. At the last minute, Imogen scrubbed both pieces with the hem of her shirt and smeared dirt on them to ruin their fingerprints. The authorities might look for Gale's and it would be better to have no prints than the wrong ones.

"You watch too much TV," Beck said to her for the third time that trip.

"Yup. It's all research." The task was serious but the mood was light; they all smiled. But Imogen knew she'd become a survivalist, willing—able—to do anything.

Their actions were disrupting the truth. But the dead were dead. Imogen, Beck, and Tilda would live with that truth forever, regardless of what anyone else knew. Or didn't.

The walk all the way from Slate to Hermit was long. With rest breaks it took them almost seven hours, but they kept a meditative pace rather than a hurried one. At one point

Imogen burst out laughing and they looked at her, expecting her to fill them in.

"Nothing. Inside joke," she mumbled, unwilling to explain that the farther away they got from Slate, the more buoyed she felt. Fearless. Alive.

Periodically one of them would start singing and they'd all join in. It was a good day, a weird kind of good, but good.

As they were cleaning up after supper, Imogen crumpled the last chicken à la king package and stuffed it into their garbage bag—which had remained strapped to Beck's pack during their entire misadventure. In the diminishing light, and completely by coincidence, she spotted among their trash...the missing Visine bottle. She fished it out, grinning. Some of her medical marijuana tincture still sloshed around inside. She slipped it into her hoodie's kangaroo pocket and wandered off for a good-night pee.

When Imogen was safely where no one could see her, she did an unthinkable thing. Praying to the rocks and the ravens for their forgiveness, she threw the Visine bottle as far as she could. It might take a million years for the plastic to decompose, but she hoped the sun goddess and Canyon spirit would understand: some things *had* to be left behind. Imogen knew she couldn't be her new self while carrying all the literal garbage of her past life.

It was their last night and again Beck and Tilda slept on either side of her. Though subtle about it, they seemed to have appointed themselves her bodyguards. Did they think she was going to fall apart? Or burst into nightmarish screams? It was sweet, if unnecessary—and a trifle funny when Imogen remembered how she'd once imagined herself as the weakling who would cower in their warrior shadows, tending to their weapons.

* * *

By the next day it was evident that they were all feeling an unburdened ease, a bolstered and triumphant energy. Even with Beck's limp, it carried them fleet-footed up the difficult trail. They paused before the steepest sections to assess who most needed one of the two remaining walking sticks, and for short step-ups they shared, passing a stick down to the next person. As happens in the Canyon, after just a few days their muscles had been trained and their skills honed; even Tilda functioned with an assured competence now.

At Santa Maria Springs they took off their boots as they had on the way down, and refilled their warmed canteens with cooler water from the trough.

"Seven days," Imogen said, wiggling her toes in a patch of sun.

That was all it had been, though time had stretched and spun and toyed with them like a cat with a mouse under its paw, indifferent to torturing a living thing until its heart gave out. They all felt the magnitude of those days. Tilda shut her eyes and tilted her face sunward. Beck looked toward the distant North Rim, hung like a picture in a frame of rock. They were both here, and there—that strange liminal zone that hovers between home and the journey, the journey and home. The present moment shared space with both past and future.

Soon they were back on the trail. Beck suggested taking another quick break when they reached the upper Hermit Basin and its little forest of juniper and pinyon pine, but instead they passed a canteen around and kept going. Their adventure was almost over; *leaving* had become a palpable thing, an invisible presence that hiked alongside them. For Imogen it was bittersweet. It certainly hadn't been the trip they'd planned—something horrible had happened, almost beyond words. But in the Canyon, nothing was *all* horrible. The beauty, the holiness of this place was everywhere, it had never abandoned them. To recognize that now filled Imogen with a resurrecting surge of joy.

Beck's Jeep was just as they'd left it. They shoved the packs in the back and it was only as they were clambering in that Imogen realized how dirty they all were.

"We're gonna make a mess of your car." Dusty red boot prints were already imprinted on the floor mats at Imogen's feet.

"It's just dirt," said Beck.

How weird it felt to sit on a cushioned seat. To move without the effort of one's own muscles. As Beck pulled out of the parking area she flicked on the radio, but after ten seconds of catastrophic news she shut it off.

Tilda, in the front passenger seat, plugged Beck's phone into the charger. It had enough juice to turn on and, without comment or question, as soon as there was a strong enough signal she placed a call. She held the phone up, in speaker mode, and they all heard it ringing.

"Hello?" Afiya's voice was a giant grin.

"Hey babe." Beck fought back tears. "We're coming home. We'll be there soon."

EPILOGUE

BACKPACKER IDENTIFIED
ARIZONA DAILY SUN (October 22, Flagstaff, AZ)

Local authorities have confirmed that the body found in an abandoned mining tunnel in a remote area of the Grand Canyon is that of missing Wisconsin backpacker Jeremy Haynes. Haynes, 39, an experienced solo hiker, was reported missing by a friend after Haynes failed to return home. Following a short search, Haynes's body was discovered near the Boucher camping area, the apparent victim of a stabbing.

Authorities are investigating a link between Haynes's murder and wanted fugitive Frederick Galen. Galen, 42, had recently been released on parole and has a long record of previous charges for burglary, fraud, aggravated assault, and armed robbery. Just days before Haynes entered the Grand Canyon, Galen was pulled over by a Texas highway patrolman for a routine traffic violation, during which the patrolman was killed. Galen's DNA was discovered at both crime scenes.

After law enforcement agencies reached out to all backcountry permit holders for Grand Canyon National Park for early-to-mid-October, separate sightings of both men were reported in and around the Hermit camp area. Haynes's body was found several miles west, and there were no other reported sightings of either man. One theory suggests Galen may have entered the Grand Canyon in a desperate effort to avoid being apprehended, and may have killed the Wisconsin man for his supplies. None of Haynes's backpacking equipment has been located.

The manhunt for Galen, who is now wanted in Texas for capital murder, is still active, though initial searches by air and on foot have yielded no further clues to his whereabouts. Due to the difficulty of the terrain, the National Park Service, in cooperation with multiple law enforcement agencies, is unsure how long it will commit manpower to ongoing backcountry searches. Galen, an inexperienced outdoorsman, is not believed to have left the Grand Canyon, nor has he contacted any members of his family. Officially he remains "at large."

Imogen had been tempted to frame the article when it came out the year before, but that would've been inappropriate: morbid at best; indiscreet at worst. At home she kept a computer-printed copy of it folded in a decorative cloisonné box. And a second copy, ratty with wear, went wherever she did, in the small pocket of the daypack she used instead of a purse. She read it one more time as she sat in her sister's office, on the edge of the sleeper sofa.

The news report shouldn't have been a talisman, and yet…Its publication so soon after their return home had given Imogen some peace. It made the aftermath easier. Since then, she'd read online that Jeremy Haynes's friends had scattered his ashes in the Canyon, his favorite place. Gale's family issued statements too (some rather colorful), apologizing to his victims, and begging the public for information regarding his whereabouts. With or without a definitive ending, Imogen half expected that someday she'd get to watch a true crime documentary about Gale's life. Maybe his disappearance would add to his legend.

She folded the news report along its worn creases and zipped it away, forcing her attention to the more aptly framed article on Beck's wall: their triumphant moment from high school. *Boom boom now watch me fly!*

Sometimes intrusive thoughts invaded her conscience, but she tried not to dwell on those final moments with Gale. Though, late at night, she occasionally felt a wicked bloom of pride that, if she really wanted to, she could plan the perfect murder. Once she would have ascribed such fantasies to her writer's imagination, but it was more than that now.

Esther's Ghost was doing well—better than expected—thanks in part to Tilda, who'd started an online book club. She'd selected *Esther's Ghost* the month of its release, which helped propel it onto *USA Today*'s bestseller list. In return, Imogen was helping her work through the organizational and brainstorming challenges of her own book. They talked regularly now, and while they sometimes found themselves in the murky waters of miscommunication, they always took the time to sort it out.

With some buzz attached to her name, Imogen was able to sell the slightly odd project she'd conceived in the Grand Canyon. The dark fairy tale poured out of her in the eight weeks after she got home, and it remained very close to her heart: another strange girl on an extraordinary adventure, who proved she was more than anyone understood her to be. It was different than anything she'd ever written, dark in spite of its whimsy, beautiful in spite of its horror, and constructed of the same fabric as her own soul.

She'd promised Beck and Afiya she'd get the guest room ready, so she stuffed her suitcase into the closet and went into the next room. She tried to be as helpful as possible whenever she visited, which she was managing to do for two weeks at a time, every three months or so. Cooking and cleaning and doing laundry were easier (and less scary) than caring for the baby, though she was getting better at that, and never missed a chance to plop down on the floor to play with her little niece. Tilda and Jalal were due to arrive imminently—Beck was picking them up at the airport—so Imogen put fresh sheets on the guest room bed. It had been hers until thirty minutes ago, but she didn't mind shifting to her sister's office with its slightly less comfortable bed but fabulous picture window.

The trio had decided to celebrate every friendiversary going forward, so they would have one guaranteed reason each year for them all to be together. While they'd agreed to be flexible with the exact date and location, today was precisely one year since they'd gathered at Beck's to prepare for entering the Grand Canyon. Tilda hadn't met the baby yet, and she was bringing Jalal—her fiancé—for the first time.

When the guest room looked tidy and welcoming, Imogen hurried to the living room on bare, silent feet—well, she was pretty sure her tread was soft. She always had some ringing in her left ear, a permanent reminder of Gale's punch to her head. A lot of living had happened under the cathedral ceiling since the baby was born, and Imogen picked up toys and pacifiers and plush animals and blankies. At seven months old, Isadora was a curious, crawling bundle of energy who scattered stuff everywhere, gurgling happily as she went. Imogen heard Afiya from the nursery, singing to her in Swahili as she changed her diaper.

From outside, a car uttered a short *beep-beep* as it pulled into the drive.

"They're here!" said Afiya and, with Isadora on her hip, she and Imogen converged on the front entryway.

The door opened and it was like a firecracker went off, tossing up people and greetings and exclamations and hugs. Isadora very agreeably allowed herself to be bounced in new arms, cooed over by new people, while Beck and Afiya beamed.

"Look at you!" said Tilda. "Aren't you the sweetest little thing ever—yes you are!"

"Yes she is," Beck agreed. Isadora sputtered, grinning as she threw back her head.

"And we are not at all biased," Afiya said, only half kidding.

"No, she is—she really really is!" said Tilda.

"She knows it, too." Imogen tickled her niece's little foot as Tilda passed the baby to Jalal, who lifted her up with silly-faced glee. Isadora was definitely the cutest, smartest, cuddliest, most loving bundle of goo ever born. Imogen said so often. She was in love with every part of her—those inquisitive brown eyes, that curly black hair, her chubby legs and arms, those grasping fingers that wanted everything. And that dimpled smile.

Imogen reached for their luggage, ready to be helpful and squirrel it off to the guest room, but Tilda stopped her.

"Wait, wait! Okay, I know we're barely in the door, but it's been killing me and I can't wait anymore." Tilda flashed Jalal a grin, excited and a bit bashful. He returned a smile almost as dopey. Tilda thrust out her belly, patted it with her hand. "I know there isn't much to see, but we're going to have one too!"

Afiya squealed and threw her arms around her—one excited mother to another. Then she hugged Jalal and it was Beck and Imogen's turn to embrace Tilda.

"So happy for you—you're going to be an awesome mom," Beck said.

"Hope so."

"Can I be Auntie Im for your baby too?"

"Of course—especially if we get all that great service we've been hearing so much about from Beck!"

They laughed, and the party finally started to move out of the entryway. Imogen gathered up their bags and suit-case and stashed them in the bedroom. When she returned, Isadora was back in Afiya's arms and Afiya was reopening the front door, about to take Jalal on the tour—which, as was tradition, started outside with the wild Western landscape. Imogen felt such happiness for her sister in that moment, that Beck had such a merry and spirited family, and that Afiya was still so proud of their home that she jumped at the chance to show it to every new guest. Or maybe she only showed such enthusiasm for extended family, and that was what Jalal was now. She was equally elated for Tilda.

It bubbled out of her, "I'm so happy for you guys!"

As if they'd been longing for it, needing it, waiting for the moment when it was just the three of them, they fell into a huddle, their heads bowed as they clung together. After a silent moment, Beck spoke.

"I've been waiting to share something too, to tell you in person, together, because only the three of us really understand what it means. I wanted to keep to the Jewish tradition of naming a baby after a recently deceased loved one—like you're named in memory of Uncle Isaac, and I'm named for our great-grandmother Rachel." In more observant families, a child would bear the actual name of a deceased relative, but the more relaxed tradition was to simply use a name that started with the same letter. Beck had shown more interest in religion in the past year—in addition to a new passion for Krav Maga.

"So Isadora Tirzah is named after the two of you—the parts of yourselves that you left behind, and the parts that will go on forever. I feel like we're all so different now, and I want my daughter to be the best parts of both of you."

"That's so beautiful, I love that." Tilda took their hands and squeezed.

A gasping sob escaped Imogen's throat. Her sister's words gave clarity to what she'd been feeling since leaving the Canyon, how the suffering of her old self had been a necessary conduit to birth the person she wanted to be. And since then the universe had been hard at work amending an imbalance. Beck was right: their time with Gale was the most frightening, uncertain thing that had ever happened to them, and now they lived more fully, more intentionally, more joyfully than had previously seemed possible.

"I love when you guys call her Izzy-Tiz," Imogen said. "But I didn't realize it was for us."

"When I'm with her, I feel like you're both here, nearby."

They remained hand-in-hand until the house tour moved inside; when Afiya and Jalal saw them together they made a light joke about "bonding time." Then Afiya led him toward the kitchen, the master bedroom, the nursery, explaining all the renovations they'd made over the years.

Jalal and Afiya didn't know about the seven days. The dark brilliance of a Canyon night. The way the ravens caught the drafts of air and floated—lazy gods, playful gods—as the sun warmed their outstretched wings. They didn't know that bad food tasted delicious when eaten after a long day with Zoroaster on the horizon. Or that the Canyon exhaled an ancient air that, like a lullaby, was a balm to weary souls. They didn't know how nature could bring you to your knees, in awe, in misery, in prayer, in everlasting gratitude.

There was so much they didn't know.

Sometimes Imogen thought of Gale. Of Crystal. What had she thought of her wayward father? Sometimes when Imogen gazed at the wonder that was her niece she imagined the baby who was probably not called Diamond, who had the DNA of a murderer coursing through her infant veins.

There but for a breach in the trail...

Anyone could tumble from the edge of the earth.